AN INTRODUCTION TO THE STUDY OF ROBERT BROWNING'S POETRY

HIRAM CORSON, LL.D.,

Professor of English Literature in the Cornell University;
Author of "An Introduction to the Study of Shakespeare",
"A Primer of English Verse, Chiefly in its Aesthetic and
Organic Character", "The Aims of Literary Study", Etc.

AN INTRODUCTION TO THE STUDY OF ROBERT BROWNING'S POETRY

BIBLIOBAZAAR

AN INTRODUCTION TO THE STUDY OF ROBERT BROWNING'S POETRY

"Subtlest Assertor of the Soul in song."

{There are several Greek phrases in this book. ASCII cannot represent the Greek characters, so if you are interested in these phrases, use the following map. Hopefully these phrases will not be mistaken for another language . . .

ASCII to Greek

A,a	alpha
B,b	beta
G,g	gamma
D,d	delta
E,e	epsilon
Z,z	zeta
H,h	eta
Q,q	theta
I,i	iota
K,k	kappa
L,l	lambda
M,m	mi/mu
N,n	ni/nu
J,j	ksi/xi
O,o	omikron/omicron
P,p	pi
R,r	rho
S,s,c	sigma
T,t	tau
U,u	ypsilon/upsilon
F,f	phi
X,x	chi/khi
Y,y	psi
W,w	omega
',`,/,\,^	Accents, follow the vowel. You figure them out.}

{The following is transcribed from a letter (from Browning to Corson) which Corson chose to use in facsimile form to begin his text. Unfortunately (or fortunately), it will be regular text here.}

19. Warwick Crescent.
      W.
      Dec. 28. '86

My dear Dr. Corson,

    I waited some days after the arrival of your Book and Letter, thinking I might be able to say more of my sense of your goodness: but I can do no more now than a week ago. You "hope I shall not find too much to disapprove of": what I ought to protest against, is "a load to sink a navy—too much honor": how can I put aside your generosity, as if cold justice—however befitting myself—would be in better agreement with your nature? Let it remain as an assurance to younger poets that, after fifty years' work unattended by any conspicuous recognition, an over-payment may be made, if there be such another munificent appreciator as I have been privileged to find, in which case let them, even if more deserving, be equally grateful.

    I have not observed anything in need of correction in the notes. The "little Tablet" was a famous "Last Supper", mentioned by Vasari, (page. 232), and gone astray long ago from the Church of S. Spirito: it turned up, according to report, in some obscure corner, while I was in Florence, and was at once acquired by a stranger. I saw it, genuine or no, a work of great beauty. (Page 156.) "A canon", in music, is a piece wherein the subject is repeated—in various keys: and being strictly obeyed in the repetition, becomes the "Canon"—the imperative law—to what follows. Fifty of such parts would be indeed a notable peal: to manage three is enough of an achievement for a good musician.

And now,—here is Christmas: all my best wishes go to you and Mrs Corson. Those of my sister also. She was indeed suffering from grave indisposition in the summer, but is happily recovered. I could not venture, under the circumstances, to expose her convalescence to the accidents of foreign travel: hence our contenting ourselves with Wales rather than Italy. Shall you be again induced to visit us? Present or absent, you will remember me always, I trust, as

Yours most affectionately
Robert Browning.

"Quanta subtilitate ipsa corda hominum reserat, intimos mentis recessus explorat, varios animi motus perscrutatur. Quod ad tragoediam antiquiorem attinet, interpretatus est, uti nostis omnes, non modo Aeschylum quo nemo sublimior, sed etiam Euripidem quo nemo humanior; quo fit ut etiam illos qui Graece nesciunt, misericordia tangat Alcestis, terrore tangat Hercules. Recentiora argumenta tragica cum lyrico quodam scribendi genere coniunxit, duas Musas et Melpomenen et Euterpen simul veneratus. Musicae miracula quis dignius cecinit? Pictoris Florentini sine fraude vitam quasi inter crepuscula vesperascentem coloribus quam vividis depinxit. Vesperi quotiens, dum foco adsidemus, hoc iubente resurgit Italia. Vesperi nuper, dum huius idyllia forte meditabar, Cami inter arundines mihi videbar vocem magnam audire clamantis, Pa\n o' me/gas ou' te/qnhken. Vivit adhuc Pan ipse, cum Marathonis memoria et Pheidippidis velocitate immortali consociatus."— Eulogium pronounced by Mr. J. E. Sandys, Public Orator at the University of Cambridge, on presenting Mr. Browning for the honorary degree of Doctor of Laws, June 10, 1879.

PREFACE.

The purpose of the present volume is to afford some aid and guidance in the study of Robert Browning's Poetry, which, being the most complexly subjective of all English poetry, is, for that reason alone, the most difficult. And then the poet's favorite art-form, the dramatic, or, rather, psychologic, monologue, which is quite original with himself, and peculiarly adapted to the constitution of his genius and to the revelation of themselves by the several "dramatis personae", presents certain structural difficulties, but difficulties which, with an increased familiarity, grow less and less. The exposition presented in the Introduction, of its constitution and skilful management, and the Arguments given of the several poems included in the volume, will, it is hoped, reduce, if not altogether remove, the difficulties of this kind. In the same section of the Introduction, certain peculiarities of the poet's diction, which sometimes give a check to the reader's understanding of a passage, are presented and illustrated.

I think it not necessary to offer any apology for my going all the way back to Chaucer, and noting the Ebb and Flow in English Poetry down to the present time, of the spirituality which constitutes the real life of poetry, and which should, as far as possible, be brought to the consciousness and appreciation of students. What I mean by spirituality is explained in my treatment of the subject. The degree to which poetry is quickened with it should always enter into an estimate of its absolute worth. It is that, indeed, which constitutes its absolute worth. The weight of thought conveyed, whatever that be, will not compensate for the absence of it.

The study of poetry, in our institutions of learning, so far as I have taken note of it, and the education induced thereby, are almost purely intellectual. The student's spiritual nature is left to take care of itself; and the consequence is that he becomes, at best, only a thinking and analyzing machine.

The spiritual claims of the study of poetry are especially demanded in the case of Browning's poetry. Browning is generally and truly regarded as the most intellectual of poets. No poetry in English literature, or in any literature, is more charged with discursive thought than his. But he is, at the same time, the most spiritual and transcendental of poets, the "subtlest assertor of the Soul in Song". His thought is never an end to itself, but is always subservient to an ulterior spiritual end—always directed towards "a presentment of the correspondency of the universe to Deity, of the natural to the spiritual, and of the actual to the ideal"; and it is all-important that students should be awakened, and made, as far as possible, responsive to this spiritual end.

The sections of the Introduction on Personality and Art were read before the Browning Society of London, in June, 1882. I have seen no reason for changing or modifying, in any respect, the views therein expressed.

The idea of personality as a quickening, regenerating power, and the idea of art as an intermediate agency of personality, are, perhaps, the most reiterated (implicitly, not explicitly) in Browning's poetry, and lead up to the dominant idea of Christianity, the idea of a Divine Personality; the idea that the soul, to use an expression from his earliest poem, 'Pauline', must "rest beneath some better essence than itself in weakness".

The notes to the poems will be found, I trust, to cover all points and features of the text which require explanation and elucidation. I have not, at any rate, wittingly passed by any real difficulties. Whether my explanations and interpretations will in all cases be acceptable, remains to be seen.

Hiram Corson.
Cascadilla Cottage, Ithaca, N.Y.
September, 1886.

NOTE TO THE SECOND EDITION.

In this edition, several errors of the first have been corrected. For the notes on "fifty-part canon", p. 156, and "a certain precious little tablet", p. 232, I am indebted to Mr. Browning.

H. C.

{p. 156—in this etext, see line 322 of "The Flight of the Duchess", in the Poems section. p. 232—see Stanza 30 of "Old Pictures in Florence", also in the Poems section.}

NOTE TO THE THIRD EDITION.

In this edition have been added, 'A Death in the Desert', with argument, notes, and commentary, a fac-simile of a letter from the poet, and a portrait copied from a photograph (the last taken of him) which he gave me when visiting him in Venice, a month before his death.

It may be of interest, and of some value, to many students of Browning's poetry, to know a reply he made, in regard to the expression in 'My Last Duchess', "I gave commands; then all smiles stopped together."

We were walking up and down the great hall of the Palazzo Rezzonico, when, in the course of what I was telling him about the study of his works in the United States, I alluded to the divided opinion as to the meaning of the above expression in 'My Last Duchess', some understanding that the commands were to put the

Duchess to death, and others, as I have explained the expression on p. 87 of this volume (last paragraph). {For etext use, section III (Browning's Obscurity) of the Introduction, sixth paragraph before the end of the section.} He made no reply, for a moment, and then said, meditatively, "Yes, I meant that the commands were that she should be put to death." And then, after a pause, he added, with a characteristic dash of expression, and as if the thought had just started in his mind, "Or he might have had her shut up in a convent." This was to me very significant. When he wrote the expression, "I gave commands", etc., he may not have thought definitely what the commands were, more than that they put a stop to the smiles of the sweet Duchess, which provoked the contemptible jealousy of the Duke. This was all his art purpose required, and his mind did not go beyond it. I thought how many vain discussions take place in Browning Clubs, about little points which are outside of the range of the artistic motive of a composition, and how many minds are occupied with anything and everything under the sun, except the one thing needful (the artistic or spiritual motive), the result being "as if one should be ignorant of nothing concerning the scent of violets, except the scent itself."

H.C.

CONTENTS

POEMS.

INTRODUCTION.

I. The Spiritual Ebb and Flow exhibited in English Poetry from Chaucer to Tennyson and Browning.

Literature, in its most restricted art-sense, is an expression in letters of the life of the spirit of man co-operating with the intellect. Without the co-operation of the spiritual man, the intellect produces only thought; and pure thought, whatever be the subject with which it deals, is not regarded as literature, in its strict sense. For example, Euclid's 'Elements', Newton's 'Principia', Spinoza's 'Ethica', and Kant's 'Critique of the Pure Reason', do not properly belong to literature. (By the "spiritual" I would be understood to mean the whole domain of the emotional, the susceptible or impressible, the sympathetic, the intuitive; in short, that mysterious something in the constitution of man by and through which he holds relationship with the essential spirit of things, as opposed to the phenomenal of which the senses take cognizance.)

The term literature is sometimes extended in meaning (and it may be so extended), to include all that has been committed to letters, on all subjects. There is no objection to such extension in ordinary speech, no more than there is to that of the signification of the word, "beauty" to what is purely abstract. We speak, for example, of the beauty of a mathematical demonstration; but beauty, in its strictest sense, is that which appeals to the spiritual nature, and must, therefore, be concrete, personal, not abstract. Art beauty is the embodiment, adequate, effective embodiment, of co-operative intellect and spirit,—"the accommodation," in Bacon's words, "of the shows of things to the desires of the mind."

It follows that the relative merit and importance of different periods of a literature should be determined by the relative degrees of spirituality which these different periods exhibit. The intellectual power of two or more periods, as exhibited in their literatures, may show no marked difference, while the spiritual vitality of these same periods may very distinctly differ. And if it be admitted that literature proper is the product of co-operative intellect and spirit (the latter being always an indispensable factor, though there can be no high order of literature that is not strongly articulated, that is not well freighted, with thought), it follows that the periods of a literature should be determined by the ebb and flow of spiritual life which they severally register, rather than by any other considerations. There are periods which are characterized by a "blindness of heart", an inactive, quiescent condition of the spirit, by which the intellect is more or less divorced from the essential, the eternal, and it directs itself to the shows of things. Such periods may embody in their literatures a large amount of thought,—thought which is conversant with the externality of things; but that of itself will not constitute a noble literature, however perfect the forms in which it may be embodied, and the general sense of the civilized world, independently of any theories of literature, will not regard such a literature as noble. It is made up of what must be, in time, superseded; it has not a sufficiently large element of the essential, the eternal, which can be reached only through the assimilating life of the spirit. The spirit may be so "cabined, cribbed, confined" as not to come to any consciousness of itself; or it may be so set free as to go forth and recognize its kinship, respond to the spiritual world outside of itself, and, by so responding, KNOW what merely intellectual philosophers call the UNKNOWABLE.

To turn now to the line of English poets who may be said to have passed the torch of spiritual life, from lifted hand to hand, along the generations. And first is

"the morning star of song, who made
His music heard below:

"Dan Chaucer, the first warbler, whose sweet breath
Preluded those melodious bursts that fill

The spacious times of great Elizabeth
With sounds that echo still."

Chaucer exhibits, in a high degree, this life of the spirit, and it is the secret of the charm which his poetry possesses for us after a lapse of five hundred years. It vitalizes, warms, fuses, and imparts a lightsomeness to his verse; it creeps and kindles beneath the tissues of his thought. When we compare Dryden's modernizations of Chaucer with the originals, we see the difference between the verse of a poet, with a healthy vitality of spirit, and, through that healthy vitality of spirit, having secret dealings with things, and verse which is largely the product of the rhetorical or literary faculty. We do not feel, when reading the latter, that any unconscious might co-operated with the conscious powers of the writer. But we DO feel this when we read Chaucer's verse.

All of the Canterbury Tales have originals or analogues, most of which have been reproduced by the London Chaucer Society. Not one of the tales is of Chaucer's own invention. And yet they may all be said to be original, in the truest, deepest sense of the word. They have been vitalized from the poet's own soul. He has infused his own personality, his own spirit-life, into his originals; he has "created a soul under the ribs of death." It is this infused vitality which will constitute the charm of the Canterbury Tales for all generations of English speaking and English reading people. This life of the spirit, of which I am speaking, as distinguished from the intellect, is felt, though much less distinctly, in a contemporary work, 'The Vision of William concerning Piers the Plowman'. What the author calls "KIND WIT", that is, "natural intelligence", has, generally, the ascendency. We meet, however, with powerful passages, wherein the thoughts are aglow with the warmth from the writer's inner spirit. He shows at times the moral indignation of a Hebrew prophet.

The 'Confessio Amantis' of John Gower, another contemporary work, exhibits comparatively little of the life of the spirit, either in its verse or in its thought. The thought rarely passes the limit of natural intelligence. The stories, which the poet drew from the 'Gesta Romanorum' and numerous other sources, can hardly be said to have been BORN AGAIN. The verse is smooth and fluent, but the reader feels it to be the product of literary skill.

It wants what can be imparted only by an unconscious might back of the consciously active and trained powers. It is this unconscious might which John Keats, in his 'Sleep and Poetry', speaks of as "might half slumbering on its own right arm", and which every reader, with the requisite susceptibility, can always detect in the verse of a true poet.

In the interval between Chaucer and Spenser, this life of the spirit is not distinctly marked in any of its authors, not excepting even Henry Howard, Earl of Surrey, whose sad fate gave a factitious interest to his writings. It is more noticeable in Thomas Sackville, Lord Buckhurst's 'Induction to the Mirror for Magistrates', which, in the words of Hallam, "forms a link which unites the school of Chaucer and Lydgate to the 'Faerie Queene'."

The Rev. James Byrne, of Trinity College, Dublin, in his lecture on 'The Influence of National Character on English Literature', remarks of Spenser: "After that dark period which separated him from Chaucer, after all the desolation of the Wars of the Roses, and all the deep trials of the Reformation, he rose on England as if, to use an image of his own,

"'At last the golden orientall gate
Of greatest heaven gan to open fayre,
And Phoebus, fresh as brydegrome to his mate,
Came dauncing forth, shaking his deawie hayre,
And hurled his glistering beams through gloomy ayre.'

"That baptism of blood and fire through which England passed at the Reformation, raised both Protestant and Catholic to a newness of life. That mighty working of heart and mind with which the nation then heaved throughout, went through every man and woman, and tried what manner of spirits they were of. What a preparation was this for that period of our literature in which man, the great actor of the drama of life, was about to appear on the stage! It was to be expected that the drama should then start into life, and that human character should speak from the stage with a depth of life never known before; but who could have imagined Shakespeare?"

And what a new music burst upon the world in Spenser's verse! His noble stanza, so admirably adapted to pictorial effect, has since been used by some of the greatest poets of the literature, Thomson, Scott, Wordsworth, Byron, Keats, Shelley, and numerous others; but none of them, except in rare instances, have drawn the music out of it which Spenser drew.

Professor Goldwin Smith well remarks, in his article on Mark Pattison's Milton, "The great growths of poetry have coincided with the great bursts of national life, and the great bursts of national life have hitherto been generally periods of controversy and struggle. Art itself, in its highest forms, has been the expression of faith. We have now people who profess to cultivate art for its own sake; but they have hardly produced anything which the world accepts as great, though they have supplied some subjects for 'Punch'."

Spenser who, of all the great English poets, is regarded by some critics as the most remote from real life, and the least reflecting his age, is, nevertheless, filled with the spirit of his age—its chivalric, romantic, patriotic, moral, and religious spirit. When he began to write, the nation had just passed through the fiery furnace of a religious persecution, and was rejoicing in its deliverance from the papistical rule of Mary. The devotion to the new queen with which it was inspired was grateful, generous, enthusiastic, and even romantic. This devotion Spenser's great poem everywhere reflects, and it has been justly pronounced to be the best exponent of the subtleties of that Calvinism which was the aristocratic form of Protestantism at that time in both France and England.

The renewed spiritual life which set in so strongly with Spenser, reached its springtide in Shakespeare. It was the secret of that sense of moral proportion which pervades his plays. Moral proportion cannot be secured through the laws of the ancients, or through any formulated theory of art. It was, I am assured, through his deep and sensitive spirit-life that Shakespeare felt the universal spirit and constitution of the world as fully, perhaps, as the human soul, in this life, is capable of feeling it. Through it he took cognizance of the workings of nature, and of the life of man, BY DIRECT ASSIMILATION OF THEIR HIDDEN PRINCIPLES,—principles which cannot be reached through an observation, by the natural intelligence, of the phenomenal. He thus became possessed of a knowledge, or rather wisdom, far beyond his conscious observation and objective experience.

Shakespeare may be regarded as the first and the last great artistic physiologist or natural historian of the passions; and he was this by virtue of the life of the spirit, which enabled him to reproduce sympathetically the whole range of human passion within himself. He was the first of the world's dramatists that exhibited the passions in their evolutions, and in their subtlest complications. And the moral proportion he preserved in exhibiting the complex and often wild play of the passions must have been largely due to the harmony of his soul with the constitution of things. What the Restoration dramatists regarded or understood as moral proportion, was not moral proportion at all, but a proportion fashioned according to merely conventional ideas of justice. Shakespeare's moral proportion appeared to them, in their low spiritual condition, a moral chaos, which they set about converting, in some of his great plays, into a cosmos; and a sad muss, if not a ridiculous muss, they made of it. Signal examples of this are the 'rifacimenti' of the Tempest by Dryden and Davenant, the King Lear by Tate, and the Antony and Cleopatra (entitled 'All for Love, or the World well Lost') by Dryden.

In Milton, though there is a noticeable, an even distinctly marked, reduction of the life of the spirit (in the sense in which I have been using these words) exhibited by Shakespeare, it is still very strong and efficient, and continues uninfluenced by the malign atmosphere around him the last fifteen years of his life, which were lived in the reign of Charles II. Within that period he wrote the 'Paradise Lost', 'Paradise Regained', and 'Samson Agonistes'. "Milton," says Emerson, "was the stair or high table-land to let down the English genius from the summits of Shakespeare."

"These heights could not be maintained. They were followed by a meanness and a descent of the mind into lower levels; the loss of wings; no high speculation. Locke, to whom the meaning of ideas was unknown, became the type of philosophy, and his "understanding" the measure, in all nations, of the English intellect. His countrymen forsook the lofty sides of Parnassus, on which they had once walked with echoing steps, and disused the studies once so beloved; the powers of thought fell into neglect."

The highest powers of thought cannot be realized without the life of the spirit. It is this, as I have already said, which has been the glory of the greatest thinkers since the world began; not their intellects, but the co-operating, unconscious power IMMANENT in their intellects.

During the Restoration period, and later, spiritual life was at its very lowest ebb. I mean, spiritual life as exhibited in the poetic and dramatic literature of the time, whose poisoned fountain-head was the dissolute court of Charles II. All the slops of that court went into the drama, all the 'sentina reipublicae', the bilge water of the ship of state. The dramatic writers of the time, to use the words of St. Paul in his letter to the Ephesians, "walked in the vanity of their mind; having the understanding darkened, being alienated from the life of God through the ignorance that was in them because of the blindness of their heart; who, being past feeling, gave themselves over unto lasciviousness, to work all uncleanness with greediness." The age, as Emerson says, had no live, distinct, actuating convictions. It was in even worse than a negative condition. As represented by its drama and poetry, it may almost be said to have repudiated the moral sentiment. A spiritual disease affected the upper classes, which continued down into the reign of the Georges. There appears to have been but little belief in the impulse which the heart imparts to the intellect, or that the latter draws greatness from the inspiration of the former. There was a time in the history of the Jews in which, it is recorded, "there was no open vision". It can be said, emphatically, that in the time of Charles II. there was no open vision. And yet that besotted, that spiritually dark age, which was afflicted with pneumatophobia, flattered itself that there had never been an age so flooded with light. The great age of Elizabeth (which designation I would apply to the period of fifty years or more, from 1575 to 1625, or somewhat later), in which the human faculties, in their whole range, both intellectual and spiritual, reached such a degree of expansion as they had never before reached in the history of the world,—that great age, I say, the age of Spenser, Sidney, Marlowe, Shakespeare, Bacon, Raleigh, Hooker, Ben Jonson, Beaumont, Fletcher, Chapman, Dekker, Ford, Herbert, Heywood, Massinger (and this list of great names might be continued),—that great age, I say, was regarded by the men of the Restoration period as barbarous in comparison with their own. But beneath all, still lay the restorative elements of the English character, which were to reassert themselves and usher in a new era of literary productiveness, the greatest since the Elizabethan age, and embodying the highest ideals of life to which the race has yet attained. We can account, to some extent, for this interregnum or spiritual life, but only to some extent. The brutal heartlessness and licentiousness of the court which the exiled Charles brought back with him, and the release from Puritan restraint, explain partly the state of things, or rather the degree to which the state of things was pushed.

In the middle of the eighteenth century, or somewhat earlier, the rise of the spiritual tide is distinctly observable. We see a reaction setting in against the soulless poetry which culminated in Alexander Pope, whose 'Rape of the Lock' is the masterpiece of that poetry. It is, in fact, the most brilliant society-poem in the literature. De Quincey pronounces it to be, though somewhat extravagantly, "the most exquisite monument of playful fancy that universal literature offers." Bishop Warburton, one of the great critical authorities of the age, believed in the infallibility of Pope, if not of THE Pope.

To notice but a few of the influences at work: Thomson sang of the Seasons, and invited attention to the beauties of the natural world, to which the previous generation had been blind and indifferent. Bishop Percy published his 'Reliques of Ancient English Poetry', thus awakening a new interest in the old ballads which had sprung from the heart of the people, and contributing much to free poetry from the yoke of the conventional and the artificial, and to work a revival of natural unaffected feeling. Thomas Tyrwhitt edited in a scholarly and appreciative manner, the Canterbury Tales of Chaucer. James McPherson published what he claimed to be translations from the poems of Ossian, the son of Fingal. Whether genuine or not, these poems indicated the tendency of the time. In Scotland, the old ballad spirit, which had continued to exist with a vigor but little abated by the influence of the artificial, mechanical school of poetry, was gathered up and intensified in the songs of him "who walked in glory and in joy, following his plow, along the mountain-side", and who is entitled to a high rank among the poetical reformers of the age.

It is not surprising that the great literary dictator in Percy's day, Dr. Samuel Johnson, should treat the old ballads with ridicule. The good man had been trained in a different school of poetry, and could not in his old age yield to the reactionary movement. Bishop Warburton, who ranked next to Johnson in literary authority, had nothing but sneering contempt to bestow upon upon the old ballads, and this feeling was shared by many others in the foremost ranks of literature and criticism. But in the face of all opposition, and aided by the yearning for literary liberty that was abroad, the old ballads grew more and more into favor. The influence of this folklore was not confined to England. It extended across the sea, and swayed the genius of such poets as Buerger and Goethe and Schiller.

Along with the poetical revival in the eighteenth century, came the great religious revival inaugurated by the Wesleys and Whitefield; and of this revival, the poetry of William Cowper was a direct product. But the two revivals were co-radical,—one was not derived from the other. The long-suppressed spiritual elements of the nation began to reassert themselves in religion and in poetry. The Church had been as sound asleep as the Muses.

Cowper belongs to the Whitefield side of the religious revival, the Evangelicals, as they were called (those that remained within the Establishment). In his poem entitled 'Hope', he vindicates the memory of Whitefield under the name Leuconomus, a translation into Greek, of White field. It was his conversion to Evangelicism which gave him his inspiration and his themes. 'The Task' has been as justly called the poem of Methodism as the 'Paradise Lost' has been called the epic of Puritanism. In it we are presented with a number of pictures of the utterly fossilized condition of the clergy of the day in the Established Church (see especially book II., vv. 326-832, in which he satirizes the clergy and the universities).

Cowper has been truly characterized by Professor Goldwin Smith, as "the apostle of feeling to a hard age, to an artificial age, the apostle of nature. He opened beneath the arid surface of a polished but soulless society, a fountain of sentiment which had long ceased to flow."

The greatest things in this world are often done by those who do not know they are doing them. This is especially true of William Cowper. He was wholly unaware of the great mission he was fulfilling; his contemporaries were wholly unaware of it. And so temporal are the world's standards, in the best of times, that spiritual regenerators are not generally recognized until long after they have passed away, when the results of what they did are fully ripe, and philosophers begin to trace the original impulses.

"Only reapers, reaping early
In among the bearded barley,
Hear a song that echoes cheerly
From the river winding clearly
    Down to towered Camelot:

And by the moon the reaper weary,
Piling sheaves in uplands airy,
Listening, whispers, 'Tis the fairy
    Lady of Shalott."

John Burroughs, in his inspiring essay on Walt Whitman entitled 'The Flight of the Eagle', quotes the following sentence from a lecture on Burns, delivered by "a lecturer from over seas", whom he does not name: "When literature becomes dozy, respectable, and goes in the smooth grooves of fashion, and copies and copies again, something must be done; and to give life to that dying literature, a man must be found not educated under its influence."

Such a man I would say was William Cowper, who, in his weakness, was

"Strong to sanctify the poet's high vocation",

and who

"Testified this solemn truth, while phrenzy desolated,—
Nor man nor angel satisfies whom only God created."

John Keats, in his poem entitled 'Sleep and Poetry', has well characterized the soulless poetry of the period between the Restoration and the poetical revival in the latter part of the eighteenth century, but more especially of the Popian period. After speaking of the greatness of his favorite poets of the Elizabethan period, he continues:—

"Could all this be forgotten? Yes, a schism
Nurtured by foppery and barbarism,
Made great Apollo blush for this his land.

Men were thought wise who could not understand
His glories: with a puling infant's force
They sway'd about upon a rocking-horse,
And thought it Pegasus."

(Alluding to the rocking-horse movement of the Popian verse.)

"Ah dismal soul'd!
The winds of heaven blew, the ocean roll'd
It's gathering waves—ye felt it not. The blue
Bar'd its eternal bosom, and the dew
Of summer nights collected still to make
The morning precious: beauty was awake!
Why were ye not awake? But ye were dead
To things ye knew not of,—were closely wed
To musty laws lined out with wretched rule
And compass vile: so that ye taught a school
Of dolts to smooth, inlay, and clip, and fit,
Till, like the certain wands of Jacob's wit,
Their verses tallied. Easy was the task:
A thousand handicraftsmen wore the mask
Of Poesy. Ill-fated, impious race!
That blasphem'd the bright Lyrist to his face,
And did not know it,—no, they went about,
Holding a poor, decrepid standard out
Mark'd with most flimsy mottoes, and in large
The name of one Boileau!"

It was these lines that raised the ire of Byron, who regarded them as an irreverent assault upon his favorite poet, Pope. In the controversy occasioned by the Rev. W. L. Bowles's strictures on the Life and Writings of Pope, Byron perversely asks, "Where is the poetry of which one-half is good? Is it the Aeneid? Is it Milton's? Is it Dryden's? Is it any one's except Pope's and Goldsmith's, of which ALL is good?"

In the first quarter of the nineteenth century, the spiritual flow which, as I have said, set in about the middle of the eighteenth century, and received its first great impulse from William Cowper, reached its high tide in Wordsworth, Coleridge, Shelley, Keats,

Southey, and Byron. These poets were all, more or less, influenced by that great moral convulsion, the French revolution, which stirred men's souls to their deepest depths, induced a vast stimulation of the meditative faculties, and contributed much toward the unfolding of the ideas "on man, on nature, and on human life", which have since so vitalized English poetry.[*]

Wordsworth exhibited in his poetry, as they had never before been exhibited, the permanent absolute relations of nature to the human spirit, interpreted the relations between the elemental powers of creation and the moral life of man, and vindicated the inalienable birthright of the lowliest of men to those inward "oracles of vital deity attesting the Hereafter." Wordsworth's poetry is, in fact, so far as it bears upon the natural world, a protest against the association theory of beauty of the eighteenth century—a theory which was an offshoot of the philosophy of Locke, well characterized by Macvicar, in his 'Philosophy of the Beautiful' (Introd., pp. xv., xvi), as "an ingenious hypothesis for the close of the eighteenth century, when the philosophy then popular did not admit, as the ground of any knowledge, anything higher than self-repetition and the transformation of sensations."

Coleridge's 'Rime of the Ancient Mariner' is an imaginative expression of that divine love which embraces all creatures, from the highest to the lowest, of the consequences of the severance of man's soul from this animating principle of the universe, and of those spiritual threshings by and through which it is brought again under its blessed influence. In his 'Cristabel' he has exhibited the dark principle of evil, lurking within the good, and ever struggling with it. We read it in the spell the wicked witch Geraldine works upon her innocent and unsuspecting protector; we read it in the strange words which Geraldine addresses to the spirit of the saintly mother who has approached to shield from harm the beloved child

---

[*]   "The agitation, the frenzy, the sorrow of the times, reacted upon the human intellect, and FORCED men into meditation. Their own nature was held up before them in a sterner form. They were compelled to contemplate an ideal of man, far more colossal than is brought forward in the tranquil aspects of society; and they were often engaged, whether they would or not, with the elementary problems of social philosophy. Mere danger forced a man into thoughts which else were foreign to his habits. Mere necessity of action forced him to decide."—Thomas De Quincey's 'Essay on Style'.

for whom she died; we read it in the story of the friendship and enmity between the Baron and Sir Roland de Vaux of Tryermaine; we read it in the vision seen in the forest by the minstrel Bard, of the bright green snake coiled around the wings and neck of a fluttering dove; and, finally, we read it in its most startling form, in the conclusion of the poem, "A little child, a limber elf, singing, dancing to itself," etc., wherein is exhibited the strange tendency to express love's excess "with words of unmeant bitterness". This dark principle of evil, we may suppose, after dwelling in the poet's mind, in an abstract form, crept into this broken poem, where it lies coiled up among the choicest and most fragrant flowers, and occasionally springs its warning rattle, and projects its forked tongue, to assure us of its ugly presence.

Both these great poems show the influence of the revival of the old English Ballads. Coleridge had drunk deep of their spirit.

Shelley and Byron were fully charged with the revolutionary spirit of the time. Shelley, of all the poets of his generation, had the most prophetic fervor in regard to the progress of the democratic spirit. All his greatest poems are informed with this fervor, but it is especially exhibited in the 'Prometheus Unbound', which is, in the words of Todhunter, "to all other lyrical poems what the ninth symphony is to all other symphonies; and more than this, for Shelley has here outsoared himself more unquestionably than Beethoven in his last great orchestral work . . . The Titan Prometheus is the incarnation of the genius of humanity, chained and suffering under the tyranny of the evil principle which at present rules over the world, typified in Jupiter; the name Prometheus, FORESIGHT, connecting him with that poetic imagination which is the true prophetic power, penetrating the mystery of things, because, as Shelley implies, it is a kind of divine Logos incarnate in man—a creative force which dominates nature by acting in harmony with her."

It is, perhaps, more correct to say of Byron, that he was charged with the spirit of revolt rather than with the revolutionary spirit. The revolutionary spirit was in him indefinite, inarticulate; he offered nothing to put in the place of the social and political evils against which he rebelled. There is nothing CONSTRUCTIVE in his poetry. But if his great passion-capital, his keen spiritual susceptibility, and his great power of vigorous expression, had been brought into the service of constructive thought, he might have been a restorative power in his generation.

The greatest loss which English poetry ever sustained, was in the premature death of John Keats. What he would have done had his life been spared, we have an assurance in what he has left us. He was spiritually constituted to be one of the subtlest interpreters of the secrets of life that the whole range of English poetry exhibits. No poet ever more deeply felt "the vital connection of beauty with truth". He realized in himself his idea of the poet expressed in his lines,—

> "'Tis the man who with a man
> Is an equal, be he king,
> Or poorest of the beggar-clan,
> Or any other wondrous thing
> A man may be 'twixt ape and Plato;
> 'Tis the man who with a bird,
> Wren, or eagle, finds his way to
> All its instincts; he hath heard
> The lion's roaring, and can tell
> What his horny throat expresseth,
> And to him the tiger's yell
> Comes articulate and presseth
> On his ear like mother tongue."*

---

*   "We often think of Shelley and Keats together, and they seem to have an attraction for minds of the same cast. They were both exposed to the same influences, those revolutionary influences in literature and religion which inaugurated a new period. Yet there is a great contrast as well as a great similarity between them, and it is interesting to remark the different spiritual results in the case of these two different minds subjected to conditions so similar in general, though different in detail. Both felt the same need, the need of ESCAPE, desiring to escape from the actual world in which they perceived more evil than good, to some other ideal world which they had to create for themselves. This is the point of their similarity; their need and motive were the same, to escape from the limitations of the present. But they escaped in different directions, Keats into the past where he reconstructed a mythical Greek world after the designs of his own fancy, Shelley into a future where he sought in a new and distant era, in a new and distant world, a refuge from the present. We may compare Keats's 'Hyperion' with Shelley's 'Prometheus', as both poems touch the same idea—the dominion of elder gods usurped by younger, for Prometheus belonged to the elder generation. The impression Keats gives us is that he represents the dethroned gods in the sad vale, "far from the fiery noon", for the pleasure of moving among them himself, and creates their lonely world as a retreat for his own spirit. Whereas in the 'Prometheus Unbound' we

Wordsworth, and the other poets I have named, Byron, Shelley, Keats, and Coleridge, made such a protest against authority in poetry as had been made in the 16th century against authority in religion; and for this authority were substituted the soul-experiences of the individual poet, who set his verse to the song that was within him, and chose such subjects as would best embody and articulate that song.

But by the end of the first quarter of the present century, the great poetical billow, which was not indeed caused by, but received an impulse from, the great political billow, the French Revolution (for they were cognate or co-radical movements), had quite spent itself, and English poetry was at a comparatively low ebb. The Poetical Revolution had done its work. A poetical interregnum of a few years' duration followed, in which there appeared to be a great reduction of the spiritual life of which poetry is the outgrowth.

Mr. Edmund W. Gosse, in his article 'On the Early Writings of Robert Browning', in the 'Century' for December, 1881, has characterized this interregnum a little too contemptuously, perhaps. There was, indeed, a great fall in the spiritual tide; but it was not such a dead-low tide as Mr. Gosse would make it.

At length, in 1830, appeared a volume of poems by a young man, then but twenty-one years of age, which distinctly marked the setting in of a new order of things. It bore the following title: 'Poems, chiefly Lyrical. By Alfred Tennyson, London: Effingham Wilson, Royal Exchange, Cornhill, 1830.' pp. 154.

The volume comprised fifty-three poems, among which were 'The Poet' and 'The Poet's Mind'. These two poems were

feel that the scenes laid in ancient days and built on Greek myths, have a direct relation to the destinies of man, and that Shelley went back into the past because he believed it was connected with the future, and because he could use it as an artistic setting for exhibiting an ideal world in the future.

"This problem of escape—to rescue the soul from the clutches of time, 'ineluctabile tempus',—which Keats and Shelley tried to resolve for themselves by creating a new world in the past and the future, met Browning too. The new way which Browning has essayed—the way in which he accepts the present and deals with it, CLOSES with time instead of trying to elude it, and discovers in the struggle that this time, 'ineluctabile tempus', is really a faithful vassal of eternity, and that its limits serve and do not enslave illimitable spirit."—From a Paper by John B. Bury, B.A., Trin. Coll., Dublin, on Browning's 'Aristophanes' Apology', read at 38th meeting of the Browning Soc., Jan. 29, 1886.

emphatically indicative of the high ideal of poetry which had been attained, and to the development of which the band of poets of the preceding generation had largely contributed.

A review of the volume, by John Stuart Mill, then a young man not yet twenty-five years of age, was published in 'The Westminster' for January, 1831. It bears testimony to the writer's fine insight and sure foresight; and it bears testimony, too, to his high estimate of the function of poetry in this world—an estimate, too, in kind and in degree, not older than this present century. The review is as important a landmark in the development of poetical criticism, as are the two poems I have mentioned, in the development of poetical ideals, in the nineteenth century.

In the concluding paragraph of the review, Mill says: "A genuine poet has deep responsibilities to his country and the world, to the present and future generations, to earth and heaven. He, of all men, should have distinct and worthy objects before him, and consecrate himself to their promotion. It is thus that he best consults the glory of his art, and his own lasting fame . . . Mr. Tennyson knows that "the poet's mind is holy ground"; he knows that the poet's portion is to be

"Dower'd with the hate of hate, the scorn of scorn,
    The love of love";

he has shown, in the lines from which we quote, his own just conception of the grandeur of a poet's destiny; and we look to him for its fulfilment . . . If our estimate of Mr. Tennyson be correct, he too is a poet; and many years hence may be read his juvenile description of that character with the proud consciousness that it has become the description and history of his own works."

Two years later, that is, in 1832 (the volume, however, is antedated 1833), appeared 'Poems by Alfred Tennyson', pp. 163. In it were contained 'The Lady of Shalott', and the untitled poems, known by their first lines, 'You ask me why, tho' ill at ease', 'Of old sat Freedom on the Heights', and 'Love thou thy Land, with Love far brought'.

In 'The Lady of Shalott' is mystically shadowed forth the relation which poetic genius should sustain to the world for whose spiritual redemption it labors, and the fatal consequences of its being seduced by the world's temptations, the lust of the flesh, and the lust of the eyes, and the pride of life.

The other poems, 'You ask me why', 'Of old sat Freedom', and 'Love thou thy land', are important as exponents of what may be called the poet's institutional creed. A careful study of his subsequent poetry will show that in these early poems he accurately and distinctly revealed the attitude toward outside things which he has since maintained. He is a good deal of an institutional poet, and, as compared with Browning, a STRONGLY institutional poet. Browning's supreme and all-absorbing interest is in individual souls. He cares but little, evidently, about institutions. At any rate, he gives them little or no place in his poetry. Tennyson is a very decided reactionary product of the revolutionary spirit which inspired some of his poetical predecessors of the previous generation. He has a horror of the revolutionary. To him, the French Revolution was "the blind hysterics of the Celt", ['In Memoriam', cix.], and "the red fool-fury of the Seine" ['I. M.', cxxvii.]. He attaches great importance to the outside arrangements of society for upholding and advancing the individual. He would "make Knowledge circle with the winds", but "her herald, Reverence", must

"fly
Before her to whatever sky
Bear seed of men and growth of minds."

He has a great regard for precedents, almost AS precedents. He is emphatically the poet of law and order. All his sympathies are decidedly, but not narrowly, conservative. He is, in short, a choice product of nineteenth century ENGLISH civilization; and his poetry may be said to be the most distinct expression of the refinements of English culture—refinements, rather than the ruder but more vital forms of English strength and power. All his ideals of institutions and the general machinery of life, are derived from England. She is

"the land that freemen till,
That sober-suited Freedom chose,
The land where, girt with friends or foes,
A man may speak the thing he will;

A land of SETTLED GOVERNMENT,
A LAND OF JUST AND OLD RENOWN,
WHERE FREEDOM BROADENS SLOWLY DOWN
FROM PRECEDENT TO PRECEDENT:

Where faction seldom gathers head,
But by degrees to fullness wrought,
The strength of some diffusive thought
Hath time and space to work and spread."

But the anti-revolutionary and the institutional features of Tennyson's poetry are not those of the higher ground of his poetry. They are features which, though primarily due, it may be, to the poet's temperament, are indirectly due to the particular form of civilization in which he has lived, and moved, and had his culture, and which he reflects more than any of his poetical contemporaries.

The most emphasized and most vitalized idea, the idea which glints forth everywhere in his poetry, which has the most important bearing on man's higher life, and which marks the height of the spiritual tide reached in his poetry, is, that the highest order of manhood is a well-poised, harmoniously operating duality of the active or intellectual or discursive, and the passive or spiritually sensitive. This is the idea which INFORMS his poem of 'The Princess'. It is prominent in 'In Memoriam' and in 'The Idylls of the King'. In 'The Princess', the Prince, speaking of the relations of the sexes, says:—

"in the long years liker must they grow;
The man be more of woman, she of man;
He gain in sweetness and in moral height,
Nor lose the wrestling thews that throw the world;
She mental breadth, nor fail in childward care,
Nor lose the childlike in the larger mind;
Till at the last she set herself to man,
Like perfect music unto noble words;
And so these twain, upon the skirts of Time,
Sit side by side, full-summ'd in all their powers,
Dispensing harvest, sowing the To-be,
Self-reverent each and reverencing each,

40

Distinct in individualities,
But like each other ev'n as those who love.
Then comes the statelier Eden back to men:
Then reign the world's great bridals, chaste and calm:
Then springs the crowning race of humankind."

To state briefly the cardinal Tennysonian idea, man must realize a WOMANLY MANLINESS, and woman a MANLY WOMANLINESS.

Tennyson presents to us his ideal man in the 109th section of 'In Memoriam'. It is descriptive of his friend, Arthur Henry Hallam. All that is most characteristic of Tennyson, even his Englishness, is gathered up in this poem of six stanzas. It is interesting to meet with such a representative and comprehensive bit in a great poet.

"HEART-AFFLUENCE in discursive talk
From household fountains never dry;
The CRITIC CLEARNESS of an eye,
That saw through all the Muses' walk;

SERAPHIC INTELLECT AND FORCE
TO SEIZE AND THROW THE DOUBTS OF MAN;
IMPASSIONED LOGIC, which outran
The bearer in its fiery course;

HIGH NATURE AMOROUS OF THE GOOD,
BUT TOUCH'D WITH NO ASCETIC GLOOM;
And passions pure in snowy bloom
Through all the years of April blood."

The first two verses of this stanza also characterize the King Arthur of the 'Idylls of the King'.* In the next stanza we have the poet's institutional Englishness:—

"A love of freedom rarely felt,
Of freedom in her regal seat

---

* See 'The Holy Grail', the concluding thirty-two verses, beginning: "And spake I not too truly, O my Knights", and ending "ye have seen that ye have seen".

Of England; not the school-boy heat,
The blind hysterics of the Celt;

And MANHOOD FUSED WITH FEMALE GRACE*
In such a sort, the child would twine
A trustful hand, unask'd, in thine,
And find his comfort in thy face;

All these have been, and thee mine eyes
Have look'd on; if they look'd in vain,
My shame is greater who remain,
Nor let thy wisdom make me wise."

Tennyson's genius was early trained by the skeptical philosophy of the age. All his poetry shows this. The 'In Memoriam' may almost be said to be the poem of nineteenth century scepticism. To this scepticism he has applied an "all-subtilizing intellect", and has translated it into the poetical "concrete", with a rare artistic skill, and more than this, has subjected it to the spiritual instincts and apperceptions of the feminine side of his nature and made it vassal to a larger faith. But it is, after all, not the vital faith which Browning's poetry exhibits, a faith PROCEEDING DIRECTLY FROM THE SPIRITUAL MAN. It is rather the faith expressed by Browning's Bishop Blougram:—

"With me faith means perpetual unbelief
Kept quiet like the snake 'neath Michael's foot,
Who stands firm just because he feels it writhe."

And Tennyson, in picturing to us in the Idylls, the passage of the soul "from the great deep to the great deep", appears to have felt it necessary to the completion of that picture (or why did he do it?), that he should bring out that doubt at the last moment. The dying Arthur is made to say:—

"I am going a long way
With these thou seest—if indeed I go

---

* The idea of 'The Princess'.

(For all my mind is clouded with a doubt)—
To the island-valley of Avilion"; etc.

Tennyson's poetry is, in fact, an expression of the highest sublimation of the scepticism which came out of the eighteenth century, which invoked the authority of the sensualistic philosophy of Locke, and has since been fostered by the science of the nineteenth; while Browning's poetry is a decided protest against, and a reactionary product of, that scepticism, that infidel philosophy (infidel as to the transcendental), and has CLOSED with it and borne away the palm.

The key-note of his poetry is struck in 'Paracelsus', published in 1835, in his twenty-third year, and, with the exception of 'Pauline' published in 1833, the earliest of his compositions: Paracelsus says (and he who knows Browning knows it to be substantially his own creed):—

"Truth is within ourselves; it takes no rise
From outward things, whate'er you may believe:
There is an inmost centre in us all,
Where truth abides in fulness; and around
Wall upon wall, the gross flesh hems it in,
This perfect, clear perception—which is truth;
A baffling and perverting carnal mesh
Blinds it, and makes all error: and 'TO KNOW'
Rather consists in opening out a way
Whence the imprisoned splendour may escape,
Than in effecting entry for a light
Supposed to be without. Watch narrowly
The demonstration of a truth, its birth,
And you trace back the effluence to its spring
And source within us, where broods radiance vast,
To be elicited ray by ray, as chance
Shall favour: chance—for hitherto, your sage
Even as he knows not how those beams are born,
As little knows he what unlocks their fount;
And men have oft grown old among their books
To die, case-hardened in their ignorance,
Whose careless youth had promised what long years
Of unremitted labour ne'er performed:

While, contrary, it has chanced some idle day,
That autumn-loiterers just as fancy-free
As the midges in the sun, have oft given vent
To truth—produced mysteriously as cape
Of cloud grown out of the invisible air.
Hence, may not truth be lodged alike in all,
The lowest as the highest? some slight film
The interposing bar which binds it up,
And makes the idiot, just as makes the sage
Some film removed, the happy outlet whence
Truth issues proudly? See this soul of ours!
How it strives weakly in the child, is loosed
In manhood, clogged by sickness, back compelled
By age and waste, set free at last by death:
Why is it, flesh enthralls it or enthrones?
What is this flesh we have to penetrate?
Oh, not alone when life flows still do truth
And power emerge, but also when strange chance
Ruffles its current; in unused conjuncture,
When sickness breaks the body—hunger, watching,
Excess, or languor—oftenest death's approach—
Peril, deep joy, or woe. One man shall crawl
Through life, surrounded with all stirring things,
Unmoved—and he goes mad; and from the wreck
Of what he was, by his wild talk alone,
You first collect how great a spirit he hid.
Therefore set free the spirit alike in all,
Discovering the true laws by which the flesh
Bars in the spirit! . . .

* * * * *

I go to gather this
The sacred knowledge, here and there dispersed
About the world, long lost or never found.
And why should I be sad, or lorn of hope?
Why ever make man's good distinct from God's?
Or, finding they are one, why dare mistrust?
Who shall succeed if not one pledged like me?
Mine is no mad attempt to build a world
Apart from His, like those who set themselves

To find the nature of the spirit they bore,
And, taught betimes that all their gorgeous dreams
Were only born to vanish in this life,
Refused to fit them to this narrow sphere,
But chose to figure forth another world
And other frames meet for their vast desires,—
Still, all a dream! Thus was life scorned; but life
Shall yet be crowned: twine amaranth! I am priest!"

And again:—

"In man's self arise
August anticipations, symbols, types
Of a dim splendour ever on before,
In that eternal circle run by life:
For men begin to pass their nature's bound,
And find new hopes and cares which fast supplant
Their proper joys and griefs; and outgrow all*
The narrow creeds of right and wrong, which fade
Before the unmeasured thirst for good; while peace
Rises within them ever more and more.
Such men are even now upon the earth,
Serene amid the half-formed creatures round,
Who should be saved by them and joined with them."

In the last three verses is indicated the doctrine of the regenerating power of exalted personalities, so prominent in Browning's poetry, and which is treated in the next paper.

There is no 'tabula rasa' doctrine in these passages, nor in any others, in the poet's voluminous works; and of all men of great intellect and learning (it is always a matter of mere insulated intellect), born in England since the days of John Locke, no one, perhaps, has been so entirely untainted with this doctrine as Robert Browning. It is a doctrine which great spiritual vitality (and that he early possessed), reaching out, as it does, beyond all experience, beyond all transformation of sensations, and all conclusions of the discursive understanding, naturally and spontaneously rejects. It simply says, "I know better", and there an end.

---

*   proper: In the sense of the Latin PROPRIUS, peculiar, private, personal.

The great function of the poet, as poet, is, with Browning, to open out a way whence the imprisoned splendor may escape, not to effect entry for a light supposed to be without; to trace back the effluence to its spring and source within us, where broods radiance vast, to be elicited ray by ray.

In 'Fifine at the Fair', published thirty-seven years after 'Paracelsus', is substantially the same doctrine:—

"Truth inside, and outside, truth also; and between
Each, falsehood that is change, as truth is permanence.
The individual soul works through the shows of sense,
(Which, ever proving false, still promise to be true)
Up to an outer soul as individual too;
And, through the fleeting, lives to die into the fixed,
And reach at length 'God, man, or both together mixed'."

In his poem entitled 'Popularity', included in his "fifty men and women", the speaker, in the monologue, "draws" his "true poet", whom HE knows, if others do not; who, though he renders, or stands ready to render, to his fellows, the supreme service of opening out a way whence the imprisoned splendor of their souls may escape, is yet locked safe from end to end of this dark world.

Though there may be, in his own time, no "reapers reaping early in among the bearded barley" and "piling sheaves in uplands airy" who hear his song, he holds the FUTURE fast, accepts the COMING AGES' duty, their present for this past. This true, creative poet, whom the speaker calls "God's glow-worm, creative in the sense of revealing, whose inmost centre, where truth abides in fulness, has that freedom of responsiveness to the divine which makes him the revealer of it to men, plays the part in the world of spirit which, in the material world was played by the fisher who, first on the coast of Tyre the old, fished up the purple-yielding murex. Until the precious liquor, filtered by degrees, and refined to proof, is flasked and priced, and salable at last, the world stands aloof. But when it is all ready for the market, the small dealers, "put blue into their line", and outdare each other in azure feats by which they secure great popularity, and, as a result, fare sumptuously; while he who fished the murex up was unrecognized, and fed, perhaps, on porridge.

Popularity.

I.

Stand still, true poet that you are!
I know you; let me try and draw you.
Some night you'll fail us: when afar
You rise, remember one man saw you,
Knew you, and named a star!*

II.

My star, God's glow-worm! Why extend
That loving hand of His which leads you,
Yet locks you safe from end to end
Of this dark world, unless He needs you,
Just saves your light to spend?

III.

His clenched hand shall unclose at last,
I know, and let out all the beauty:
My poet holds the future fast,
Accepts the coming ages' duty,
Their present for this past.

IV.

That day, the earth's feast-master's brow
Shall clear, to God the chalice raising;
"Others give best at first, but Thou
Forever set'st our table praising,
Keep'st the good wine till now!"

V.

Meantime, I'll draw you as you stand,
With few or none to watch and wonder:
I'll say—a fisher, on the sand
By Tyre the old, with ocean-plunder,
A netful, brought to land.

VI.

Who has not heard how Tyrian shells

---

* named: Announced.

Enclosed the blue, that dye of dyes
Whereof one drop worked miracles,
And colored like Astarte's eyes
Raw silk the merchant sells?

VII.

And each by-stander of them all
Could criticise, and quote tradition
How depths of blue sublimed some pall—
To get which, pricked a king's ambition;
Worth sceptre, crown, and ball.

VIII.

Yet there's the dye, in that rough mesh,
The sea has only just o'er-whispered!
Live whelks, each lip's beard dripping fresh,
As if they still the water's lisp heard
Through foam the rock-weeds thresh.

IX.

Enough to furnish Solomon
Such hangings for his cedar-house,
That, when gold-robed he took the throne
In that abyss of blue, the Spouse
Might swear his presence shone

X.

Most like the centre-spike of gold
Which burns deep in the blue-bell's womb
What time, with ardors manifold,
The bee goes singing to her groom,
Drunken and overbold.

XI.

Mere conchs! not fit for warp or woof!
Till cunning come to pound and squeeze
And clarify,—refine to proof*

---

*   Original reading:
"Till art comes,—comes to pound and squeeze
And clarify,—refines to proof."

The liquor filtered by degrees,
While the world stands aloof.

XII.
And there's the extract, flasked and fine,
And priced and salable at last!
And Hobbs, Nobbs, Stokes, and Nokes combine
To paint the future from the past,
Put blue into their line.*

XIII.
Hobbs hints blue,—straight he turtle eats:
Nobbs prints blue,—claret crowns his cup:
Nokes outdares Stokes in azure feats,—
Both gorge. Who finished the murex up?
What porridge had John Keats?

The spiritual ebb and flow exhibited in English poetry (the highest tide being reached in Tennyson and Browning) which I have endeavored cursorily to present, bear testimony to the fact that human nature WILL assert its wholeness in the civilized man. And there must come a time, in the progress of civilization, when this ebb and flow will be less marked than it has been heretofore, by reason of a better balancing, which will be brought about, of the intellectual and the spiritual. Each will have its due activity. The man of intellectual pursuits will not have a starved spiritual nature; and the man of predominant spiritual functions will not have an intellect weakened into a submissiveness to formulated, stereotyped, and, consequently, lifeless dogmas.

Robert Browning is in himself the completest fulfilment of this equipoise of the intellectual and the spiritual, possessing each in an exalted degree; and his poetry is an emphasized expression of his own personality, and a prophecy of the ultimate results of Christian civilization.

---

* "Line" is perhaps meant to be used equivocally,—their line of business or line of their verse.

II. The Idea of Personality and of Art as an intermediate agency of Personality, as embodied in Browning's Poetry.

1. General Remarks.

"Subsists no law of Life outside of Life.

* * * * *

The Christ himself had been no Lawgiver,
Unless he had given the LIFE, too, with the law."

The importance of Robert Browning's poetry, as embodying the profoundest thought, the subtlest and most complex sentiment, and, above all, the most quickening spirituality of the age, has, as yet, notwithstanding the great increase within the last few years of devoted students, received but a niggardly recognition when compared with that received by far inferior contemporary poets. There are, however, many indications in the poetical criticism of the day that upon it will ere long be pronounced the verdict which is its due. And the founding of a society in England in 1881, "to gather together some at least of the many admirers of Robert Browning, for the study and discussion of his works, and the publication of papers on them, and extracts from works illustrating them" has already contributed much towards paying a long-standing debt.

Mr. Browning's earliest poems, 'Pauline' (he calls it in the preface to the reprint of it in 1868 "a boyish work", though it exhibits the great basal thought of all his subsequent poetry), was published in 1833, since which time he has produced the largest body of poetry produced by any one poet in English literature; and the range of thought and passion which it exhibits is greater than that of any other poet, without a single exception, since the days of Shakespeare. And he is the most like Shakespeare in his deep interest in human nature in all its varieties of good and evil. Though endowed with a powerful, subtle, and restless intellect, he has throughout his voluminous poetry made the strongest protest that has been made in these days against mere intellect. And his poetry has, therefore, a peculiar value in an age like the present—an age exhibiting "a condition of humanity which has thrown itself wholly on its intellect and its genius in physics, and has done marvels in material science and invention, but at the expense of the interior divinity." It is the human heart, that is, the intuitive, the non-discursive side of man, with its hopes and its prophetic aspirations, as opposed to the analytic, the discursive understanding, which is to him a subject of the deepest and most scrutinizing interest. He knows that its deepest depths are "deeper than did ever plummet sound"; but he also knows that it is in these depths that life's greatest secrets must be sought. The philosophies excogitated by the insulated intellect help nothing toward even a glimpse of these secrets. In one of his later poems, that entitled 'House', he has intimated, and forcibly intimated, his sense of the impossibility of penetrating to the Holy of Holies of this wondrous human heart, though assured as he is that all our hopes in regard to the soul's destiny are warmed and cherished by what radiates thence. He quotes, in the last stanza of this poem, from Wordsworth's sonnet on the Sonnet, "With this same key Shakespeare unlocked his heart," and then adds, "DID Shakespeare? If so, the less Shakespeare he!"

Mrs. Browning, in the Fifth Book of her 'Aurora Leigh', has given a full and very forcible expression to the feeling which has caused the highest dramatic genius of the present day to seek refuge in the poem and the novel. "I will write no plays; because the drama, less sublime in this, makes lower appeals, defends more menially, adopts the standard of the public taste to chalk its height on, wears a dog-chain round its regal neck, and learns to carry and fetch the fashions of the day, to please the day; . . . 'Tis that, honoring to its worth the drama, I would fear to keep it down to the level of the footlights . . . The growing drama has outgrown such toys of simulated stature, face, and speech, it also, peradventure, may outgrow the simulation of the painted scene, boards, actors, prompters, gaslight, and costume; and TAKE FOR A WORTHIER STAGE, THE SOUL ITSELF, ITS SHIFTING FANCIES AND CELESTIAL LIGHTS, WITH ALL ITS GRAND ORCHESTRAL SILENCES TO KEEP THE PAUSES OF THE RHYTHMIC SOUNDS."

Robert Browning's poetry is, in these days, the fullest realization of what is expressed in the concluding lines of this passage: he has taken for a worthier stage, the soul itself, its shifting fancies and celestial lights, more than any other poet of the age. And he has worked with a thought-and-passion capital greater than the combined thought-and-passion capital of the richest of his poetical contemporaries. And he has thought nobly of the soul, and has treated it as, in its essence, above the fixed and law-bound system of things which we call nature; in other words, he has treated it as supernatural. "Mind," he makes the Pope say, in 'The Ring and the Book',—and his poetry bears testimony to its being his own conviction and doctrine,—"Mind is not matter, nor from matter, but above." With every student of Browning, the recognition and acceptance of this must be his starting-point. Even that which impelled the old dog, in his poem entitled 'Tray' ('Dramatic Lyrics', First Series), to rescue the beggar child that fell into the river, and then to dive after the child's doll, and bring it up, after a long stay under water, the poet evidently distinguishes from matter,—regards as "not matter nor from matter, but above":—

"And so, amid the laughter gay,
Trotted my hero off,—old Tray,—
Till somebody, prerogatived
With reason, reasoned: 'Why he dived,
His brain would show us, I should say.

John, go and catch—or, if needs be,
Purchase that animal for me!
By vivisection, at expense
Of half-an-hour and eighteen pence,
How brain secretes dog's soul, we'll see!"

In his poem entitled 'Halbert and Hob' ('Dramatic Lyrics', First Series), quoting from Shakespeare's 'King Lear', "Is there a reason in nature for these hard hearts?" the poet adds, "O Lear, That a reason OUT of nature must turn them soft, seems clear!"

Mind is, with Browning, SUPERNATURAL, but linked with, and restrained, and even enslaved by, the natural. The soul, in its education, that is, in its awakening, becomes more and more independent of the natural, and, as a consequence, more responsive to higher souls and to the Divine. ALL SPIRIT IS MUTUALLY

ATTRACTIVE, and the degree of attractiveness results from the degree of freedom from the obstructions of the material, or the natural. Loving the truth implies a greater or less degree of that freedom of the spirit which brings it into SYMPATHY with the true. "If ye abide in My word," says Christ (and we must understand by "word" His own concrete life, the word made flesh, and living and breathing), "if ye abide in My word" (that is, continue to live My life), "then are ye truly My disciples; and ye shall know the truth, and the truth shall make you free" (John viii. 32).

In regard to the soul's INHERENT possessions, its microcosmic potentialities, Paracelsus is made to say (and this may be taken, too, as the poet's own creed), "Truth is WITHIN ourselves; it takes no rise from outward things, whate'er you may believe: there is an inmost centre in us all, where truth abides in fulness; and around, wall upon wall, the gross flesh hems it in, this perfect, clear perception—which is truth. A baffling and perverting carnal mesh blinds it, and makes all error: and, TO KNOW, rather consists in opening out a way whence the imprisoned splendour may escape, than in effecting entry for a light supposed to be without."

All possible thought is IMPLICIT in the mind, and waiting for release—waiting to become EXPLICIT. "Seek within yourself," says Goethe, "and you will find everything; and rejoice that, without, there lies a Nature that says yea and amen to all you have discovered in yourself." And Mrs. Browning, in the person of Aurora Leigh, writes: "The cygnet finds the water; but the man is born in ignorance of his element, and feels out blind at first, disorganized by sin in the blood,—his spirit-insight dulled and crossed by his sensations. Presently we feel it quicken in the dark sometimes; then mark, be reverent, be obedient,—for those dumb motions of imperfect life are oracles of vital Deity attesting the Hereafter. Let who says 'The soul's a clean white paper', rather say, a palimpsest, a prophet's holograph defiled, erased, and covered by a monk's,—the Apocalypse by a Longus! poring on which obscure text, we may discern perhaps some fair, fine trace of what was written once, some off-stroke of an alpha and omega expressing the old Scripture."

This "fair, fine trace of what was written once", it was the mission of Christ, it is the mission of all great personalities, of all the concrete creations of Genius, to bring out into distinctness and vital glow. It is not, and cannot be, brought out,—and this fact is emphasized in the poetry of Browning,—it cannot be brought out, through what is born and resides in the brain: it is brought out, either directly or indirectly, by the attracting power of magnetic personalities, the ultimate, absolute personality being the God-man, Christ, qea/nqrwpos.

The human soul is regarded in Browning's poetry as a complexly organized, individualized divine force, destined to gravitate towards the Infinite. How is this force, with its numberless checks and counter-checks, its centripetal and centrifugal tendencies, best determined in its necessarily oblique way? How much earthly ballast must it carry, to keep it sufficiently steady, and how little, that it may not be weighed down with materialistic heaviness? How much certainty must it have of its course, and how much uncertainty, that it may shun the "torpor of assurance",[*] and not lose the vigor which comes of a dubious and obstructed road, "which who stands upon is apt to doubt if it's indeed a road."[**] "Pure faith indeed," says Bishop Blougram, to Gigadibs, the literary man, "you know not what you ask! naked belief in God the Omnipotent, Omniscient, Omnipresent, sears too much the sense of conscious creatures, to be borne. It were the seeing him, no flesh shall dare. Some think, Creation's meant to show him forth: I say, it's meant to hide him all it can, and that's what all the blessed Evil's for. Its use in time is to environ us, our breath, our drop of dew, with shield enough against that sight till we can bear its stress. Under a vertical sun, the exposed brain and lidless eye and disimprisoned heart less certainly would wither up at once, than mind, confronted with the truth of Him. But time and earth case-harden us to live; the feeblest sense is trusted most: the child feels God a moment, ichors o'er the place, plays on and grows to be a man like us. With me, faith means perpetual unbelief kept quiet like the snake 'neath Michael's foot, who stands calm just because he feels it writhe."[***]

---

[*]   'The Ring and the Book', The Pope, v. 1853.
[**]   'Bishop Blougram's Apology', vv. 198, 199.
[***]   'Bishop Blougram's Apology', vv. 650-671.

There is a remarkable passage to the same effect in 'Paracelsus', in which Paracelsus expatiates on the "just so much of doubt as bade him plant a surer foot upon the sun-road."

And in 'Easter Day':—

"You must mix some uncertainty
With faith, if you would have faith BE."

And the good Pope in 'The Ring and the Book', alluding to the absence of true Christian soldiership, which is revealed by Pompilia's case, says: "Is it not this ignoble CONFIDENCE, cowardly hardihood, that dulls and damps, makes the old heroism impossible? Unless . . . what whispers me of times to come? What if it be the mission of that age my death will usher into life, to SHAKE THIS TORPOR OF ASSURANCE FROM OUR CREED, reintroduce the DOUBT discarded, bring the formidable danger back we drove long ago to the distance and the dark?"

True healthy doubt means, in Browning, that the spiritual nature is sufficiently quickened not to submit to the conclusions of the insulated intellect. It WILL reach out beyond them, and assert itself, whatever be the resistance offered by the intellect. Mere doubt, without any resistance from the intuitive, non-discursive side of our nature, is the dry-rot of the soul. The spiritual functions are "smothered in surmise". Faith is not a matter of blind belief, of slavish assent and acceptance, as many no-faith people seem to regard it. It is what Wordsworth calls it, "a passionate intuition", and springs out of quickened and refined sentiment, out of inborn instincts which are as cultivable as are any other elements of our complex nature, and which, too, may be blunted beyond a consciousness of their possession. And when one in this latter state denies the reality of faith, he is not unlike one born blind denying the reality of sight.

A reiterated lesson in Browning's poetry, and one that results from his spiritual theory, is, that the present life is a tabernacle-life, and that it can be truly lived only as a tabernacle-life; for only such a life is compatible with the ever-continued aspiration and endeavor which is a condition of, and inseparable from, spiritual vitality.

Domizia, in the tragedy of 'Luria', is made to say:—

"How inexhaustibly the spirit grows!
One object, she seemed erewhile born to reach
With her whole energies and die content,—
So like a wall at the world's edge it stood,
With naught beyond to live for,—is that reached?—
Already are new undream'd energies
Outgrowing under, and extending farther
To a new object,—there's another world!"

The dying John in 'A Death in the Desert', is made to say:—

"I say that man was made to grow, not stop;
That help he needed once, and needs no more,
Having grown up but an inch by, is withdrawn:
For he hath new needs, and new helps to these.
This imports solely, man should mount on each
New height in view; the help whereby he mounts,
The ladder-rung his foot has left, may fall,
Since all things suffer change save God the Truth.
Man apprehends him newly at each stage
Whereat earth's ladder drops, its service done;
And nothing shall prove twice what once was proved."

And again:—

"Man knows partly but conceives beside,
Creeps ever on from fancies to the fact,
And in this striving, this converting air
Into a solid he may grasp and use,
Finds progress, man's distinctive mark alone,
Not God's, and not the beasts': God is, they are,
Man partly is and wholly hopes to be.
Such progress could no more attend his soul
Were all it struggles after found at first
And guesses changed to knowledge absolute,
Than motion wait his body, were all else
Than it the solid earth on every side,
Where now through space he moves from rest to rest.
Man, therefore, thus conditioned, must expect
He could not, what he knows now, know at first;

What he considers that he knows to-day,
Come but to-morrow, he will find misknown;
Getting increase of knowledge, since he learns
Because he lives, which is to be a man,
Set to instruct himself by his past self:
First, like the brute, obliged by facts to learn,
Next, as man may, obliged by his own mind,
Bent, habit, nature, knowledge turned to law.
God's gift was that man should conceive of truth
And yearn to gain it, catching at mistake,
As midway help till he reach fact indeed.
The statuary ere he mould a shape
Boasts a like gift, the shape's idea, and next
The aspiration to produce the same;
So, taking clay, he calls his shape thereout,
Cries ever, 'Now I have the thing I see':
Yet all the while goes changing what was wrought,
From falsehood like the truth, to truth itself.
How were it had he cried, 'I see no face,
No breast, no feet i' the ineffectual clay'?
Rather commend him that he clapped his hands,
And laughed, 'It is my shape and lives again!'
Enjoyed the falsehood touched it on to truth,
Until yourselves applaud the flesh indeed
In what is still flesh-imitating clay.
Right in you, right in him, such way be man's!
God only makes the live shape at a jet.
Will ye renounce this fact of creatureship?
The pattern on the Mount subsists no more,
Seemed awhile, then returned to nothingness,
But copies, Moses strove to make thereby
Serve still and are replaced as time requires:
By these make newest vessels, reach the type!
If ye demur, this judgment on your head,
Never to reach the ultimate, angels' law,
Indulging every instinct of the soul
There where law, life, joy, impulse are one thing."

Browning has given varied and beautiful expressions to these
ideas throughout his poetry.

The soul must rest in nothing this side of the infinite. If it does rest in anything, however relatively noble that thing may be, whether art, or literature, or science, or theology, even, it declines in vitality—it torpifies. However great a conquest the combatant may achieve in any of these arenas, "striding away from the huge gratitude, his club shouldered, lion-fleece round loin and flank", he must be "bound on the next new labour, height o'er height ever surmounting—destiny's decree!"*

> "Rejoice that man is hurled
> From change to change unceasingly,
> His soul's wings never furled!"***

But this tabernacle-life, which should ever look ahead, has its claims which must not be ignored, and its standards which must not be too much above present conditions. Man must "fit to the finite his infinity" ('Sordello'). Life may be over-spiritual as well as over-worldly. "Let us cry, 'All good things are ours, nor soul helps flesh more, now, than flesh helps soul!'"*** The figure the poet employs in 'The Ring and the Book' to illustrate the art process, may be as aptly applied to life itself—the greatest of all arts. The life-artist must know how to secure the proper degree of malleability in this mixture of flesh and soul. He must mingle gold with gold's alloy, and duly tempering both effect a manageable mass. There may be too little of alloy in earth-life as well as too much—too little to work the gold and fashion it, not into a ring, but ring-ward. "On the earth the broken arcs; in the heaven a perfect round" ('Abt Vogler'). "Oh, if we draw a circle premature, heedless of far gain, greedy for quick returns of profit, sure, bad is our bargain" ('A Grammarian's Funeral').

'An Epistle containing the Strange Medical Experiences of Karshish, the Arab Physician', is one of Browning's most remarkable psychological studies. It may be said to polarize the idea, so often presented in his poetry, that doubt is a condition of the vitality of faith. In this poem, the poet has treated a supposed case of a spiritual knowledge "increased beyond the fleshly faculty—heaven

---

*   'Aristophanes' Apology', p. 31, English ed.
**   'James Lee's Wife', sect. 6.
*** 'Rabbi Ben Ezra'.

opened to a soul while yet on earth, earth forced on a soul's use while seeing heaven", a spiritual state, less desirable and far less favorable to the true fulfilment of the purposes of earth-life, than that expressed in the following lines from 'Easter Day':—

"A world of spirit as of sense
Was plain to him, yet not TOO plain,
Which he could traverse, not remain
A GUEST IN:—else were permanent
Heaven on earth, which its gleams were meant
To sting with hunger for full light", etc.

The Epistle is a subtle representation of a soul conceived with absolute spiritual standards, while obliged to live in a world where all standards are relative and determined by the circumstances and limitations of its situation.

The spiritual life has been too distinctly revealed for fulfilling aright the purposes of earth-life, purposes which the soul, while in the flesh, must not ignore, since, in the words of Rabbi Ben Ezra, "all good things are ours, nor soul helps flesh more, now, than flesh helps soul." The poem may also be said to represent what is, or should be, the true spirit of the man of science. In spite of what Karshish writes, apologetically, he betrays his real attitude throughout, towards the wonderful spiritual problem involved.

It is, as many of Browning's Monologues are, a double picture—one direct, the other reflected, and the reflected one is as distinct as the direct. The composition also bears testimony to Browning's own soul-healthfulness. Though the spiritual bearing of things is the all-in-all, in his poetry, the robustness of his nature, the fulness and splendid equilibrium of his life, protect him against an inarticulate mysticism. Browning is, in the widest and deepest sense of the word, the healthiest of all living poets; and in general constitution the most Shakespearian.

What he makes Shakespeare say, in the Monologue entitled 'At the Mermaid', he could say, with perhaps greater truth, in his own person, than Shakespeare could have said it:—

"Have you found your life distasteful?
My life did and does smack sweet.

Was your youth of pleasure wasteful?
Mine I save and hold complete.
Do your joys with age diminish?
When mine fail me, I'll complain.
Must in death your daylight finish?
My sun sets to rise again.

I find earth not gray but rosy,
Heaven not grim but fair of hue.
Do I stoop? I pluck a posy.
Do I stand and stare? All's blue."

It is the spirit expressed in these lines which has made his poetry so entirely CONSTRUCTIVE. With the destructive spirit he has no affinities. The poetry of despair and poets with the dumps he cannot away with.

Perhaps the most comprehensive passage in Browning's poetry, expressive of his ideal of a complete man under the conditions of earth-life, is found in 'Colombe's Birthday', Act IV. Valence says of Prince Berthold:—

"He gathers earth's WHOLE GOOD into his arms, standing, as man, now, stately, strong and wise—marching to fortune, not surprised by her: one great aim, like a guiding star above—which tasks strength, wisdom, stateliness, to lift his manhood to the height that takes the prize; a prize not near—lest overlooking earth, he rashly spring to seize it—nor remote, so that he rests upon his path content: but day by day, while shimmering grows shine, and the faint circlet prophesies the orb, he sees so much as, just evolving these, the stateliness, the wisdom, and the strength to due completion, will suffice this life, and lead him at his grandest to the grave."

Browning fully recognizes, to use an expression in his 'Fra Lippo Lippi', fully recognizes "the value and significance of flesh." A healthy and well-toned spiritual life is with him the furthest removed from asceticism. To the passage from his 'Rabbi Ben Ezra' already quoted, "all good things are ours, nor soul helps flesh more, now, than flesh helps soul", should be added what David sings to Saul, in the poem entitled 'Saul'. Was the full physical life ever more beautifully sung?

"Oh! our manhood's prime vigour! no spirit feels waste,
Not a muscle is stopped in its playing, nor sinew unbraced.
Oh, the wild joys of living! the leaping from rock up to rock,
The strong rending of boughs from the fir-tree, the cool
    silver shock
Of the plunge in a pool's living water, the hunt of the bear,
And the sultriness showing the lion is couched in his lair.
And the meal, the rich dates yellowed over with gold dust
    divine,
And the locust-flesh steeped in the pitcher, the full draught
    of wine,
And the sleep in the dried river-channel where bulrushes tell
That the water was wont to go warbling so softly and well.
How good is man's life, the mere living! how fit to employ
All the heart and the soul and the senses for ever in joy!"

Though this is said in the person of the beautiful shepherd-boy, David, whoever has lived any time with Browning, through his poetry, must be assured that it is also an expression of the poet's own experience of the glory of flesh. He has himself been an expression of the fullest physical life: and now, in his five and seventieth year, since the 7th of last May, he preserves both mind and body in a magnificent vigor. If his soul had been lodged in a sickly, rickety body, he could hardly have written these lines from 'Saul'. Nor could he have written 'Caliban upon Setebos', especially the opening lines: "Will sprawl, now that the heat of day is best, flat on his belly in the pit's much mire, with elbows wide, fists clenched to prop his chin. And, while he kicks both feet in the cool slush, and feels about his spine small eft-things course, run in and out each arm, and make him laugh: and while above his head a pompion-plant, coating the cave-top as a brow its eye, creeps down to touch and tickle hair and beard, and now a flower drops with a bee inside, and now a fruit to snap at, catch and crunch,—he looks out o'er yon sea which sunbeams cross and recross till they weave a spider-web (meshes of fire, some great fish breaks at times), and talks to his own self, howe'er he please, touching that other, whom his dam called God."

There's a grand passage in 'Balaustion's Adventure: including a transcript from Euripides', descriptive of Herakles as he returns, after his conflict with Death, leading back Alkestis, which shows the poet's sympathy with the physical. The passage is more valuable as revealing that sympathy, from the fact that it's one of his additions to Euripides:—

> "there stood the strength,
> Happy as always; something grave, perhaps;
> The great vein-cordage on the fret-worked brow,
> Black-swollen, beaded yet with battle-drops
> The yellow hair o' the hero!—his big frame
> A-quiver with each muscle sinking back
> Into the sleepy smooth it leaped from late.
> Under the great guard of one arm, there leant
> A shrouded something, live and woman-like,
> Propped by the heart-beats 'neath the lion-coat.
> When he had finished his survey, it seemed,
> The heavings of the heart began subside,
> The helping breath returned, and last the smile
> Shone out, all Herakles was back again,
> As the words followed the saluting hand."

It is not so much the glory of flesh which Euripides represents in Herakles, as the indulgence of appetite, at a time, too, when that indulgence is made to appear the more culpable and gross.

This idea of "the value and significance of flesh", it is important to note, along with the predominant spiritual bearing of Browning's poetry. It articulates everywhere the spiritual, so to speak—makes it healthy and robust, and protects it against volatility and from running into mysticism.

2. The Idea of Personality as embodied in Browning's Poetry.

A cardinal idea in Browning's poetry is the regeneration of men through a personality who brings fresh stuff for them to mould, interpret, and prove right,—new feeling fresh from God—whose life re-teaches them what life should be, what faith is, loyalty and simpleness, all once revealed, but taught them so long since that they have but mere tradition of the fact,—truth copied falteringly from copies faint, the early traits all dropped away. ('Luria'.) The intellect plays a secondary part. Its place is behind the instinctive, spiritual antennae which conduct along their trembling lines, fresh stuff for the intellect to stamp and keep—fresh instinct for it to translate into law.

"A people is but the attempt of many to rise to the completer life of one." ('A Soul's Tragedy'.)

Only the man who supplies new feeling fresh from God, quickens and regenerates the race, and sets it on the King's highway from which it has wandered into by-ways—not the man of mere intellect, of unkindled soul, that supplies only stark-naked thought. Through the former, "God stooping shows sufficient of His light for those i' the dark to rise by." ('R. and B., Pompilia'.) In him men discern "the dawn of the next nature, the new man whose will they venture in the place of theirs, and whom they trust to find them out new ways to the new heights which yet he only sees." ('Luria'.) It is by reaching towards, and doing fealty to, the greater spirit which attracts and absorbs their own, that, "trace by trace old memories reappear, old truth returns, their slow thought does its work, and all's re-known." ('Luria'.)

> "Some existence like a pact
> And protest against Chaos, . . .
>
> . . . The fullest effluence of the finest mind,
> All in degree, no way diverse in kind
> From minds above it, minds which, more or less
> Lofty or low, move seeking to impress
> Themselves on somewhat; but one mind has climbed
> Step after step, by just ascent sublimed.
> Thought is the soul of act, and, stage by stage,
> Is soul from body still to disengage,
> As tending to a freedom which rejects
> Such help, and incorporeally affects
> The world, producing deeds but not by deeds,
> Swaying, in others, frames itself exceeds,
> Assigning them the simpler tasks it used
> To patiently perform till Song produced
> Acts, by thoughts only, for the mind: divest
> Mind of e'en Thought, and, lo, God's unexpressed
> Will dawns above us!" ('Sordello'.)

A dangerous tendency of civilization is that towards crystallization—towards hardened, inflexible conventionalisms which "refuse the soul its way".

Such crystallization, such conventionalisms, yield only to the dissolving power of the spiritual warmth of life-full personalities.

The quickening, regenerating power of personality is everywhere exhibited in Browning's poetry. It is emphasized in 'Luria', and in the Monologues of the Canon Caponsacchi and Pompilia, in the 'Ring and the Book'; it shines out, or glints forth, in 'Colombe's Birthday', in 'Saul', in 'Sordello', and in all the Love poems. I would say, en passant, that Love is always treated by Browning as a SPIRITUAL claim; while DUTY may be only a worldly one. SEE especially the poem entitled 'Bifurcation'. In 'Balaustion's Adventure: including a transcipt from Euripides', the regenerating power of personality may be said to be the leavening idea, which the poet has introduced into the Greek play. It is entirely absent in the original. It baptizes, so to speak, the Greek play, and converts it into a Christian poem. It is the "new truth" of the poet's 'Christmas Eve'.

After the mourning friends have spoken their words of consolation to the bereaved husband, the last word being, "Dead, thy wife—living, the love she left", Admetos "turned on the comfort, with no tears, this time. HE WAS BEGINNING TO BE LIKE HIS WIFE. I told you of that pressure to the point, word slow pursuing word in monotone, Alkestis spoke with; so Admetos, now, solemnly bore the burden of the truth. And as the voice of him grew, gathered strength, and groaned on, and persisted to the end, we felt how deep had been descent in grief, and WITH WHAT CHANGE HE CAME UP NOW TO LIGHT, and left behind such littleness as tears."

And when Alkestis was brought back by Herakles, "the hero twitched the veil off: and there stood, with such fixed eyes and such slow smile, Alkestis' silent self! It was the crowning grace of that great heart to keep back joy: procrastinate the truth until the wife, who had made proof and found the husband wanting, might essay once more, hear, see, and feel him RENOVATED now—ABLE TO DO, NOW, ALL HERSELF HAD DONE, RISEN TO THE HEIGHT OF HER: so, hand in hand, the two might go together, live and die." (Compare with this the restoration of Hermione to her husband, in 'The Winter's Tale', Act V.)

A good intellect has been characterized as the chorus of Divinity. Substitute for "good intellect", an exulted magnetic personality, and the thought is deepened. An exalted magnetic personality is the chorus of Divinity, which, in the great Drama of Humanity, guides and interprets the feelings and sympathies of other souls and thus adjusts their attitudes towards the Divine. It is not the highest function of such a personality to TEACH, but rather to INFORM, in the earlier and deeper sense of the word. Whatever mere doctrine he may promulgate, is of inferior importance to the spontaneous action of his concrete life, in which the True, the Beautiful, and the Good, breathe and live. What is born in the brain dies there, it may be; at best, it does not, and cannot of itself, lead up to the full concrete life. It is only through the spontaneou and unconscious fealty which an inferior does to a superior soul (a fealty resulting from the responsiveness of spirit to spirit), that the former is slowly and silently transformed into a more or less approximate image of the latter. The stronger personality leads the weaker on by paths which the weaker knows not, upward he leads him, though his steps be slow and vacillating. Humility, in the Christian sense, means this fealty to the higher. It doesn't mean self-abasement, self-depreciation, as it has been understood to mean, by both the Romish and the Protestant Church. Pride, in the Christian sense, is the closing of the doors of the soul to a great magnetic guest.

Browning beautifully expresses the transmission of personality in his 'Saul'. But according to Browning's idea, personality cannot strictly be said to be transmitted. Personality rather evokes its LIKE from other souls, which are "all in degree, no way diverse in kind." ('Sordello'.)

David has reached an advanced stage in his symbolic song to Saul. He thinks now what next he shall urge "to sustain him where song had restored him?—Song filled to the verge his cup with the wine of this life, pressing all that it yields of mere fruitage, the strength and the beauty: beyond, on what fields glean a vintage more potent and perfect to brighten the eye and bring blood to the lip, and commend them the cup they put by?" So once more the string of the harp makes response to his spirit, and he sings:—

"In our flesh grows the branch of this life, in our soul it
   bears fruit.

Thou hast marked the slow rise of the tree,—how its stem
   trembled first

Till it passed the kid's lip, the stag's antler; then safely
   outburst

The fan-branches all round; and thou mindest when these,
   too, in turn

Broke a-bloom and the palm-tree seemed perfect; yet more
   was to learn,

E'en the good that comes in with the palm-fruit. Our dates
   shall we slight,

When their juice brings a cure for all sorrow? or care for
   the plight

Of the palm's self whose slow growth produced them?
   Not so! stem and branch

Shall decay, nor be known in their place, while the palm-
   wine shall staunch

Every wound of man's spirit in winter. I pour thee such
   wine.

Leave the flesh to the fate it was fit for! the spirit be thine!

By the spirit, when age shall o'ercome thee, thou still shalt
   enjoy

More indeed, than at first when, inconscious, the life of a
   boy.

Crush that life, and behold its wine running! each deed thou
   hast done

Dies, revives, goes to work in the world; until e'en as the sun

Looking down on the earth, though clouds spoil him,
   though tempests efface,

Can find nothing his own deed produced not, must
   everywhere trace

The results of his past summer-prime,—SO, EACH RAY
   OF THY WILL,

EVERY FLASH OF THY PASSION AND PROWESS,
   LONG OVER, SHALL THRILL

THY WHOLE PEOPLE, THE COUNTLESS, WITH
   ARDOUR, TILL THEY TOO GIVE FORTH

A LIKE CHEER TO THEIR SONS: WHO IN TURN,
   FILL THE SOUTH AND THE NORTH

WITH THE RADIANCE THY DEED WAS THE
GERM OF."

In the concluding lines is set forth what might be characterized
as the apostolic succession of a great personality—the succession
of those "who in turn fill the South and the North with the radiance
his deed was the germ of."

What follows in David's song gives expression to the other
mode of transmitting a great personality—that is, through records
that "give unborn generations their due and their part in his being",
and also to what those records owe their effectiveness, and are
saved from becoming a dead letter.

> "Is Saul dead? In the depth of the vale make his tomb—bid
> arise
> A grey mountain of marble heaped four-square, till, built to
> the skies,
> Let it mark where the great First King slumbers: whose fame
> would ye know?
> Up above see the rock's naked face, where the record shall go
> In great characters cut by the scribe,—Such was Saul, so he
> did;
> With the sages directing the work, by the populace chid,—
> For not half, they'll affirm, is comprised there! Which fault to
> amend,
> In the grove with his kind grows the cedar, whereon they shall
> spend
> (See, in tablets 'tis level before them) their praise, and record
> With the gold of the graver, Saul's story,—the statesman's
> great word
> Side by side with the poet's sweet comment. The river's a-
> wave
> With smooth paper-reeds grazing each other when prophet-
> winds rave:
> So the pen gives unborn generations their due and their part
> In thy being! Then, first of the mighty, thank God that thou
> art!"

What is said in this passage is applicable to the record we
have of Christ's life upon earth. Christianity has only to a very

limited extent been perpetuated through the letter of the New Testament. It has been perpetuated chiefly through transmissions of personalities, through apostolic succession, in a general sense, and through embodiments of his spirit in art and literature—"the stateman's great word", "the poet's sweet comment". Were it not for this transmission of the quickening power of personality, the New Testament would be to a great extent a dead letter. It owes its significance to the quickened spirit which is brought to the reading of it. The personality of Christ could not be, through a plastic sympathy, moulded out of the New Testament records, without the aid of intermediate personalities.

The Messianic idea was not peculiar to the Jewish race—the idea of a Person gathering up within himself, in an effective fulness and harmony, the restorative elements of humanity, which have lost their power through dispersion and consequent obscuration. There have been Messiahs of various orders and ranks in every age,—great personalities that have realized to a greater or less extent (though there has been but one, the God-Man, who fully realized), the spiritual potentialities in man, that have stood upon the sharpest heights as beacons to their fellows. In the individual the species has, as it were, been gathered up, epitomized, and intensified, and he has thus been a prophecy, and to some extent a fulfilment of human destiny.

"A poet must be earth's ESSENTIAL king", as Sordello asserts, and he is that by virtue of his exerting or shedding the influence of his essential personality. "If caring not to exert the proper essence of his royalty, he, the poet, trifle malapert with accidents instead—good things assigned as heralds of a better thing behind"—he is "deposed from his kingly throne, and his glory is taken from him". Of himself, Sordello says: "The power he took most pride to test, whereby all forms of life had been professed at pleasure, forms already on the earth, was but a means of power beyond, whose birth should, in its novelty, be kingship's proof. Now, whether he came near or kept aloof the several forms he longed to imitate, not there the kingship lay, he sees too late. Those forms, unalterable first as last, proved him her copier, not the protoplast of nature: what could come of being free by action to exhibit tree for tree, bird, beast, for beast and bird, or prove earth bore one veritable man or woman more? Means to an end such proofs are: what the end?"

The answer given involves the great Browning idea of the quickening power of personality: "Let essence, whatsoe'er it be, extend—never contract!"

By "essence" we must understand that which "constitutes man's self, is what Is", as the dying John, in 'A Death in the Desert', expresses it—that which backs the active powers and the conscious intellect, "subsisting whether they assist or no".

"Let essence, whatsoe'er it be, extend—never contract!" Sordello says. "Already you include the multitude"; that is, you gather up in yourself, in an effective fulness and harmony, what lies scattered and ineffective in the multitude; "then let the mulitude include yourself"; that is, be substantiated, essenced with yourself; "and the result were new: themselves before, the multitude turn YOU" (become yourself). "This were to live and move and have, in them, your being, and secure a diadem you should transmit (because no cycle yearns beyond itself, but on itself returns) when the full sphere in wane, the world o'erlaid long since with you, shall have in turn obeyed some orb still prouder, some displayer, still more potent than the last, of human will, and some new king depose the old."

This is a most important passage to get hold of in studying Browning. It may be said to gather up Browning's philosophy of life in a nutshell.

There's a passage to the same effect in 'Balaustion's Adventure', in regard to the transmission of the poet's essence. The enthusiastic Rhodian girl, Balaustion, after she has told the play of Euripides, years after her adventure, to her four friends, Petale, Phullis, Charope, and Chrusion, says:—

"I think I see how . . . you, I, or any one, might mould a new Admetos, new Alkestis. Ah, that brave bounty of poets, the one royal race that ever was, or will be, in this world! They give no gift that bounds itself, and ends i' the giving and the taking: theirs so breeds i' the heart and soul of the taker, so transmutes the man who only was a man before, that he grows god-like in his turn, can give—he also: share the poet's privilege, bring forth new good, new beauty from the old. As though the cup that gave the wine, gave too the god's prolific giver of the grape, that vine, was wont to find out, fawn around his footstep, springing still to bless the dearth, at bidding of a Mainad."

3. Art as an Intermediate Agency of Personality.

If Browning's idea of the quickening, the regeneration, the rectification of personality, through a higher personality, be fully comprehended, his idea of the great function of Art, as an intermediate agency of personality, will become plain. To emphasize the latter idea may be said to be the ultimate purpose of his masterpiece, 'The Ring and the Book'.

The complexity of the circumstances involved in the Roman murder case, adapts it admirably to the poet's purpose—namely, to exhibit the swervings of human judgment in spite of itself, and the conditions upon which the rectification of that judgment depends.

This must be taken, however, as only the articulation, the framework, of the great poem. It is richer in materials, of the most varied character, than any other long poem in existence. To notice one feature of the numberless features of the poem, which might be noticed, Browning's deep and subtle insight into the genius of the Romish Church is shown in it more fully than in any other of his poems,—though special phases of that genius are distinctly exhibited in numerous poems: a remarkable one being 'The Bishop orders his Tomb at St. Praxed's Church'. It is questionable whether any work of any kind has ever exhibited that genius more fully and distinctly than 'The Ring and the Book' exhibits it. The reader breathes throughout the ecclesiastical atmosphere of the Eternal City.

To return from this digression, the several monologues of which the poem consists, with the exception of those of the Canon Caponsacchi, Pompilia, and the Pope, are each curious and subtle and varied exponents of the workings, without the guidance of instinct at the heart, of the prepossessed, prejudiced intellect, and of the sources of its swerving into error. What is said of the "feel after the vanished truth" in the monologue entitled 'Half Rome'— the speaker being a jealous husband—will serve to characterize, in a general way, "the feel after truth" exhibited in the other monologues: "honest enough, as the way is: all the same, harboring in the CENTRE OF ITS SENSE a hidden germ of failure, shy but sure, should neutralize that honesty and leave that feel for truth at fault, as the way is too. Some prepossession, such as starts amiss, by but a hair's-breadth at the shoulder-blade, the arm o' the feeler, dip he ne'er so brave; and so leads waveringly, lets fall wide o' the mark his finger meant to find, and fix truth at the bottom, that deceptive speck."

The poet could hardly have employed a more effective metaphor in which to embody the idea of mental swerving. The several monologues all going over the same ground, are artistically justified in their exhibiting, each of them, a quite distinct form of this swerving. For the ultimate purpose of the poet, it needed to be strongly emphasized. The student of the poem is amazed, long before he gets over all these monologues, at the Protean capabilities of the poet's own intellect. It takes all conceivable attitudes toward the case, and each seems to be a perfectly easy one.

These monologues all lead up to the great moral of the poem, which is explicitly set forth at the end, namely, "that our human speech is naught, our human testimony false, our fame and human estimation, words and wind. Why take the artistic way to prove so much? Because, it is the glory and good of Art, that Art remains the one way possible of speaking truth, to mouths like mine, at least. How look a brother in the face and say, Thy right is wrong, eyes hast thou yet art blind, thine ears are stuffed and stopped, despite their length: and, oh, the foolishness thou countest faith! Say this as silvery as tongue can troll—the anger of the man may be endured, the shrug, the disappointed eyes of him are not so bad to bear—but here's the plague, that all this trouble comes of telling truth, which truth, by when it reaches him, looks false, seems to be just the thing it would supplant, nor recognizable by whom it left: while falsehood would have done the work of truth. But Art,— wherein man nowise speaks to men, only to mankind,—Art may tell a truth obliquely, DO THE THING SHALL BREED THE THOUGHT", that is, bring what is IMPLICIT within the soul, into the right attitude to become EXPLICIT—bring about a silent adjustment through sympathy induced by the concrete; in other words, prepare the way for the perception of the truth—"do the thing shall breed the thought, nor wrong the thought missing the mediate word"; meaning, that Art, so to speak, is the word made flesh,—IS the truth, and, as Art, has nothing directly to do with the explicit. "So may you paint your picture, twice show truth, beyond mere imagery on the wall,—so, note by note, bring music from your mind, deeper than ever the Andante dived,—so write a book shall mean beyond the facts, suffice the eye and save the soul beside."

And what is the inference the poet would have us draw from this passage? It is, that the life and efficacy of Art depends on the personality of the artist, which "has informed, transpierced, thridded, and so thrown fast the facts else free, as right through ring and ring runs the djereed and binds the loose, one bar without a break." And it is really this fusion of the artist's soul, which kindles, quickens, INFORMS those who contemplate, respond to, reproduce sympathetically within themselves the greater spirit which attracts and absorbs their own. The work of Art is apocalyptic of the artist's own personality. It CANNOT be impersonal. As is the temper of his spirit, so is, MUST be, the temper of his Art product.* It is hard to believe, almost impossible to believe, that 'Titus Andronicus' could have been written by Shakespeare, the external testimony to the authorship, notwithstanding. Even if he had written it as a burlesque of such a play as Marlow's 'Jew of Malta', he could not have avoided some revelation of that sense of moral proportion which is omnipresent in his Plays. But I can find no Shakespeare in 'Titus Andronicus'. Are we not certain what manner of man Shakespeare was from his Works (notwithstanding that critics are ever asserting their impersonality)—far more certain than if his biography had been written by one who knew him all his life, and sustained to him the most intimate relations? We know Shakespeare—or he CAN be known, if the requisite conditions are met, better, perhaps, than any other great author that ever lived— know, in the deepest sense of the word, in a sense other than that in which we know Dr. Johnson, through Boswell's Biography. The moral proportion which is so signal a characteristic of his Plays could not have been imparted to them by the conscious intellect. It was SHED from his spiritual constitution.

By "speaking truth" in Art's way, Browning means, inducing a right ATTITUDE toward, a full and free SYMPATHY with, the

---

* "And long it was not after, when I was confirmed in this opinion, that he who would not be frustrate of his hope to write well hereafter in laudable things, ought himself to be a true poem."—Milton's 'Apology for Sinectymnuus'.

True, which is a far more important and effective way of speaking truth than delivering truth 'in re'. A work of Art, worthy of the name, need not be true to fact, but must be true in its spiritual attitude, and being thus true, it will tend to induce a corresponding attitude in those who do fealty to it. It will have the influence, though in an inferior degree, it may be, of a magnetic personality. Personality is the ultimate source of spiritual quickening and adjustment. Literature and all forms of Art are but the intermediate agencies of personalities. The artist cannot be separated from his art. As is the artist so MUST be his art. The 'aura', so to speak, of a great work of Art, must come from the artist's own personality. The spiritual worth of Shakespeare's 'Winter's Tale' is not at all impaired by the fact that Bohemia is made a maritime country, that Whitsun pastorals and Christian burial, and numerous other features of Shakespeare's own age, are introduced into pagan times, that Queen Hermione speaks of herself as a daughter of the Emperor of Russia, that her statue is represented as executed by Julio Romano, an Italian painter of the 16th century, that a puritan sings psalms to hornpipes, and, to crown all, that messengers are sent to consult the oracle of Apollo, at Delphi, which is represented as an island! All this jumble, this gallimaufry, I say, does not impair the spiritual worth of the play. As an Art-product, it invites a rectified attitude toward the True and the Sweet.

If we look at the letter of the trial scene in 'The Merchant of Venice', it borders on the absurd; but if we look at its spirit, we see the Shakespearian attitude of soul which makes for righteousness, for the righteousness which is inherent in the moral constitution of the universe.

The inmost, secretest life of Shakespeare's Plays came from the personality, the inmost, secretest life, of the man Shakespeare. We might, with the most alert sagacity, note and tabulate and aggregate his myriad phenomenal merits as a dramatic writer, but we might still be very far from that something back of them all, or rather that IMMANENT something, that mystery of personality, that microcosmos, that "inmost centre, where truth abides in fulness", as Browning makes Paracelsus characterize it, "constituting man's self, is what Is", as he makes the dying John characterize it, in 'A Death in the Desert', that "innermost of the inmost, most interior of the interne", as Mrs. Browning characterizes it, "the hidden Soul", as

Dallas characterizes it, which is projected into, and constitutes the soul of, the Plays, and which is reached through an unconscious and mystic sympathy on the part of him who habitually communes with and does fealty to them. That personality, that living force, co-operated spontaneously and unconsciously with the conscious powers, in the creative process; and when we enter into a sympathetic communion with the concrete result of that creative process, our own mysterious personalities, being essentially identical with, though less quickened than, Shakespeare's, respond, though it may be but feebly, to his. This response is the highest result of the study of Shakespeare's works.

It is a significant fact that Shakespearian critics and editors, for nearly two centuries, have been a 'genus irritabile', to which genus Shakespeare himself certainly did not belong. The explanation may partly be, that they have been too much occupied with the LETTER, and have fretted their nerves in angry dispute about readings and interpretations; as theologians have done in their study of the sacred records, instead of endeavoring to reach, through the letter, the personality of which the letter is but a manifestation more or less imperfect. To KNOW a personality is, of course, a spiritual knowledge—the result of sympathy, that is, spiritual responsiveness. Intellectually it is but little more important to know one rather than another personality. The highest worth of all great works of genius is due to the fact that they are apocalyptic of great personalities.

Art says, as the Divine Person said, whose personality and the personalities fashioned after it, have transformed and moulded the ages, "Follow me!" Deep was the meaning wrapt up in this command: it was, Do as I do, live as I live, not from an intellectual perception of the principles involved in my life, but through a full sympathy, through the awakening, vitalizing, actuating power of the incarnate Word.

Art also says, as did the voice from the wilderness, inadequately translated, "REPENT ye, for the kingdom of heaven is at hand". (Metanoei^te h'/ggike ga\r h' Basilei/a tw^n ou'ranw^n.) Rather, be transformed, or, as De Quincey puts it, "Wheel into a new centre your spiritual system; GEOCENTRIC has that system been up to this hour—that is, having earth and the earthly for its starting-point; henceforward make it HELIOCENTRIC (that is, with the sun, or the heavenly, for its principle of motion)."

The poetry of Browning everywhere says this, and says it more emphatically than that of any other poet in our literature. It says everywhere, that not through knowledge, not through a sharpened intellect, but through repentance, in the deeper sense to which I have just alluded, through conversion, through wheeling into a new centre its spiritual system, the soul attains to saving truth. Salvation with him means that revelation of the soul to itself, that awakening, quickening, actuating, attitude-adjusting, of the soul, which sets it gravitating toward the Divine.

Browning's idea of Conversion is, perhaps, most distinctly expressed in a passage in the Monologue of the Canon Caponsacchi, in 'The Ring and the Book', wherein he sets forth the circumstances under which his soul was wheeled into a new centre, after a life of dalliance and elegant folly, and made aware of "the marvellous dower of the life it was gifted and filled with". He has been telling the judges, before whom he has been summoned, the story of the letters forged by Guido to entrap him and Pompilia, and of his having seen "right through the thing that tried to pass for truth and solid, not an empty lie". The conclusion and the resolve he comes to, are expressed in the soliloquy which he repeats to the judges, as having uttered at the time: "So, he not only forged the words for her but words for me, made letters he called mine: what I sent, he retained, gave these in place, all by the mistress messenger! As I recognized her, at potency of truth, so she, by the crystalline soul, knew me, never mistook the signs. Enough of this—let the wraith go to nothingness again, here is the orb, have only thought for her!" What follows admits us to the very HEART of Browning's poetry—admits us to the great Idea which is almost, in these days, strange to say, peculiarly his—which no other poet, certainly, of this intellectual, analytic, scientific age, with its "patent, truth-extracting processes", has brought out with the same degree of distinctness— the great Idea which may be variously characterized as that of soul-kindling, soul-quickening, adjustment of soul-attitude, regeneration, conversion, through PERSONALITY—a kindling, quickening, adjustment, regeneration, conversion in which THOUGHT is not even a coefficient. As expressed in Sordello, "Divest mind of e'en thought, and lo, God's unexpressed will dawns above us!" "Thought?" the Canon goes on to say, "Thought? nay, Sirs, what shall follow was not thought: I have thought sometimes, and thought long and hard. I have stood before, gone round a serious thing, tasked my whole mind to touch it and clasp it close, . . . God and man, and what duty I owe both,—I dare say I have confronted these in thought: but no such faculty helped here. I put forth no thought,—powerless, all that night I paced the city: it was the first Spring. By the INVASION I LAY PASSIVE TO, in rushed new things, the old were rapt away; alike abolished—the imprisonment of the outside air, the inside weight o' the world that pulled me down. Death meant, to spurn the ground, soar to the sky,—die well and you do that. The very immolation made the bliss; death was the heart of life, and all the harm my folly had crouched to avoid, now proved a veil hiding all gain my wisdom strove to grasp . . . Into another state, under new rule I knew myself was passing swift and sure; whereof the initiatory pang approached, felicitous annoy, as bitter-sweet as when the virgin band, the victors chaste, feel at the end the earthy garments drop, and rise with something of a rosy shame into immortal nakedness: so I lay, and let come the proper throe would thrill into the ecstasy and out-throb pain. I' the gray of the dawn it was I found myself facing the pillared front o' the Pieve—mine, my church: it seemed to say for the first time, 'But am not I the Bride, the mystic love o' the Lamb, who took thy plighted troth, my priest, to fold thy warm heart on my heart of stone and freeze thee nor unfasten any more? This is a fleshly woman,—let the free bestow their life blood, thou art pulseless now!' . . . Now, when I found out first that life and death are means to an end, that passion uses both, indisputably mistress of the man whose form of worship is self-sacrifice—now, from the stone lungs sighed the scrannel voice, 'Leave that live passion, come be dead with me!' As if, i' the fabled garden, I had gone on great adventure, plucked in ignorance hedge-fruit, and feasted to satiety, laughing at such high fame for hips and haws, and scorned the achievement: then come all at once o' the prize o' the place, the thing of perfect gold, the apple's self: and, scarce my eye on that, was 'ware as well of the sevenfold dragon's watch. Sirs, I obeyed. Obedience was too strange,—this new thing that had been STRUCK INTO ME BY

THE LOOK OF THE LADY, to dare disobey the first authoritative word. 'Twas God's. I had been LIFTED TO THE LEVEL OF HER, could take such sounds into my sense. I said, 'We two are cognizant o' the Master now; it is she bids me bow the head: how true, I am a priest! I see the function here; I thought the other way self-sacrifice: this is the true, seals up the perfect sum. I pay it, sit down, silently obey.'"

Numerous and varied expressions of the idea of conversion set forth in this passage, occur in Browning's poetry, evidencing his deep sense of this great and indispensable condition of soul-life, of being born anew (or from above, as it should be rendered in the Gospel, a'/nwqen, that is, through the agency of a higher personality), in order to see the kingdom of God—evidencing his conviction that "the kingdom of God cometh not with observation: for lo! the kingdom of God is within you." In the poem entitled 'Cristina', the speaker is made to say,—

"Oh, we're sunk enough here, God knows! but not quite so sunk
that moments,
Sure tho' seldom, are denied us, when the spirit's true endowments
Stand out plainly from its false ones, and apprise it if pursuing
Or the right way or the wrong way, to its triumph or undoing.

There are flashes struck from midnights, there are fire-flames noon-days kindle,
Whereby piled-up honors perish, whereby swollen ambitions dwindle,
While just this or that poor impulse, which for once had play unstifled,
Seems the sole work of a life-time that away the rest have trifled."

And again, when the Pope in 'The Ring and the Book' has come to the decision to sign the death-warrant of Guido and his accomplices, he says: "For the main criminal I have no hope except in such a SUDDENNESS OF FATE. I stood at Naples once, a night so dark I could have scarce conjectured there was earth anywhere, sky or sea or world at all: but the night's black was burst through by a blaze—thunder struck blow on blow, earth groaned and bore, through her whole length of mountain visible: there lay the city thick and plain with spires, and, like a ghost disshrouded, white the sea. SO MAY THE TRUTH BE FLASHED OUT BY ONE BLOW, AND GUIDO SEE, ONE INSTANT, AND BE SAVED. Else I avert my face, nor follow him into that sad obscure sequestered state where God UNMAKES BUT TO REMAKE the soul he else made first in vain; which must not be. Enough, for I may die this very night: and how should I dare die, this man let live? Carry this forthwith to the Governor!"

Browning is the most essentially Christian of living poets. Though he rarely speaks 'in propria persona' in his poetry, any one who has gone over it all, can have no doubt as to his own most vital beliefs. What the Beauty-loving Soul in Tennyson's 'Palace of Art' say of herself, cannot be suspected even, of Browning:—

> "I take possession of man's mind and deed.
> I care not what the sects may brawl.
> I sit as God holding no form of creed,
> But contemplating all."

Religion with him is, indeed, the all-in-all; but not any particular form of it as a finality. This is not a world for finalities of any kind, as he constantly teaches us: it is a world of broken arcs, not of perfect rounds. Formulations of some kind he would, no doubt, admit there must be, as in everything else; but with him all formulations and tabulations of beliefs, especially such as "make square to a finite eye the circle of infinity",* are, at the best, only PROVISIONAL, and, at the worst, lead to spiritual standstill, spiritual torpor, "a ghastly smooth life, dead at heart."** The essential nature of Christianity is contrary to special prescription, do this or do that, believe this or believe that. Christ gave no recipes. Christianity is with Browning, and this he sets forth again and again, a LIFE, quickened and motived and nourished by the Personality

---

*   'Christmas Eve'.
**   'Easter Day'.

of Christ. And all that he says of this Personality can be accepted by every Christian, whatever theological view he may entertain of Christ. Christ's teachings he regards but as INCIDENTS of that Personality, and the records we have of his sayings and doings, but a fragment, a somewhat distorted one, it may be, out of which we must, by a mystic and plastic sympathy,* aided by the Christ spirit which is immanent in the Christian world, mould the Personality, and do fealty to it. The Christian must endeavor to be able to say, with the dying John, in Browning's 'Death in the Desert', "To me that story,—ay, that Life and Death of which I wrote 'it was'—to me, it is."

The poem entitled 'Christmas Eve' contains the fullest and most explicit expression, in Browning, of his idea of the personality of Christ, as being the all-in-all of Christianity.

> "The truth in God's breast
> Lies trace for trace upon ours impressed:
> Though He is so bright and we so dim,
> We are made in His image to witness Him:
> And were no eye in us to tell,
> Instructed by no inner sense,
> The light of Heaven from the dark of Hell,
> That light would want its evidence,—
> Though Justice, Good, and Truth, were still
> Divine, if, by some demon's will,
> Hatred and wrong had been proclaimed
> Law through the worlds, and Right misnamed,
> No mere exposition of morality
> Made or in part or in totality,
> Should win you to give it worship, therefore:
> And if no better proof you will care for,
> —Whom do you count the worst man upon earth?
> Be sure, he knows, in his conscience, more
> Of what Right is, than arrives at birth
> In the best man's acts that we bow before:
> And thence I conclude that the real God-function
> Is to furnish a motive and injunction
> For practising what we know already.

---

* 'plastic' in the 1800's sense of 'pliable', not 'fake'.—A.L..

And such an injunction and such a motive
As the God in Christ, do you waive, and 'heady,
High-minded', hang your tablet votive
Outside the fane on a finger-post?
Morality to the uttermost,
Supreme in Christ as we all confess,
Why need WE prove would avail no jot
To make Him God, if God he were not?
Where is the point where Himself lays stress?
Does the precept run 'Believe in Good,
In Justice, Truth, now understood
For the first time'?—or 'Believe in ME,
Who lived and died, yet essentially
Am Lord of Life'?* Whoever can take
The same to his heart and for mere love's sake
Conceive of the love,—that man obtains
A new truth; no conviction gains
Of an old one only, made intense
By a fresh appeal to his faded sense."

If all Christendom could take this remarkable poem of 'Christmas Eve' to its heart, its tolerance, its Catholic spirit, and, more than all, the fealty it exhibits to the Personality who essentially is Lord of Life, what a revolution it would undergo! and what a mass of dogmatic and polemic theology would become utterly obsolete! The most remarkable thing, perhaps, about the vast body of Christian theology which has been developed during the eighteen centuries which have elapsed since Christ was in the flesh, is, that it is occupied so largely, it might almost be said, exclusively, with what Christ and his disciples TAUGHT, and with fierce discussions about the manifold meanings which have been ingeniously extorted from the imperfect RECORD of what he taught. British museum libraries of polemics have been written in

---

*   "Subsists no law of life outside of life."

* * * * *

"The Christ himself had been no Lawgiver,
Unless he had given the LIFE, too, with the law."
Mrs. Browning's 'Aurora Leigh'.

defence of what Christ himself would have been indifferent to, and written with an animosity towards opponents which has been crystallized in a phrase now applied in a general way to any intense hate—ODIUM THEOLOGICUM.

If the significance of Christ's mission, or a large part of it, is to be estimated by his teachings, from those teachings important deductions must be made, as many of them had been delivered long before his time.

Browning has something to say on this point, in this same poem of 'Christmas Eve':—

"Truth's atmosphere may grow mephitic
When Papist struggles with Dissenter,
Impregnating its pristine clarity,
—One, by his daily fare's vulgarity,
Its gust of broken meat and garlic;
—One, by his soul's too-much presuming
To turn the frankincense's fuming
An vapors of the candle starlike
Into the cloud her wings she buoys on.
Each that thus sets the pure air seething,
May poison it for healthy breathing—
But the Critic leaves no air to poison;
Pumps out by a ruthless ingenuity
Atom by atom, and leaves you—vacuity.
Thus much of Christ, does he reject?
And what retain? His intellect?
What is it I must reverence duly?
Poor intellect for worship, truly,
Which tells me simply what was told
(If mere morality, bereft
Of the God in Christ, be all that's left)
Elsewhere by voices manifold;
With this advantage, that the stater
Made nowise the important stumble
Of adding, he, the sage and humble,
Was also one with the Creator."

Browning's poetry is instinct with the essence of Christianity—the LIFE of Christ. There is no other poetry, there is no writing of any form, in this age, which so emphasizes the fact (and it's the most consoling of all facts connected with the Christian religion), that the Personality, Jesus Christ, is the impregnable fortress of Christianity. Whatever assaults and inroads may be made upon the original records by Goettingen professors, upon the august fabric of the Church, with its creeds and dogmas, and formularies, and paraphernalia, this fortress will stand forever, and mankind will forever seek and find refuge in it.

The poem entitled 'Cleon' bears the intimation (there's nothing directly expressed thereupon), that Christianity is something distinct from, and beyond, whatever the highest civilization of the world, the civilization of Greece, attained to before Christ. Through him the world obtained "a new truth—no conviction gained of an old one merely, made intense by a fresh appeal to the faded sense."

Cleon, the poet, writes to Protos in his Tyranny (that is, in the Greek sense, Sovereignty). Cleon must be understood as representing the ripe, composite result, as an individual, of what constituted the glory of Greece—her poetry, sculpture, architecture, painting, and music, and also her philosophy. He acknowledges the gifts which the King has lavished upon him. By these gifts we are to understand the munificent national patronage accorded to the arts. "The master of thy galley still unlades gift after gift; they block my court at last and pile themselves along its portico royal with sunset, like a thought of thee."

By the slave women that are among the gifts sent to Cleon, seems to be indicated the degradation of the spiritual by its subjection to earthly ideals, as were the ideals of Greek art. This is more particularly indicated by the one white she-slave, the lyric woman, whom further on in his letter, Cleon promises to the King he will make narrate (in lyric song we must suppose) his fortunes, speak his great words, and describe his royal face.

He continues, that in such an act of love,—the bestowal of princely gifts upon him whose song gives life its joy,—men shall remark the King's recognition of the use of life—that his spirit is equal to more than merely to help on life in straight ways, broad enough for vulgar souls, by ruling and the rest. He ascribes to the King, in the building of his tower (and by this must be understood the building up of his own selfhood), a higher motive than work for mere work's sake,—that higher motive being, the luring hope of some EVENTUAL REST atop of it (the tower), whence, all the tumult of the building hushed, the first of men may look out to the east.*

By the eventual rest atop of the tower, is indicated the aim of the Greek civilization, to reach a calm within the finite, while the soul is constituted and destined to gravitate forever towards the infinite—to "force our straitened sphere . . . display completely here the mastery another life should learn." ('Sordello'.) The eventual rest in this world is not the Christian ideal. Earth-life, whatever its reach, and whatever its grasp, is to the Christian a broken arc, not a perfect round.

Cleon goes on to recount his accomplishments in the arts, and what he has done in philosophy, in reply to the first requirement of Protos's letter, Protos, as it appears, having heard of, and wonderingly enumerated, the great things Cleon has effected; and he has written to know the truth of the report. Cleon replies, that the epos on the King's hundred plates of gold is his, and his the little chaunt so sure to rise from every fishing-bark when, lights at prow, the seamen haul their nets; that the image of the sun-god on the light-house men turn from the sun's self to see, is his; that the Poecile, o'erstoried its whole length with painting, is his, too; that he knows the true proportions of a man and woman, not observed before; that he has written three books on the soul, proving absurd all written hitherto, and putting us to ignorance again; that in music he has combined the moods, inventing one; that, in brief, all arts are his, and so known and recognized. At this he writes the King to marvel not. We of these latter days, he says, being more COMPOSITE, appear not so great as our forerunners who, in their simple way, were greater in a certain single direction, than we; but our composite way is greater. This life of men on earth, this sequence of the soul's achievements here, he finds reason to

---

* Tennyson uses a similar figure in 'The Two Voices'. The speaker, who is meditating whether "to be or not to be", says:—

> "Were this not well, to bide mine hour,
> Though watching from a ruined tower
> How grows the day of human power."

The ruined tower is his own dilapidated selfhood, whence he takes his outlook upon the world.

believe, was intended to be viewed eventually as a great whole, the individual soul being only a factor toward the realization of this great whole—toward spelling out, so to speak, Zeus's idea in the race. Those divine men of old, he goes on to say, reached each at one point, the outside verge that rounds our faculty, and where they reached, who could do more than reach? I have not chaunted, he says, verse like Homer's, nor swept string like Terpander, nor carved and painted men like Phidias and his friend; I am not great as they are, point by point; but I have entered into sympathy with these four, running these into one soul, who, separate, ignored each other's arts. The wild flower was the larger—I have dashed rose-blood upon its petals, pricked its cup's honey with wine, and driven its seed to fruit, and show a better flower, if not so large.

And now he comes to the important questions in the King's letter—whether he, the poet, his soul thus in men's hearts, has not attained the very crown and proper end of life—whether, now life closeth up, he faces death with success in his right hand,—whether he fears death less than he, the King, does himself, the fortunate of men, who assigns the reason for thinking that he does, that he, the poet, leaves much behind, his life stays in the poems men shall sing, the pictures men shall study; while the King's life, complete and whole now in its power and joy, dies altogether with his brain and arm, as HE leaves not behind, as the poet does, works of art embodying the essence of his life which, through those works, will pass into the lives of men of all succeeding times. Cleon replies that if in the morning of philosophy, the King, with the light now in him, could have looked on all earth's tenantry, from worm to bird, ere man appeared, and if Zeus had questioned him whether he would improve on it, do more for visible creatures than was done, he would have answered, "Ay, by making each grow conscious in himself: all's perfect else, life's mechanics can no further go, and all this joy in natural life is put, like fire from off thy fingers into each, so exquisitely perfect is the same. But 'tis pure fire—and they mere matter are; it has THEM, not they IT: and so I choose, for man, that a third thing shall stand apart from both, a quality arise within the soul, which, intro-active, made to supervise and feel the force it has, may view itself and so be happy." But it is this quality, Cleon continues, which makes man a failure. This sense of sense, this spirit consciousness, grew the only life worth calling life, the pleasure-house, watch-tower, and treasure-fortress of the soul, which whole surrounding flats of natural life seemed only fit to yield subsistence to; a tower that crowns a country. But alas! the soul now climbs it just to perish there, for thence we have discovered that there's a world of capability for joy, spread round about us, meant for us, inviting us; and still the soul craves all, and still the flesh replies, "Take no jot more than ere you climbed the tower to look abroad! Nay, so much less, as that fatigue has brought deduction to it." After expatiating on this sad state of man, he arrives at the same conclusion as the King in his letter: "I agree in sum, O King, with thy profound discouragement, who seest the wider but to sigh the more. Most progress is most failure! thou sayest well."

And now he takes up the last point of the King's letter, that he, the King, holds joy not impossible to one with artist-gifts, who leaves behind living works. Looking over the sea, as he writes, he says, "Yon rower with the moulded muscles there, lowering the sail, is nearer it than I." He presents with clearness, and with rigid logic, the DILEMMA of the growing soul; shows the vanity of living in works left behind, and in the memory of posterity, while he, the feeling, thinking, acting man, shall sleep in his urn. The horror of the thought makes him dare imagine at times some future state unlimited in capability for joy, as this is in DESIRE for joy. But no! Zeus had not yet revealed such a state; and alas! he must have done so were it possible!

He concludes, "Live long and happy, and in that thought die, glad for what was! Farewell." And then, as a matter of minor importance, he informs the King, in a postscript, that he cannot tell his messenger aright where to deliver what he bears to one called Paulus. Protos, it must be understood, having heard of the fame of Paul, and being perplexed in the extreme, has written the great apostle to know of his doctrine. But Cleon writes that it is vain to suppose that a mere barbarian Jew, one circumcised, hath access to a secret which is shut from them, and that the King wrongs their philosophy in stooping to inquire of such an one. "Oh, he finds adherents, who does not. Certain slaves who touched on this same isle, preached him and Christ, and, as he gathered from a bystander, their doctrines could be held by no sane man."

There is a quiet beauty about this poem which must insinuate itself into the feelings of every reader. In tone it resembles the

'Epistle of Karshish, the Arab Physician'. The verse of both poems is very beautiful. No one can read these two poems, and 'Bishop Blougram's Apology', and 'The Bishop orders his Tomb at St. Praxed's Church', and not admit that Browning is a master of blank verse in its most difficult form—a form far more difficult than that of the epic blank verse of Milton, or the Idyllic blank verse of Tennyson, argumentative and freighted with thought, and, at the same time, almost chatty, as it is, and bearing in its course exquisitely poetical conceptions. The same may be said of much of the verse of 'The Ring and the Book', especially that of the monologues of the Canon Caponsacchi, Pompilia, the Pope, and Count Guido Franceschini. But this by the way.

'Cleon' belongs to a grand group of poems, in which Browning shows himself to be, as I've said, the most essentially Christian of living poets—the poet who, more emphatically than any of his contemporaries have done, has enforced the importance, the indispensableness of a new birth, the being born from above (a'/nwqen) as the condition not only of soul vitality and progress, but also of intellectual rectitude. In this group of poems are embodied the profoundest principles of education—principles which it behoves the present generation of educators to look well to. The acquisition of knowledge is a good thing, the sharpening of the intellect is a good thing, the cultivation of philosophy is a good thing; but there is something of infinitely more importance than all these—it is, the rectification, the adjustment, through that mysterious operation we call sympathy, of the unconscious personality, the hidden soul, which co-operates with the active powers, with the conscious intellect, and, as this unconscious personality is rectified or unrectified, determines the active powers, the conscious intellect, for righteousness or unrighteousness.

The attentive reader of Browning's poetry must soon discover how remarkably homogeneous it is in spirit. There are many authors, and great authors too, the reading of whose collected works gives the impression of their having "tried their hand" at many things. No such impression is derivable from the voluminous poetry of Browning. Wide as is its range, one great and homogeneous spirit pervades and animates it all, from the earliest to the latest. No other living poet gives so decided an assurance of having a BURDEN to deliver. An appropriate general title to his works would be, 'The

Burden of Robert Browning to the 19th Century'. His earliest poems show distinctly his ATTITUDE toward things. We see in what direction the poet has set his face—what his philosophy of life is, what soul-life means with him, what regeneration means, what edification means in its deepest sense of building up within us the spiritual temple. And if he had left this world after writing no more than those poems of his youth, 'Pauline' and 'Paracelsus', a very fair 'ex-pede-Herculem' estimate might have been made of the possibilities which he has since so grandly realized.

III. Mr. Browning's "Obscurity".

It was long the FASHION—and that fashion has not yet passed away—with skimming readers and perfunctory critics to charge Mr. Browning with being "wilfully obscure, unconscientiously careless, and perversely harsh."

There are readers and readers. One class, constituting, perhaps, not more than one-tenth of one per cent, or a thousandth part of the whole number, "read, mark, learn, and inwardly digest"; the remaining ninety-nine and nine-tenths per cent, through a habit of loose and indiscriminate reading, are unequal to the sustained concentration of mind demanded by the higher poetry, the language of which is characterized by a severe economy of expression—a closeness of texture, resulting from the elliptical energy of highly impassioned thought.

Reading is, perhaps, more superficial at the present day than it ever was before. There is an almost irresistible temptation to reverse the "multum legendum esse non multa" of Quintilian, overwhelmed as we are with books, magazines, and newspapers, which no man can number, and of which thousands and tens of thousands of minds endeavor to gobble up all they can; and yet, from want of all digestive and assimilating power, they are pitiably famished and deadened.

Sir John Lubbock has lately been interested in the preparation of a list of the best hundred books, and to that end has solicited the aid of a number of prominent scholars. Prof. Edward Dowden remarks thereupon, in an article on 'The Interpretation of Literature', "It would have been more profitable for us had we been advised how to read any one of the hundred; for what, indeed, does it matter whether we read the best books or the worst, if we lack the power or the instinct or the skill by which to reach the heart of any of them? Books for most readers are, as Montaigne says, 'a languid pleasure'; and so they must be, unless they become living powers, with a summons or a challenge for our spirit, unless we embrace them or wrestle with them."

To return from this digression to the charge against Browning of obscurity. And, first, it should be said that Browning has so much material, such a large thought and passion capital, that we never find him making a little go a great way, by means of EXPRESSION, or rather concealing the little by means of rhetorical tinsel. We can never justly demand of him what the Queen in 'Hamlet' demands of Polonius, "more matter with less art". His thought is wide-reaching and discursive, and the motions of his mind rapid and leaping. The connecting links of his thought have often to be supplied by an analytic reader whose mind is not up to the required tension to spring over the chasm. He shows great faith in his reader and "leaves the mere rude explicit details", as if he thought,

> "'tis but brother's speech
> We need, speech where an accent's change gives each
> The other's soul."*

A truly original writer like Browning, original, I mean, in his spiritual attitudes, is always more of less difficult to the uninitiated, for the reason that he demands of his reader new standpoints, new habits of thought and feeling; says, virtually, to his reader, Metanoei^te; and until these new standpoints are taken, these new habits of thought and feeling induced, the difficulty, while appearing to the reader at the outset, to be altogether objective, will really be, to a great extent, subjective, that is, will be in himself.

---

*   'Sordello'.

Goethe, in his 'Wahrheit und Dichtung', says:—

"Wer einem Autor Dunkelheit vorwerfen will, sollte erst sein eigenes Innere besuchen, ob es denn da auch recht hell ist. In der Daemmerung wird eine sehr deutliche Schrift unlesbar."*

And George Henry Lewes, in his 'Life of Goethe', well says:—

"A masterpiece excites no sudden enthusiasm; it must be studied much and long, before it is fully comprehended; we must grow up to it, for it will not descend to us. Its emphasis grows with familiarity. We never become disenchanted; we grow more and more awe-struck at its infinite wealth. We discover no trick, for there is none to discover. Homer, Shakespeare, Raphael, Beethoven, Mozart, never storm the judgment; but once fairly in possession, they retain it with unceasing influence."

And Professor Dowden, in the article from which I have just quoted, says:—

"Approaching a great writer in this spirit of courageous and affectionate fraternity, we need all our forces and all our craft for the friendly encounter. If we love ease and lethargy, let us turn in good time and fly. The interpretation of literature, like the interpretation of Nature, is no mere record of facts; it is no catalogue of the items which make up a book—such catalogues and analyses of contents encumber our histories of literature with some of their dreariest pages. The interpretation of literature exhibits no series of dead items, but rather the life and power of one mind at play upon another mind duly qualified to receive and manifest these. Hence, one who would interpret the work of a master must summon up all his powers, and must be alive at as many points as possible. He who approaches his author as a whole, bearing upon life as a whole, is himself alive at the greatest possible number of points, will be the best and truest interpreter. For he will grasp what is central, and at the same time will be sensitive to the value of all details, which details he will perceive not isolated, but in connection with one

---

* He who would charge an author with obscurity, should first look into his own mind, to know whether it is quite clear there. In the dusk a very distinct handwriting becomes illegible.

another, and with the central life to which they belong and from which they proceed."

In his poem entitled 'Pacchiarotto, and how he worked in distemper', Mr. Browning turns upon his critics, whom he characterizes as "the privileged fellows, in the drabs, blues, and yellows" (alluding to the covers of the leading British Reviews), and especially upon Alfred Austin, the author of that work of wholesale condemnation, 'The Poetry of the Period', and gives them a sound and well-deserved drubbing. At the close of the onset he says:—

"Was it 'grammar' wherein you would 'coach' me—
You,—pacing in even that paddock
Of language allotted you ad hoc,
With a clog at your fetlocks,—you—scorners
Of me free from all its four corners?
Was it 'clearness of words which convey thought?'
Ay, if words never needed enswathe aught
But ignorance, impudence, envy
And malice—what word-swathe would then vie
With yours for a clearness crystalline?
But had you to put in one small line
Some thought big and bouncing—as noddle
Of goose, born to cackle and waddle
And bite at man's heel as goose-wont is,
Never felt plague its puny os frontis—
You'd know, as you hissed, spat and sputtered,
Clear 'quack-quack' is easily uttered!"

In a letter written to Mr. W. G. Kingsland, in 1868, Mr. Browning says:—

"I can have little doubt that my writing has been in the main too hard for many I should have been pleased to communicate with; but I never designedly tried to puzzle people, as some of my critics have supposed. On the other hand, I never pretended to offer such literature as should be a substitute for a cigar or a game at dominoes to an idle man. So, perhaps, on the whole I get my deserts, and something over—not a crowd, but a few I value more."[*]

It was never truer of any author than it is true of Browning, that 'Le style c'est l'homme'; and Browning's style is an expression of the panther-restlessness and panther-spring of his impassioned intellect. The musing spirit of a Wordsworth or a Tennyson he partakes not of.

Mr. Richard Holt Hutton's characterization of the poet's style, as a "crowded note-book style", is not a particularly happy one. In the passage, which he cites from Sordello, to illustrate the "crowded note-book style", occurs the following parenthesis:—

"(To be by him themselves made act,
Not watch Sordello acting each of them.)"

"What the parenthesis means," he says, "I have not the most distant notion. Mr. Browning might as well have said, 'to be by him her himself herself themselves made act', etc., for any vestige of meaning I attach to this curious mob of pronouns and verbs. It is exactly like the short notes of a speech intended to be interpreted afterwards by one who had heard and understood it himself."[**]

At first glance, this parenthesis is obscure; but the obscurity is not due to its being "exactly like the short notes of a speech", etc. It is due to what the "obscurity" of Mr. Browning's language, as language, is, in nine cases out of ten, due, namely, to the COLLOCATION of the words, not to an excessive economy of words. He often exercises a liberty in the collocation of his words which is beyond what an uninflected language like the English admits of, without more or less obscurity. There are difficult passages in Browning which, if translated into Latin, would present no difficulty at all; for in Latin, the relations of words are more independent of their collocation, being indicated by their inflections.

The meaning of the parenthesis is, and, independently of the context, a second glance takes it in (the wonder is, Mr. Hutton didn't take it in),—

---

[*]   'Browning Society Papers', III., p. 344.
[**]   'Essays Theological and Literary'. Vol. II., 2d ed., rev. and enl., p. 175.

"To be themselves made by him [to] act,
Not each of them watch Sordello acting."

There are two or three characteristics of the poet's diction which may be noticed here:—

1. The suppression of the relative, both nominative and accusative or dative, is not uncommon; and, until the reader becomes familiar with it, it often gives, especially if the suppression is that of a subject relative, a momentary, but only a momentary, check to the understanding of a passage.

The following examples are from 'The Ring and the Book':—

"Checking the song of praise in me, had else
Swelled to the full for God's will done on earth."
I. The Ring and the Book, v. 591.

i.e., which had (would have) else swelled to the full, etc.

"This that I mixed with truth, motions of mine
That quickened, made the inertness malleolable
O' the gold was not mine,"—
I. The Ring and the Book, v. 703.

"Harbouring in the centre of its sense
A hidden germ of failure, shy but sure,
Should neutralize that honesty and leave
That feel for truth at fault, as the way is too."
I. The Ring and the Book, v. 851.

"Elaborate display of pipe and wheel
Framed to unchoak, pump up and pour apace
Truth in a flowery foam shall wash the world."
I. The Ring and the Book, v. 1113.

"see in such
A star shall climb apace and culminate,"
III. The Other Half Rome, v. 846.

"Guido, by his folly, forced from them
The untoward avowal of the trick o' the birth,
Would otherwise be safe and secret now."
IV. Tertium Quid, v. 1599.

"so I
Lay, and let come the proper throe would thrill
Into the ecstasy and outthrob pain."
VI. Giuseppe Caponsacchi, v. 972.

"blind?
Ay, as a man would be inside the sun,
Delirious with the plentitude of light
Should interfuse him to the finger-ends"—
X. The Pope, 1564.

"You have the sunrise now, joins truth to truth."
X. The Pope, 1763.

"One makes fools look foolisher fifty-fold
By putting in their place the wise like you,
To take the full force of an argument
Would buffet their stolidity in vain."
XI. Guido, 858.

Here the infinitive "To take" might be understood, at first
look, as the subject of "Would buffet"; but it depends on "putting",
etc., and the subject relative "that" is suppressed: "an argument
[that] would buffet their stolidity in vain."

"Will you hear truth can do no harm nor good?"
XI. Guido, 1915.

"I who, with outlet for escape to heaven,
Would tarry if such flight allowed my foe
To raise his head, relieved of that firm foot
Had pinned him to the fiery pavement else!"
XI. Guido, 2099.

i.e., "that firm foot [that] had (would have) pinned."

. . ."ponder, ere ye pass,
Each incident of this strange human play
Privily acted on a theatre,
Was deemed secure from every gaze but God's,"—
              XII. The Book and the Ring, v. 546.

"As ye become spectators of this scene—

                    * * * * *

—A soul made weak by its pathetic want
Of just the first apprenticeship to sin,
Would thenceforth make the sinning soul secure
From all foes save itself, that's truliest foe,"—
              XII. The Book and the Ring, v. 559.

i.e., "sin, [that] would."

"Was he proud,—a true scion of the stock
Which bore the blazon, shall make bright my page"—
              XII. The Book and the Ring, v. 821.

2. The use of the infinitive without the prepositive "to", is
frequently extended beyond present usage, especially in 'Sordello'
and 'The Ring and the Book'. The following are examples:—

"Who fails, through deeds howe'er diverse, RE-TRACK
My purpose still, my task?"
              Sordello, p. 168.

"failed Adelaide SEE then
Who was the natural chief, the man of men?"
              Sordello, p. 175.

"but when
'Twas time expostulate, attempt withdraw
Taurello from his child," . . .
              Sordello, p. 180.

Here are two infinitives, with the prepositive omitted,
"expostulate" and "attempt", both dependent on the noun "time",

and another, "withdraw", without the prepositive, dependent on "attempt": "but when 'twas time [to] expostulate, [to] attempt [to] withdraw", etc.

> "For thus he ventured, to the verge,
> Push a vain mummery." . . .
>> Sordello, p. 190.

i.e., for thus he ventured [to] push to the verge a vain mummery.

>> "as yet
> He had inconsciously contrived FORGET
> I' the whole, to dwell o' the points" . . .
>> Sordello, p. 190.

> "Grown bestial, dreaming how BECOME divine."
>> Sordello, p. 191.

> "And the whole music it was framed AFFORD,"—
>> Sordello, p. 203.

> "Was such a lighting-up of faith, in life,
> Only allowed initiate, set man's step
> In the true way by help of the great glow?"
>> R. and B. X. The Pope, v. 1815.

i.e. only allowed [to] initiate, [to] set man's step, etc.

> "If I might read instead of print my speech,—
> Ay, and enliven speech with many a flower
> Refuses obstinately blow in print."
>> R. and B. IX.
>> Johannes-Baptista Bottinius, v. 4.

Here the subject relative of "refuses" is omitted, and the verb followed by an infinitive without the prepositive: "many a flower [that] refuses obstinately [to] blow in print."

3. Instead of the modern analytic form, the simple form of the past subjunctive derived from the Anglo-Saxon inflectional form, and identical with that of the past indicative, is frequently

employed, the context only showing that it is the subjunctive. (See Abbott's 'Shakespearian Grammar', 361 et seq.)

> "Would we some prize might hold
> To match those manifold
> Possessions of the brute,—gain most, as we did best!"
> > Rabbi Ben Ezra, St. xi.

i.e., as we should do best.

> "Thus were abolished Spring and Autumn both,"
> > I. The Ring and the Book, 1358.

i.e., would be abolished.

> "His peevishness had promptly put aside
> Such honor and refused the proffered boon," . . .
> > II. Half Rome (R. and B.), 369.

i.e., would have promptly put aside.

> "(What daily pittance pleased the plunderer dole.)"
> > X. The Pope (R. and B.), 561.

i.e., as the context shows, [it] might please the plunderer [to] dole.

> "succession to the inheritance
> Which bolder crime had lost you:"
> > IV. Tertium Quid (R. and B.), 1104.

i.e., would have lost you.

But the verbs "be" and "have" are chiefly so used, and not often beyond what present usage allows.*

4. The use of the dative, or indirect object, without "to" or "for".

---

*   * Tennyson uses "saw" = 'viderem', in the following passage:

> "But since I did not see the Holy Thing,
> I sware a vow to follow it till I saw."
> > Sir Percivale in 'The Holy Grail'.

Such datives are very frequent, and scarcely need illustration. The poet has simply carried the use of them beyond the present general usage of the language. But there's a noticeable one in the Pope's Monologue, in 'The Ring and the Book', vv. 1464-1466: The Archbishop of Arezzo, to whom poor Pompilia has applied, in her distress, for protection against her brutal husband, thinks it politic not to take her part, but send her back to him and enjoin obedience and submission. The Pope, in his Monologue, represents the crafty Archbishop as saying, when Pompilia cries, "Protect me from the wolf!"

> "No, thy Guido is rough, heady, strong,
> Dangerous to disquiet: let him bide!
> He needs some bone to mumble, help amuse
> The darkness of his den with: so, the fawn
> Which limps up bleeding to my foot and lies,
> —Come to me daughter!—thus I throw him back!"

i.e., thus I throw back [to] him the fawn which limps up bleeding to my foot and lies. The parenthesis, "Come to me, daughter", being interposed, and which is introduced as preparatory to his purpose, adds to the difficulty of the construction.

There are, after all, but comparatively few instances in Browning's poetry, where these features of his diction can be fairly condemned. They often impart a crispness to the expressions in which they occur.

The contriving spirit of the poet's language often results in great complexity of construction. Complexity of construction may be a fault, and it may not. It may be justified by the complexity of the thought which it bears along. "Clear quack-quack is easily uttered." But where an author's thought is nimble, far-reaching, elliptical through its energy, and discursive, the expression of it must be more or less complex or involved; he will employ subordinate clauses, and parentheses, through which to express the outstanding, restricting, and toning relations of his thought, that is, if he is a master of perspective, and ranks his grouped thoughts according to their relative importance.

The poet's apostrophe to his wife in the spirit-world, which closes the long prologue to 'The Ring and the Book' (vv. 1391-

1416), and in which he invokes her aid and benediction, in the work he has undertaken, presents a greater complexity of construction than is to be met with anywhere else in his works; and of this passage it may be said, as it may be said of any other having a complex construction, supposing this to be the only difficulty, that it's hard rather than obscure, and demands close reading. But, notwithstanding its complex structure and the freight of thought conveyed, the passage has a remarkable LIGHTSOMENESS of movement, and is a fine specimen of blank verse. The unobtrusive, but distinctly felt, alliteration which runs through it, contributes something toward this lightsomeness. The first two verses have a Tennysonian ring:—

> "O lyric Love, half-angel and half-bird
> And all a wonder and a wild desire,—
> Boldest of hearts that ever braved the sun,
> Took sanctuary within the holier blue,
> 5 And sang a kindred soul out to his face,—
> Yet human at the red-ripe of the heart—
> When the first summons from the darkling earth
> Reached thee amid thy chambers, blanched their blue,
> And bared them of the glory—to drop down,
> 10 To toil for man, to suffer or to die,—
> This is the same voice: can thy soul know change?
> Hail then, and hearken from the realms of help!
> Never may I commence my song, my due
> To God who best taught song by gift of thee,
> 15 Except with bent head and beseeching hand—
> That still, despite the distance and the dark,
> What was, again may be; some interchange
> Of grace, some splendour once thy very thought,
> Some benediction anciently thy smile:
> 20 —Never conclude, but raising hand and head
> Thither where eyes, that cannot reach, yet yearn
> For all hope, all sustainment, all reward,
> Their utmost up and on,—so blessing back
> In those thy realms of help, that heaven thy home,
> 25 Some whiteness which, I judge, thy face makes proud,

Some wanness where, I think, thy foot may fall!"[*]

"his", v. 5, the sun's. "Yet human", v. 6: though 'kindred' to the sun, yet proved 'human' . . . 'when the first summons', etc. "This is the same voice", v. 11, i.e., a voice of the same import as was "the first summons"—one invoking help. The nouns "interchange", "splendour", "benediction", vv. 17, 18, 19, are appositives of "what", v. 17. "Never conclude", v. 20, to be construed with "commence", v. 13: "Never [may I] conclude". "Their utmost up and on", v. 23, to be construed with "yearn", v. 21. "so", v. 23, looks back to "raising hand and head", etc. "Some whiteness" . . . v. 25, "Some wanness" . . . v. 26, to be construed with "blessing back".

See an elaborate analysis of this Invocation, by Dr. F. J. Furnivall, read at the forty-eighth meeting of the Browning Society, February 25, 1887, being No. 39 of the Society's Papers.

But, after all, the difficulties in Browning which result from the construction of the language, be that what it may, are not the main difficulties, as has been too generally supposed. THE MAIN DIFFICULTIES ARE QUITE INDEPENDENT OF THE CONSTRUCTION OF THE LANGUAGE.

Many readers, especially those who take an intellectual attitude toward all things, in the heavens above and in the earth beneath, suppose that they are prepared to understand almost

---

[*]   In the last three verses of 'The Ring and the Book' the poet again addresses his "Lyric Love" to express the wish that the Ring, which he has rounded out of the rough ore of the Roman murder case, might but lie "in guardianship" outside hers,

> "Thy rare gold ring of verse (the poet praised)
> Linking our England to his Italy."

The reference is to the inscription on Casa Guidi, Via Maggiore, 9. Florence:

QUI SCRISSE E MORI
ELISABETTA BARRETT BROWNING
CHE IN CUORE DI DONNA CONCILIAVA
SCIENZA DI DOTTO E SPIRITO DI POETA
E FECE DEL SUO VERSO AUREO ANELLO
FRA ITALIA E INGHILTERRA
PONE QUESTO MEMORIA
FIRENZE GRATA
1861.

anything which is understandable if it is only PUT right. This is a most egregious mistake, especially in respect to the subtle and complex spiritual experiences which the more deeply subjective poetry embodies. What De Quincey says in his paper on Kant,* of the comprehension of the higher philosophical truths, can, with still better reason, be said of the responsiveness to the higher spiritual truths: "No complex or very important truth was ever yet transferred in full development from one mind to another: truth of that character is not a piece of furniture to be shifted; it is a seed which must be sown, and pass through the several stages of growth. No doctrine of importance can be transferred in a matured shape into any man's understanding from without: it must arise by an act of genesis within the understanding itself."

And so it may be said in regard to the responsiveness to the higher spiritual truths—I don't say COMPREHENSION of the higher spiritual truths (that word pertains rather to an intellectual grasp), but RESPONSIVENESS to the higher spiritual truths. Spiritual truths must be spiritually responded to; they are not and cannot be intellectually comprehended. The condition of such responsiveness it may require a long while to fulfil. New attitudes of the soul, a meta/noia, may be demanded, before such responsiveness is possible. And what some people may regard in the higher poetry as obscure, by reason of the mode of its presentation on the part of the poet, may be only relatively so—that is, the obscurity may be wholly due to the wrong attitudes, or the no attitudes, of their own souls, and to the limitations of their spiritual experiences. In that case "the patient must minister to himself".

While on the subject of "obscurity", I must notice a difficulty which the reader at first experiences in his study of Browning's poetry—a difficulty resulting from the poet's favorite art-form, the dramatic or psychologic monologue.** The largest portion of his

---

*   'Letters to a Young Man'. Letter V.
**   The dramatic monologue differs from a soliloquy in this: while there is but one speaker, the presence of a silent second person is supposed, to whom the arguments of the speaker are addressed. Perhaps such a situation may be termed a novelty of invention in our Poet. It is obvious that the dramatic monologue gains over the soliloquy in that it allows the artist greater room in which to work out his conception of character. We cannot gaze long at a solitary figure on a canvas, however powerfully treated, without feeling some need of relief. In the same way a soliloquy (comp. the great soliloquies of Shakespeare) cannot be protracted to

voluminous poetry is in this form. Some speaker is made to reveal his character, and, sometimes, by reflection, or directly, the character of some one else—to set forth some subtle and complex soul-mood, some supreme, all-determining movement or experience of a life; or, it may be, to RATIOCINATE subtly on some curious question of theology, morals, philosophy, or art. Now it is in strictly preserving the monologue character that obscurity often results. A monologue often begins with a startling abruptness, and the reader must read along some distance before he gathers what the beginning means. Take the monologue of Fra Lippo Lippi for example. The situation is necessarily left more or less unexplained. The poet says nothing 'in propria persona', and no reply is made to the speaker by the person or persons addressed. Sometimes a look, a gesture, or a remark, must be supposed on the part of the one addressed, which occasions a responsive remark. Sometimes the speaker IMPUTES a question; and the reader is sometimes obliged to stop and consider whether a question is imputed by the speaker to the one he is addressing, or is a direct question of his own. This is often the case throughout 'The Ring and the Book'. But to the initiated, these features of the monologue present little or no difficulty, and they conduce to great compactness of composition—a closeness of texture which the reader comes in time to enjoy, and to prefer to a more loosely woven diction.

The monologue entitled 'My Last Duchess. Ferrara' is a good example of the constitution of this art-form. It is one of the most perfect in artistic treatment, and exhibits all the features I have just noticed. Originally, this monologue and that now entitled 'Count Gismond. Aix in Provence', had the common title, 'Italy and France', the former being No. I. Italy; the latter, No. II. France. The poet, no doubt, afterward thought that the Duke of the one monologue, and the Count of the other, could not justly be presented as representatives, respectively, of Italy and France. In

---

any great length without wearying the listener. The thoughts of a man in self-communion are apt to run in a certain circle, and to assume a monotony. The introduction of a second person acting powerfully upon the speaker throughout, draws the latter forth into a more complete and varied expression of his mind. The silent person in the background, who may be all the time master of the situation, supplies a powerful stimulus to the imagination of the reader.—Rev. Prof. E. Johnson's "Paper on 'Bishop Blougram's Apology'" ('Browning Soc. Papers', Pt. III., p. 279).

giving the monologues new titles, 'My Last Duchess' and 'Count Gismond', he added to the one, 'Ferrara', and to the other, 'Aix in Provence', thus locally restricting the order of character which they severally represent.

In 'My Last Duchess', the speaker is a soulless VIRTUOSO— a natural product of a proud, arrogant, and exclusive aristocracy, on the one hand, and on the other, of an old and effete city, like Ferrara, where art, rather than ministering to soul-life and true manliness of character, has become an end to itself—is valued for its own sake.

The Duke is showing, with the weak pride of the mere virtuoso, a portrait of his last Duchess, to some one who has been sent to negotiate another marriage. We see that he is having an entertainment or reception of some kind in his palace, and that he has withdrawn from the company with the envoy to the picture-gallery on an upper floor. He has pulled aside the curtain from before the portrait, and in remarking on the expression which the artist, Fra Pandolf, has given to the face, he is made to reveal a fiendish jealousy on his part, occasioned by the sweetness and joyousness of his late Duchess, who, he thought, should show interest in nothing but his own fossilized self. "She had," he says, "a heart—how shall I say?—too soon made glad, too easily impressed; she liked whate'er she looked on, and her looks went everywhere. Sir, 'twas all one! My favour at her breast, the dropping of the daylight in the West, the bough of cherries some officious fool broke in the orchard for her, the white mule she rode with round the terrace—all and each would draw from her alike the approving speech, or blush, at least. She thanked men,—good! but thanked somehow—I know not how—as if she ranked my gift of a nine-hundred-years-old name with anybody's gift."

Her fresh interest in things, and the sweet smile she had for all, due to a generous soul-life, proved fatal to the lovely Duchess: "Oh sir, she smiled, no doubt, whene'er I passed her; but who passed without much the same smile? This grew; I gave commands; then all smiles stopped together."

He succeeded, and he seems to be proud of it, in shutting off all her life-currents, pure, and fresh, and sparkling, as they were, and we must suppose that she than sank slowly and uncomplainingly away. What a deep pathos there is in "then all smiles stopped together"!*

The contemptible meanness and selfishness of jealousy were never exhibited with greater power, than they are exhibited in this short monologue—a power largely due to the artistic treatment. The jealousy of Leontes, in 'The Winter's Tale', of Shakespeare, is nobility itself, in comparison with the Duke's. How distinctly, while indirectly, the sweet Duchess is, with a few masterly touches, placed before us! The poet shows his artistic skill especially in his indirect, reflected portraitures.

This short composition, comprising as it does but fifty-six lines, is, of itself, sufficient to prove the poet a consummate artist. Tennyson's TECHNIQUE is quite perfect, almost "faultily faultless", indeed; but in no one of his compositions has he shown an equal degree of art-power, in the highest sense of the word.

{'My Last Duchess'}

"That's my last Duchess painted on the wall,
Looking as if she were alive. I call
That piece a wonder, now: Fra Pandolf's hands
Worked busily a day, and there she stands.
Will't please you sit and look at her? I said,
'Fra Pandolf' by design: for never read
Strangers like you that pictured countenance,
The depth and passion of its earnest glance,
But to myself they turned (since none puts by
The curtain I have drawn for you, but I)
And seemed as they would ask me, if they durst,
How such a glance came there; so, not the first
Are you to turn and ask thus. Sir, 'twas not
Her husband's presence only, called that spot
Of joy into the Duchess' cheek: perhaps
Fra Pandolf chanced to say 'Her mantle laps
Over my lady's wrist too much', or 'Paint
Must never hope to reproduce the faint

---

* "I gave commands" certainly must not be understood to mean commands for her death, as it is understood by the writer of the articles in 'The Saint Paul's Magazine' for December, 1870, and January, 1871. {See Preface: Note to the Third Edition.}

Half-flush that dies along her throat': such stuff
Was courtesy, she thought, and cause enough
For calling up that spot of joy. She had
A heart—how shall I say?—too soon made glad,
Too easily impressed; she liked whate'er
She looked on, and her looks went everywhere.
Sir, 'twas all one! My favour at her breast,
The dropping of the daylight in the West,
The bough of cherries some officious fool
Broke in the orchard for her, the white mule
She rode with round the terrace—all and each
Would draw from her alike the approving speech,
Or blush, at least. She thanked men,—good! but thanked
Somehow—I know not how—as if she ranked
My gift of a nine-hundred-years-old name
With anybody's gift. Who'd stoop to blame
This sort of trifling? Even had you skill
In speech—(which I have not)—to make your will
Quite clear to such an one, and say, 'Just this
Or that in you disgusts me; here you miss,
Or there exceed the mark'—and if she let
Herself be lessoned so, nor plainly set
Her wits to yours, forsooth, and made excuse,
—E'en then would be some stooping; and I choose
Never to stoop. Oh sir, she smiled, no doubt,
Whene'er I passed her; but who passed without
Much the same smile? This grew; I gave commands;
Then all smiles stopped together. There she stands
As if alive. Will't please you rise? We'll meet
The company below, then. I repeat,
The Count your master's known munificence
Is ample warrant that no just pretence
Of mine for dowry will be disallowed;
Though his fair daughter's self, as I avowed
At starting, is my object. Nay, we'll go
Together down, sir. Notice Neptune, though,
Taming a sea-horse, thought a rarity,
Which Claus of Innsbruck cast in bronze for me!'*

---

*   Claus of Innsbruck and also Fra Pandolf (v. 3) are imaginary artists.

The last ten verses illustrate well the poet's skilful management of his difficult art-form. After the envoy has had his look at the portrait, the Duke, thinking it time to return to his guests, says "Will't please you rise? We'll meet the company below, then." His next speech, which indicates what he has been talking about, during the envoy's study of the picture, must be understood as uttered while they are moving toward the stairway. The next, "Nay, we'll go together down, sir", shows that they have reached the head of the stairway, and that the envoy has politely motioned the Duke to lead the way down. This is implied in the "Nay". The last speech indicates that on the stairway is a window which affords an outlook into the courtyard, where he calls the attention of the envoy to a Neptune, taming a sea-horse, cast in bronze for him by Claus of Innsbruck. The pride of the virtuoso is also implied in the word, "though".

It should be noticed, also, that the Duke values his wife's picture wholly as a picture, not as the "counterfeit presentment" and reminder of a sweet and lovely woman, who might have blessed his life, if he had been capable of being blessed. It is to him a picture by a great artist, and he values it only as such. He says, parenthetically, "since none puts by the curtain I have drawn for you, but I." It's too precious a work of art to be entrusted to anybody else.

IV. Browning's Verse.

It seems to be admitted, even by many of the poet's most devoted students, that his verse is, in its general character, harsh and rugged. To judge it fairly, one must free his mind of many merely conventional canons in regard to verse. Pure music is absolute. The music of verse moves, or should move, under the conditions of the thought which articulates it. It should serve as a chorus to the thought, expressing a mystic sympathy with it. Verse may be very musical, and yet more or less mechanical; that is, it may CLOTHE thought and sentiment, but not be a part of it, not EMBODY it.

Unrippled verse, which many readers demand, MUST be more or less mechanical. Such verse flows according to its own sweet will, independently of the thought-articulation. But the thought-articulation may be so flimsy that it's well enough for the verse so to flow.

The careful student of Browning's language-shaping must discover—the requisite susceptibility to vitality of form being supposed—that his verse is remarkably organic: often, indeed, more organic, even when it appears to be clumsy, than the "faultily faultless" verse of Tennyson. The poet who has written 'In a Gondola', 'By the Fireside', 'Meeting at Night', 'Parting at Morning', 'Gold Hair', 'May and Death', 'Love among the Ruins', 'Home Thoughts from Abroad', 'Home Thoughts from the Sea', the Incantation in 'The Flight of the Duchess' (some of which are both song and picture), and many, many more that might be named, certainly has the very highest faculty of word and verse music, of music, too, that is entirely new in English Poetry; and it can be shown that he always exercises that faculty WHENEVER THERE'S A REAL ARTISTIC OCCASION FOR IT, not otherwise. Verse-music is never with him a mere literary indulgence. The grotesquerie of rhythm and rhyme which some of his poems exhibit, is as organic as any other feature of his language-shaping, and shows the rarest command of language. He has been charged with having "failed to reach continuous levels of musical phrasing". It's a charge which every one who appreciates Browning's verse in its higher forms (and its higher forms are not those which are addressed especially to the physical ear) will be very ready to admit. In the general tenor of his poetry, he is ABOVE the Singer,—he is the Seer and Revealer, who sees great truths beyond the bounds of the territory of general knowledge, instead of working over truths within that territory; and no seer of modern times has had his eyes more clearly purged with euphrasy and rue. Poetry is with him, in the language of Mr. E. Paxton Hood ('Eclectic and Congregational Rev.', Dec., 1868), "no jingle of words, or pretty amusement for harpsichord or piano, but rather a divine trigonometry, a process of celestial triangulation, a taking observations of celestial places and spheres, an attempt to estimate our world, its place, its life amidst the boundless immeasurable sweeps of space and time; or if describing, then describing the animating stories of the giants, how they fought and fell, or conquered . . . a great all-inclusive strength of song, which is as a battle march to warriors, or as the refreshment of brooks and dates to the spent and toiling soldiers on their way, is more than the pretty idyll, whose sweet and plaintive story pleases the idle hour or idle ear."

The Rev. Prof. E. Johnson, in the section entitled 'Poets of the Ear and of the Eye', of his valuable paper on 'Conscience and Art in Browning' ('Browning Soc. Papers', Part III., pp. 345-380), has ably shown that "the economy of music is a necessity of Browning's Art"—that music, instead of ever being an end to itself, is with him a means to a much higher end. He says:—

"All poetry may be classified according to its form or its contents. Formal classification is easy, but of little use. When we have distinguished compositions as dramatic, lyrical, or characterized a poet in like manner, we have done little. What we want to ascertain is the peculiar quality of the imaginative stuff with which he plastically works, and to appreciate its worth. This is always a great task, but one particularly necessary in the case of Browning, because the stuff in which he has wrought is so novel in the poet's hands. Psychology itself is comparatively a new and modern study, as a distinct science; but a psychological poet, who has made it his business to clothe psychic abstractions 'in sights and sounds', is entirely a novel appearance in literature.

"Now that phrase 'clothing in sights and sounds' may yield us the clue to the classification we are seeking. The function of artists, that is, musicians, poets in the narrower sense, and painters, is to clothe Truth in sights and sounds for the hearing and seeing of us all. Their call to do this lies in their finer and fuller aesthetic faculty. The sense of hearing and that of seeing stand in polar opposition, and thus a natural scale offers itself by which we may rank and arrange our artists. At the one end of the scale is the acoustic artist, i.e., the musician. At the other end of the scale is the optic artist, the painter and sculptor. Between these, and comprising both these activities in his own, is the poet, who is both acoustic and optic artist. He translates the sounds of the world, both external and internal,—the tumult of storms, the murmurs of waves, the SUSURRUS of the woodland, the tinkling of brooks, the throbbing of human hearts, the cries of all living creatures; all those groans of pain, stammers of desire, shrieks of despair, yawns even of languor, which are ever breaking out of the heart of things; and beside all this, the hearsay, commonplace, proverbial lore of the world. He turns these into melodies which shall be caught up by those who listen. In short, he converts by his alchemy the common stuff of pain and of joy into music. But he is optic as well as acoustic; that is, he calls up at the same time by his art a procession of images which march or dance across the theatre of the listener's fancy. Now the question of classification on this scheme comes to this, Does the particular poet who invites our attention deal more with the aesthesis of the ear or with that of the eye? Does he more fill our ear with sweet tunes or our fancy with shapes and colours? Does he compel us to listen and shut our eyes, or to open our eyes wide and dispense with all but the faintest musical accompaniment? What sense, in short, does he mainly address himself to? Goethe said that he was a 'seeing' man; W. von Humboldt, the great linguist, that he was a 'listening' man. The influence of Milton's blindness on his poetry was noticed by Lessing. The short-sightedness of Wieland has also been detected in his poetry.

"If we apply these tests to Browning, there can be, I think, no doubt as to the answer. He is, in common with all poets, both musician and painter, but much more the latter than the former. He is never for a moment the slave of his ear, if I may so express it. We know that he has, on the contrary, the mastery of music. But music helps and supports his imagination, never controls it. Music is to Browning an inarticulate revelation of the truth of the supersensual world, the 'earnest of a heaven'. He is no voluptuary in music. Music is simply the means by which the soul wings its way into the azure of spiritual theory and contemplation. Take only 'Saul' and 'Abt Vogler' in illustration. 'Saul' is a magnificent interpretation of the old theme, a favorite with the mystics, that evil spirits are driven out by music. But in this interpretation it is not the mere tones, the thrumming on the harp, it is the religious movement of the intelligence, it is the truth of Divine love throbbing in every chord, which constitutes the spell. And so in 'Abt Vogler'; the abbot's instrument is only the means whereby he strikes out the light of faith and hope within him. Not to dwell upon this point, I would only say that it seems clear that Browning has the finest acoustic gifts, and could, if he had chosen, have scattered musical bons-bons through every page. But he has printed no 'versus inopes rerum, nugaeque canorae' (Hor. ad Pis.). He has had higher objects in view, and has dispensed better stuff than that which lingers in the ear, and tends to suppress rather than support the higher activity of thought.

"When for a moment he shuts his eyes, and falls purely into the listening or 'musing' mood, he becomes the instrument of a rich deep music, breaking out of the heart of the unseen world, as in the Dirge of unfaithful Poets in 'Paracelsus', or the Gypsy's Incantation in the 'Flight of the Duchess', or the Meditation at the crisis of Sordello's temptation.

"When the keen inquisitive intelligence is in its full waking activity there grows 'more of the words' and thought, and 'less of the music', to invert a phrase of the poet's. The melody ceases, the rhythm is broken, as in all intense, earnest conversation. At times only the tinkle of the pairing rhymes, of which Browning has made a most witty use, reminds that we are called to partake a mood in which commonplace associations are melting into the ideal. I believe the economy of music is a necessity of Browning's art; and it would be only fair, if those who attack him on this ground would consider how far thought of such quality as his admits of being chanted, or otherwise musically accompanied. In plain words the problem is, how far the pleasures of sound and of sense can be united in poetry; and it will be found in every case that a poet sacrifices something either to the one or to the other. Browning has said something in his arch way on this point. In effect, he remarks, Italian prose can render a simple thought more sweetly to the ear than either Greek or English verse. It seems clear from many other of his critical remarks that he considers the demand for music in preference to thought in poetry, as the symptom of a false taste.

"Browning's poetry is to be gazed at, rather than listened to and recited, for the most part. It is infinitely easier to listen for an hour to spiritual music than to fix one's whole attention for a few minutes on a spiritual picture. In the latter act of mind we find a rich musical accompaniment distracting, while a slight musical accompaniment is probably helpful. And perhaps we may characterize Browning's poetry as a series of spiritual pictures with a faint musical accompaniment.

"For illustration by extreme contrast, Milton may be compared with Browning. Milton was a great hearsay poet, Browning repeats no hearsay. In reading Milton, the difficulty is to keep up the mental tension where there is so little thought, strictly speaking. With Browning the highest tension is exacted.

"He is pre-eminently the looker, the seer, the 'maker-see'; the reporter, the painter of the scenery and events of the soul. And if the sense of vision is our noblest, and we instinctively express the acts of intelligence in terms drawn from physical vision, the poet who leans most towards the 'SEER of Power and Love in the absolute, Beauty and Goodness in the concrete', takes the higher rank. This is no matter for bigotry of taste. Singers and seers, musicians and reporters, and reproducers of every degree, who have something to tell us or to show us of the 'world as God has made it, where all is beauty', we have need of all. But of singers there are many, of seers there are few, that is all."

In the most difficult form of verse, namely, blank verse, Browning has shown himself a great master, and has written some of the very best in the literature. And great as is the extent of his blank verse, the 'Ring and the Book' alone containing 21,116 verses, it never entirely lapses into prose.

One grand merit of blank verse is in the SWEEP of it; another, in its pause-melody, which can be secured only by a skilful recurrence of an unbroken measure; without this, variety of pause ceases to be variety, and results in a metrical chaos; a third is in its lightsomeness of movement, its go, when well-freighted with thought. All these merits are found united in much of Browning's blank verse, especially in that of 'The Ring and the Book'. As an example of this, take the following passage from the monologue of the Canon Caponsacchi. It gives expression to his vision of Count Guido's spiritual down-sliding; "in the lowest deep a lower deep still threatening to devour him, opens wide":—

> "And thus I see him slowly and surely edged
> Off all the table-land whence life upsprings
> Aspiring to be immortality,
> As the snake, hatched on hill-top by mischance,
> Despite his wriggling, slips, slides, slidders down
> Hill-side, lies low and prostrate on the smooth
> Level of the outer place, lapsed in the vale:
> So I lose Guido in the loneliness,

Silence, and dusk, till at the doleful end,
At the horizontal line, creation's verge,
From what just is to absolute nothingness—
Lo, what is this he meets, strains onward still?
What other man, deep further in the fate,
Who, turning at the prize of a foot-fall
To flatter him and promise fellowship,
Discovers in the act a frightful face—
Judas, made monstrous by much solitude!
The two are at one now! Let them love their love
That bites and claws like hate, or hate their hate
That mops and mows and makes as it were love!
There, let them each tear each in devil's-fun,
Or fondle this the other while malice aches—
Both teach, both learn detestability!
Kiss him the kiss, Iscariot! Pay that back,
That smatch o' the slaver blistering on your lip—
By the better trick, the insult he spared Christ—
Lure him the lure o' the letters, Aretine!
Lick him o'er slimy-smooth with jelly-filth
O' the verse-and-prose pollution in love's guise!
The cockatrice is with the basilisk!
There let him grapple, denizens o' the dark,
Foes or friends, but indissolubly bound,
In their one spot out of the ken of God
Or care of man for ever and ever more!"

Browning has distinctly indicated the standard by which he estimates art-work, in the closing paragraph of his Essay 'On the Poet objective and subjective; on the latter's aim; on Shelley as man and poet'.

"I would rather," he says, "consider Shelley's poetry as a sublime fragmentary essay towards a presentment of the correspondency of the universe to Deity, of the natural to the spiritual, and of the actual to the ideal, than I would isolate and separately appraise the worth of many detachable portions which might be acknowledged AS UTTERLY PERFECT IN A LOWER MORAL POINT OF VIEW, UNDER THE MERE CONDITIONS OF ART. It would be easy to take my stand on successful instances of objectivity in Shelley: there is the unrivalled 'Cenci'; there is the 'Julian and

Maddalo' too; there is the magnificent 'Ode to Naples': why not regard, it may be said, the less organized matter as the radiant elemental foam and solution, out of which would have been evolved, eventually, creations as perfect even as those? But I prefer to look for the highest attainment, not simply the high,—and, seeing it, I hold by it. There is surely enough of the work 'Shelley' to be known enduringly among men, and, I believe, to be accepted of God, as human work may; and AROUND THE IMPERFECT PROPORTIONS OF SUCH, THE MOST ELABORATED PRODUCTIONS OF ORDINARY ART MUST ARRANGE THEMSELVES AS INFERIOR ILLUSTRATIONS."

The italics are mine. I would say, but without admitting imperfect art on the part of Browning, for I regard him as one of the greatest of literary artists, that HE must be estimated by the standard presented in this passage, by the "presentment", everywhere in his poetry, "of the correspondency of the universe to Deity, of the natural to the spiritual, and of the actual to the ideal."

The same standard is presented in 'Andrea del Sarto', in 'Old Pictures in Florence', and in other of his poems.

V. Arguments of the Poems.

* It has not been thought necessary, in these Arguments, to use quotation marks wherever expressions from the poems are incorporated; and especially where they are adapted in construction to the place where they are introduced.

Wanting is—What?

"Love, the soul of soul, within the soul", the Christ-spirit, the spirit of the "Comer" (o' e'rxo/menos, Matt. 11:3), completes incompletion, reanimates that which without it is dead, and admits to a fellowship with the soul of things; 'Ubi caritas, ibi claritas'. See passage from 'Fifine at the Fair', quoted under 'My Star'.

My Star.

The following passage from 'Fifine at the Fair', section 55, is an expansion of the idea involved in 'My Star', and is the best commentary which can be given on it:—

> "I search but cannot see
> What purpose serves the soul that strives, or world it tries
> Conclusions with, unless the fruit of victories
> Stay, one and all, stored up and guaranteed its own
> For ever, by some mode whereby shall be made known
> The gain of every life. Death reads the title clear—
> What each soul for itself conquered from out things here:
> Since, IN THE SEEING SOUL, ALL WORTH LIES, I
>   ASSERT,—
> AND NOUGHT I' THE WORLD, WHICH, SAVE FOR
>   SOUL THAT SEES, INERT
> WAS, IS, AND WOULD BE EVER,—STUFF FOR
>   TRANSMUTING—NULL
> AND VOID UNTIL MAN'S BREATH EVOKE THE
>   BEAUTIFUL—
> BUT, TOUCHED ARIGHT, PROMPT YIELDS EACH
>   PARTICLE, ITS TONGUE
> OF ELEMENTAL FLAME,—no matter whence flame
>   sprung
> From gums and spice, or else from straw and rottenness,
> So long as soul has power to make them burn, express
> What lights and warms henceforth, leaves only ash behind,
> Howe'er the chance: if soul be privileged to find
> Food so soon that, at first snatch of eye, suck of breath,
> It shall absorb pure life:" etc.

The Flight of the Duchess.

In 'The Flight of the Duchess' we are presented with a generous soul-life, as exhibited by the sweet, glad Duchess, linked with fossil conventionalism and mediaevalsim, and an inherited authority which brooks no submissiveness, as exhibited by the Duke, her husband, "out of whose veins ceremony and pride have driven the blood, leaving him but a fumigated and embalmed self". The scene of the poem is a "rough north land", subject to a Kaiser of Germany. The story is so plainly told that no prose summary of it could make it plainer. Its deeper meaning centres in the incantation of the old gypsy woman, in which is mystically shadowed forth the long and painful discipline through which the soul must pass before being fully admitted to the divine arcanum, "how love is the only good in the world".

The poem is one which readily lends itself to an allegorical interpretation. For such an interpretation, the reader is referred to Mrs. Owen's paper, read before the Browning Society of London, and contained in the Society's Papers, Part IV., pp. 49* et seq. It is too long to be given here.

The Last Ride Together.

"The speaker is a man who has to give up the woman he loves; but his love is probably reciprocated, however inadequately, for his appeal for 'a last ride together' is granted. The poem reflects his changing moods and thoughts as 'here we are riding, she and I'. 'Fail I alone in words and deeds? Why, all men strive, and who succeeds?' Careers, even careers called 'successful', pass in review—statesmen, poets, sculptors, musicians—each fails in his ideal, for ideals are not attainable in this life of incompletions. But faith gains something for a man. He has loved this woman. That is something gained. If this life gave all, what were there to look forward to? 'Now, heaven and she are beyond this ride.' Again,—and this is his closing reflection,—

"'What if heaven be, that, fair and strong'", etc.
—Browning Soc. Papers, V., 144*.

By the Fireside.

Perhaps in no other of Mr. Browning's poems are the spiritual uses of "the love of wedded souls" more fully set forth than in the poem, 'By the Fireside'.

The Monologue is addressed by a happy husband to his "perfect wife, my Leonor". He looks forward to what he will do when the long, dark autumn evenings come—the evenings of declining age, when the pleasant hue of his soul shall have dimmed, and the music of all its spring and summer voices shall be dumb in life's November. In his "waking dreams" he will "live o'er again" the happy life he has spent with his loved and loving companion. Passing out where the backward vista ends, he will survey, with her, the pleasant wood through which they have journeyed together. To the hazel-trees of England, where their childhood passed, succeeds a rarer sort, till, by green degrees, they at last slope to Italy, and youth,—Italy, the woman-country, loved by earth's male-lands. She being the trusted guide, they stand at last in the heart of things, the heaped and dim woods all around them, the single and slim thread of water slipping from slab to slab, the ruined chapel perched half-way up in the Alpine gorge, reached by the one-arched bridge where the water is stopped in a stagnant pond, where all day long a bird sings, and a stray sheep drinks at times. Here, where at afternoon, or almost eve, the silence grows conscious to that degree, one half feels it must get rid of what it knows, they walked side by side, arm in arm, and cheek to cheek; cross silent the crumbling bridge, pity and praise the sweet chapel, read the dead builder's date, 'five, six, nine, recross the bridge, take the path again—but wait! Oh moment one and infinite! the west is tender, with its one star, the chrysolite! the sights and sounds, the lights and shades, make up a spell; a moment after, and unseen hands are hanging the night around them fast, but they know that a bar has been broken between life and life, that they are mixed at last in spite of the mortal screen.

> "The forests had done it; there they stood;
> We caught for a moment the powers at play:
> They had mingled us so, for once and for good,
> Their work was done—we might go or stay,
> They relapsed to their ancient mood."

Browning everywhere lays great stress on those moments of exalted feeling, when the soul has an unchecked play and is revealed to itself. See in the section of the Introduction on Personality and Art, the passage quoted from the Canon's Monologue in 'The Ring and the Book', and the remarks on conversion.

Mr. Nettleship, in his 'Essays on Browning's Poetry', has traced somewhat minutely the symbolical meaning which he sees in the scenery and circumstances of 'By the Fireside'. Readers are referred to these Essays.

Prospice.

The speaker in this noble monologue is one who, having fought a good fight and finished his course, lived and wrought thoroughly in sense, and soul, and intellect, is now ready and eager to encounter the 'Arch-Fear', Death; and then he will clasp again his Beloved, the soul of his soul, who has gone before. He leaves the rest to God.

With this monologue should be read the mystical description, in 'The Passing of Arthur' (Tennyson's Idylls of the King), of "the last, dim, weird battle of the west", beginning,—

"A deathwhite mist slept over sand and sea."

Amphibian.

This poem is the Prologue to 'Fifine at the Fair'.

Amphibian is one who unites both lives within himself, the material and the spiritual, in complete concord and mutual subservience—one who "lives and likes life's way", and can also free himself of tether, leave the solid land, and, unable to fly, swim "in the sphere which overbrims with passion and thought",—the sphere of poetry. Such an one may be said to be Browning's ideal man. "The value and significance of flesh" is everywhere recognized in his poetry. "All good things are ours," Rabbi Ben Ezra is made to say, "nor soul helps flesh more, now, than flesh helps soul." The full physical life, in its relation to the spiritual, was never more beautifully sung than it is sung by David, in the poem of 'Saul'. See the passage beginning, "Oh! our manhood's prime vigor!" and the passage in 'Balaustion's Adventure', descriptive of Hercules, as he returns, after his conflict with Death, leading back Alkestis.

James Lee's Wife.

The original title in 'Dramatis Personae' (first published in 1864) was 'James Lee'.

The poem consists of a succession of soliloquies (rather than monologues*), separated, it must be supposed, by longer or shorter intervals of time, and expressive of subjective states induced in a wife whose husband's love, if it ever were love, indeed, gradually declines to apathy and finally entire deadness. What manner of man James Lee was, is only faintly intimated. The interest centres in, is wholly confined to, the experiences of the wife's heart, under the circumstances, whatever they were.

The scene is a cottage on a "bitter coast of France".

I. 'James Lee's Wife speaks at the Window'.—The first misgivings of her heart are expressed; and these misgivings are responded to by the outer world. Summer has stopped. Will the summer of her husband's love stop too, and be succeeded by cheerless winter? The revolt of her heart against such a thought is expressed in the third stanza.

II. 'By the Fireside'.—Here the faintly indefinite misgiving expressed in the first soliloquy has become a gloomy foreboding of ill; "the heart shrinks and closes, ere the stroke of doom has attained it."

The fire on the hearth is built of shipwreck wood, which tells of a "dim dead woe befallen this bitter coast of France", and omens to her foreboding heart the shipwreck of their home. The ruddy shaft of light from the casement must, she thinks, be seen by sailors who envy the warm safe house and happy freight. But there are ships in port which go to ruin,

"All through worms i' the wood, which crept,
Gnawed our hearts out while we slept:
           That is worse."

Her mind reverts to the former occupants of their house, as if she felt an influence shed within it by some unhappy woman

---

* For the distinction between the soliloquy and the monologue, see the passage given in a note, from Rev. Prof. Johnson's paper on 'Bishop Blougram's Apology', under the treatment of the monologue, p. 85 {part III of Intro.}

who, like herself, in Love's voyage, saw planks start and open hell beneath.

III. 'In the Doorway'.—As she looks out from the doorway, everything tells of the coming desolation of winter, and reflects the desolation which, she feels, is coming upon herself. The swallows are ready to depart, the water is in stripes, black, spotted white with the wailing wind. The furled leaf of the fig-tree, in front of their house, and the writhing vines, sympathize with her heart and her spirit:—

"My heart shrivels up and my spirit shrinks curled."

But there is to them two, she thinks, no real outward want, that should mar their peace, small as is their house, and poor their field. Why should the change in nature bring change to the spirit which should put life in the darkness and cold?

"Oh, live and love worthily, bear and be bold!
Whom Summer made friends of, let Winter estrange."

IV. 'Along the Beach'.—It does not appear that she anywhere in the poem addresses her husband, face to face. It is soliloquy throughout. In this section it does appear, more than in the others, that she is directly addressing him; but it's better to understand it as a mental expostulation. He wanted her love, and got it, in its fulness; though an expectation of all harvest and no dearth was not involved in that fulness of love.

Though love greatens and even glorifies, she knew there was much in him waste, with many a weed, and plenty of passions run to seed, but a little good grain too. And such as he was she took him for hers; and he found her his, to watch the olive and wait the vine of his nature; and when rivers of oil and wine came not, the failure only proved that he was her whole world, all the same. But he has been averse to, and has resented, the tillage of his nature to which she has lovingly devoted herself, feeling it to be a bondage;

"And 'tis all an old story, and my despair
Fit subject for some new song:"

such as the one with which she closes this soliloquy, representing a love which cares only for outside charms (which, later in the poem, we learn she has not) and looks not deeper.

V. 'On the Cliff'.—Leaning on the barren turf, which is dead to the roots, and looking at a rock, flat as an anvil's face, and left dry by the surf, with no trace of living thing about it (Death's altar by the lone shore), she sees a cricket spring gay, with films of blue, upon the parched turf, and a beautiful butterfly settle and spread its two red fans, on the rock. And then there is to her, wholly taken up, as she is, with their beauty,

> "No turf, no rock; in their ugly stead,
> See, wonderful blue and red!"

and they symbolize to her, Love settling unawares upon men, the level and low, the burnt and bare, in themselves (as are the turf and the rock).

VI. 'Reading a Book, under the Cliff'.—The first six stanzas of this section she reads from a book.[*]

Her experiences have carried her beyond what these Lines convey, and she speaks of them somewhat sarcastically and ironically. This "young man", she thinks, will be wiser in time,

> "for kind
> Calm years, exacting their accompt
> Of pain, mature the mind:"

and then the wind, when it begins among the vines, so low, so low, will have for him another language; such as this:—

> "Here is the change beginning, here the lines
> Circumscribe beauty, set to bliss
> The limit time assigns."

---

[*]   They were composed by Mr. Browning when in his 23d year, and published in 1836, in 'The Monthly Repository', vol. x., pp. 270, 271, and entitled simply 'Lines'. They were revised and introduced into this section of 'James Lee', which was published in 'Dramatis Personae' in 1864.

This is the language SHE has learned: We cannot draw one beauty into our hearts' core, and keep it changeless. This is the old woe of the world; the tune, to whose rise and fall we live and die. RISE WITH IT, THEN! REJOICE THAT MAN IS HURLED FROM CHANGE TO CHANGE UNCEASINGLY, HIS SOUL'S WINGS NEVER FURLED! To this philosophy of life has she been brought. But she must still sadly reflect how bitter it is for man not to grave, on his soul, one fair, good, wise thing just as he grasped it! For himself death's wave; while time washes (ah, the sting!) o'er all he'd sink to save.

This reflection must be understood, in her own case, as prompted by her unconquerable wifely love. It is this which points the sting.

VII. 'Among the Rocks'.—The brown old earth, in autumn, when all the glories of summer are fading, or have faded, wears a good gigantic smile, looking not backward, but forward, with his feet in the ripples of the sea-wash, and listening to the sweet twitters of the 'white-breasted sea-lark'. The entire stanza has a mystical meaning and must be interpreted in its connection.

She has reached, in this soliloquy, high ground:—

> "If you loved only what were worth your love,
> Love were clear gain, and wholly well for you:
> Make the low nature better by your throes!
> GIVE EARTH YOURSELF, GO UP FOR GAIN ABOVE!"

The versification of the first stanza of this section is very lovely, and subtly responsive to the feeling. It exhibits the completest inspiration. No mere metrical skill, nor metrical sensibility even, could have produced it.

VIII. 'Beside the Drawing-Board'.—She is seated at her drawing-board, and has turned from the poor coarse hand of some little peasant girl she has called in as a model, to work, but with poor success, after a clay cast of a hand by Leonardo da Vinci, who

> "Drew and learned and loved again,
> While fast the happy moments flew,

Till beauty mounted into his brain
And on the finger which outvied
His art, he placed the ring that's there,
Still by fancy's eye descried,
In token of a marriage rare:
For him on earth his art's despair,
For him in heaven his soul's fit bride."

Her effort has taught her a wholesome lesson: "the worth of flesh and blood at last!" There's something more than beauty in a hand. Da Vinci would not have turned from the poor coarse hand of the little girl who has been standing by in wondering patience. He, great artist as he was, owed all he achieved to his firm grasp upon, and struggle with, and full faith in, the real. She imagines him saying:—

"Shall earth and the cramped moment-space
Yield the heavenly crowning grace?
Now the parts and then the whole!*
Who art thou with stinted soul
And stunted body, thus to cry
'I love,—shall that be life's strait dole?
I must live beloved or die!'
This peasant hand that spins the wool
And bakes the bread, why lives it on,
Poor and coarse with beauty gone,—
What use survives the beauty? Fool!"

She has been brought to the last stage of initiation into the mystery of Life. But, as is shown in the next and final section of the poem, the wifely heart has preserved its vitality, has, indeed, grown in vitality, and cherishes a hope which shows its undying love, and is not without a touch of pathos.

IX. 'On Deck'.—In Sections V.-VIII. the soliloquies are not directed to the husband, as they are in I.-IV. In this last, he is again mentally addressed. She is on board the vessel which is to convey, or is conveying, her to her English home, or somewhere else. As

---

*   "On the earth the broken arcs; in the heaven, a perfect round."—Abt Vogler.

there is nothing in her for him to remember, nothing in her art efforts he cares to see, nothing she was that deserves a place in his mind, she leaves him, sets him free, as he has long shown to her he has wished to be. She, conceding his attitude toward her, asks him to concede, in turn, that such a thing as mutual love HAS been. There's a slight retaliation here of the wounded spirit. But her heart, after all, MUST have its way; and it cherishes the hope that his soul, which is now cabined, cribbed, confined, may be set free, through some circumstance or other, and she may then become to him what he is to her. And then, what would it matter to her that she was ill-favored? All sense of this would be sunk in the strange joy that he possessed her as she him, in heart and brain. Hers has been a love that was life, and a life that was love. Could one touch of such love for her come in a word of look of his, why, he might turn into her ill-favoredness, she would know nothing of it, being dead to joy.

A Tale.
(The Epilogue to 'The Two Poets of Croisic'.)

The speaker in this monologue is the wife of a poet, and she tells the story to her husband, of the little cricket that came to the aid of the musician who was contending for a prize, when one of the strings of his lyre snapped. So he made a statue for himself, and on the lyre he held perched his partner in the prize. If her poet-husband gain a prize in poetry, she asks, will some ticket when his statue's built tell the gazer 'twas a cricket helped his crippled lyre; that when one string which made "love" sound soft, was snapt in twain, she perched upon the place left vacant and duly uttered, "Love, Love, Love", whene'er the bass asked the treble to atone for its somewhat sombre drone?

Confessions.

The speaker is a dying man, who replies very decidedly in the negative to the question of the attendant priest as to whether he views the world as a vale of tears. The memory of a past love, which is running through his mind, still keeps the world bright. Of the stolen interviews with the girl he loved he makes confession, using the physic bottles which stand on a table by the bedside to illustrate his story.

The monologue is a choice bit of grotesque humor touched with pathos.

Respectability.

By the title of the poem is meant respectability according to the standard of the beau monde.

The speaker is a woman, as is indicated in the third stanza. The monologue is addressed to her lover.

Stanza 1 shows that they have disregarded the conventionalities of the beau monde. Had they conformed to them, many precious months and years would have passed before they found out the world and what it fears. One cannot well judge of any state of things while in it. It must be looked at from the outside.

Stanza 2. The idea is repeated in a more special form in the first four verses of the stanza; and in the last four their own non-conventional and Bohemian life is indicated.

Stanza 3, vv. 1-4. The speaker knows that this beau monde does not proscribe love, provided it be in accordance with the proprieties which IT has determined upon and established. v. 5. "The world's good word!" a contemptuous exclamation: what's the world's good word worth? "the Institute!" (the reference is, of course, to the French Institute), the Institute! with all its authoritative, dictatorial learnedness! v.6. Guizot and Montalembert were both members of the Institute, and being thus in the same boat, Guizot conventionally receives Montalembert. vv. 7 and 8. These two unconventional Bohemian lovers, strolling together at night, at their own sweet will, see down the court along which they are strolling, three lampions flare, which indicate some big place or other where the "respectables" do congregate; and the woman says to her companion, with a humorous sarcasm, "Put forward your best foot!" that is, we must be very correct passing along here in this brilliant light.

By the two lovers are evidently meant George Sand (the speaker) and Jules Sandeau, with whom she lived in Paris, after she left her husband, M. Dudevant. They took just such unconventional night-strolls together, in the streets of Paris.

Home-Thoughts from Abroad.

An Englishman, in some foreign land, longs for England, now that April's there, with its peculiar English charms; and then will come May, with the white-throat and the swallows, and, most delightful of all, the thrush, with its rapturous song! And the buttercups, far brighter than the gaudy melon-flower he has before him!

Home-Thoughts from the Sea.

A paean, inspired by the sight, from the sea, of Cape Trafalgar and Gibraltar, both objects of patriotic pride to an Englishman; the one associated with the naval victory gained by the English fleet, under Nelson, over the combined French and Spanish fleets; the other, England's greatest stronghold.

The first four verses make a characteristic Turner picture.

Old Pictures in Florence.

The speaker in the monologue is looking down upon Florence, in the valley beneath, from a villa on one of the surrounding heights. The startling bell-tower Giotto raised more than startles him. (For an explanation of this, see note under Stanza 2.) Although the poem presents a general survey of the old Florentine masters, the THEME of the poem is really Giotto, who received the affectionate homage of the Florentines, in his own day, and for whom the speaker has a special love. The poem leads up to the prophesied restoration of Freedom to Florence, the return of Art, that departed with her, and the completion of the Campanile, which will vindicate Giotto and Florence together, and crown the restoration of freedom to the city, and its liberation from the hated Austrian rule.

Mrs. Browning's 'Casa Guidi Windows' should be read in connection with this monologue. The strong sympathy which is expressed in the last few stanzas of the monologue, with Italian liberty, is expressed in 'Casa Guidi Windows' at a white heat.

"We find," says Professor Dowden, "a full confession of Mr. Browning's creed with respect to art in the poem entitled 'Old Pictures in Florence'. He sees the ghosts of the early Christian masters, whose work has never been duly appreciated, standing sadly by each mouldering Italian Fresco; and when an imagined interlocutor inquires what is admirable in such work as this, the poet answers that the glory of Christian art lies in its rejecting a limited perfection, such as that of the art of ancient Greece, the subject of which was finite, and the lesson taught by which was submission, and in its daring to be incomplete, and faulty, faulty because its subject was great with infinite fears and hopes, and because it must needs teach man not to submit but to aspire."

Pictor Ignotus.
[Florence, 15—.]

An unknown painter reflects, but without envy, upon the praise which has been bestowed on a youthful artist,—what that praise involves. He himself was conscious of all the power, and more, which the youth has shown; no bar stayed, nor fate forbid, to exercise it, nor would flesh have shrunk from seconding his soul. All he saw he could have put upon canvas;

> "Each face obedient to its passion's law,
> Each passion clear proclaimed without a tongue."

And when he thought how sweet would be the earthly fame which his work would bring him, "the thought grew frightful, 'twas so wildly dear!" But a vision flashed before him and changed that thought. Along with the loving, trusting ones were cold faces, that begun to press on him and judge him. Such as these would buy and sell his pictures for garniture and household-stuff. His pictures, so sacred to his soul, would be the subject of their prate, "This I love, or this I hate, this likes me more, and this affects me less!" To avoid such sacrilege, he has chosen his portion. And if his heart sometimes sinks, while at his monotonous work of painting endless cloisters and eternal aisles, with the same series, Virgin, Babe, and Saint, with the same cold, calm, beautiful regard, at least no merchant traffics in his heart. Guarded by the sanctuary's gloom, from vain tongues, his pictures may die, surely, gently die.

> "O youth, men praise so,—holds their praise its worth?
> Tastes sweet the water with such specks of earth?"

Andrea del Sarto.
(Called "The Faultless Painter".)

In this monologue, "the faultless painter" (Andrea Senza Errori, as he was surnamed by the Italians) is the speaker. He addresses his worthless wife, Lucrezia, upon whom he weakly dotes, and for whom he has broken faith with his royal patron, Francis I. of France, in order that he might meet her demands for money, to be spent upon her pleasures. He laments that he has fallen below himself as an artist, that he has not realized the possibilities of his genius, half accusing, from the better side of his nature, and half excusing, in his uxoriousness, the woman who has had no sympathy with him in the high ideals which, with her support, he might have realized, and thus have placed himself beside Angelo and Rafael. "Had the mouth then urged 'God and the glory! never care for gain. The present by the future, what is that? Live for fame, side by side with Angelo—Rafael is waiting. Up to God all three!' I might have done it for you."

In his 'Comparative Study of Tennyson and Browning'*, Professor Edward Dowden, setting forth Browning's doctrines on the subject of Art, remarks:—

"The true glory of art is, that in its creation there arise desires and aspirations never to be satisfied on earth, but generating new desires and new aspirations, by which the spirit of man mounts to God Himself. The artist (Mr. Browning loves to insist on this point) who can realize in marble or in color, or in music, his ideal, has thereby missed the highest gain of art. In 'Pippa Passes' the regeneration of the young sculptor's work turns on his finding that in the very perfection which he had attained lies ultimate failure. And one entire poem, 'Andrea del Sarto', has been devoted to the exposition of this thought. Andrea is 'the faultless painter'; no line of his drawing ever goes astray; his hand expressed adequately and accurately all that his mind conceives; but for this very reason,

---

* Originally a lecture, delivered in 1868, and published in 'Afternoon Lectures on Literature and Art' (Dublin), 5th series, 1869; afterwards revised, and included in the author's 'Studies in Literature, 1789-1877'. It is one of the best criticisms of Browning's poetry that have yet been produced. Every Browning student should make a careful study of it.

precisely because he is 'the faultless painter', his work lacks the highest qualities of art:—

> "'A man's reach should exceed his grasp,
> Or what's a Heaven for? all is silver-grey,
> Placid and perfect with my art—the worse.'

"And in the youthful Raphael, whose technical execution fell so far below his own, Andrea recognizes the true master:—

> "'Yonder's a work, now, of that famous youth', etc.

"In Andrea del Sarto," says Vasari, "art and nature combined to show all that may be done in painting, where design, coloring, and invention unite in one and the same person. Had this master possessed a somewhat bolder and more elevated mind, had he been as much distinguished for higher qualifications as he was for genius and depth of judgment in the art he practised, he would, beyond all doubt, have been without an equal. But there was a certain timidity of mind, a sort of diffidence and want of force in his nature, which rendered it impossible that those evidences of ardor and animation which are proper to the more exalted character, should ever appear in him; nor did he at any time display one particle of that elevation which, could it but have been added to the advantages wherewith he was endowed, would have rendered him a truly divine painter: wherefore the works of Andrea are wanting in those ornaments of grandeur, richness, and force, which appear so conspicuously in those of many other masters. His figures are, nevertheless, well drawn, they are entirely free from errors, and perfect in all their proportions, and are for the most part simple and chaste: the expression of his heads is natural and graceful in women and children, while in youths and old men it is full of life and animation. The draperies of this master are beautiful to a marvel, and the nude figures are admirably executed, the drawing is simple, the coloring is most exquisite, nay, it is truly divine."

Mr. Ernest Radford, quoting this passage, in the Browning Society's 'Illustrations to Browning's Poems', remarks that "nearly the whole POEM of 'Andrea del Sarto' is a mere translation into the SUBJECTIVE Mood (if I may so say) of this passage in which the painter's work is criticised from an external standpoint . . .

"Recent researches into Andrea's life throw doubt upon a good deal that Vasari has written concerning the unhappiness of his marriage and the manner of his death. And the biographer himself modifies, in his second edition, the account he had given of the fair Lucrezia. Vasari, it should be said, was a pupil of Andrea, and therefore must, in this instance, have had special opportunities of knowledge, though he may, on the same account, have had some special 'animus' when he wrote. For the purposes of his poem, Browning is content to take the traditional account of the matter, which, after all, seems to substantially accurate. The following is from the first edition:—

"At that time there was a most beautiful girl in Via di San Gallo, who was married to a cap-maker, and who, though born of a poor and vicious father, carried about her as much pride and haughtiness, as beauty and fascination. She delighted in trapping the hearts of men, and amongst others ensnared the unlucky Andrea, whose immoderate love for her soon caused him to neglect the studies demanded by his art, and in great measure to discontinue the assistance which he had given to his parents.

"Certain pictures of Andrea's which had been painted for the King of France were received with much favor, and an invitation to Andrea soon followed their delivery, to 'go and paint at the French Court'. He went accordingly, and 'painted proudly', as Browning relates, and prospered every way. But one day, being employed on the figure of a St. Jerome doing penance, which he was painting for the mother of the King, there came to him certain letters from Florence; these were written him by his wife; and from that time (whatever may have been the cause) he began to think of leaving France. He asked permission to that effect from the French King accordingly, saying that he desired to return to Florence, but that, when he had arranged his affairs in that city, he would return without fail to his Majesty; he added, that when he came back, his wife should accompany him, to the end that he might remain in France the more quietly; and that he would bring with him pictures and sculptures of great value. The King, confiding in these promises, gave him money for the purchase of those pictures and sculptures,

Andrea taking an oath on the gospels to return within the space of a few months, and that done he departed to his native city.

"He arrived safely in Florence, enjoying the society of his beautiful wife, and that of his friends, with the sight of his native city, during several months; but when the period specified by the King, and that at which he ought to have returned, had come and passed, he found himself at the end, not only of his own money, but, what with building" (the "melancholy little house they built to be so gay with") "indulging himself with various pleasures, and doing no work, of that belonging to the French monarch also, the whole of which he had consumed. He was, nevertheless, determined to return to France, but the prayers and tears of his wife had more power than his own necessities, or the faith which he had pledged to the King."

"And so for a pretty woman's sake, was a great nature degraded. And out of sympathy with its impulses, broad, and deep, and tender as only the greatest can show, 'Andrea del Sarto', our great, sad poem, was written."

The monologue exhibits great perfection of finish. Its composition was occasioned, as Mr. Furnivall learned from the poet himself (see 'Browning Society's Papers', Part II., p. 161), by the portrait of Andrea del Sarto and his wife, painted by himself, and now in the Pitti Palace, in Florence. Mr. Browning's friend, and his wife's friend, Mr. John Kenyon (the same to whom Mrs. Browning dedicated 'Aurora Leigh'), had asked the poet to buy him a copy of Andrea del Sarto's picture. None could be got, and so Mr. Browning put into a poem what the picture had said to himself, and sent it to Mr. Kenyon. It was certainly a worthy substitute.

Fra Lippo Lippi.

The Italian artist, Lippi, is the speaker. Lippi was one of the representatives of the protest made in the fifteenth century against the conventional spiritualization in the art of his time. In the monologue he gives expression to his faith in the real, in the absolute spiritual significance of the lineaments of the human face, and in the forms of nature. The circumstances under which this faith is expressed, are somewhat droll. Lippi was a wild fellow and given to excesses of various kinds. When a boy he took refuge against starvation in the convent of the Carmelites, in Florence, and became a monk; but he proved unfaithful to his religious vows, and, impelled by his genius for art, made his escape from the convent, having first profited by the work of Masaccio, and devoted himself to painting. After many romantic experiences, and having risen to distinction in his art, he returned to Florence and became known to Cosimo de' Medici, in whose employ he is at the time he is presented to us in the monologue. It appears he had been shut up by his patron, for three weeks, in order to be kept at work, "a-painting for the great man, saints and saints and saints again. I could not paint all night—Ouf! I leaned out of window for fresh air. There came a hurry of feet, and little feet, a sweep of lutestrings, laughs, and whiffs of song,"—etc. In his eagerness to join in the fun, he tears into shreds curtain, and counterpane, and coverlet, makes a rope, descends, and comes up with the fun hard by Saint Laurence, hail fellow, well met. On his way back toward daybreak, he is throttled by the police, and it is to them the monologue is addressed. He ingratiates himself with them by telling his history, and by his talk on art, and a most interesting and deeply significant talk it is, the gist of it being well expressed in a passage of Mrs. Browning's 'Aurora Leigh', "paint a body well, you paint a soul by implication, like the grand first Master . . . Without the spiritual, observe, the natural's impossible;—no form, no motion! Without sensuous, spiritual is inappreciable;—no beauty or power! And in this twofold sphere the two-fold man (and still the artist is intensely a man) holds firmly by the natural, to reach the spiritual beyond it,—fixes still the type with mortal vision, to pierce through, with eyes immortal, to the antetype, some call the ideal,—better called the real, and certain to be called so presently when things shall have their names."

Browning has closely followed, in the monologue, the art-historian, Giorgio Vasari, as the following extracts will show (the translation is that of Mrs. Jonathan Foster, in the Bohn Library):—

"The Carmelite monk, Fra Filippo di Tommaso Lippi (1412-1469)[*] was born at Florence in a bye-street called Ardiglione, under

---

[*]   The date of birth differs in the biographies, it being variously given as 1400, 1406, 1410, and 1412. But the latter appears to be the one generally accepted.

the Canto alla Cuculia, and behind the convent of the Carmelites. By the death of his father he was left a friendless orphan at the age of two years, his mother having also died shortly after his birth. The child was for some time under the care of a certain Mona Lapaccia, his aunt, the sister of his father, who brought him up with very great difficulty till he had attained his eighth year, when, being no longer able to support the burden of his maintenance, she placed him in the above-named convent of the Carmelites. Here, in proportion as he showed himself dexterous and ingenious in all works performed by hand, did he manifest the utmost dulness and incapacity in letters, to which he would never apply himself, nor would he take any pleasure in learning of any kind. The boy continued to be called by his worldly name of Filippo,* and being placed with others, who like himself were in the house of the novices, under the care of the master, to the end that the latter might see what could be done with him; in place of studying, he never did anything but daub his own books, and those of the other boys, with caricatures, whereupon the prior determined to give him all means and every opportunity for learning to draw. The chapel of the Carmine had then been newly painted by Masaccio, and this being exceedingly beautiful, pleased Fra Filippo greatly, wherefore he frequented it daily for his recreation, and, continually practising there, in company with many other youths, who were constantly drawing in that place, he surpassed all the others by very much in dexterity and knowledge . . . Proceeding thus, and improving from day to day, he had so closely followed the manner of Masaccio, and his works displayed so much similarity to those of the latter, that many affirmed the spirit of Masaccio to have entered the body of Fra Filippo . . .

"It is said that Fra Filippo was much addicted to the pleasures of sense, insomuch that he would give all he possessed to secure the gratification of whatever inclination might at the moment be predominant; . . . It was known that, while occupied in the pursuit of his pleasures, the works undertaken by him received little or none of his attention; for which reason Cosimo de' Medici, wishing him to execute a work in his own palace, shut him up, that he

---

* It was customary, on entering a convent, to change the baptismal name for some other.

might not waste his time in running about; but having endured this confinement for two days, he then made ropes with the sheets of his bed, which he cut to pieces for that purpose, and so having let himself down from a window, escaped, and for several days gave himself up to his amusements. When Cosimo found that the painter had disappeared, he caused him to be sought, and Fra Filippo at last returned to his work, but from that time forward Cosimo gave him liberty to go in and out at his pleasure, repenting greatly of having previously shut him up, when he considered the danger that Fra Filippo had incurred by his folly in descending from the window; and ever afterwards laboring to keep him to his work by kindness only, he was by this means much more promptly and effectually served by the painter, and was wont to say that the excellencies of rare genius were as forms of light and not beasts of burden."

A Face.

The speaker imagines the head of a beautiful girl he knows, "painted upon a background of pale gold, such as the Tuscan's early art prefers", and details the picture as he would have it.

The Bishop orders his Tomb.
The Bishop orders his Tomb at St. Praxed's Church.*
    [Rome, 15—.]

The dying Bishop pleads with his natural sons that they give him the sumptuous tomb they stand pledged to,—such a tomb as will excite the envy of his old enemy Gandolf, who cheated him out of a favorite niche in St. Praxed's Church, by dying before him, and securing it for his tomb.

It is not necessary to suppose that the natural sons are present. His, perhaps, delirious mind is occupied with the precious marbles and stones and other luxuries he has loved to much, and with his old rival and enemy, Gandolf.

---

* First published in 'Hood's Magazine', March, 1845, No. III., vol. iii., pp. 237-239, under the title 'The Tomb at St. Praxed's (Rome, 15—)'. "This poem and 'The Flight of the Duchess' were sent by Browning to help make up the numbers of the magazine while Hood lay dying."—Furnivall's 'Bibliography of Robert Browning', p. 48.

John Ruskin, in his 'Modern Painters' (Vol. IV., chap. XX., Section 32), remarks:—

"Robert Browning is unerring in every sentence he writes of the Middle Ages; always vital, right, and profound; so that in the matter of art, . . . there is hardly a principle connected with the mediaeval temper, that he has not struck upon in those seemingly careless and too rugged rhymes of his. There is a curious instance, by the way, in a short poem* referring to this very subject of tomb and image sculpture; all illustrating just one of those phases of local human character which, though belonging to Shakespeare's own age, he [Shakespeare] never noticed, because it was specially Italian and un-English; connected also closely with the influence of mountains on the heart, and therefore with our immediate inquiries.** I mean the kind of admiration with which a southern artist regarded the STONE he worked in; and the pride which populace or priest took in the possession of precious mountain substance, worked into the pavements of their cathedrals, and the shafts of their tombs.

"Observe, Shakespeare, in the midst of architecture and tombs of wood, or freestone, or brass, naturally thinks of GOLD as the best enriching and ennobling substance for them; in the midst also of the fever of the Renaissance he writes, as every one else did, in praise of precisely the most vicious master of that school—Giulio Romano***; but the modern poet, living much in Italy, and quit of the Renaissance influence, is able fully to enter into the Italian feeling, and to see the evil of the Renaissance tendency, not because he is greater than Shakespeare, but because he is in another element, and has seen other things . . .

"I know no other piece of modern English, prose or poetry, in which there is so much told, as in these lines ['The Bishop orders his Tomb'], of the Renaissance spirit,—its worldliness, inconsistency, pride, hypocrisy, ignorance of itself, love of art, of luxury, and of good Latin. It is nearly all that I said of the Central Renaissance in thirty pages of the 'Stones of Venice' put into as many lines, Browning's being also the antecedent work. The worst of it is that

*   'The Bishop orders his Tomb in St. Praxed's Church'.
**   'The Mountain Glory', the subject of the chapter from which this is taken.
*** 'Winter's Tale', V. 2. 106.

this kind of concentrated writing needs so much SOLUTION before the reader can fairly get the good of it, that people's patience fails them, and they give the thing up as insoluble; though, truly, it ought to be to the current of common thought like Saladin's talisman, dipped in clear water, not soluble altogether, but making the element medicinable."

Professor Dowden, in regard to Mr. Browning's doctrines on the subject of art, remarks:—

"It is always in an unfavorable light that he depicts the virtuoso or collector, who, conscious of no unsatisfied aspirations such as those which make the artist's joy and sorrow, rests in the visible products of art, and looks up to nothing above or beyond them . . . The unbelieving and worldly spirit of the dying Bishop, who orders his tomb at St. Praxed's, his sense of the vanity of the world simply because the world is passing out of his reach, the regretful memory of the pleasures of his youth, the envious spite towards Gandolf, who robbed him of the best position for a tomb, and the dread lest his reputed sons should play him false and fail to carry out his designs, are united with a perfect appreciation of Renaissance art, and a luxurious satisfaction, which even a death-bed cannot destroy, in the splendor of voluptuous form and color. The great lump of lapis lazuli,

> "'Big as a Jew's head cut off at the nape,
> Blue as a vein o'er the Madonna's breast',

must poise between his sculptured knees; the black basalt must contrast with the bas-relief in bronze below:—

> "'St. Praxed in a glory, and one Pan
> Ready to twitch the Nymph's last garment off';

the inscription must be 'choice Latin, picked phrase, Tully's every word'."

A Toccata of Galuppi's.

The speaker is listening to a Toccata of Galuppi's, and the music tells him of how they lived once in Venice, where the merchants were the kings. He was never out of England, yet it's as if he SAW it all, through what is addressed to the ear alone.

But the music does more than reflect the life of mirth and folly which was led in the gay and voluptuous city. It has an undertone of sadness; its lesser thirds so plaintive, its sixths diminished, sigh on sigh, tell the votaries of pleasure something; its suspensions, its solutions, its commiserating sevenths, awaken in them the question of their hold on life. That question the music answers.

Abt Vogler.

(After he has been extemporizing upon the musical instrument of his invention.)

The Abbe Georg Joseph Vogler was born at Wuerzburg (Bavaria), June 15, 1749; appointed Kappelmeister to the King of Sweden, in 1786. While in this capacity, the "musical instrument of his invention", called the Orchestrion, was constructed;* went to London with his organ, in 1790, and gave a series of successful concerts, realizing some 1200 Pounds, and making a name as an organist; commissioned to reconstruct the organ of the Pantheon on the plan of his Orchestrion; and later, received like commissions at Copenhagen and at Neu Ruppin in Prussia; founded a school of music at Copenhagen, and published there many works; in 1807 was appointed by the Grand Duke, Louis I., Kappelmeister at Darmstadt; founded there his last school, two of his pupils being Weber and Meyerbeer; died in 1814. Browning presents Vogler as a great extemporizer, in which character he appears to have been the most famous. For a further account, see Miss Eleanor Marx's paper on the Abbe Vogler, from which the above facts have been derived ('Browning Soc. Papers', Pt. III., pp. 339-343). Her authorities are Fetis's 'Biogr. Univ. des Musiciens' and Nisard's 'Vie de l'Abbe Vogler'.

Mrs. Turnbull, in her paper on 'Abt Vogler' ('Browning Soc. Papers', Pt. IV., pp. 469-476), has so well traced the argument of

---

* "This was a very compact organ, in which four key-boards of five octaves each, and a pedal board of thirty-six keys, with swell complete, were packed into a cube of nine feet. See Fetis's 'Biographie Universelle des Musiciens'.—G. Grove." 'Note to Miss Marx's Art. on Vogler'.

the monologue, that I cannot do better than quote the portion of her paper in which she presents it:—

"Abt Vogler has been extemporizing on his instrument, pouring out through it all his feelings of yearning and aspiration; and now, waking from his state of absorption, excited, and trembling with excess of emotion, he breaks out into the wish, 'Would it might tarry!' In verses [stanzas] one and two he compares the music he has made to a palace, which Solomon (as legends of the Koran relate) summoned all creatures, by the magic name on his ring, to raise for the princess he loved; so all the keys, joyfully submitting to the magic power of the master, combine to aid him, the low notes rushing in like demons to give him the base on which to build his airy structure; the high notes like angels throwing decoration of carving and tracery on pinnacle and flying buttress, till in verse three its outline, rising ever higher and higher, shows in the clouds like St. Peter's dome, illuminated and towering into the vasty sky; and it seems as if his soul, upborne on the surging waves of music, had reached its highest elevation. But no. Influences from without, inexplicable, unexpected, join to enhance his own attempts; the heavens themselves seem to bow down and to flash forth inconceivable splendors on his amazed spirit, till the limitations of time and space are gone—'there is no more near nor far'.

". . . In this strange fusion of near and far, of heaven and earth, presences hover, spirits of those long dead or of those yet to be, lured by the power of music to return to life, or to begin it. Figures are dimly descried in the fervor and passion of music, even as of old in the glare and glow of the fiery furnace.

"Verses four and five are a bold attempt to describe the indescribable, to shadow forth that strange state of clairvoyance when the soul shakes itself free from all external impressions, which Vogel tells us was the case with Schubert, and which is true of all great composers—'whether in the body or out of the body, I cannot say'.

"In the sixth verse we come to a comparison of music with the other arts. Poetry, painting, and sculpture deal with actual form, and the tangible realities of life. They are subject to laws, and we know how they are produced; can watch the painting grow beneath the artist's touches, or the poem take shape line by line.

"True it needs the soul of the artist to combine and to interfuse the elements with which he wishes to create any true work of art, but music is almost entirely independent of earthly element in which to clothe and embody itself. It does not allow of a realistic conception, but without intermediate means is in a direct line from God, and enables us to comprehend that Power which created all things out of nothing, with whom TO WILL and TO DO are one and the same.

"Schopenhauer says, 'There is no sound in Nature fit to serve the musician as a model, or to supply him with more than an occasional suggestion for his sublime purpose. He approaches the original sources of existence more closely than all other artists, nay, even than Nature herself.'

"Heine has also noticed this element of miracle, which coincides exactly with Browning's view expressed in the lines:—

> "'Here is the finger of God, a flash of the will that can,
> Existent behind all laws, that made them, and, lo, they are!'

Now, these seven verses contain the music of the poem; in the remaining ones we pass to Browning's Platonic philosophy.

"In the eighth verse a sad thought of the banished music obtrudes—'never to be again'. So wrapt was he in the emotions evoked, he had no time to think of what tones called them up, and now all is past and gone. His magic palace, unlike that of Solomon, has 'melted into air, into thin air', and, 'like the baseless fabric of a vision', only the memory of it is left . . . And, depressed by this saddest of human experiences, . . . he turns away impatient from the promise of more and better, to demand from God the same— the very same. Browning with magnificent assurance answers, 'yes, you shall have the same'.

> "'Fool! all that is at all,
> Lasts ever, past recall.'

> "'Ay, what was, shall be.'

". . . the ineffable Name which built the palace of King Solomon, which builds houses not made with hands—houses of flesh which souls inhabit, craving for a heart and a love to fill them, can and will satisfy their longings; . . . I know no other words in the English language which compresses into small compass such a body of high and inclusive thought as verse nine. (1) God the sole changeless, to whom we turn with passionate desire as the one abiding-place, as we find how all things suffer loss and change, ourselves, alas! the greatest. (2) His power and love able and willing to satisfy the hearts of His creatures—the thought expatiated on by St. Augustine and George Herbert here crystallized in one line:— 'Doubt that Thy power can fill the heart that Thy power expands?' (3) Then the magnificent declaration, 'There shall never be one lost good'—the eternal nature of goodness, while its opposite evil . . . is a non-essential which shall one day pass away entirely, and be swallowed up of good . . .

"Now follows an announcement, as by tongue of prophet or seer, that we shall at last find all our ideals complete in the mind of God, not put forth timorously, but with triumphant knowledge— knowledge gained by music whose creative power has for the moment revealed to us the permanent existence of these ideals.

"The sorrow and pain and failure which we are all called upon to suffer here, . . . are seen to be proofs and evidences of this great belief. Without the discords how should we learn to prize the harmony?

"Carried on the wings of music and high thought, we have ascended one of those Delectable mountains—Pisgah-peaks from which

"'Our souls have sight of that immortal sea

Which brought us hither';

and whence we can descry, however faintly, the land that is very far off to which we travel, and we would fain linger, nay, abide, on the mount, building there our tabernacles.

"But it cannot be. That fine air is difficult to breathe long, and life, with its rounds of custom and duty, recalls us. So we descend with the musician, through varying harmonies and sliding modulations . . . deadening the poignancy of the minor third in the more satisfying reassuring chord of the dominant ninth, which again finds its rest on the key-note—C major—the common chord, so sober and uninteresting that it well symbolizes the common level of life, the prosaic key-note to which unfortunately most of our lives are set.

"We return, however, strengthened and refreshed, braced to endure the wrongs which we know shall be one day righted, to acquiesce in the limited and imperfect conditions of earth, which we know shall be merged at last in heaven's perfect round, and to accept with patience the renunciation demanded of us here, knowing

> "'All we have willed, or hoped, or dreamed of good shall exist.'"

In his 'Introductory Address to the Browning Society', the Rev. J. Kirkman, of Queen's College, Cambridge, says of 'Abt Volger':—

"The spiritual transcendentalism of music, the inscrutable relation between the seen and the eternal, of which music alone unlocks the gate by inarticulate expression, has never had an articulate utterance from a poet before 'Abt Vogler'. This is of a higher order of composition, quite nobler, than the merely fretful rebellion against the earthly condition imposed here below upon heavenly things, seen in 'Master Hughes' [of Saxe-Gotha]. In that and other places, I am not sure that persons of musical ATTAINMENT, as distinguished from musical SOUL AND SYMPATHY, do not rather find a professional gratification at the technicalities . . . than get conducted to 'the law within the law'. But in 'Abt Vogler', the understanding is spell-bound, and carried on the wings of the emotions, as Ganymede in the soft down of the eagle, into the world of spirit . . .

"The beautiful utterances of Richter alone approach to the value of Browning's on music. Well does he deserve remembrance for the remark, that 'Music is the only language incapable of expressing anything impure', and for many others. They all [the poets quoted in the passage omitted above], comparatively, speak FROM OUTSIDE; Browning speaks FROM INSIDE, as if an angel came to give all the hints we could receive,

> "'Of that imperial palace when we came.'

He speaks of music as Dante does of Heaven, Hell, and Purgatory, because he has been there. Even the musical Milton, whose best line is, 'In linked sweetness long drawn out', whose best special treatment of music is in the occasional poem, 'At a solemn music', has given us nothing of the nature of 'Abt Vogler'. It should be perfectly learnt by heart; and it will be ever whispering analogies to the soul in daily life. Because, of course, the mystery of life and the mystery of music make one of the most fundamental transcendental harmonies breathed into our being."

'Touch him ne'er so lightly', etc.

In the first stanza some one describes admiringly a writer of mushroom poems. In the second stanza another gives the genesis of a poem which becomes a nation's heritage.

Memorabilia.

The speaker is one to whom Shelley is an almost ideal being. He can hardly think of him as a man of flesh and blood. He meets some one who has actually seen him and talked with him; and it's all so strange to him, and he expresses so much surprise at it, that it moves the laughter of the other, and he breaks off and speaks of crossing a moor. Only a hand's breadth of it shines alone 'mid the blank miles round about; for there he picked up, and put inside his breast, a moulted feather, an eagle-feather. He forgets the rest. There is, in fact, nothing more for him to remember. The eagle-feather causes an isolated flash of association with the poet of the atmosphere, the winds, and the clouds,

"The meteoric poet of air and sea."

How it strikes a Contemporary.

The speaker, a Spaniard, it must be supposed, describes to his companion the only poet he knew in his life, who roamed along the promenades and through the by-streets and lanes and alleys of Valladolid, an old dog, bald and blindish, at his heels. He appeared interested in whatever he looked on, and his looks went everywhere, taking in the cobbler at his trade, the man slicing lemons into drink, the coffee-roaster's brazier, and the boys turning its winch; books on stalls, strung-up fly-leaf ballads, posters by the wall;

> "'If any beat a horse, you felt he saw;
> If any cursed a woman, he took note.'
> Yet stared at nobody,—you stared at him,
> And found, less to your pleasure than surprise,
> He seemed to know you, and expect as much."

Popular imagination is active as to who and what he is; perhaps a spy, or it may be "a recording chief-inquisitor, the town's true master if the town but knew", who by letters keeps "our Lord the King" well informed "of all thought, said, and acted"; but of the King's approval of these letters there has been no evidence of any kind.

The speaker found no truth in one of the popular reports, namely, that this strange man lived in great luxury and splendor. On the contrary, he lived in the plainest, simplest manner; played a game of cribbage with his maid, in the evening, and, when the church clock struck ten, went straight off to bed. It seems that while the belief of the people was, that this man kept up a correspondence with their earthly Lord, the King, noting all that went on, the speaker, in the monologue is aware that it was the Heavenly King with whom he corresponded. In the last paragraph of his monologue he expresses the wish that he might have looked in, yet had haply been afraid, when this man came to die, and seen, ministering to him, the heavenly attendants,—

> "who line the clean gay garret sides,
> And stood about the neat low truckle-bed
> With the heavenly manner of relieving guard.
> Here had been, mark, the general-in-chief,
> Thro' a whole campaign of the world's life and death,
> Doing the King's work all the dim day long,

* * * * *

And, now the day was won, relieved at once!"

He then adds that there was

"'No further show or need of that old coat,
You are sure, for one thing! Bless us, all the while
How sprucely WE are dressed out, you and I!'"

we who are so inferior to that divine poet; but,

"A second, and the angels alter that."

"Transcendentalism"
.A poem in twelve books.

This monologue is addressed by a poet to a brother-poet whom he finds fault with for speaking naked thoughts instead of draping them in sights and sounds. If boys want images and melody, grown men, you think, want abstract thought. Far from it. The objects which throng our youth, we see and hear, quite as a matter of course. But what of it, if you could tell what they mean? The German Boehme, with his affinities for the abstract, never cared for plants until, one day, he noticed they could speak; that the daisy colloquized with the cowslip on SUCH themes! themes found extant in Jacob's prose. But when life's summer passes while reading prose in that tough book he wrote, getting some sense or other out of it, who helps, then, to repair our loss? Another Boehme, say you, with a tougher book and subtler abstract meanings of what roses say? Or some stout Mage like John of Halberstadt, who MADE THINGS Boehme WROTE THOUGHTS about? Ah, John's the man for us! who instead of giving us the wise talk of roses, scatters all around us the roses themselves, pouring heaven into this shut house of life. So come, the harp back to your heart again, instead of speaking dry words across its strings. Your own boy-face bent over the finer chords, and following the cherub at the top that points to God with his paired half-moon wings, is a far better poem than your poem with all its naked thoughts.

Apparent Failure.

The poet, it appears, speaks here in his own person. Sauntering about Paris, he comes upon the Doric little Morgue, the dead-house, where they show their drowned. He enters, and sees through the screen of glass, the bodies of three men who committed suicide, the day before, by drowning themselves in the Seine.

In the last stanza, he gives expression to his hopeful philosophy, which recognizes "some soul of goodness, in things evil";* which sees in human nature, "potentiality of final deliverance from the evil in it, given only time enough for the work". In this age of professed and often, no doubt, affected, agnosticism and pessimism, Browning is the foremost apostle of Hope. He, more than any other great author of the age, whether philosopher, or poet, or divine, has been inspired with the faith that

> "a sun will pierce
> The thickest cloud earth ever stretched;
> That, after Last, returns the First,
> Though a wide compass round be fetched;
> That what began best, can't end worst,
> Nor what God blessed once, prove accurst."

Compare with this, the following stanzas from Tennyson's 'In Memoriam', Section 54:—

> "Oh yet we trust that somehow good
> Will be the final goal of ill,
> To pangs of nature, sins of will,
> Defects of doubt, and taints of blood.
>
> That nothing walks with aimless feet;
> That not one life shall be destroyed,
> Or cast as rubbish to the void,
> When God hath made the pile complete.

* * * * *

---

*   'Henry V.', IV. 1. 4.

Behold, we know not anything;
I can but trust that good shall fall
At last—far off—at last, to all,
And every winter change to spring."

Rabbi Ben Ezra.

Accompany me, my young friend, in my survey of life from youth to old age.

The present life does not rise to its best and then decline to its worst; "the best is yet to be, the last of life, for which the first was made."

The indecisions, perplexities, and yearnings, the hopes and fears of youth, I do not remonstrate against. They are the conditions of vitality and growth, distinguish man's life from the limited completeness of the "low kinds" of creation, "finished and finite clods untroubled by a spark"; and should be prized as inseparable from his high rank in existence.

Life would have nothing to boast of, were man formed but to experience an unalloyed joy, to find always and never to seek. Care irks not the crop-full bird, and doubt frets not the maw-crammed beast. But man is disturbed by a divine spark which is his title to a nearer relationship with God who gives than with his creatures that receive.

The rebuffs he meets with should be welcomed. Life's true success is secured through obstacles, and seeming failures, and unfulfilled aspirations. He is but a brute whose soul is conformed to his flesh, whose spirit works for the play of arms and legs. The test of the body's worth should be, the extent to which it can project the soul on its lone way.

But we must not calculate soul-profits all the time. Gifts of every kind which belong to our nature should prove their use, their own good in themselves. I own that the past was for me profuse of power on every side, of perfection at every turn, which my eyes and ears took in, and my brain treasured up. The heart should beat in harmony with this life, and feel how good it is to live and learn, and see the whole design. I who once saw only Power, now see Love perfect also, and am thankful that I was a man, and trust what my Maker will do with me.

This flesh is pleasant, and the soul can repose in it, after its own activities. It is the solid land to which it can return when wearied with its flights; and we often wish, in our yearnings for rest, that we might hold some prize to match those manifold possessions of the brute, might gain most as we should do best; but the realization of such a wish is not compatible with the dignity of our nature.

Flesh and soul must be mutually subservient; one must not be merely subjected to the other, not even the inferior to the superior. Let us cry, "All good things are ours, nor soul helps flesh more, now, than flesh helps soul."

Let, then, youth enter into its heritage, and use and enjoy it; let it then pass into an approved manhood, "for aye removed from the developed brute; a God, though in the germ"; let it pass fearless and unperplexed as to what weapons to select, what armor to indue for the battle which awaits that approved manhood.

Youth ended, let what it has resulted in, be taken account of; wherein it succeeded, wherein it failed; and having proved the past, let it face the future, satisfied in acting to-morrow what is learned to-day.

As it was better that youth should awkwardly strive TOWARD making, than repose in what it found made, so is it better that age, exempt from strife, should know, than tempt further. As in youth, age was waited for, so in age, wait for death, without fear, and with the absolute soul-knowledge which is independent of the reasoning intellect of youth. It is this absolute soul-knowledge which severs great minds from small, rather than intellectual power.

Human judgments differ. Whom shall my soul believe? One conclusion may, at least, be rested in: a man's true success must not be estimated by things done, which had their price in the world; but by that which the world's coarse thumb and finger failed to plumb; by his immature instincts and unsure purposes which weighed not as his work in the world's estimation, yet went toward making up the main amount of his real worth; by thoughts which could not be contained in narrow acts, by fancies which would not submit to the bonds of language; by all that he strived after and could not attain, by all that was ignored by men with only finite and realizable aims: such are God's standards of his worth.

All the true acquisitions of the soul, all the reflected results of its energizing after the unattainable in this life, all that has truly BEEN, belong to the absolute, and are permanent amid all earth's changes. It is, indeed, through these changes, through the dance of plastic circumstance, that the permanent is secured. They are the machinery, the Divine Potter's wheel, which gives the soul its bent, tries it, and turns it forth a cup for the Master's lips, sufficiently impressed.

> "So take and use Thy work!
> Amend what flaws may lurk,
> What strain o' the stuff, what warpings past the aim!
> My times be in Thy hand!
> Perfect the cup as planned!
> Let age approve of youth, and death complete the same."

The following account of Rabbi Ben Ezra, I take from Dr. F. J. Furnivall's 'Bibliography of Rober Browning' ('Browning Soc. Papers', Part II., p. 162):—

"Rabbi Ben Ezra, or Ibn Ezra, was a learned Jew, 1092-1167 A.D. Ibn Ezra and Maimonides, whom he is said to have visited in Egypt, were two of the four great Philosophers or Lights of the Jews in the Middle Ages. Ibn Ezra was born at Toledo in Spain, about 1092 or 1093 A.D., or in 1088 according to Graetz, 'Geschichte der Juden', vi. 198. He was poor, but studied hard, composed poems wherewith to 'Adorn my own, my Hebrew nation', married, had a son Isaac (a poet too), travelled to Africa, the Holy Land, Rome in 1140, Persia, India, Italy, France, England. He wrote many treatises on Hebrew Grammar, astronomy, mathematics, &c., commentaries on the books of the Bible, &c.—many of them in Rome—and two pamphlets in England 'for a certain Salomon of London'. Joseph of Maudeville was one of his English pupils. He died in 1167, at the age of 75, either in Kalahorra, on the frontier of Navarre, or in Rome. His commentary on Isaiah has been englished by M. Friedlaender, and published by the Society of Hebrew Literature, Truebner, 1873. From the Introduction to that book I take these details. Ibn Ezra believed in a future life. In his commentary on Isaiah 55:3, 'AND YOUR SOUL SHALL LIVE', he says, 'That is, your soul shall live forever after the death of the body, or you will receive new life through Messiah, when you will return to the Divine Law.' See also on Isaiah 39:18. Of the potter's clay passage, Isaiah 29:16, he has only a translation, 'Shall man be esteemed as the potter's clay', and no comment that could ever have given Browning a hint for his use of the metaphor in his poem, even if he had ever seen Ibn Ezra's commentary. See Rabbi Ben Ezra's fine 'Song of Death' in stanzas 12-20 of the grimly humorous Holy-Cross Day."

A Grammarian's Funeral.

---

* "Grammarian" mustn't be understood here in its restricted modern sense; it means rather one devoted to learning, or letters, in general.

Shortly after the revival of learning in Europe.

The devoted disciples of a dead grammarian are bearing his body up a mountain-side for burial on its lofty summit, "where meteors shoot, clouds form, lightnings are loosened, stars come and go! Lofty designs must close in like effects: loftily lying, leave him,—still loftier than the world suspects, living and dying".

This poem is INFORMED throughout with the poet's iterated doctrine in regard to earth life,—to the relativity of that life. The grammarian, in his hunger and thirst after knowledge and truth, thought not of time. "What's time? Leave Now for dogs and apes! Man has Forever." "Oh, if we draw a circle premature, heedless of far gain, greedy for quick returns of profit, sure bad is our bargain!"

The poem "exhibits something of the life of the Scaligers and the Casaubons, of many an early scholar, like Roger Bacon's friend, Pierre de Maricourt, working at some region of knowledge, and content to labor without fame so long as he mastered thoroughly whatever he undertook" ('Contemporary Rev.', iv., 135).

But the grammarian was true to one side only of Browning's philosophy of life. He disregarded the claims of the physical life, and became "soul-hydropic with a sacred thirst".[*]

The lyrico-dramatic verse of this monologue is especially noticeable. There is a march in it, exhibiting the spirit with which the bearers of the corpse are conveying it up the mountain-side.

An Epistle containing the Strange Medical Experience of
Karshish, the Arab Physician.

Karshish, the Arab physician, has been journeying in quest of knowledge pertaining to his art, and writes to his all-sagacious master, Abib, ostensibly about the specimens he has gathered of medicinal plants and minerals, and the observations he has made; but his real interest, which he endeavors to conceal by passing to matters of greater import to him, as he would have his sage at home believe, is in what he pronounces "a case of mania, subinduced by epilepsy". His last letter brought his journeyings to Jericho. He is now on his way to Jerusalem, and has reached Bethany, where he passes the night.

The case of mania which so interests him,—far more than he is willing to admit,—is that of Lazarus, whose firm conviction rests that he was dead (in fact they buried him) and then restored to life by a Nazarene physician of his tribe, who afterwards perished in a tumult. The man Lazarus is witless, he writes, of the relative value of all things. Vast armaments assembled to besiege his city, and the passing of a mule with gourds, are all one to him; while at some trifling fact, he'll gaze, rapt with stupor, as if it had for him prodigious import. Should his child sicken unto death, why look for scarce abatement of his cheerfulness, or suspension of his daily craft; while a word, gesture, or glance from that same child at play or laid asleep, will start him to an agony of fear, exasperation, just as like! The law of the life, it seems, to which he was temporarily admitted, has become to him the law of this earthly life; his heart and brain move there, his feet stay here. He appears to be perfectly

---

[*]   "Every lust is a kind of hydropic distemper, and the more we drink the more we shall thirst."—Tillotson, quoted in 'Webster'.

submissive to the heavenly will, and awaits patiently for death to restore his being to equilibrium. He is by no means apathetic, but loves both old and young, affects the very brutes and birds and flowers of the field. This man, so restored to life, regards his restorer as, who but God himself, Creator and Sustainer of the world, that came and dwelt in flesh on it awhile, taught, healed the sick, broke bread at his own house, then died! Here Karshish breaks off and asks pardon for writing of such trivial matters, when there are so important ones to treat of, and states that he noticed on the margin of a pool blue-flowering borage abounding, the Aleppo sort, very nitrous. But he returns again to the subject, and tries to explain the peculiar interest, and awe, indeed, the man has inspired him with. Perhaps the journey's end, and his weariness, he thinks, may have had something to do with it. He then relates the weird circumstances under which he met him, and concludes by saying that the repose he will have at Jerusalem shall make amends for the time his letter wastes, his master's and his own. Till when, once more thy pardon and farewell!

But in spite of himself, his suppressed interest in the strange case MUST have full expression, and he gives way to all reserve and ejaculates in a postscript:—

> "The very God! think, Abib; dost thou think?
> So, the All-Great, were the All-Loving too—
> So, through the thunder comes a human voice
> Saying, 'O heart I made, a heart beats here!
> Face, my hands fashioned, see it in myself.
> Thou hast no power nor may'st conceive of mine,
> But love I gave thee, with myself to love,
> And thou must love me who have died for thee!'
> The madman saith He said so: it is strange."

See before, p. 41 {about one-fifth into Part II of the Introduction}, some remarks on the psychological phase of the monologue.

"The monologue is a signal example of 'emotional ratiocination'. There is a flash of ecstasy through the strangely cautious description of Karshish; every syllable is weighed and thoughtful, everywhere the lines swell into perfect feeling."—Robert Buchanan.

"As an example of our poet's dramatic power in getting right at the heart of a man, reading what is there written, and then looking through his eyes and revealing it all in the man's own speech, nothing can be more complete in its inner soundings and outer-keeping, than the epistle containing the 'Strange Medical Experience of Karshish, the Arab Physician', who has been picking up the crumbs of learning on his travels in the Holy Land, and writes to Abib, the all-sagacious, at home. It is so solemnly real and so sagely fine."—N. Brit. Rev., May, 1861.

A Martyr's Epitaph.

A wonderfully effective expression, effective through its pathetic simplicity, of the peaceful spirit of a Christian, who has triumphed over persecution and death, and passed to his reward.

Soliloquy of the Spanish Cloister.

The speaker in this monologue is a Spanish monk, whose jealousy toward a simple and unoffending brother has, in the seclusion of the cloister, developed into a festering malignity. If hate, he says, could kill a man, his hate would certainly kill Brother Laurence. He is watching this brother, from a window of the cloister, at work in the garden. He looks with contempt upon his honest toil; repeats mockingly to himself, his simple talk when at meals, about the weather and the crops; sneers at his neatness, and orderliness, and cleanliness; imputes to him his own libidinousness. He takes credit to himself in laying crosswise, in Jesu's praise, his knife and fork, after refection, and in illustrating the Trinity, and frustrating the Arian, by drinking his watered orange-pulp in three sips, while Laurence drains his at one gulp. Now he notices Laurence's tender care of the melons, of which it appears the good man has promised all the brethren a feast; "so nice!" He calls to him, from the window, "How go on your flowers? None double? Not one fruit-sort can you spy?" Laurence, it must be understood, kindly answers him in the negative, and then he chuckles to himself, "Strange!—and I, too, at such trouble, keep 'em close-nipped on the sly!" He thinks of devising means of causing him to trip on a great text in Galatians, entailing "twenty-nine distinct damnations, one sure, if another fails"; or of slyly putting his "scrofulous French novel" in his way, which will make him "grovel hand and foot in Belial's gripe". In his malignity, he is ready to pledge his soul to Satan (leaving a flaw in the indenture), to see blasted that rose-acacia Laurence is so proud of. Here the vesper-bell interrupts his filthy and blasphemous eructations, and he turns up his eyes and folds his hands on his breast, mumbling "Plena gratia ave Virgo!" and right upon the prayer, his disgust breaks out, "Gr-r-r—you swine!"

This monologue affords a signal illustration of the poet's skill in making a speaker, while directly revealing his own character, reflect very distinctly the character of another. This has been seen in 'My Last Duchess', given as an example of the constitution of this art-form, in the section of the Introduction on 'Browning's Obscurity'.

"The 'Soliloquy of the Spanish Cloister', is a picture (ghastly in its evident truth) of superstition which has survived religion; of a heart which has abandoned the love of kindred and friends, only to lose itself in a wilderness of petty spite, terminating in an abyss of diabolical hatred. The ordinary providential helps to goodness have been rejected; the ill-provided adventurer has sought to scale the high snow-peaks of saintliness,—he has missed his footing,—and the black chasm which yawns beneath, has ingulfed him."—E. J. H[asell], in St. Paul's Magazine, December, 1870.

An able writer in 'The Contemporary Review', Vol. IV., p. 140, justly remarks:—

"No living writer—and we do not know any one in the past who can be named, in this respect, in the same breath with him [Browning]—approaches his power of analyzing and reproducing the morbid forms, the corrupt semblances, the hypocrisies, formalisms, and fanaticisms of man's religious life. The wildness of an Antinomian predestinarianism has never been so grandly painted as in 'Johannes Agricola in Meditation'; the white heat of the persecutor glares on us, like a nightmare spectre, in 'The Herctic's Tragedy'. More subtle forms are drawn with greater elaboration. If 'Bishop Blougram's Apology', in many of its circumstances and touches, suggests the thought of actual portraiture, recalling a form and face once familiar to us, . . . it is also a picture of a class of minds which we meet with everywhere. Conservative scepticism that persuades itself that it believes, cynical acuteness in discerning the weak points either of mere secularism or dreaming mysticism, or passionate eagerness to reform, avoiding dangerous extremes, and taking things as they are because they are comfortable, and lead to wealth, enjoyment, reputation,—this, whether a true account or not of the theologian to whom we have referred . . . is yet to be found under many eloquent defences of the faith, many fervent and scornful denunciations of criticism and free thought . . . In 'Calaban upon Setebos', if it is more than the product of Mr. Browning's fondness for all abnormal forms of spiritual life, speculating among other things on the religious thoughts of a half brute-like savage, we must see a protest against the thought that man can rise by himself to true thoughts of God, and develop a pure theology out of his moral consciousness. So far it is a witness for the necessity of a revelation, either through the immediate action of the Light that lighteth every man, or that which has been given to mankind in spoken or written words, by The WORD that was in the beginning. In the 'Death in the Desert', in like manner, we have another school of thought analyzed with a corresponding subtlety . . . The 'Death in the Dessert' is worth studying in its bearing upon the mythical school of interpretation, and as a protest, we would fain hope, from Mr. Browning's own mind against the thought that because the love of God has been revealed in Christ, and has taught us the greatness of all true human love, therefore,

"'We ourselves make the love, and Christ was not.'

"In one remarkable passage at the close of 'The Legend of Pornic', Mr. Browning, speaking apparently in his own person, proclaims his belief in one great Christian doctrine, which all pantheistic and atheistic systems formally repudiate, and which many semi-Christian thinkers implicitly reject:—

"'The candid incline to surmise of late
That the Christian faith may be false, I find,

For our 'Essays and Reviews'* debate
Begins to tell on the public mind,
And Colenso's** words have weight.

"'I still, to suppose it true, for my part,
See reasons and reasons: this, to begin—
'Tis the faith that launched point-blank her dart
At the head of a lie,—taught Original Sin,
The Corruption of Man's Heart.'"

Holy-Cross Day.

On which the Jews were forced to attend an annual Christian sermon in Rome.

The argument is sufficiently shown by what is prefixed to this poem. The 'Diary by the Bishop's Secretary, 1600', is presumably imaginary.

Saul.

This is, in every respect, one of Browning's grandest poems; and in all that is included in the idea of EXPRESSION, is quite perfect.

The portion of Scripture which is the germ of the poem, and it is only the germ, is contained in the First Book of Samuel 16:14-23.

To the present consolation which David administers to Saul, with harp and song, and the Scripture story does not go beyond this, is added the assurance of the transmission of his personality, and of the influence of his deeds; first, through those who have been quickened by them, and who will, in turn, transmit that quickening—"Each deed thou hast done, dies, revives, goes to work

---

*   A volume which appeared in 1860, made up of essays and reviews, the several authors having "written in entire independence of each other, and without concert or comparison". These essays and reviews offset the extreme high church doctrine of the Tracts for the Times.

**   John W. Colenso, Bishop of Natal, in South Africa; he published works questioning the inspiration and historical accuracy of certain parts of the Bible, among which was 'The Pentateuch, and the Book of Joshua critically examined'.

in the world: . . . each ray of thy will, every flash of thy passion and prowess, long over, shall thrill thy whole people, the countless, with ardor, till they too give forth a like cheer to their sons: who, in turn, fill the South and the North with the radiance thy deed was the germ of"; and, then, through records that will give unborn generations their due and their part in his being.

The consolation is, moreover, carried beyond that afforded by earthly fame and influence. David's yearnings to give Saul "new life altogether, as good, ages hence, as this moment,—had love but the warrant, love's heart to dispense", pass into a prophecy, based on his own loving desires, of the God-Man who shall throw open to Saul the gates of that new life.

With this prophecy, David leaves Saul. On his way home, in the night, he represents himself as attended by witnesses, cohorts to left and to right. At the dawn, all nature, the forests, the wind, beasts and birds, even the serpent that slid away silent, appear to him aware of the new law; the little brooks, witnessing, murmured with all but hushed voices, "E'en so, it is so!"

A Death in the Desert.

'A Death in the Desert' appears to have been inspired by the controversies in regard to the historical foundations of Christianity, and, more especially, in regard to the character and the authorship of the Fourth Gospel—controversies which received their first great impulse from the 'Leben Jesu' of David Friedrich Strauss, first published in 1835. An English translation of the fourth edition, 1840, by Marian Evans (George Eliot), was published in London, in 1846.

The immediate occasion of the composition of 'A Death in the Desert' was, perhaps, the publication, in 1863, of Joseph Ernest Renan's 'Vie de Jesus'. 'A Death in the Desert' was included in the poet's 'Dramatis Personae', published in the following year.

"In style, the poem a little recalls 'Cleon'; with less of harmonious grace and clear classic outline, it possesses a certain stilled sweetness, a meditative tenderness, all its own, and beautifully appropriate to the utterance of the 'beloved disciple'."—Arthur Symons.

During a persecution of the Christians, the aged John of Patmos has been secretly conveyed, by some faithful disciples, to a cave in the desert, where he is dying. Revived temporarily by the tender ministrations of his disciples, he is enabled to tell over his past labors in the service of his beloved Master, to refute the Antichrist already in the world, and to answer the questions which, with his far-reaching spiritual vision, he foresees will be raised in regard to Christ's nature, life, doctrine, and miracles, as recorded in the Gospel he has written. These services he feels to be due from him, in his dying hour, as the sole survivor of Christ's apostles and intimate companions.

This is the only composition in which Browning deals directly with historical Christianity; and its main purpose may, in brief, be said to be, to set forth the absoluteness of Christianity, which cannot be affected by any assaults made upon its external, historical character.

The doctrine of the trinal unity of man (the what Does, what Knows, what Is) ascribed to John (vv. 82-104), and upon which his discourse may be said to proceed, leads up the presentation of the final stage of the Christian life on earth—that stage when man has won his way to the kingdom of the "what Is" within himself, and when he no longer needs the outward supports to his faith which he needed before he passed from the "what Knows". Christianity is a religion which is only secondarily a doctrine addressed to the "what Knows". It is, first of all, a religion whose fountain-head is a Personality in whom all that is spiritually potential in man, was realized, and in responding to whom the soul of man is quickened and regenerated. And the Church, through the centuries, has been kept alive, not by the letter of the New Testament, for the letter killeth, but by a succession of quickened and regenerated spirits, "the noble Living and the noble Dead", through whom the Christ has been awakened and developed in other souls.

POEMS.

Wanting is—What?

Wanting is—what?
Summer redundant,
Blueness abundant,
—Where is the spot?
Beamy the world, yet a blank all the same,   [5]
—Framework which waits for a picture to frame:
What of the leafage, what of the flower?
Roses embowering with nought they embower!
Come then, complete incompletion, O Comer,
Pant through the blueness, perfect the summer!   [10]
Breathe but one breath
Rose-beauty above,
And all that was death
Grows life, grows love,
Grows love!   [15]

———

4. spot: defect, imperfection.

9. O Comer: o' e'rxo/menos, Matt. 3:11; 11:3; 21:9; 23:39;
Luke 19:38; John 1:15; 3:31; 12:13. Without love, the Christ-spirit,
the spirit of the Comer, man sees, at best, only dynamic action,
blind force, in nature; but

"love greatens and glorifies
Till God's a-glow, to the loving eyes,
In what was mere earth before."
James Lee's Wife (Along the Beach).

My Star.

All that I know
    Of a certain star
Is, it can throw

156

(Like the angled spar)
Now a dart of red,   [5]
    Now a dart of blue;
Till my friends have said
    They would fain see, too,
My star that dartles the red and the blue!
Then it stops like a bird; like a flower, hangs furled: [10]
    They must solace themselves with the Saturn above it.
What matter to me if their star is a world?
    Mine has opened its soul to me; therefore I love it.

———

10. Then it stops like a bird: it beats no longer with emotion responsive to loving eyes, but stops, as a bird stops its song when disturbed.

The Flight of the Duchess.

1.

You're my friend:
I was the man the Duke spoke to;
I helped the Duchess to cast off his yoke, too:
So, here's the tale from beginning to end,
My friend!   [5]

———

2. I was the man: see vv. 440 and 847. He's proud of the honor done him.

2.

Ours is a great wild country:
If you climb to our castle's top,
I don't see where your eye can stop;
For when you've passed the corn-field country,
Where vineyards leave off, flocks are packed,   [10]
And sheep-range leads to cattle-tract,
And cattle-tract to open-chase,
And open-chase to the very base
O' the mountain where, at a funeral pace,
Round about, solemn and slow,
One by one, row after row,
Up and up the pine-trees go,
So, like black priests up, and so
Down the other side again
To another greater, wilder country,   [20]
That's one vast red drear burnt-up plain,
Branched through and through with many a vein
Whence iron's dug, and copper's dealt;
Look right, look left, look straight before,—
Beneath they mine, above they smelt,
Copper-ore and iron-ore,
And forge and furnace mould and melt,
And so on, more and ever more,
Till at the last, for a bounding belt,
Comes the salt sand hoar of the great seashore,   [30]
—And the whole is our Duke's country.

3.

I was born the day this present Duke was—
(And O, says the song, ere I was old!)
In the castle where the other Duke was—
(When I was happy and young, not old!)
I in the kennel, he in the bower:
We are of like age to an hour.
My father was huntsman in that day:
Who has not heard my father say,
That, when a boar was brought to bay,   [40]
Three times, four times out of five,

With his huntspear he'd contrive
To get the killing-place transfixed,
And pin him true, both eyes betwixt?
And that's why the old Duke would rather
He lost a salt-pit than my father,
And loved to have him ever in call;
That's why my father stood in the hall
When the old Duke brought his infant out
To show the people, and while they passed   [50]
The wondrous bantling round about,
Was first to start at the outside blast
As the Kaiser's courier blew his horn,
Just a month after the babe was born.
"And," quoth the Kaiser's courier, "since
The Duke has got an heir, our Prince
Needs the Duke's self at his side":
The Duke looked down and seemed to wince,
But he thought of wars o'er the world wide,
Castles a-fire, men on their march,   [60]
The toppling tower, the crashing arch;
And up he looked, and a while he eyed
The row of crests and shields and banners
Of all achievements after all manners,
And "Ay", said the Duke with a surly pride.
The more was his comfort when he died
At next year's end, in a velvet suit,
With a gilt glove on his hand, his foot
In a silken shoe for a leather boot,
Petticoated like a herald,   [70]
In a chamber next to an ante-room,
Where he breathed the breath of page and groom,
What he called stink, and they, perfume:
—They should have set him on red Berold
Mad with pride, like fire to manage!
They should have got his cheek fresh tannage
Such a day as to-day in the merry sunshine!
Had they stuck on his fist a rough-foot merlin!
(Hark, the wind's on the heath at its game!
Oh for a noble falcon-lanner   [80]

To flap each broad wing like a banner,
And turn in the wind, and dance like flame!)
Had they broached a cask of white beer from Berlin!
—Or if you incline to prescribe mere wine,
Put to his lips when they saw him pine,
A cup of our own Moldavia fine,
Cotnar for instance, green as May sorrel
And ropy with sweet,—we shall not quarrel.

—

74. Berold: the old Duke's favorite hunting-horse.

78. merlin: a species of hawk.

80. falcon-lanner: a long-tailed species of hawk, 'falco laniarius'.

4.

So, at home, the sick tall yellow Duchess
Was left with the infant in her clutches,   [90]
She being the daughter of God knows who:
And now was the time to revisit her tribe.
Abroad and afar they went, the two,
And let our people rail and gibe
At the empty hall and extinguished fire,
As loud as we liked, but ever in vain,
Till after long years we had our desire,
And back came the Duke and his mother again.

5.

And he came back the pertest little ape
That ever affronted human shape;   [100]
Full of his travel, struck at himself.
You'd say, he despised our bluff old ways?
—Not he! For in Paris they told the elf
That our rough North land was the Land of Lays,
The one good thing left in evil days;
Since the Mid-Age was the Heroic Time,
And only in wild nooks like ours

Could you taste of it yet as in its prime,
And see true castles with proper towers,
Young-hearted women, old-minded men,   [110]
And manners now as manners were then.
So, all that the old Dukes had been, without knowing it,
This Duke would fain know he was, without being it;
'Twas not for the joy's self, but the joy of his showing it,
Nor for the pride's self, but the pride of our seeing it,
He revived all usages thoroughly worn-out,
The souls of them fumed-forth, the hearts of them torn-out:
And chief in the chase his neck he perilled,
On a lathy horse, all legs and length,
With blood for bone, all speed, no strength;   [120]
—They should have set him on red Berold
With the red eye slow consuming in fire,
And the thin stiff ear like an abbey spire!

———

101. struck at himself: astonished at his own importance.
119. lathy: long and slim.

6.

Well, such as he was, he must marry, we heard;
And out of a convent, at the word,
Came the lady, in time of spring.
—Oh, old thoughts they cling, they cling!
That day, I know, with a dozen oaths
I clad myself in thick hunting-clothes
Fit for the chase of urox or buffle   [130]
In winter-time when you need to muffle.
But the Duke had a mind we should cut a figure,
And so we saw the lady arrive:
My friend, I have seen a white crane bigger!
She was the smallest lady alive,
Made in a piece of nature's madness,
Too small, almost, for the life and gladness
That over-filled her, as some hive
Out of the bears' reach on the high trees

Is crowded with its safe merry bees: [140]
In truth, she was not hard to please!
Up she looked, down she looked, round at the mead,
Straight at the castle, that's best indeed
To look at from outside the walls:
As for us, styled the "serfs and thralls",
She as much thanked me as if she had said it,
(With her eyes, do you understand?)
Because I patted her horse while I led it;
And Max, who rode on her other hand,
Said, no bird flew past but she inquired   [150]
What its true name was, nor ever seemed tired—
If that was an eagle she saw hover,
And the green and gray bird on the field was the plover,
When suddenly appeared the Duke:
And as down she sprung, the small foot pointed
On to my hand,—as with a rebuke,
And as if his backbone were not jointed,
The Duke stepped rather aside than forward,
And welcomed her with his grandest smile;
And, mind you, his mother all the while   [160]
Chilled in the rear, like a wind to nor'ward;
And up, like a weary yawn, with its pulleys
Went, in a shriek, the rusty portcullis;
And, like a glad sky the north-wind sullies,
The lady's face stopped its play,
As if her first hair had grown gray;
For such things must begin some one day.

—

130. urox: wild bull; Ger. 'auer-ochs'. buffle: buffalo.

7.

In a day or two she was well again;
As who should say, "You labor in vain!
This is all a jest against God, who meant   [170]
I should ever be, as I am, content
And glad in his sight; therefore, glad I will be."

So, smiling as at first went she.

8.

She was active, stirring, all fire—
Could not rest, could not tire—
To a stone she might have given life!
(I myself loved once, in my day)
—For a shepherd's, miner's, huntsman's wife,
(I had a wife, I know what I say)
Never in all the world such an one! [180]
And here was plenty to be done,
And she that could do it, great or small,
She was to do nothing at all.
There was already this man in his post,
This in his station, and that in his office,
And the Duke's plan admitted a wife, at most,
To meet his eye, with the other trophies,
Now outside the hall, now in it,
To sit thus, stand thus, see and be seen,
At the proper place in the proper minute, [190]
And die away the life between.
And it was amusing enough, each infraction
Of rule—(but for after-sadness that came)
To hear the consummate self-satisfaction
With which the young Duke and the old dame
Would let her advise, and criticise,
And, being a fool, instruct the wise,
And, childlike, parcel out praise or blame:
They bore it all in complacent guise,
As though an artificer, after contriving [200]
A wheel-work image as if it were living,
Should find with delight it could motion to strike him!
So found the Duke, and his mother like him:
The lady hardly got a rebuff—
That had not been contemptuous enough,
With his cursed smirk, as he nodded applause,
And kept off the old mother-cat's claws.

180. such an one: i.e., for a shepherd's, miner's, huntsman's
wife.

9.

So, the little lady grew silent and thin,
Paling and ever paling,
As the way is with a hid chagrin;   [210]
And the Duke perceived that she was ailing,
And said in his heart, "'Tis done to spite me,
But I shall find in my power to right me!"
Don't swear, friend! The old one, many a year,
Is in hell; and the Duke's self . . . you shall hear.

10.

Well, early in autumn, at first winter-warning,
When the stag had to break with his foot, of a morning,
A drinking-hole out of the fresh tender ice,
That covered the pond till the sun, in a trice,
Loosening it, let out a ripple of gold,   [220]
And another and another, and faster and faster,
Till, dimpling to blindness, the wide water rolled,
Then it so chanced that the Duke our master
Asked himself what were the pleasures in season,
And found, since the calendar bade him be hearty,
He should do the Middle Age no treason
In resolving on a hunting-party,
Always provided, old books showed the way of it!
What meant old poets by their strictures?
And when old poets had said their say of it,   [230]
How taught old painters in their pictures?
We must revert to the proper channels,
Workings in tapestry, paintings on panels,
And gather up woodcraft's authentic traditions:
Here was food for our various ambitions,

As on each case, exactly stated—
To encourage your dog, now, the properest chirrup,
Or best prayer to St. Hubert on mounting your stirrup—
We of the household took thought and debated.
Blessed was he whose back ached with the jerkin   [240]
His sire was wont to do forest-work in;
Blesseder he who nobly sunk "ohs"
And "ahs" while he tugged on his grandsire's trunk-hose;
What signified hats if they had no rims on,
Each slouching before and behind like the scallop,
And able to serve at sea for a shallop,
Loaded with lacquer and looped with crimson?
So that the deer now, to make a short rhyme on't,
What with our Venerers, Prickers, and Verderers,
Might hope for real hunters at length
       and not murderers,   [250]
And oh the Duke's tailor, he had a hot time on't!

—

238. St. Hubert: patron saint of huntsmen.

247. lacquer: yellowish varnish.

249. Venerers, Prickers, and Verderers: huntsmen, light-horsemen, and guardians of the vert and venison in the Duke's forest.

11.

Now you must know that when the first dizziness
Of flap-hats and buff-coats and jack-boots subsided,
The Duke put this question, "The Duke's part provided,
Had not the Duchess some share in the business?"
For out of the mouth of two or three witnesses
Did he establish all fit-or-unfitnesses;
And, after much laying of heads together,
Somebody's cap got a notable feather
By the announcement with proper unction   [260]
That he had discovered the lady's function;
Since ancient authors gave this tenet,
"When horns wind a mort and the deer is at siege,

Let the dame of the castle prick forth on her jennet,
And with water to wash the hands of her liege
In a clean ewer with a fair towelling,
Let her preside at the disembowelling."
Now, my friend, if you had so little religion
As to catch a hawk, some falcon-lanner,
And thrust her broad wings like a banner   [270]
Into a coop for a vulgar pigeon,
And if day by day and week by week
You cut her claws, and sealed her eyes,
And clipped her wings, and tied her beak,
Would it cause you any great surprise
If, when you decided to give her an airing,
You found she needed a little preparing?—
I say, should you be such a curmudgeon,
If she clung to the perch, as to take it in dudgeon?
Yet when the Duke to his lady signified,   [280]
Just a day before, as he judged most dignified,
In what a pleasure she was to participate,—
And, instead of leaping wide in flashes,
Her eyes just lifted their long lashes,
As if pressed by fatigue even he could not dissipate,
And duly acknowledged the Duke's forethought,
But spoke of her health, if her health were worth aught,
Of the weight by day and the watch by night,
And much wrong now that used to be right,
So, thanking him, declined the hunting,—   [290]
Was conduct ever more affronting?
With all the ceremony settled—
With the towel ready, and the sewer
Polishing up his oldest ewer,
And the jennet pitched upon, a piebald,
Black-barred, cream-coated, and pink eye-balled,—
No wonder if the Duke was nettled!
And when she persisted nevertheless,—
Well, I suppose here's the time to confess
That there ran half round our lady's chamber   [300]
A balcony none of the hardest to clamber;
And that Jacynth the tire-woman, ready in waiting,

Staid in call outside, what need of relating?
And since Jacynth was like a June rose, why, a fervent
Adorer of Jacynth of course was your servant;
And if she had the habit to peep through the casement,
How could I keep at any vast distance?
And so, as I say, on the lady's persistence,
The Duke, dumb stricken with amazement,
Stood for a while in a sultry smother,   [310]
And then, with a smile that partook of the awful,
Turned her over to his yellow mother
To learn what was decorous and lawful;
And the mother smelt blood with a cat-like instinct,
As her cheek quick whitened through all its quince-tint.
Oh, but the lady heard the whole truth at once!
What meant she?—Who was she?—Her duty and station,
The wisdom of age and the folly of youth, at once,
Its decent regard and its fitting relation—
In brief, my friends, set all the devils in hell free   [320]
And turn them out to carouse in a belfry
And treat the priests to a fifty-part canon,
And then you may guess how that tongue of hers ran on!
Well, somehow or other it ended at last,
And, licking her whiskers, out she passed;
And after her,—making (he hoped) a face
Like Emperor Nero or Sultan Saladin,
Stalked the Duke's self with the austere grace
Of ancient hero or modern paladin,
From door to staircase—oh, such a solemn   [330]
Unbending of the vertebral column!

—

263. wind a mort: announce that the deer is taken.

273. sealed: more properly spelt 'seeled', a term in falconry;
Lat. 'cilium', an eyelid; 'seel', to close up the eyelids of a hawk, or
other bird (Fr. 'ciller les yeux'). "Come, seeling Night, Skarfe vp the
tender Eye of pittiful Day." 'Macbeth', III. II. 46.

322. fifty-part canon: "A canon, in music, is a piece wherein

the subject is repeated, in various keys: and being strictly
obeyed in the repetition, becomes the 'canon'—the imperative

LAW—to what follows. Fifty of such parts would be indeed a notable peal:to manage three is enough of an achievement for a good musician."—From Poet's Letter to the Editor.

12.

However, at sunrise our company mustered;
And here was the huntsman bidding unkennel,
And there 'neath his bonnet the pricker blustered,
With feather dank as a bough of wet fennel;
For the court-yard walls were filled with fog
You might cut as an axe chops a log—
Like so much wool for color and bulkiness;
And out rode the Duke in a perfect sulkiness,
Since, before breakfast, a man feels but queasily,   [340]
And a sinking at the lower abdomen
Begins the day with indifferent omen.
And lo! as he looked around uneasily,
The sun ploughed the fog up and drove it asunder,
This way and that, from the valley under;
And, looking through the court-yard arch,
Down in the valley, what should meet him
But a troop of gypsies on their march?
No doubt with the annual gifts to greet him.

13.

Now, in your land, gypsies reach you, only [350]
After reaching all lands beside;
North they go, South they go, trooping or lonely,
And still, as they travel far and wide,
Catch they and keep now a trace here, a trace there,
That puts you in mind of a place here, a place there.
But with us, I believe they rise out of the ground,
And nowhere else, I take it, are found
With the earth-tint yet so freshly embrowned;
Born, no doubt, like insects which breed on
The very fruit they are meant to feed on.   [360]
For the earth—not a use to which they don't turn it,

The ore that grows in the mountain's womb,
Or the sand in the pits like a honeycomb,
They sift and soften it, bake it and burn it—
Whether they weld you, for instance, a snaffle
With side-bars never a brute can baffle;
Or a lock that's a puzzle of wards within wards;
Or, if your colt's fore foot inclines to curve inwards,
Horseshoes they hammer which turn on a swivel
And won't allow the hoof to shrivel.   [370]
Then they cast bells like the shell of the winkle
That keep a stout heart in the ram with their tinkle;
But the sand—they pinch and pound it like otters;
Commend me to gypsy glass-makers and potters!
Glasses they'll blow you, crystal-clear,
Where just a faint cloud of rose shall appear,
As if in pure water you dropped and let die
A bruised black-blooded mulberry;
And that other sort, their crowning pride,
With long white threads distinct inside,   [380]
Like the lake-flower's fibrous roots which dangle
Loose such a length and never tangle,
Where the bold sword-lily cuts the clear waters,
And the cup-lily couches with all the white daughters:
Such are the works they put their hand to,
The uses they turn and twist iron and sand to.
And these made the troop, which our Duke saw sally
Toward his castle from out of the valley,
Men and women, like new-hatched spiders,
Come out with the morning to greet our riders.   [390]
And up they wound till they reached the ditch,
Whereat all stopped save one, a witch
That I knew, as she hobbled from the group,
By her gait directly and her stoop,
I, whom Jacynth was used to importune
To let that same witch tell us our fortune.
The oldest gypsy then above ground;
And, sure as the autumn season came round,
She paid us a visit for profit or pastime,
And every time, as she swore, for the last time.   [400]

And presently she was seen to sidle
Up to the Duke till she touched his bridle,
So that the horse of a sudden reared up
As under its nose the old witch peered up
With her worn-out eyes, or rather eye-holes,
Of no use now but to gather brine,
And began a kind of level whine
Such as they used to sing to their viols
When their ditties they go grinding
Up and down with nobody minding;   [410]
And then, as of old, at the end of the humming
Her usual presents were forthcoming
—A dog-whistle blowing the fiercest of trebles
(Just a seashore stone holding a dozen fine pebbles),
Or a porcelain mouth-piece to screw on a pipe-end,—
And so she awaited her annual stipend.
But this time, the Duke would scarcely vouchsafe
A word in reply; and in vain she felt
With twitching fingers at her belt
For the purse of sleek pine-martin pelt,   [420]
Ready to put what he gave in her pouch safe,—
Till, either to quicken his apprehension,
Or possibly with an after-intention,
She was come, she said, to pay her duty
To the new Duchess, the youthful beauty.
No sooner had she named his lady,
Than a shine lit up the face so shady,
And its smirk returned with a novel meaning—
For it struck him, the babe just wanted weaning;
If one gave her a taste of what life was and sorrow, [430]
She, foolish to-day, would be wiser to-morrow;
And who so fit a teacher of trouble
As this sordid crone bent well-nigh double?
So, glancing at her wolf-skin vesture
(If such it was, for they grow so hirsute
That their own fleece serves for natural fur-suit)
He was contrasting, 'twas plain from his gesture,
The life of the lady so flower-like and delicate
With the loathsome squalor of this helicat.

I, in brief, was the man the Duke beckoned   [440]
From out of the throng; and while I drew near
He told the crone—as I since have reckoned
By the way he bent and spoke into her ear
With circumspection and mystery—
The main of the lady's history,
Her frowardness and ingratitude;
And for all the crone's submissive attitude
I could see round her mouth the loose plaits tightening,
And her brow with assenting intelligence brightening,
As though she engaged with hearty good will   [450]
Whatever he now might enjoin to fulfil,
And promised the lady a thorough frightening.
And so, just giving her a glimpse
Of a purse, with the air of a man who imps
The wing of the hawk that shall fetch the hernshaw,
He bade me take the gypsy mother
And set her telling some story or other
Of hill and dale, oak-wood or fernshaw,
To while away a weary hour
For the lady left alone in her bower,   [460]
Whose mind and body craved exertion
And yet shrank from all better diversion.

———

354. Catch they and keep: i.e., in their expression, or bearing, or manner.

407. level: monotonous.

439. helicat: for hell-cat? hag or witch.

454. imps: repairs a wing by inserting feathers; 'impen' or 'ympen', in O. E., means to ingraft. "It often falls out that a hawk breaks her wing and train-feathers, so that others must be set in their steads, which is termed 'ymping' them."—The Gentleman's Recreation, Part 2, Hawking, 1686.

14.

Then clapping heel to his horse, the mere curveter,
Out rode the Duke, and after his hollo

Horses and hounds swept, huntsman and servitor,
And back I turned and bade the crone follow.
And what makes me confident what's to be told you
Had all along been of this crone's devising,
Is, that, on looking round sharply, behold you,
There was a novelty quick as surprising: [470]
For first, she had shot up a full head in stature,
And her step kept pace with mine nor faltered,
As if age had foregone its usurpature,
And the ignoble mien was wholly altered,
And the face looked quite of another nature,
And the change reached too, whatever the change meant,
Her shaggy wolf-skin cloak's arrangment:
For where its tatters hung loose like sedges,
Gold coins were glittering on the edges,
Like the band-roll strung with tomans [480]
Which proves the veil a Persian woman's:
And under her brow, like a snail's horns newly
Come out as after the rain he paces,
Two unmistakable eye-points duly
Live and aware looked out of their places.
So, we went and found Jacynth at the entry
Of the lady's chamber standing sentry;
I told the command and produced my companion,
And Jacynth rejoiced to admit any one,
For since last night, by the same token, [490]
Not a single word had the lady spoken:
They went in both to the presence together,
While I in the balcony watched the weather.

———

463. curveter: a leaping horse.
480. tomans: Persian coins.
490. by the same token: by a presentiment or forewarning of
the same.

15.

And now, what took place at the very first of all,

172

I cannot tell, as I never could learn it:
Jacynth constantly wished a curse to fall
On that little head of hers and burn it
If she knew how she came to drop so soundly
Asleep of a sudden, and there continue
The whole time, sleeping as profoundly   [500]
As one of the boars my father would pin you
'Twixt the eyes where life holds garrison,
—Jacynth, forgive me the comparison!
But where I begin my own narration
Is a little after I took my station
To breathe the fresh air from the balcony,
And, having in those days a falcon eye,
To follow the hunt through the open country,
From where the bushes thinlier crested
The hillocks, to a plain where's not one tree.   [510]
When, in a moment, my ear was arrested
By—was it singing, or was it saying,
Or a strange musical instrument playing
In the chamber?—and to be certain
I pushed the lattice, pulled the curtain,
And there lay Jacynth asleep,
Yet as if a watch she tried to keep,
In a rosy sleep along the floor
With her head against the door;
While in the midst, on the seat of state,   [520]
Was a queen—the gypsy woman late,
With head and face downbent
On the lady's head and face intent:
For, coiled at her feet like a child at ease,
The lady sat between her knees,
And o'er them the lady's clasped hands met,
And on those hands her chin was set,
And her upturned face met the face of the crone
Wherein the eyes had grown and grown
As if she could double and quadruple   [530]
At pleasure the play of either pupil
—Very like, by her hands' slow fanning,
As up and down like a gor-crow's flappers

They moved to measure, or bell-clappers.
I said, "Is it blessing, is it banning,
Do they applaud you or burlesque you—
Those hands and fingers with no flesh on?"
But, just as I thought to spring in to the rescue,
At once I was stopped by the lady's expression:
For it was life her eyes were drinking   [540]
From the crone's wide pair above unwinking,
—Life's pure fire, received without shrinking,
Into the heart and breast whose heaving
Told you no single drop they were leaving,
—Life that, filling her, passed redundant
Into her very hair, back swerving
Over each shoulder, loose and abundant,
As her head thrown back showed the white throat curving;
And the very tresses shared in the pleasure,
Moving to the mystic measure,   [550]
Bounding as the bosom bounded.
I stopped short, more and more confounded,
As still her cheeks burned and eyes glistened,
As she listened and she listened:
When all at once a hand detained me,
The selfsame contagion gained me,
And I kept time to the wondrous chime,
Making out words and prose and rhyme,
Till it seemed that the music furled
Its wings like a task fulfilled, and dropped   [560]
From under the words it first had propped,
And left them midway in the world,
Word took word as hand takes hand,
I could hear at last, and understand,
And when I held the unbroken thread,
The gypsy said:—

"And so at last we find my tribe.
And so I set thee in the midst,
And to one and all of them describe
What thou saidst and what thou didst,   [570]
Our long and terrible journey through,

174

And all thou art ready to say and do
In the trials that remain:
I trace them the vein and the other vein
That meet on thy brow and part again,
Making our rapid mystic mark;
And I bid my people prove and probe
Each eye's profound and glorious globe,
Till they detect the kindred spark
In those depths so dear and dark, [580]
Like the spots that snap and burst and flee,
Circling over the midnight sea.
And on that round young cheek of thine
I make them recognize the tinge,
As when of the costly scarlet wine
They drip so much as will impinge
And spread in a thinnest scale afloat
One thick gold drop from the olive's coat
Over a silver plate whose sheen
Still through the mixture shall be seen. [590]
For so I prove thee, to one and all,
Fit, when my people ope their breast,
To see the sign, and hear the call,
And take the vow, and stand the test
Which adds one more child to the rest—
When the breast is bare and the arms are wide,
And the world is left outside.
For there is probation to decree,
And many and long must the trials be
Thou shalt victoriously endure, [600]
If that brow is true and those eyes are sure;
Like a jewel-finder's fierce assay
Of the prize he dug from its mountain tomb,—
Let once the vindicating ray
Leap out amid the anxious gloom,
And steel and fire have done their part,
And the prize falls on its finder's heart;
So, trial after trial past,
Wilt thou fall at the very last
Breathless, half in trance [610]

With the thrill of the great deliverance,
Into our arms forevermore;
And thou shalt know, those arms once curled
About thee, what we knew before,
How love is the only good in the world.
Henceforth be loved as heart can love,
Or brain devise, or hand approve!
Stand up, look below,
It is our life at thy feet we throw
To step with into light and joy; [620]
Not a power of life but we employ
To satisfy thy nature's want;
Art thou the tree that props the plant,
Or the climbing plant that seeks the tree—
Canst thou help us, must we help thee?
If any two creatures grew into one,
They would do more than the world has done;
Though each apart were never so weak,
Ye vainly through the world should seek
For the knowledge and the might [630]
Which in such union grew their right:
So, to approach at least that end,
And blend,—as much as may be, blend
Thee with us or us with thee,—
As climbing plant or propping tree,
Shall some one deck thee over and down,
Up and about, with blossoms and leaves?
Fix his heart's fruit for thy garland crown,
Cling with his soul as the gourd-vine cleaves,
Die on thy boughs and disappear [640]
While not a leaf of thine is sere?
Or is the other fate in store,
And art thou fitted to adore,
To give thy wondrous self away,
And take a stronger nature's sway?
I foresee and could foretell
Thy future portion, sure and well:
But those passionate eyes speak true, speak true,
Let them say what thou shalt do!

Only be sure thy daily life,   [650]
In its peace or in its strife,
Never shall be unobserved;
We pursue thy whole career,
And hope for it, or doubt, or fear,—
Lo, hast thou kept thy path or swerved,
We are beside thee in all thy ways,
With our blame, with our praise,
Our shame to feel, our pride to show,
Glad, angry—but indifferent, no!
Whether it be thy lot to go,   [660]
For the good of us all, where the haters meet
In the crowded city's horrible street;
Or thou step alone through the morass
Where never sound yet was
Save the dry quick clap of the stork's bill,
For the air is still, and the water still,
When the blue breast of the dipping coot
Dives under, and all is mute.
So at the last shall come old age,
Decrepit as befits that stage;   [670]
How else wouldst thou retire apart
With the hoarded memories of thy heart,
And gather all the very least
Of the fragments of life's earlier feast,
Let fall through eagerness to find
The crowning dainties yet behind?
Ponder on the entire past
Laid together thus at last,
When the twilight helps to fuse
The first fresh with the faded hues,   [680]
And the outline of the whole,
As round eve's shades their framework roll,
Grandly fronts for once thy soul.
And then as, 'mid the dark, a gleam
Of yet another morning breaks,
And like the hand which ends a dream,
Death, with the might of his sunbeam,
Touches the flesh and the soul awakes,

Then"—

        Ay, then indeed something would happen!
But what? For here her voice changed like a bird's;   [690]
There grew more of the music and less of the words;
Had Jacynth only been by me to clap pen
To paper and put you down every syllable
With those clever clerkly fingers,
All I've forgotten as well as what lingers
In this old brain of mine that's but ill able
To give you even this poor version
Of the speech I spoil, as it were, with stammering!
—More fault of those who had the hammering
Or prosody into me and syntax,   [700]
And did it, not with hobnails but tintacks!
But to return from this excursion,—
Just, do you mark, when the song was sweetest,
The peace most deep and the charm completest,
There came, shall I say, a snap—
And the charm vanished!
And my sense returned, so strangely banished,
And, starting as from a nap,
I knew the crone was bewitching my lady,
With Jacynth asleep; and but one spring made I   [710]
Down from the casement, round to the portal,
Another minute and I had entered,—
When the door opened, and more than mortal
Stood, with a face where to my mind centred
All beauties I ever saw or shall see,
The Duchess: I stopped as if struck by palsy.
She was so different, happy and beautiful,
I felt at once that all was best,
And that I had nothing to do, for the rest,
But wait her commands, obey and be dutiful.   [720]
Not that, in fact, there was any commanding;
I saw the glory of her eye,
And the brow's height and the breast's expanding,
And I was hers to live or to die.
As for finding what she wanted,
You know God Almighty granted

Such little signs should serve wild creatures
To tell one another all their desires,
So that each knows what his friend requires,
And does its bidding without teachers.   [730]
I preceded her; the crone
Followed silent and alone;
I spoke to her, but she merely jabbered
In the old style; both her eyes had slunk
Back to their pits; her stature shrunk;
In short, the soul in its body sunk
Like a blade sent home to its scabbard.
We descended, I preceding;
Crossed the court with nobody heeding;
All the world was at the chase,   [740]
The court-yard like a desert-place,
The stable emptied of its small fry;
I saddled myself the very palfrey
I remember patting while it carried her,
The day she arrived and the Duke married her.
And, do you know, though it's easy deceiving
One's self in such matters, I can't help believing
The lady had not forgotten it either,
And knew the poor devil so much beneath her
Would have been only too glad, for her service,   [750]
To dance on hot ploughshares like a Turk dervise,
But, unable to pay proper duty where owing it,
Was reduced to that pitiful method of showing it.
For though, the moment I began setting
His saddle on my own nag of Berold's begetting
(Not that I meant to be obtrusive),
She stopped me, while his rug was shifting,
By a single rapid finger's lifting,
And, with a gesture kind but conclusive,
And a little shake of the head, refused me,—   [760]
I say, although she never used me,
Yet when she was mounted, the gypsy behind her,
And I ventured to remind her,
I suppose with a voice of less steadiness
Than usual, for my feeling exceeded me,

—Something to the effect that I was in readiness
Whenever God should please she needed me,—
Then, do you know, her face looked down on me
With a look that placed a crown on me,
And she felt in her bosom,—mark, her bosom—   [770]
And, as a flower-tree drops its blossom,
Dropped me . . . ah! had it been a purse
Of silver, my friend, or gold that's worse,
Why, you see, as soon as I found myself
So understood,—that a true heart so may gain
Such a reward,—I should have gone home again,
Kissed Jacynth, and soberly drowned myself!
It was a little plait of hair
Such as friends in a convent make
To wear, each for the other's sake,—   [780]
This, see, which at my breast I wear,
Ever did (rather to Jacynth's grudgment),
And ever shall, till the Day of Judgment.
And then,—and then,—to cut short,—this is idle,
These are feelings it is not good to foster,—
I pushed the gate wide, she shook the bridle,
And the palfrey bounded,—and so we lost her.

—

501. you: ethical dative; there are several examples in the
poem, and of "me"; see especially v. 876.

586. impinge: to strike or fall upon or against; in the following
passage used ethically:—

"For I find this black mark impinge the man,
That he believes in just the vile of life."
—The Ring and the Book: The Pope, v. 511.

567-689. "When higher laws draw the spirit out of itself into
the life of others; when grief has waked in it, not a self-centred
despair, but a divine sympathy; when it looks from the narrow
limits of its own suffering to the largeness of the world and the
sorrows it can lighten, we can dimly apprehend that it has taken
flight and has found its freedom in a region whither earth-bound

spirits cannot follow it. Surely the Gypsy's message was this—if the Duchess would leave her own troubles and throw herself into the life of others, she would be free. None can give true sympathy but those who have suffered and learnt to love, therefore she must be proved,—'Fit when my people ope their breast', etc. (vv. 592-601). Passing from the bondage she has endured she will still have trials, but the old pain will have no power to touch her. She has learnt all it can teach, and the world will be richer for it. The Gypsy Queen will not foretell what her future life may be; the true powers of self-less love are not yet gauged, and the power of the union of those that truly love has never been tried. 'If any two creatures grew into one', etc. (vv. 626-631). Love at its highest is not yet known to us, but the passionate eyes of the Duchess tell us it will not be a life of quiescence. Giving herself out freely for the good of all she can never be alone again,—'We are beside thee in all thy ways'. The great company of those who need her, the gypsy band of all human claims. Death to such a life is but 'the hand that ends a dream'. What was to come after not even the Gypsy Queen could tell." —Mrs. Owen ('Browning Soc. Papers', Part IV. p. 52*).

712. had: past subj., should have.

753. that pitiful method: i.e., patting her palfrey.

784. And then,—and then: his feelings overcome him.

16.

When the liquor's out why clink the cannikin?
I did think to describe you the panic in
The redoubtable breast of our master the manikin,   [790]
And what was the pitch of his mother's yellowness,
How she turned as a shark to snap the spare-rib
Clean off, sailors say, from a pearl-diving Carib,
When she heard, what she called the flight of the feloness
—But it seems such child's play,
What they said and did with the lady away!
And to dance on, when we've lost the music,
Always made me—and no doubt makes you—sick.
Nay, to my mind, the world's face looked so stern
As that sweet form disappeared through the postern, [800]
She that kept it in constant good humor,

It ought to have stopped; there seemed nothing to do more.
But the world thought otherwise and went on,
And my head's one that its spite was spent on:
Thirty years are fled since that morning,
And with them all my head's adorning.
Nor did the old Duchess die outright,
As you expect, of suppressed spite,
The natural end of every adder
Not suffered to empty its poison-bladder: [810]
But she and her son agreed, I take it,
That no one should touch on the story to wake it,
For the wound in the Duke's pride rankled fiery;
So, they made no search and small inquiry:
And when fresh gypsies have paid us a visit, I've
Noticed the couple were never inquisitive,
But told them they're folks the Duke don't want here,
And bade them make haste and cross the frontier.
Brief, the Duchess was gone and the Duke was glad of it,
And the old one was in the young one's stead,   [820]
And took, in her place, the household's head,
And a blessed time the household had of it!
And were I not, as a man may say, cautious
How I trench, more than needs, on the nauseous,
I could favor you with sundry touches
Of the paint-smutches with which the Duchess
Heightened the mellowness of her cheek's yellowness
(To get on faster) until at last her
Cheek grew to be one master-plaster
Of mucus and fucus from mere use of ceruse: [830]
In short, she grew from scalp to udder
Just the object to make you shudder.

---

793. Carib: a Caribbee, a native of the Caribbean islands.

17.

You're my friend—
What a thing friendship is, world without end!

How it gives the heart and soul a stir-up
As if somebody broached you a glorious runlet,
And poured out, all lovelily, sparklingly, sunlit,
Our green Moldavia, the streaky syrup,
Cotnar as old as the time of the Druids—
Friendship may match with that monarch of fluids;   [840]
Each supples a dry brain, fills you its ins-and-outs,
Gives your life's hour-glass a shake when the thin sand doubts
Whether to run on or stop short, and guarantees
Age is not all made of stark sloth and arrant ease.
I have seen my little lady once more,
Jacynth, the gypsy, Berold, and the rest of it,
For to me spoke the Duke, as I told you before;
I always wanted to make a clean breast of it:
And now it is made—why, my heart's blood, that went trickle,
Trickle, but anon, in such muddy driblets,   [850]
Is pumped up brisk now, through the main ventricle,
And genially floats me about the giblets.
I'll tell you what I intend to do:
I must see this fellow his sad life through—
He is our Duke, after all,
And I, as he says, but a serf and thrall.
My father was born here, and I inherit
His fame, a chain he bound his son with;
Could I pay in a lump I should prefer it,
But there's no mine to blow up and get done with: [860]
So, I must stay till the end of the chapter.
For, as to our middle-age-manners-adapter,
Be it a thing to be glad on or sorry on,
Some day or other, his head in a morion
And breast in a hauberk, his heels he'll kick up,
Slain by an onslaught fierce of hiccup.
And then, when red doth the sword of our Duke rust,
And its leathern sheath lie o'ergrown with a blue crust,
Then I shall scrape together my earnings;
For, you see, in the churchyard Jacynth reposes,   [870]
And our children all went the way of the roses:
It's a long lane that knows no turnings.
One needs but little tackle to travel in;

So, just one stout cloak shall I indue:
And for a staff, what beats the javelin
With which his boars my father pinned you?
And then, for a purpose you shall hear presently,
Taking some Cotnar, a tight plump skinful,
I shall go journeying, who but I, pleasantly!
Sorrow is vain and despondency sinful.   [880]
What's a man's age? He must hurry more, that's all;
Cram in a day, what his youth took a year to hold:
When we mind labor, then only, we're too old—
What age had Methusalem when he begat Saul?
And at last, as its haven some buffeted ship sees
(Come all the way from the north-parts with sperm oil),
I hope to get safely out of the turmoil
And arrive one day at the land of the gypsies,
And find my lady, or hear the last news of her
From some old thief and son of Lucifer,   [890]
His forehead chapleted green with wreathy hop,
Sunburned all over like an Aethiop.
And when my Cotnar begins to operate
And the tongue of the rogue to run at a proper rate,
And our wine-skin, tight once, shows each flaccid dent,
I shall drop in with—as if by accident—
"You never knew, then, how it all ended,
What fortune good or bad attended
The little lady your Queen befriended?"
—And when that's told me, what's remaining?   [900]
This world's too hard for my explaining.
The same wise judge of matters equine
Who still preferred some slim four-year-old
To the big-boned stock of mighty Berold,
And, for strong Cotnar, drank French weak wine,
He also must be such a lady's scorner!
Smooth Jacob still robs homely Esau:
Now up, now down, the world's one seesaw.
—So, I shall find out some snug corner
Under a hedge, like Orson the wood-knight,   [910]
Turn myself round and bid the world goodnight;
And sleep a sound sleep till the trumpet's blowing

Wakes me (unless priests cheat us laymen)
To a world where will be no further throwing
Pearls before swine that can't value them. Amen!

——

845. I have seen: i.e., in imagination, while telling the story.

864. morion: a sort of helmet.

884. What age had Methusalem: the old man forgets his Bible.

906. He also must be such a lady's scorner: he who is such a poor judge of horses and wines.

910. Orson the wood-knight (Fr. 'ourson', a small bear): twin-brother of Valentine, and son of Bellisant. The brothers were born in a wood near Orleans, and Orson was carried off by a bear, which suckled him with her cubs. When he grew up, he became the terror of France, and was called "The Wild Man of the Forest". Ultimately he was reclaimed by his brother Valentine, overthrew the Green Knight, his rival in love, and married Fezon, daughter of the duke of Savary, in Aquitaine.—'Romance of Valentine and Orson' (15th cent.). Brewer's 'Reader's Handbook' and 'Dictionary of Phrase and Fable'.

The Last Ride Together.

1.

I said—Then, dearest, since 'tis so,
Since now at length my fate I know,
Since nothing all my love avails,
Since all, my life seemed meant for, fails,
Since this was written and needs must be—
My whole heart rises up to bless
Your name in pride and thankfulness!
Take back the hope you gave,—I claim
Only a memory of the same,
—And this beside, if you will not blame,
Your leave for one more last ride with me.

—St. 1. Browning has no moping melancholy lovers. His lovers generally reflect his own manliness; and when their passion is unrequited, they acknowledge the absolute value of love to their own souls. As Mr. James Thomson, in his 'Notes on the Genius of Robert Browning', remarks ('B. Soc. Papers', Part II., p. 246), "Browning's passion is as intense, noble, and manly as his intellect is profound and subtle, and therefore original. I would especially insist on its manliness, because our present literature abounds in so-called passion which is but half-sincere or wholly insincere sentimentalism, if it be not thinly disguised prurient lust, and in so-called pathos which is maudlin to nauseousness. The great unappreciated poet last cited [George Meredith] has defined passion as 'noble strength on fire'; and this is the true passion of great natures and great poets; while sentimentalism is ignoble weakness dallying with fire; . . . Browning's passion is of utter self-sacrifice, self-annihilation, self-vindicated by its irresistible intensity. So we read it in 'Time's Revenges', so in the scornful condemnation of the weak lovers in 'The Statue and the Bust', so in 'In a Balcony', and 'Two in the Campagna', with its

"'Infinite passion and the pain
Of finite hearts that yearn.'

Is the love rejected, unreturned? No weak and mean upbraidings of the beloved, no futile complaints; a solemn resignation to immitigable Fate; intense gratitude for inspiring love to the unloving beloved. So in 'A Serenade at the Villa'; so in 'One Way of Love', with its

"'My whole life long I learned to love.
This hour my utmost art I prove
And speak my passion.—Heaven or Hell?
She will not give me Heaven? 'Tis well!
Lose who may—I still can say,
Those who win Heaven, blest are they!'

So in 'The Last Ride Together', with its

"'I said—Then, dearest, since 'tis so,'" etc.

2.

My mistress bent that brow of hers;
Those deep dark eyes where pride demurs
When pity would be softening through,
Fixed me a breathing-while or two
    With life or death in the balance: right!
The blood replenished me again;
My last thought was at least not vain:
I and my mistress, side by side,
Shall be together, breathe and ride,
So, one day more am I deified.
    Who knows but the world may end to-night?

3.

Hush! if you saw some western cloud
All billowy-bosomed, over-bowed
By many benedictions—sun's
And moon's and evening-star's at once—
    And so, you, looking and loving best,
Conscious grew, your passion drew
Cloud, sunset, moonrise, star-shine too,
Down on you, near and yet more near,
Till flesh must fade for heaven was here!—
Thus leant she and lingered—joy and fear
    Thus lay she a moment on my breast.

4.

Then we began to ride. My soul
Smoothed itself out, a long-cramped scroll
Freshening and fluttering in the wind.
Past hopes already lay behind.
    What need to strive with a life awry?
Had I said that, had I done this,
So might I gain, so might I miss.

Might she have loved me? just as well
She might have hated, who can tell!
Where had I been now if the worst befell?
    And here we are riding, she and I.

5.

Fail I alone, in words and deeds?
Why, all men strive and who succeeds?
We rode; it seemed my spirit flew,
Saw other regions, cities new,
    As the world rushed by on either side.
I thought,—All labor, yet no less
Bear up beneath their unsuccess.
Look at the end of work, contrast
The petty done, the undone vast,
This present of theirs with the hopeful past!
    I hoped she would love me: here we ride.

6.

What hand and brain went ever paired?
What heart alike conceived and dared?
What act proved all its thought had been?
What will but felt the fleshy screen?
    We ride and I see her bosom heave.
There's many a crown for who can reach.
Ten lines, a statesman's life in each!
The flag stuck on a heap of bones,
A soldier's doing! what atones?
They scratch his name on the Abbey-stones.
    My riding is better, by their leave.

7.

What does it all mean, poet? Well,
Your brains beat into rhythm, you tell
What we felt only; you expressed
You hold things beautiful the best,

And pace them in rhyme so, side by side.
'Tis something, nay 'tis much: but then,
Have you yourself what's best for men?
Are you—poor, sick, old ere your time—
Nearer one whit your own sublime
Than we who have never turned a rhyme?
    Sing, riding's a joy! For me, I ride.

8.

And you, great sculptor—so, you gave
A score of years to Art, her slave,
And that's your Venus, whence we turn
To yonder girl that fords the burn!
    You acquiesce, and shall I repine?
What, man of music, you grown gray
With notes and nothing else to say,
Is this your sole praise from a friend,
"Greatly his opera's strains intend,
But in music we know how fashions end!"
    I gave my youth; but we ride, in fine.

9.

Who knows what's fit for us? Had fate
Proposed bliss here should sublimate
My being—had I signed the bond—
Still one must lead some life beyond,
    Have a bliss to die with, dim-descried.
This foot once planted on the goal,
This glory-garland round my soul,
Could I descry such? Try and test!
I sink back shuddering from the quest.
Earth being so good, would heaven seem best?
    Now, heaven and she are beyond this ride.

10.

And yet—she has not spoke so long!

What if heaven be that, fair and strong
At life's best, with our eyes upturned
Whither life's flower is first discerned,
       We, fixed so, ever should so abide?
What if we still ride on, we two,
With life forever old yet new,
Changed not in kind but in degree,
'The instant made eternity,—
And heaven just prove that I and she
       Ride, ride together, forever ride?

By the Fireside.

1.

How well I know what I mean to do
       When the long dark autumn evenings come;
And where, my soul, is thy pleasant hue?
       With the music of all thy voices, dumb
In life's November too!

——

St. 1, v. 3. is: present used for the future, shall then be.

2.

I shall be found by the fire, suppose,
       O'er a great wise book, as beseemeth age;
While the shutters flap as the cross-wind blows,
       And I turn the page, and I turn the page,
Not verse now, only prose!

——

St. 2. Not verse now, only prose: he shall have reached the
"years which bring the philosophic mind".

3.

Till the young ones whisper, finger on lip,

"There he is at it, deep in Greek:
    Now then, or never, out we slip
        To cut from the hazels by the creek
    A mainmast for our ship!"

4.

I shall be at it indeed, my friends!
    Greek puts already on either side
Such a branch-work forth as soon extends
    To a vista opening far and wide,
And I pass out where it ends.

—

St. 4. Greek puts already such a branch-work forth as will soon extend to a vista opening far and wide, and he will pass out where it ends and retrace the paths he has trod through life's pleasant wood.

5.

The outside frame, like your hazel-trees —
    But the inside-archway widens fast,
And a rarer sort succeeds to these,
    And we slope to Italy at last
And youth, by green degrees.

6.

I follow wherever I am led,
    Knowing so well the leader's hand:
Oh woman-country, wooed not wed,
    Loved all the more by earth's male-lands,
Laid to their hearts instead!

—

St. 5, 6. He will pass first through his childhood, in England, represented by the hazels, and on, by green degrees, to youth and

Italy, where, knowing so well the leader's hand, and assured as to whither she will conduct him, he will follow wherever he is led.

7.

Look at the ruined chapel again
     Half-way up in the Alpine gorge!
Is that a tower, I point you plain,
     Or is it a mill, or an iron forge
Breaks solitude in vain?

———

St. 7. Look: to be construed with "follow".

8.

A turn, and we stand in the heart of things;
     The woods are round us, heaped and dim;
From slab to slab how it slips and springs,
     The thread of water single and slim,
Through the ravage some torrent brings!

9.

Does it feed the little lake below?
     That speck of white just on its marge
Is Pella; see, in the evening-glow,
     How sharp the silver spear-heads charge
When Alp meets heaven in snow!

10.

On our other side is the straight-up rock;
     And a path is kept 'twixt the gorge and it
By bowlder-stones, where lichens mock
     The marks on a moth, and small ferns fit
Their teeth to the polished block.

11.

Oh the sense of the yellow mountain-flowers,
 And thorny balls, each three in one,
The chestnuts throw on our path in showers!
 For the drop of the woodland fruit's begun,
These early November hours,

12.

That crimson the creeper's leaf across
 Like a splash of blood, intense, abrupt,
O'er a shield else gold from rim to boss,
 And lay it for show on the fairy-cupped
Elf-needled mat of moss,

13.

By the rose-flesh mushrooms, undivulged
 Last evening — nay, in to-day's first dew
Yon sudden coral nipple bulged,
 Where a freaked fawn-colored flaky crew
Of toad-stools peep indulged.

14.

And yonder, at foot of the fronting ridge
 That takes the turn to a range beyond,
Is the chapel reached by the one-arched bridge,
 Where the water is stopped in a stagnant pond
Danced over by the midge.

15.

The chapel and bridge are of stone alike,
 Blackish-gray and mostly wet;
Cut hemp-stalks steep in the narrow dike.
 See here again, how the lichens fret
And the roots of the ivy strike!

16.

Poor little place, where its one priest comes
    On a festa-day, if he comes at all,
To the dozen folk from their scattered homes,
    Gathered within that precinct small
By the dozen ways one roams —

17.

To drop from the charcoal-burners' huts,
    Or climb from the hemp-dressers' low shed,
Leave the grange where the woodman stores his nuts,
    Or the wattled cote where the fowlers spread
Their gear on the rock's bare juts.

18.

It has some pretension too, this front,
    With its bit of fresco half-moon-wise
Set over the porch, Art's early wont:
    'Tis John in the Desert, I surmise,
But has borne the weather's brunt —

19.

Not from the fault of the builder, though,
    For a pent-house properly projects
Where three carved beams make a certain show,
    Dating — good thought of our architect's —
'Five, six, nine, he lets you know.

20.

And all day long a bird sings there,
    And a stray sheep drinks at the pond at times;

The place is silent and aware;
    It has had its scenes, its joys and crimes,
But that is its own affair.

———

St. 20. aware: self-conscious.

". . .in green ruins, in the desolate walls
Of antique palaces, where Man hath been,

            *   *   *   *   *

There the true Silence is, self-conscious and alone."
              — Hood's 'Sonnet on Silence'.

21.

My perfect wife, my Leonor,
    O heart, my own, Oh eyes, mine too,
Whom else could I dare look backward for,
    With whom beside should I dare pursue
The path gray heads abhor?

———

St. 21. He digresses here, and does not return to the subject till the 31st stanza, "What did I say?—that a small bird sings". The path gray heads abhor: this verse and the following stanza are, with most readers, the CRUX of the poem; "gray heads" must be understood with some restriction: many gray heads, not all, abhor —gray heads who went along through their flowery youth as if it had no limit, and without insuring, in Love's true season, the happiness of their lives beyond youth's limit, "life's safe hem", which to cross without such insurance, is often fatal. And these, when they reach old age, shun retracing the path which led to the gulf wherein their youth dropped.

22.

For it leads to a crag's sheer edge with them;
    Youth, flowery all the way, there stops—
Not they; age threatens and they contemn,

Till they reach the gulf wherein youth drops,
One inch from our life's safe hem!

23.

With me, youth led . . . I will speak now,
    No longer watch you as you sit
Reading by firelight, that great brow
    And the spirit-small hand propping it,
Mutely, my heart knows how—

— St. 23. With me: the speaker continues, youth led:—we
are told whither, in St. 25, v. 4, "to an age so blest that, by its side,
youth seems the waste instead". I will speak now: up to this point
his reflections have been silent, his wife, the while, reading, mutely,
by fire-light, his heart knows how, that is, with her heart secretly
responsive to his own. The mutual responsiveness of their hearts
is expressed in St. 24.

24.

When, if I think but deep enough,
    You are wont to answer, prompt as rhyme;
And you, too, find without rebuff
    Response your soul seeks many a time,
Piercing its fine flesh-stuff.

25.

My own, confirm me! If I tread
    This path back, is it not in pride
To think how little I dreamed it led
    To an age so blest that, by its side,
Youth seems the waste instead?

26.

My own, see where the years conduct!
    At first, 'twas something our two souls

Should mix as mists do; each is sucked
    In each now: on, the new stream rolls,
Whatever rocks obstruct.

27.

    Think, when our one soul understands
The great Word which makes all things new,
    When earth breaks up and heaven expands,
    How will the change strike me and you
In the house not made with hands?

28.

Oh I must feel your brain prompt mine,
    Your heart anticipate my heart,
You must be just before, in fine,
    See and make me see, for your part,
New depths of the divine!

— St. 28. "The conviction of the eternity of marriage meets us again and again in Browning's poems; e.g., 'Prospice', 'Any Wife to any Husband', 'The Epilogue to Fifine'." The union between two complementary souls cannot be dissolved. "Love is all, and Death is nought!"

29.

But who could have expected this
    When we two drew together first
Just for the obvious human bliss,
    To satisfy life's daily thirst
With a thing men seldom miss?

30.

Come back with me to the first of all,
    Let us lean and love it over again,
Let us now forget and now recall,
    Break the rosary in a pearly rain,

And gather what we let fall!

31.

What did I say?—that a small bird sings
    All day long, save when a brown pair
Of hawks from the wood float with wide wings
    Strained to a bell: 'gainst noonday glare
You count the streaks and rings.

—

St. 31. Here he returns to the subject broken off at St. 21.

32.

But at afternoon or almost eve
    'Tis better; then the silence grows
To that degree, you half believe
    It must get rid of what it knows,
Its bosom does so heave.

33.

Hither we walked then, side by side,
    Arm in arm and cheek to cheek,
And still I questioned or replied,
    While my heart, convulsed to really speak,
Lay choking in its pride.

34.

Silent the crumbling bridge we cross,
    And pity and praise the chapel sweet,
And care about the fresco's loss,
    And wish for our souls a like retreat,
And wonder at the moss.

35.

Stoop and kneel on the settle under,
    Look through the window's grated square:
Nothing to see! For fear of plunder,
    The cross is down and the altar bare,
As if thieves don't fear thunder.

36.

We stoop and look in through the grate,
    See the little porch and rustic door,
Read duly the dead builder's date;
    Then cross the bridge that we crossed before,
Take the path again—but wait!

37.

Oh moment one and infinite!
    The water slips o'er stock and stone;
The West is tender, hardly bright:
    How gray at once is the evening grown—
One star, its chrysolite!

38.

We two stood there with never a third,
    But each by each, as each knew well:
The sights we saw and the sounds we heard,
    The lights and the shades made up a spell
Till the trouble grew and stirred.

— St. 37, 38. "Mr. Browning's most characteristic feeling for nature appears in his rendering of those aspects of sky, or earth, or sea, of sunset, or noonday, or dawn, which seem to acquire some sudden and passionate significance; which seem to be charged with some spiritual secret eager for disclosure; in his rendering of those moments which betray the passion at the heart of things, which thrill and tingle with prophetic fire. When lightning searches for the guilty lovers, Ottima and Sebald [in 'Pippa Passes'], like an angelic sword plunged into the gloom, when the tender twilight with its one chrysolite star, grows aware, and the light and shade make up a spell, and the forests by their mystery, and sound, and silence, mingle together two human lives forever ['By the Fireside'], when the apparition of the moon-rainbow appears gloriously after storm, and Christ is in his heaven ['Christmas Eve'], when to David the stars shoot out the pain of pent knowledge and in the grey of the hills at morning there dwells a gathered intensity ['Saul'],—then nature rises from her sweet ways of use and wont, and shows herself the Priestess, the Pythoness, the Divinity which she is. Or rather, through nature, the Spirit of God addresses itself to the spirit of man."—Edward Dowden.

39.

Oh, the little more, and how much it is!
    And the little less, and what worlds away!
How a sound shall quicken content to bliss,
    Or a breath suspend the blood's best play,
And life be a proof of this!

40.

Had she willed it, still had stood the screen
    So slight, so sure, 'twixt my love and her:
I could fix her face with a guard between,
    And find her soul as when friends confer,
Friends—lovers that might have been.

41.

For my heart had a touch of the woodland time,
    Wanting to sleep now over its best.
Shake the whole tree in the summer-prime,
    But bring to the last leaf no such test!
"Hold the last fast!" runs the rhyme.

42.

For a chance to make your little much,
    To gain a lover and lose a friend,
Venture the tree and a myriad such,
    When nothing you mar but the year can mend:
But a last leaf—fear to touch!

43.

Yet should it unfasten itself and fall
    Eddying down till it find your face
At some slight wind—best chance of all!
    Be your heart henceforth its dwelling-place
You trembled to forestall!

44.

Worth how well, those dark gray eyes,
    That hair so dark and dear, how worth
That a man should strive and agonize,
    And taste a veriest hell on earth
For the hope of such a prize!

45.

You might have turned and tried a man,
    Set him a space to weary and wear,
And prove which suited more your plan,
    His best of hope or his worst despair,
Yet end as he began.

46.

But you spared me this, like the heart you are,
    And filled my empty heart at a word.
If two lives join, there is oft a scar,
    They are one and one, with a shadowy third;
One near one is too far.

47.

A moment after, and hands unseen
    Were hanging the night around us fast;
But we knew that a bar was broken between
    Life and life: we were mixed at last
In spite of the mortal screen.

48.

The forests had done it; there they stood;
    We caught for a moment the powers at play:
They had mingled us so, for once and good,
    Their work was done—we might go or stay,
They relapsed to their ancient mood.

49.

How the world is made for each of us!
    How all we perceive and know in it
Tends to some moment's product thus,
    When a soul declares itself—to wit,
By its fruit, the thing it does!

— St. 49. "Those periods of life which appear most full of moral purpose to Mr. Tennyson, are periods of protracted self-control, and those moments stand eminent in life in which the spirit has struggled victoriously in the cause of conscience against impulse and desire. With Mr. Browning the moments are most glorious in which the obscure tendency of many years has been revealed by the lightning of sudden passion, or in which a resolution that changes the current of life has been taken in reliance upon that insight which vivid emotion bestows; and those periods of our history are charged most fully with moral purpose, which take their direction from moments such as these . . . In such a moment the somewhat dull youth of 'The Inn Album' rises into the justiciary of the Highest; in such a moment Polyxena with her right woman's-manliness, discovers to Charles his regal duty, and infuses into her weaker husband, her own courage of heart ['King Victor and King

Charles']; and rejoicing in the remembrance of a moment of high devotion which determined the issues of a life, the speaker of 'By the Fireside' exclaims,— 'How the world is made for each of us!'" etc.—Edward Dowden.

50.

Be hate that fruit, or love that fruit,
    It forwards the general deed of man,
And each of the Many helps to recruit
    The life of the race by a general plan;
Each living his own, to boot.

51.

I am named and known by that moment's feat;
    There took my station and degree;
So grew my own small life complete,
    As nature obtained her best of me—
One born to love you, sweet!

52.

And to watch you sink by the fireside now
    Back again, as you mutely sit
Musing by fire-light, that great brow
    And the spirit-small hand propping it,
Yonder, my heart knows how!

53.

So, earth has gained by one man the more,
    And the gain of earth must be heaven's gain too;
And the whole is well worth thinking o'er
    When autumn comes: which I mean to do
One day, as I said before.

Prospice.

—

* 'Prospice' (look forward) is a challenge to spiritual conflict, exultant with the certainty of victory, glowing with the prospective joy of reunion with one whom death has sent before.—Mrs. Orr.

—

Fear death?—to feel the fog in my throat,
    The mist in my face,
When the snows begin, and the blasts denote
    I am nearing the place,
The power of the night, the press of the storm,
    The post of the foe;
Where he stands, the Arch Fear in a visible form,
    Yet the strong man must go:
For the journey is done and the summit attained,
    And the barriers fall, [10]
Though a battle's to fight ere the guerdon be gained,
    The reward of it all.
I was ever a fighter, so—one fight more,
    The best and the last!
I would hate that death bandaged my eyes, and forbore,
    And bade me creep past.
No! let me taste the whole of it, fare like my peers
    The heroes of old,
Bear the brunt, in a minute pay glad life's arrears
    Of pain, darkness, and cold. [20]
For sudden the worst turns the best to the brave,
    The black minute's at end,
And the elements' rage, the fiend-voices that rave,
    Shall dwindle, shall blend,
Shall change, shall become first a peace out of pain,
    Then a light, then thy breast,
O thou soul of my soul! I shall clasp thee again, .
    And with God be the rest!

25. first a peace out of pain: original reading, "first a peace, then a joy".

Amphibian.

1.

The fancy I had to-day,
 Fancy which turned a fear!
I swam far out in the bay,
 Since waves laughed warm and clear.

2.

I lay and looked at the sun,
 The noon-sun looked at me:
Between us two, no one
 Live creature, that I could see.

3.

Yes! There came floating by
 Me, who lay floating too,
Such a strange butterfly!
 Creature as dear as new:

4.

Because the membraned wings
 So wonderful, so wide,
So sun-suffused, were things
 Like soul and naught beside.

5.

A handbreadth over head!
   All of the sea my own,
It owned the sky instead;
   Both of us were alone.

6.

I never shall join its flight,
   For naught buoys flesh in air.
If it touch the sea—goodnight!
   Death sure and swift waits there.

7.

Can the insect feel the better
   For watching the uncouth play
Of limbs that slip the fetter,
   Pretend as they were not clay?

8.

Undoubtedly I rejoice
   That the air comports so well
With a creature which had the choice
   Of the land once. Who can tell?

9.

What if a certain soul
   Which early slipped its sheath,
And has for its home the whole
   Of heaven, thus look beneath,

10.

Thus watch one who, in the world,
   Both lives and likes life's way,

Nor wishes the wings unfurled
    That sleep in the worm, they say?

11.

But sometimes when the weather
    Is blue, and warm waves tempt
To free one's self of tether,
    And try a life exempt

12.

From worldly noise and dust,
    In the sphere which overbrims
With passion and thought,—why, just
    Unable to fly, one swims!

13.

By passion and thought upborne,
    One smiles to one's self—"They fare
Scarce better, they need not scorn
    Our sea, who live in the air!"

14.

Emancipate through passion
    And thought, with sea for sky,
We substitute, in a fashion,
    For heaven—poetry:

—

St. 14. for: instead of.

15.

Which sea, to all intent,
    Gives flesh such noon-disport

As a finer element
    Affords the spirit-sort.

16.

Whatever they are, we seem:
    Imagine the thing they know;
All deeds they do, we dream;
    Can heaven be else but so?

17.

And meantime, yonder streak
    Meets the horizon's verge;
That is the land, to seek
    If we tire or dread the surge:

———

St. 17. We can return from the sea of passion and thought, that is, poetry, or a deep spiritual state, to the solid land again, of material fact.

18.

Land the solid and safe—
    To welcome again (confess!)
When, high and dry, we chafe
    The body, and don the dress.

———

St. 18. Man, in his earth life, cannot always be "high contemplative", and indulge in "brave translunary things"; he must welcome again, it must be confessed, "land the solid and safe". "Other heights in other lives, God willing" ('One Word More').

19.

Does she look, pity, wonder
    At one who mimics flight,

Swims—heaven above, sea under,
    Yet always earth in sight?

—

St. 19. does she: the "certain soul" in 9th St., "which early slipped its sheath".

James Lee's Wife.

I. James Lee's Wife speaks at the Window.

—

* In the original ed., 1864, the heading to this section was 'At the Window'; changed in ed. of 1868.

—

1.

Ah, Love, but a day,
    And the world has changed!
The sun's away,
    And the bird estranged;
The wind has dropped,
    And the sky's deranged:
Summer has stopped.

—

St. 1. Ah, Love, but a day: Rev. H. J. Bulkeley, in his paper on 'James Lee's Wife' ('Browning Soc. Papers', iv., p. 457), explains, "One day's absence from him has caused the world to change." It's better to understand that something has occurred to cause the world to change in a single day; that James Lee has made some new revelation of himself, which causes the wife's heart to have misgivings, and with these misgivings comes the eager desire expressed in St. 3, to show her love, when he returns, more strongly than ever.

2.

Look in my eyes!
　　Wilt thou change too?
Should I fear surprise?
　　Shall I find aught new
In the old and dear,
　　In the good and true,
With the changing year?

3.

Thou art a man,
　　But I am thy love.
For the lake, its swan;
　　For the dell, its dove;
And for thee—(oh, haste!)
　　Me, to bend above,
Me, to hold embraced.

II. By the Fireside.

1.

Is all our fire of shipwreck wood,
　　Oak and pine?
Oh, for the ills half-understood,
　　The dim dead woe
　　Long ago
Befallen this bitter coast of France!
Well, poor sailors took their chance;
　　I take mine.

2.

A ruddy shaft our fire must shoot
　　O'er the sea;
Do sailors eye the casement—mute
　　Drenched and stark,

From their bark—
And envy, gnash their teeth for hate
O' the warm safe house and happy freight
    —Thee and me?

3.

God help you, sailors, at your need!
    Spare the curse!
For some ships, safe in port indeed,
    Rot and rust,
    Run to dust,
All through worms i' the wood, which crept,
Gnawed our hearts out while we slept:
    That is worse.

4.

Who lived here before us two?
    Old-world pairs.
Did a woman ever—would I knew!—
    Watch the man
    With whom began
Love's voyage full-sail,—(now, gnash your teeth!)
When planks start, open hell beneath
    Unawares?

III. In the Doorway.

1.

The swallow has set her six young on the rail,
    And looks seaward:
The water's in stripes like a snake, olive-pale
    To the leeward,—
On the weather-side, black, spotted white with the wind.
"Good fortune departs, and disaster's behind",—
Hark, the wind with its wants and its infinite wail!

—

St. 1. Note the truth of color in vv. 3-5.

2.

Our fig-tree, that leaned for the saltness, has furled
    Her five fingers,
Each leaf like a hand opened wide to the world
    Where there lingers
No glint of the gold, Summer sent for her sake:
How the vines writhe in rows, each impaled on its stake!
My heart shrivels up and my spirit shrinks curled.

———

St. 2. her five fingers: referring to the shape of the fig-leaf.

3.

Yet here are we two; we have love, house enough,
    With the field there,
This house of four rooms, that field red and rough,
    Though it yield there,
For the rabbit that robs, scarce a blade or a bent;
If a magpie alight now, it seems an event;
And they both will be gone at November's rebuff.

———

St. 3. a bent: a bit of coarse grass; A.-S. 'beonet', an adduced
form; Ger. 'binse'.

4.

But why must cold spread? but wherefore bring change
    To the spirit,
God meant should mate his with an infinite range,
    And inherit
His power to put life in the darkness and cold?
Oh, live and love worthily, bear and be bold!
Whom Summer made friends of, let Winter estrange!

—

St. 4. Whom Summer made friends of, etc.: i.e., let Winter (Adversity) estrange those whom Summer (Prosperity) made friends of, but let it not estrange us.

IV. Along the Beach.

1.

I will be quiet and talk with you,
    And reason why you are wrong.
You wanted my love—is that much true?
And so I did love, so I do:
    What has come of it all along?

2.

I took you—how could I otherwise?
    For a world to me, and more;
For all, love greatens and glorifies
Till God's a-glow, to the loving eyes,
    In what was mere earth before.

—

St. 2. love greatens and glorifies: see the poem, "Wanting is—what?"

3.

Yes, earth—yes, mere ignoble earth!
    Now do I misstate, mistake?
Do I wrong your weakness and call it worth?
Expect all harvest, dread no dearth,
    Seal my sense up for your sake?

4.

Oh Love, Love, no, Love! not so, indeed
    You were just weak earth, I knew:
With much in you waste, with many a weed,
And plenty of passions run to seed,
    But a little good grain too.

5.

And such as you were, I took you for mine:
    Did not you find me yours,
To watch the olive and wait the vine,
And wonder when rivers of oil and wine
    Would flow, as the Book assures?

———

St. 5. yours, to watch the olive and wait the vine: "olive" and
    "vine" are used metaphorically for the capabilities of her
    husband's nature.

6.

Well, and if none of these good things came,
    What did the failure prove?
The man was my whole world, all the same,
With his flowers to praise or his weeds to blame,
    And, either or both, to love.

———

    St. 6. The failure of fruit in her husband proved the absoluteness
of her love, proved that he was her all, notwithstanding.

7.

Yet this turns now to a fault—there! there!
    That I do love, watch too long,
And wait too well, and weary and wear;

And 'tis all an old story, and my despair
Fit subject for some new song:

—

St. 7. Yet this turns now to a fault: i.e., her watching the olive
and waiting the vine of his nature. there! there!: I've come out
plainly with the fact.

8.

"How the light, light love, he has wings to fly
At suspicion of a bond:
My wisdom has bidden your pleasure good-bye,
Which will turn up next in a laughing eye,
And why should you look beyond?"

—

St. 8. bond: refers to what is said in St. 7; why should you look
beyond?: i.e., beyond a laughing eye, which does not "watch" and
"wait", and thus "weary" and "wear".

V. On the Cliff.

1.

I leaned on the turf,
I looked at a rock
Left dry by the surf;
For the turf, to call it grass were to mock:
Dead to the roots, so deep was done
The work of the summer sun.

2.

And the rock lay flat
As an anvil's face:
No iron like that!

Baked dry; of a weed, of a shell, no trace:
Sunshine outside, but ice at the core,
Death's altar by the lone shore.

3.

On the turf, sprang gay
With his films of blue,
No cricket, I'll say,
But a warhorse, barded and chanfroned too,
The gift of a quixote-mage to his knight,
Real fairy, with wings all right.

———

St. 3. No cricket, I'll say: but to my lively admiration, a warhorse,
barded and chanfroned too: see Webster's Dict., s.v. "chamfrain".
{also chamfron: armor for a horse's head}.

4.

On the rock, they scorch
Like a drop of fire
From a brandished torch,
Fall two red fans of a butterfly:
No turf, no rock,—in their ugly stead,
See, wonderful blue and red!

———

St. 4. they: i.e., the 'two red fans'. no turf, no rock: i.e., the eye
is taken up entirely with cricket and butterfly; blue and red refer
respectively to cricket and butterfly.

5.

Is it not so
With the minds of men?
The level and low,
The burnt and bare, in themselves; but then

With such a blue and red grace, not theirs,
Love settling unawares!

St. 5. Love: settling on the minds of men, the level and low, the burnt and bare, is compared to the cricket and the butterfly settling on the turf and the rock.

VI. Reading a Book under the Cliff.

———

* In the original ed., 1864, the heading to this section was 'Under the Cliff'; changed in ed. of 1868.

———

1.

"Still ailing, Wind? Wilt be appeased or no?
    Which needs the other's office, thou or I?
Dost want to be disburthened of a woe,
    And can, in truth, my voice untie
Its links, and let it go?

2.

"Art thou a dumb, wronged thing that would be righted,
    Entrusting thus thy cause to me? Forbear!
No tongue can mend such pleadings; faith, requited
    With falsehood,—love, at last aware
Of scorn,—hopes, early blighted,—

3.

"We have them; but I know not any tone
    So fit as thine to falter forth a sorrow:
Dost think men would go mad without a moan,
    If they knew any way to borrow
A pathos like thy own?

4.

"Which sigh wouldst mock, of all the sighs? The one
    So long escaping from lips starved and blue,
That lasts while on her pallet-bed the nun
    Stretches her length; her foot comes through
The straw she shivers on;

5.

"You had not thought she was so tall: and spent,
    Her shrunk lids open, her lean fingers shut
Close, close, their sharp and livid nails indent
    The clammy palm; then all is mute:
That way, the spirit went.

6.

"Or wouldst thou rather that I understand
    Thy will to help me?—like the dog I found
Once, pacing sad this solitary strand,
    Who would not take my food, poor hound,
But whined, and licked my hand."

—

St. 1-6. See foot-note to the Argument of this section.

7.

All this, and more, comes from some young man's pride
    Of power to see,—in failure and mistake,
Relinquishment, disgrace, on every side,—
    Merely examples for his sake,
Helps to his path untried:

8.

Instances he must—simply recognize?
    Oh, more than so!—must, with a learner's zeal,

Make doubly prominent, twice emphasize,
    By added touches that reveal
The god in babe's disguise.

9.

Oh, he knows what defeat means, and the rest!
    Himself the undefeated that shall be:
Failure, disgrace, he flings them you to test,—
    His triumph, in eternity
Too plainly manifest!

—

St. 7-9. She reflects, ironically and sarcastically, upon the confidence of the young poet, resulting from his immaturity, in his future triumph over all obstacles. Inexperienced as he is, he feels himself the god in babe's disguise, etc. He will learn after a while what the wind means in its moaning. The train of thought in St. 11-16 is presented in the Argument.

10.

Whence, judge if he learn forthwith what the wind
    Means in its moaning—by the happy prompt
Instinctive way of youth, I mean; for kind
    Calm years, exacting their accompt
Of pain, mature the mind:

11.

And some midsummer morning, at the lull
    Just about daybreak, as he looks across
A sparkling foreign country, wonderful
    To the sea's edge for gloom and gloss,
Next minute must annul,—

12.

Then, when the wind begins among the vines,
    So low, so low, what shall it say but this?
"Here is the change beginning, here the lines
    Circumscribe beauty, set to bliss
The limit time assigns."

13.

Nothing can be as it has been before;
    Better, so call it, only not the same.
To draw one beauty into our hearts' core,
    And keep it changeless! such our claim;
So answered,—Never more!

14.

Simple? Why this is the old woe o' the world;
    Tune, to whose rise and fall we live and die.
Rise with it, then! Rejoice that man is hurled
    From change to change unceasingly,
His soul's wings never furled!

15.

That's a new question; still replies the fact,
    Nothing endures: the wind moans, saying so;
We moan in acquiescence: there's life's pact,
    Perhaps probation—do I know?
God does: endure his act!

16.

Only, for man, how bitter not to grave
    On his soul's hands' palms one fair good wise thing
Just as he grasped it! For himself, death's wave;
    While time first washes—ah, the sting!—
O'er all he'd sink to save.

VII. Among the Rocks.

1.

Oh, good gigantic smile o' the brown old earth,
    This autumn morning! How he sets his bones
To bask i' the sun, and thrusts out knees and feet
For the ripple to run over in its mirth;
    Listening the while, where on the heap of stones
The white breast of the sea-lark twitters sweet.

2.

That is the doctrine, simple, ancient, true;
    Such is life's trial, as old earth smiles and knows.
If you loved only what were worth your love,
Love were clear gain, and wholly well for you:
    Make the low nature better by your throes!
Give earth yourself, go up for gain above!

VIII. Beside the Drawing-Board.

1.

"As like as a Hand to another Hand!"
    Whoever said that foolish thing,
Could not have studied to understand
    The counsels of God in fashioning,
Out of the infinite love of his heart,
This Hand, whose beauty I praise, apart
From the world of wonder left to praise,
If I tried to learn the other ways
Of love, in its skill, or love, in its power.
    "As like as a Hand to another Hand":   [10]
    Who said that, never took his stand,
Found and followed, like me, an hour,
The beauty in this,—how free, how fine
To fear, almost,—of the limit-line!
As I looked at this, and learned and drew,

Drew and learned, and looked again,
While fast the happy minutes flew,
    Its beauty mounted into my brain,
    And a fancy seized me; I was fain
To efface my work, begin anew,   [20]
Kiss what before I only drew;
Ay, laying the red chalk 'twixt my lips,
    With soul to help if the mere lips failed,
    I kissed all right where the drawing ailed,
Kissed fast the grace that somehow slips
Still from one's soulless finger-tips.

—

* Lines 27-87 {below—the rest of this section except the last two
lines} were added in the edition of 1868; they clear up the obscurity
of this section of the poem, as it stood in the original edition of
1864.

—

2.

'Tis a clay cast, the perfect thing,
    From Hand live once, dead long ago:
Princess-like it wears the ring
    To fancy's eye, by which we know   [30]
That here at length a master found
    His match, a proud lone soul its mate,
As soaring genius sank to ground
    And pencil could not emulate
The beauty in this,—how free, how fine
To fear almost!—of the limit-line.
Long ago the god, like me
The worm, learned, each in our degree:
Looked and loved, learned and drew,
    Drew and learned and loved again,   [40]
While fast the happy minutes flew,
    Till beauty mounted into his brain
And on the finger which outvied
    His art he placed the ring that's there,

Still by fancy's eye descried,
     In token of a marriage rare:
For him on earth, his art's despair,
For him in heaven, his soul's fit bride.

3.

Little girl with the poor coarse hand
     I turned from to a cold clay cast—   [50]
I have my lesson, understand
     The worth of flesh and blood at last!
Nothing but beauty in a Hand?
     Because he could not change the hue,
     Mend the lines and make them true
To this which met his soul's demand,—
     Would Da Vinci turn from you?
I hear him laugh my woes to scorn—
"The fool forsooth is all forlorn
Because the beauty, she thinks best,   [60]
Lived long ago or was never born,—
Because no beauty bears the test
In this rough peasant Hand! Confessed
'Art is null and study void!'
So sayest thou? So said not I,
Who threw the faulty pencil by,
And years instead of hours employed,
Learning the veritable use
Of flesh and bone and nerve beneath
Lines and hue of the outer sheath,   [70]
If haply I might reproduce
One motive of the mechanism,
Flesh and bone and nerve that make
The poorest coarsest human hand
An object worthy to be scanned
A whole life long for their sole sake.
Shall earth and the cramped moment-space
Yield the heavenly crowning grace?

Now the parts and then the whole!
Who art thou, with stinted soul   [80]
And stunted body, thus to cry
'I love,—shall that be life's strait dole?
I must live beloved or die!'
This peasant hand that spins the wool
And bakes the bread, why lives it on,
Poor and coarse with beauty gone,—
What use survives the beauty? Fool!"

Go, little girl with the poor coarse hand!
I have my lesson, shall understand.

IX. On Deck.

1.

There is nothing to remember in me,
    Nothing I ever said with a grace,
Nothing I did that you care to see,
    Nothing I was that deserves a place
In your mind, now I leave you, set you free.

—

St. 1. Nothing I did that you care to see: refers to her art-
work.

2.

Conceded! In turn, concede to me,
    Such things have been as a mutual flame.
Your soul's locked fast; but, love for a key,
    You might let it loose, till I grew the same
In your eyes, as in mine you stand: strange plea!

3.

For then, then, what would it matter to me
    That I was the harsh, ill-favored one?

We both should be like as pea and pea;
    It was ever so since the world begun:
So, let me proceed with my reverie.

—

St. 3. Here it is indicated that she had not the personal charms which were needed to maintain her husband's interest. A pretty face was more to him than a deep loving soul.

4.

How strange it were if you had all me,
    As I have all you in my heart and brain,
You, whose least word brought gloom or glee,
    Who never lifted the hand in vain
Will hold mine yet, from over the sea!

5.

Strange, if a face, when you thought of me,
    Rose like your own face present now,
With eyes as dear in their due degree,
    Much such a mouth, and as bright a brow,
Till you saw yourself, while you cried "'Tis She!"

6.

Well, you may, you must, set down to me
    Love that was life, life that was love;
A tenure of breath at your lips' decree,
    A passion to stand as your thoughts approve,
A rapture to fall where your foot might be.

—

St. 6. vv. 3-5 express the entire devotion and submissiveness of her love.

7.

But did one touch of such love for me
    Come in a word or a look of yours,
Whose words and looks will, circling, flee
    Round me and round while life endures,—
Could I fancy "As I feel, thus feels He";

8.

Why, fade you might to a thing like me,
    And your hair grow these coarse hanks of hair,
Your skin, this bark of a gnarled tree,—
    You might turn myself!—should I know or care,
When I should be dead of joy, James Lee?

A Tale.

Epilogue to 'The Two Poets of Croisic'.

1.

What a pretty tale you told me
    Once upon a time
—Said you found it somewhere (scold me!)
    Was it prose or was it rhyme,
Greek or Latin? Greek, you said,
While your shoulder propped my head.

2.

Anyhow there's no forgetting
    This much if no more,
That a poet (pray, no petting!)
    Yes, a bard, sir, famed of yore,
Went where suchlike used to go,
Singing for a prize, you know.

3.

Well, he had to sing, nor merely
    Sing but play the lyre;
Playing was important clearly
    Quite as singing: I desire,
Sir, you keep the fact in mind
For a purpose that's behind.

4.

There stood he, while deep attention
    Held the judges round,
—Judges able, I should mention,
    To detect the slightest sound
Sung or played amiss: such ears
Had old judges, it appears!

5.

None the less he sang out boldly,
    Played in time and tune,
Till the judges, weighing coldly
    Each note's worth, seemed, late or soon,
Sure to smile "In vain one tries
Picking faults out: take the prize!"

6.

When, a mischief! Were they seven
    Strings the lyre possessed?
Oh, and afterwards eleven,
    Thank you! Well, sir,—who had guessed
Such ill luck in store?—it happed
One of those same seven strings snapped.

7.

All was lost, then! No! a cricket
        (What "cicada"? Pooh!)
—Some mad thing that left its thicket
        For mere love of music—flew
With its little heart on fire,
Lighted on the crippled lyre.

—

St. 7. "Cicada": do you say? Pooh!: that's bringing the mysterious little thing down to the plane of entomology.

8.

So that when (Ah joy!) our singer
        For his truant string
Feels with disconcerted finger,
        What does cricket else but fling
Fiery heart forth, sound the note
Wanted by the throbbing throat?

9.

Ay and, ever to the ending,
        Cricket chirps at need,
Executes the hand's intending,
        Promptly, perfectly,—indeed
Saves the singer from defeat
With her chirrup low and sweet.

10.

Till, at ending, all the judges
        Cry with one assent
"Take the prize—a prize who grudges
        Such a voice and instrument?
Why, we took your lyre for harp,
So it shrilled us forth F sharp!"

11.

Did the conqueror spurn the creature,
    Once its service done?
That's no such uncommon feature
    In the case when Music's son
Finds his Lotte's power too spent
For aiding soul-development.

—

St. 11. when Music's son, etc.: a fling at Goethe.

12.

No! This other, on returning
    Homeward, prize in hand,
Satisfied his bosom's yearning:
    (Sir, I hope you understand!)
—Said "Some record there must be
Of this cricket's help to me!"

13.

So, he made himself a statue:
    Marble stood, life-size;
On the lyre, he pointed at you,
    Perched his partner in the prize;
Never more apart you found
Her, he throned, from him, she crowned.

14.

That's the tale: its application?
    Somebody I know
Hopes one day for reputation
    Through his poetry that's—Oh,
All so learned and so wise
And deserving of a prize!

15.

If he gains one, will some ticket,
    When his statue's built,
Tell the gazer "'Twas a cricket
    Helped my crippled lyre, whose lilt
Sweet and low, when strength usurped
Softness' place i' the scale, she chirped?

16.

"For as victory was nighest,
    While I sang and played,—
With my lyre at lowest, highest,
    Right alike,—one string that made
'Love' sound soft was snapt in twain,
Never to be heard again,—

17.

"Had not a kind cricket fluttered,
    Perched upon the place
Vacant left, and duly uttered
    'Love, Love, Love', whene'er the bass
Asked the treble to atone
For its somewhat sombre drone."

18.

But you don't know music! Wherefore
    Keep on casting pearls
To a—poet? All I care for
    Is—to tell him that a girl's
"Love" comes aptly in when gruff
Grows his singing. (There, enough!)

Confessions.

1.

What is he buzzing in my ears?
    "Now that I come to die,
Do I view the world as a vale of tears?"
    Ah, reverend sir, not I!

2.

What I viewed there once, what I view again
    Where the physic bottles stand
On the table's edge,—is a suburb lane,
    With a wall to my bedside hand.

3.

That lane sloped, much as the bottles do,
    From a house you could descry
O'er the garden-wall: is the curtain blue
    Or green to a healthy eye?

4.

To mine, it serves for the old June weather
    Blue above lane and wall;
And that farthest bottle labelled "Ether"
    Is the house o'er-topping all.

5.

At a terrace, somewhat near the stopper,
    There watched for me, one June,
A girl: I know, sir, it's improper,
    My poor mind's out of tune.

6.

Only, there was a way . . . you crept
    Close by the side, to dodge
Eyes in the house, two eyes except:
    They styled their house "The Lodge".

7.

What right had a lounger up their lane?
    But, by creeping very close,
With the good wall's help,—their eyes might strain
    And stretch themselves to Oes,

8.

Yet never catch her and me together,
    As she left the attic, there,
By the rim of the bottle labelled "Ether",
    And stole from stair to stair,

9.

And stood by the rose-wreathed gate. Alas,
    We loved, sir—used to meet:
How sad and bad and mad it was—
    But then, how it was sweet!

Respectability.

1.

Dear, had the world in its caprice
    Deigned to proclaim "I know you both,
    Have recognized your plighted troth,
Am sponsor for you: live in peace!"—
How many precious months and years
    Of youth had passed, that speed so fast,

Before we found it out at last,
The world, and what it fears?

2.

How much of priceless life were spent
    With men that every virtue decks,
    And women models of their sex,
Society's true ornament,—
Ere we dared wander, nights like this,
    Through wind and rain, and watch the Seine,
    And feel the Boulevart break again
To warmth and light and bliss?

3.

I know! the world proscribes not love;
    Allows my finger to caress
    Your lips' contour and downiness,
Provided it supply a glove.
The world's good word!—the Institute!
    Guizot receives Montalembert!
    Eh? Down the court three lampions flare:
Put forward your best foot!

—

St. 3. Guizot: Francois Pierre Guillaume Guizot, French statesman and historian, b. 1787, d. 1874. Montalembert: Charles Forbes Rene, Comte de Montalembert, French statesman, orator, and political writer, b. 1810, d. 1870. Guizot receives Montalembert: i.e., on purely conventional grounds.

Home Thoughts, from Abroad.

1.

Oh, to be in England now that April's there,
And whoever wakes in England sees, some morning,
  unaware,
That the lowest boughs and the brushwood sheaf
Round the elm-tree bole are in tiny leaf,
While the chaffinch sings on the orchard bough
In England—now!
And after April, when May follows
And the white-throat builds, and all the swallows!
Hark, where my blossomed pear-tree in the hedge
Leans to the field and scatters on the clover [10]
Blossoms and dewdrops—at the bent spray's edge—
That's the wise thrush: he sings each song twice over
Lest you should think he never could recapture
The first fine careless rapture!
And though the fields look rough with hoary dew,
And will be gay when noontide wakes anew
The buttercups, the little children's dower
—Far brighter than this gaudy melon-flower!

{despite this stanza being numbered 1, there is apparently no 2.}

Home Thoughts, from the Sea.

Nobly, nobly Cape Saint Vincent to the north-west died away;
Sunset ran, one glorious blood-red, reeking into Cadiz Bay; Bluish
mid the burning water, full in face Trafalgar lay; In the dimmest
north-east distance, dawned Gibraltar grand and gray; "Here and
here did England help me,—how can I help England?"—say,
Whoso turns as I, this evening, turn to God to praise and pray,
While Jove's planet rises yonder, silent over Africa.

Old Pictures in Florence.

1.

The morn when first it thunders in March,
    The eel in the pond gives a leap, they say.
As I leaned and looked over the aloed arch
    Of the villa-gate this warm March day,
No flash snapped, no dumb thunder rolled
    In the valley beneath where, white and wide
And washed by the morning water-gold,
    Florence lay out on the mountain-side.

———

St. 1. washed by the morning water-gold: the water of the Arno, gilded by the morning sun;

> "I can but muse in hope, upon this shore
> Of golden Arno, as it shoots away
> Through Florence' heart beneath her bridges four."
> —Casa Guidi Windows.

2.

River and bridge and street and square
    Lay mine, as much at my beck and call,
Through the live translucent bath of air,
    As the sights in a magic crystal-ball.
And of all I saw and of all I praised,
    The most to praise and the best to see
Was the startling bell-tower Giotto raised:
    But why did it more than startle me?

———

St. 2. the startling bell-tower Giotto raised: the Campanile of the Cathedral, or Duomo, of Florence (La Cattedrale di S. Maria del Fiore), begun in 1334.

"The characteristics of Power and Beauty occur more of less in different buildings, some in one and some in another. But all together, and all in their highest possible relative degrees, they exist, as far as I know, only in one building of the world, the Campanile of Giotto."—Ruskin. But why did it more than startle me?: There's a rumor "that a certain precious little tablet which Buonarotti eyed like a lover" has been discovered by somebody. If this rumor is true, the speaker feels that Giotto, whom he has so loved, has played him false, in not favoring him with the precious find. See St. 30. "The opinion which his contemporaries entertained of Giotto, as the greatest genius in the arts which Italy in that age possessed, has been perpetuated by Dante in the lines in which the illuminator, Oderigi, says:—

> "'In painting Cimabue fain had thought
> To lord the field; now Giotto has the cry,
> So that the other's fame in shade is brought'
> (Dante, 'Purg.' xi. 93).

"Giotto di Bondone was born at Del Colle, a village in the commune of Vespignano near Florence, according to Vasari, A.D. 1276, but more probably A.D. 1266. He went through his apprenticeship under Cimabue, and practised as a painter and architect not only in Florence, but in various parts of Italy, in free cities as well as in the courts of princes . . . On April 12, 1334, Giotto was appointed by the civic authorities of Florence, chief master of the Cathedral works, the city fortifications, and all public architectural undertakings, in an instrument of which the wording constitutes the most affectionate homage to the 'great and dear master'. Giotto died January 8, 1337." —Woltmann and Woermann's History of Painting.

For a good account of the Campanile, see Susan and Joanna Horner's 'Walks in Florence', v. I, pp. 62-66; Art. in 'Macmillan's Mag.', April, 1877, by Sidney Colvin,—'Giotto's Gospel of Labor'.

3.

Giotto, how, with that soul of yours,
    Could you play me false who loved you so?

Some slights if a certain heart endures
　　Yet it feels, I would have your fellows know!
I' faith, I perceive not why I should care
　　To break a silence that suits them best,
But the thing grows somewhat hard to bear
　　When I find a Giotto join the rest.

4.

On the arch where olives overhead
　　Print the blue sky with twig and leaf
(That sharp-curled leaf which they never shed),
　　'Twixt the aloes, I used to learn in chief,
And mark through the winter afternoons,
　　By a gift God grants me now and then,
In the mild decline of those suns like moons,
　　Who walked in Florence, besides her men.

—

St. 4. By a gift God grants me now and then: the gift of
spiritual vision.

5.

They might chirp and chaffer, come and go
　　For pleasure or profit, her men alive—
My business was hardly with them, I trow,
　　But with empty cells of the human hive;
—With the chapter-room, the cloister-porch,
　　The church's apsis, aisle or nave,
Its crypt, one fingers along with a torch,
　　Its face set full for the sun to shave.

6.

Wherever a fresco peels and drops,
　　Wherever an outline weakens and wanes
Till the latest life in the painting stops,
　　Stands One whom each fainter pulse-tick pains:

One, wishful each scrap should clutch the brick,
     Each tinge not wholly escape the plaster,
—A lion who dies of an ass's kick,
     The wronged great soul of an ancient Master.

———

St. 6. "He sees the ghosts of the early Christian masters, whose work has never been duly appreciated, standing sadly by each mouldering Italian Fresco."—Dowden.

7.

For oh, this world and the wrong it does!
     They are safe in heaven with their backs to it,
The Michaels and Rafaels, you hum and buzz
     Round the works of, you of the little wit!
Do their eyes contract to the earth's old scope,
     Now that they see God face to face,
And have all attained to be poets, I hope?
     'Tis their holiday now, in any case.

8.

Much they reck of your praise and you!
     But the wronged great souls—can they be quit
Of a world where their work is all to do,
     Where you style them, you of the little wit,
Old Master This and Early the Other,
     Not dreaming that Old and New are fellows:
A younger succeeds to an elder brother,
     Da Vincis derive in good time from Dellos.

———

St. 8. Much they reck of your praise and you!: the Michaels and Rafaels. Leonardo da Vinci (b. at Vinci, in the Val d'Arno, below Florence, 1452); "in him the two lines of artistic descent, tracing from classic Rome and Christian Byzantium, meet."—Heaton's 'History of Painting'. Dello di Niccolo Delli, painter and sculptor, fl. first half 15th cent.

9.

And here where your praise might yield returns,
    And a handsome word or two give help,
Here, after your kind, the mastiff girns,
    And the puppy pack of poodles yelp.
What, not a word for Stefano there,
    Of brow once prominent and starry,
Called Nature's Ape and the world's despair
    For his peerless painting? (see Vasari.)

—

St. 9. "Stefano is extolled by Vasari as having left Giotto himself far behind, but it is very difficult to ascertain what were really his works."—Heaton. "Stefano appears from Landinio's Commentary on Dante to have been called 'scimia della natura', the ape of nature, which seems to refer to the strong realistic tendencies common to the school."—Woltmann and Woermann's History of Painting. Giorgio Vasari, an Italian painter of Arezzo, b. 1512, d. 1574; author of 'Vite de' piu excellenti pittori scultori ed architettori'. Florence, 1550.

10.

There stands the Master. Study, my friends,
    What a man's work comes to! So he plans it,
Performs it, perfects it, makes amends
    For the toiling and moiling, and then, 'sic transit'!
Happier the thrifty blind-folk labor,
    With upturned eye while the hand is busy,
Not sidling a glance at the coin of their neighbor!
    'Tis looking downward makes one dizzy.

11.

"If you knew their work you would deal your dole."
    May I take upon me to instruct you?
When Greek Art ran and reached the goal,

Thus much had the world to boast 'in fructu'—
The Truth of Man, as by God first spoken,
    Which the actual generations garble,
Was re-uttered, and Soul (which Limbs betoken)
    And Limbs (Soul informs) made new in marble.

—

St. 11. "If you knew their work", etc.. The speaker imputes this remark to some one; the meaning is, if you really knew these old Christian painters, you would deal them your mite of praise, damn them, perhaps, with faint praise, and no more. The poet then proceeds to instruct this person.

12.

So, you saw yourself as you wished you were,
    As you might have been, as you cannot be;
Earth here, rebuked by Olympus there:
    And grew content in your poor degree
With your little power, by those statues' godhead,
    And your little scope, by their eyes' full sway,
And your little grace, by their grace embodied,
    And your little date, by their forms that stay.

13.

You would fain be kinglier, say, than I am?
    Even so, you will not sit like Theseus.
You would prove a model? The Son of Priam
    Has yet the advantage in arms' and knees' use.
You're wroth—can you slay your snake like Apollo?
    You're grieved—still Niobe's the grander!
You live—there's the Racers' frieze to follow:
    You die—there's the dying Alexander.

—

St. 13. Theseus: a reclining statue from the eastern pediment of the Parthenon, now in the British Museum. The Son of Priam:

probably the Paris of the Aeginetan Sculptures (now in the Glyptothek at Munich), which is kneeling and drawing the bow.

Apollo: "A word on the line about Apollo the snake-slayer, which my friend Professor Colvin condemns, believing that the God of the Belvedere grasps no bow, but the Aegis, as described in the 15th Iliad. Surely the text represents that portentous object (qou^rin, deinh/n, a'mfida/seian, a'riprepe/'—marmare/hn) as 'shaken violently' or 'held immovably' by both hands, not a single one, and that the left hand:—

a'lla\ su/ g' e'n xei/ressi la/b' ai'gi/da qusano/essan
th\n ma/l' e'pi/ssei/wn fobe/ein h'/rwas 'Axaiou/s.

and so on, th\n a'/r' o'/ g' e'n xei/ressin e'/xwn— xersi\n e'/x' a'tre/ma, k.t.l. Moreover, while he shook it he 'shouted enormously', sei^s', e'pi\ d' au'to\s au'/se ma/la me/ga, which the statue does not. Presently when Teukros, on the other side, plies the bow, it is to/j'on e'/xwn e'n xeiri\ pali/ntonon. Besides, by the act of discharging an arrow, the right arm and hand are thrown back as we see,—a quite gratuitous and theatrical display in the case supposed. The conjecture of Flaxman that the statue was suggested by the bronze Apollo Alexikakos of Kalamis, mentioned by Pausanias, remains probable; though the 'hardness' which Cicero considers to distinguish the artist's workmanship from that of Muron is not by any means apparent in our marble copy, if it be one.—Feb. 16, 1880."—The Poet's Note.

Niobe: group of ancient sculpture, in the gallery of the Uffizi Palace, in Florence, representing Niobe mourning the death of her children. the Racers' frieze: the frieze of the Parthenon is perhaps meant, the reference being to the FULNESS OF LIFE exhibited by the men and horses. the dying Alexander: "'The Dying Alexander', at Florence. This well-known, beautiful, and deeply affecting head, which bears a strong resemblance to the Alexander Helios of the Capitol —especially in the treatment of the hair—has been called by Ottfried Mueller a riddle of archaeology. It is no doubt a Greek original, and one of the most interesting remains of ancient art, but we cannot take it for granted that it is intended for Alexander, and still less that it is the work of Lysippus. It is difficult to imagine that the favored and devoted artist of the mighty conqueror would choose to portray his great master in a painful and impotent struggle with disease and death. This consideration makes it extremely improbable that it was executed during the lifetime of Alexander, and the whole character of the work, in which free pathos is the prevailing element, and its close resemblance in style to the heads on coins of the period of the Diadochi, point to a later age than that of Lysippus." —'Greek and Roman Sculpture' by Walter Copland Perry. London, 1882. p. 484.

14.

So, testing your weakness by their strength,
    Your meagre charms by their rounded beauty,
Measured by Art in your breadth and length,
    You learned—to submit is a mortal's duty.
—When I say "you", 'tis the common soul,
    The collective, I mean: the race of Man
That receives life in parts to live in a whole,
    And grow here according to God's clear plan.

—

St. 14. common: general.

15.

Growth came when, looking your last on them all,
    You turned your eyes inwardly one fine day
And cried with a start—What if we so small
    Be greater and grander the while than they?
Are they perfect of lineament, perfect of stature?
    In both, of such lower types are we
Precisely because of our wider nature;
    For time, theirs—ours, for eternity.

16.

To-day's brief passion limits their range;
    It seethes with the morrow for us and more.
They are perfect—how else? they shall never change:

We are faulty—why not? we have time in store.
The Artificer's hand is not arrested
    With us; we are rough-hewn, nowise polished.
They stand for our copy, and, once invested
    With all they can teach, we shall see them abolished.

17.

'Tis a life-long toil till our lump be leaven—
    The better! What's come to perfection perishes.
Things learned on earth, we shall practise in heaven:
    Works done least rapidly, Art most cherishes.
Thyself shalt afford the example, Giotto!
    Thy one work, not to decrease or diminish,
Done at a stroke, was just (was it not?) "O!"
    Thy great Campanile is still to finish.

—

St. 15-17. "Greek art had ITS lesson to teach, and it taught it. It reasserted the dignity of the human form. It re-stated THE TRUTH of the soul which informs the body, and the body which expresses it. Men saw in its creations their own qualities carried to perfection, and were content to know that such perfection was possible and to renounce the hope of attaining it. In this experience the first stage was progress, the second was stagnation. Progress began again when men looked on these images of themselves and said: 'we are not inferior to these. We are greater than they. For what has come to perfection perishes, and we are imperfect because eternity is before us; because we were made to GROW.'"—Mrs. Orr's Handbook to the Works of R. B.

St. 17. "O!": Boniface VIII. (not Benedict IX., as Vasari has it), wishing to employ Giotto, sent a courtier to obtain some proof of his skill. The latter requesting a drawing to send to his Holiness, Giotto took a sheet of paper and a pencil dipped in red color; then resting his elbow on his side, to form a compass, with one turn of his hand he drew a circle so perfect and exact, that it was a marvel to behold. This done, he turned to the courtier, saying, "Here is your drawing." The courtier seems to have thought that Giotto was fooling him; but the pope was easily convinced, by the roundness

of the O, of the greatness of Giotto's skill. This incident gave rise
to the proverb, "Tu sei piu tondo che l' O di Giotto", the point of
which lies in the word 'tondo', signifying slowness of intellect, as
well as a circle. —Adapted from Vasari and Heaton.

18.

Is it true that we are now, and shall be hereafter,
    But what and where depend on life's minute?
Hails heavenly cheer or infernal laughter
    Our first step out of the gulf or in it?
Shall Man, such step within his endeavor,
    Man's face, have no more play and action
Than joy which is crystallized forever,
    Or grief, an eternal petrifaction?

—

St. 18. life's minute: life's short span.

19.

On which I conclude, that the early painters,
    To cries of "Greek Art and what more wish you?"—
Replied, "To become now self-acquainters,
    And paint man, man, whatever the issue!
Make new hopes shine through the flesh they fray,
    New fears aggrandize the rags and tatters:
To bring the invisible full into play,
    Let the visible go to the dogs—what matters?"

20.

Give these, I exhort you, their guerdon and glory
    For daring so much, before they well did it.
The first of the new, in our race's story,
    Beats the last of the old; 'tis no idle quiddit.
The worthies began a revolution,
    Which if on earth you intend to acknowledge,

Why, honor them now! (ends my allocution)
  Nor confer your degree when the folks leave college.

21.

There's a fancy some lean to and others hate—
  That, when this life is ended, begins
New work for the soul in another state,
  Where it strives and gets weary, loses and wins:
Where the strong and the weak, this world's congeries,
  Repeat in large what they practised in small,
Through life after life in unlimited series;
  Only the scale's to be changed, that's all.

22.

Yet I hardly know. When a soul has seen
  By the means of Evil that Good is best,
And, through earth and its noise, what is heaven's serene,—
  When our faith in the same has stood the test,—
Why, the child grown man, you burn the rod,
  The uses of labor are surely done;
There remaineth a rest for the people of God:
  And I have had troubles enough, for one.

23.

But at any rate I have loved the season
  Of Art's spring-birth so dim and dewy;
My sculptor is Nicolo the Pisan,
  My painter—who but Cimabue?
Nor even was man of them all indeed,
  From these to Ghiberti and Ghirlandajo,
Could say that he missed my critic-meed.
  So, now to my special grievance—heigh-ho!

—

St. 23. Nicolo the Pisan: Nicolo Pisano, architect and sculptor,
b. ab. 1207, d. 1278; the church and monastery of the Holy Trinity,

at Florence, and the church of San Antonio, at Padua, are esteemed his best architectural works, and his bas-reliefs in the Cathedral of Sienna, his best sculptural. Cimabue: Giovanni Cimabue, 1240-1302, "ends the long Byzantine succession in Italy . . . In him 'the spirit of the years to come' is decidedly manifest; but he never entirely succeeded in casting off the hereditary Byzantine asceticism."— Heaton. Giotto was his pupil. Ghiberti: Lorenzo Ghiberti, the great Florentine sculptor, 1381-1455; his famous masterpiece, the eastern doors of the Florentine Baptistery, of San Giovanni, of which Michael Angelo said that they were worthy to be the gates of Paradise. Ghirlandajo: Domenico Bigordi, called Ghirlandajo, or the garland-maker, celebrated painter, b. in Florence, 1449, d. 1494; "in treatment, drawing, and modelling, G. excels any fresco-painter since Masaccio; shares with the two Lippis, father and son, a fondness for introducing subordinate groups which was unknown to Massaccio."—Woltmann and Woermann's History of Painting.

24.

Their ghosts still stand, as I said before,
    Watching each fresco flaked and rasped,
Blocked up, knocked out, or whitewashed o'er:
    —No getting again what the Church has grasped!
The works on the wall must take their chance;
    "Works never conceded to England's thick clime!"
(I hope they prefer their inheritance
    Of a bucketful of Italian quicklime.)

25.

When they go at length, with such a shaking
    Of heads o'er the old delusion, sadly
Each master his way through the black streets taking,
    Where many a lost work breathes though badly—
Why don't they bethink them of who has merited?
    Why not reveal, while their pictures dree
Such doom, how a captive might be out-ferreted?
    Why is it they never remember me?

—

St. 25. dree: endure (A. S. "dreo'gan").

26.

Not that I expect the great Bigordi,
    Nor Sandro to hear me, chivalric, bellicose;
Nor the wronged Lippino; and not a word I
    Say of a scrap of Fra Angelico's:
But are you too fine, Taddeo Gaddi,
    To grant me a taste of your intonaco,
Some Jerome that seeks the heaven with a sad eye?
    Not a churlish saint, Lorenzo Monaco?

—

St. 26. Bigordi: Ghirlandajo; see above. {note to St. 23.}
Sandro: Sandro Filipepi, called Botticelli (1437-1515), "belonged in
feeling, to the older Christian school, tho' his religious sentiment
was not quite strong enough to resist entirely the paganizing
influence of the time" (Heaton); became a disciple of Savonarola.
Lippino: Filippino Lippi, son of Fra Filippo (1460-1505), "added
to his father's bold naturalism a dramatic talent in composition,
which places his works above the mere realisms of Fra Filippo, and
renders him worthy to be placed next to Masaccio in the line of
progress."—Heaton. Fra Angelico: see under the Monologue of
Fra Lippo Lippi. Taddeo Gaddi: "foremost amongst these ('The
Giotteschi') stands the name of T. G. (1300, living in 1366), the
son of Gaddo Gaddi, and godson of Giotto; was an architect as
well as painter, and was on the council of Works of S. Maria del
Fiore, after Giotto's death, and carried out his design for the bell-
tower."—Heaton. intonaco: rough-casting. Lorenzo Monaco: see
under the Monologue of Fra Lippo Lippi.

27.

Could not the ghost with the close red cap,
    My Pollajolo, the twice a craftsman,
Save me a sample, give me the hap
    Of a muscular Christ that shows the draughtsman?

No Virgin by him the somewhat petty,
    Of finical touch and tempera crumbly—
Could not Alesso Baldovinetti
    Contribute so much, I ask him humbly?

—

St. 27. Pollajolo: "Antonio Pollajuolo (ab. 1430-1498) was a sculptor and goldsmith, more than a painter; . . . his master-work in pictorial art is the Martyrdom of St. Sebastian, in the Nat. Gal., painted for the Pucci Chapel in the Church of San Sebastiano de' Servi, at Florence. 'This painting', says Vasari, 'has been more extolled than any other ever executed by Antonio'. It is, however, unpleasantly hard and obtrusively anatomical. Pollajuolo is said to have been the first artist who studied anatomy by means of dissection, and his sole aim in this picture seems to have been to display his knowledge of muscular action. He was an engraver as well as goldsmith, sculptor, and painter."—Heaton. tempera: see Webster, s. vv. "tempera" and "distemper". {paint types} Alesso Baldovinetti: Florentine painter, b. 1422, or later, d. 1499; worked in mosaic, particularly as a restorer of old mosaics, besides painting; he made many experiments in both branches of art, and attempted to work fresco 'al secco', and varnish it so as to make it permanent, but in this he failed. His works were distinguished for extreme minuteness of detail. "In the church of the Annunziata in Florence, he executed an historical piece in fresco, but finished 'a secco', wherein he represented the Nativity of Christ, painted with such minuteness of care, that each separate straw in the roof of a cabin, figured therein, may be counted, and every knot in these straws distinguished."—Vasari. His remaining works are much injured by scaling or the abrasion of the colors.

28.

Margheritone of Arezzo,
    With the grave-clothes garb and swaddling barret
(Why purse up mouth and beak in a pet so,
    You bald old saturnine poll-clawed parrot?)
Not a poor glimmering Crucifixion,
    Where in the foreground kneels the donor?

If such remain, as is my conviction,
    The hoarding it does you but little honor.

—

St. 28. Margheritone: Margaritone; painter, sculptor, and architect, of Arezzo (1236-1313); the most important of his remaining pictures is a Madonna, in the London National Gallery, from Church of St. Margaret, at Arezzo, "said to be a characteristic work, and mentioned by Vasari, who praises its small figures, which he says are executed 'with more grace and finished with greater delicacy' than the larger ones. Nothing, however, can be more unlike nature, than the grim Madonna and the weird starved Child in her arms (see 'Wornum's Catal. Nat. Gal.', for a description of this painting). Margaritone's favorite subject was the figure of St. Francis, his style being well suited to depict the chief ascetic saint. Crucifixions were also much to his taste, and he represented them in all their repulsive details. Vasari relates that he died at the age of 77, afflicted and disgusted at having lived to see the changes that had taken place in art, and the honors bestowed on the new artists."—Heaton. His monument to Pope Gregory X. in the Cathedral of Arezzo, is ranked among his best works. "Browning possesses the 'Crucifixion' by M. to which he alludes, as also the pictures of Alesso Baldovinetti, and Taddeo Gaddi, and Pollajuolo described in the poem." —Browning Soc. Papers, Pt. II., p. 169.

29.

They pass; for them the panels may thrill,
    The tempera grow alive and tinglish;
Their pictures are left to the mercies still
    Of dealers and stealers, Jews and the English,
Who, seeing mere money's worth in their prize,
    Will sell it to somebody calm as Zeno
At naked High Art, and in ecstasies
    Before some clay-cold vile Carlino!

—

St. 29. tempera: see Webster, s.v. {a type of paint} tinglish: sharp? Zeno: founder of the Stoic philosophy. Carlino: some

249

expressionless picture by Carlo, or Carlino, Dolci. His works show an extreme finish, often with no end beyond itself; some being, to use Ruskin's words, "polished into inanity".

30.

No matter for these! But Giotto, you,
    Have you allowed, as the town-tongues babble it—
Oh, never! it shall not be counted true—
    That a certain precious little tablet
Which Buonarroti eyed like a lover,
    Was buried so long in oblivion's womb
And, left for another than I to discover,
    Turns up at last! and to whom?—to whom?

—

St. 30. a certain precious little tablet: "The 'little tablet' was a famous 'Last Supper', mentioned by Vasari, and gone astray long ago from the Church of S. Spirito: it turned up, according to report, in some obscure corner, while I was in Florence, and was at once acquired by a stranger. I saw it, genuine or no, a work of great beauty."—From Poet's Letter to the Editor. Buonarotti: Michael Angelo (more correctly, Michel Agnolo) Buonarotti, b. 6th of March, 1475, at Castel Caprese, near Florence; d. at Rome, 18th of Feb., 1564. and to whom?—to whom?: a contemptuous repetition.

31.

I, that have haunted the dim San Spirito,
    (Or was it rather the Ognissanti?)
Patient on altar-step planting a weary toe!
    Nay, I shall have it yet! Detur amanti!
My Koh-i-noor—or (if that's a platitude)
    Jewel of Giamschid, the Persian Sofi's eye;
So, in anticipative gratitude,
    What if I take up my hope and prophesy?

St. 31. San Spirito: a church of the 14th century, in Florence. Ognissanti: i.e., "All Saints", in Florence. I shall have it yet!: I shall make a happy find yet. Detur amanti!: let it be given to the loving one. Koh-i-noor: "Mountain of Light", a celebrated diamond, "the diamond of the great Mogul", presented to Queen Victoria, in 1850. See Art. on the Diamond, 'N. Brit. Rev.' Vol. 18, p. 186, and Art., Diamond, 'Encycl. Brit.'; used here, by metonymy, for a great treasure. Jewel of Giamschid: the 'Deria-i-noor', or 'the Sea of Light', one of the largest of known diamonds, belonging to the king of Persia, is probably referred to. See 'N. Brit. Rev.', Vol. 18, p. 217.

32.

When the hour grows ripe, and a certain dotard
    Is pitched, no parcel that needs invoicing,
To the worse side of the Mont St. Gothard,
    We shall begin by way of rejoicing;
None of that shooting the sky (blank cartridge),
    Nor a civic guard, all plumes and lacquer,
Hunting Radetzky's soul like a partridge
    Over Morello with squib and cracker.

St. 32. a certain dotard: Joseph Wenzel Radetzky, b. Nov. 2, 1766, d. Jan. 5, 1858, in his 92d year; governed the Austrian possessions in Italy to Feb. 28, 1857. Morello: Monte Morello, the highest of the spurs of the Apennines, to the north of Florence.

33.

This time we'll shoot better game and bag 'em hot:
    No mere display at the stone of Dante,
But a kind of sober Witanagemot
    (Ex: "Casa Guidi", 'quod videas ante')

Shall ponder, once Freedom restored to Florence,
　　How Art may return that departed with her.
Go, hated house, go each trace of the Loraine's,
　　And bring us the days of Orgagna hither!

———

St. 33. the stone of Dante: see 'Casa Guidi Windows', Pt. I,
Sect. XIV., XV. Witanagemot: A. S. 'witena gemo^t': an assembly of
wise men, a parliament. Casa Guidi: Mrs. Browning's 'Casa Guidi
Windows', a poem named from the house in Florence in which she
lived, and giving her impressions of events in Tuscany at the time.
the Loraine's: the "hated house" included the Cardinals of Guise,
or Lorraine, and the Dukes of Guise, a younger branch of the
house of Lorraine. Orgagna: Andrea di Cione (surnamed Orcagna,
or Arcagnolo, approximate dates of b. and d. 1315-1376), one of
the most noted successors of Giotto, and allied to him in genius;
though he owed much to Giotto, he showed great independence
of spirit in his style.

34.

How we shall prologuize, how we shall perorate,
　　Utter fit things upon art and history,
Feel truth at blood-heat and falsehood at zero rate,
　　Make of the want of the age no mystery;
Contrast the fructuous and sterile eras,
　　Show—monarchy ever its uncouth cub licks
Out of the bear's shape into Chimaera's,
　　While Pure Art's birth is still the republic's!

35.

Then one shall propose in a speech (curt Tuscan,
　　Expurgate and sober, with scarcely an "issimo"),
To end now our half-told tale of Cambuscan,
　　And turn the bell-tower's ALT to ALTISSIMO;
And, fine as the beak of a young beccaccia,
　　The Campanile, the Duomo's fit ally,

Shall soar up in gold full fifty braccia,
　　Completing Florence, as Florence, Italy.

———

St. 35. an "issimo": any adjective in the superlative degree. to end: complete. our half-told tale of Cambuscan: by metonymy for the unfinished Campanile of Giotto;

"Or call up him that left half-told
　The story of Cambuscan bold."
　　　　—Milton's 'Il Penseroso'.

An allusion to Chaucer, who left the 'Squire's Tale' in the 'Canterbury Tales' unfinished. The poet follows Milton's accentuation of the word "Cambuscan", on the penult; it's properly accented on the ultimate. beccaccia: woodcock. the Duomo's fit ally: "There is, as far as I know, only one Gothic building in Europe, the Duomo of Florence, in which the ornament is so exquisitely finished as to enable us to imagine what might have been the effect of the perfect workmanship of the Renaissance, coming out of the hands of men like Verocchio and Ghiberti, had it been employed on the magnificent framework of Gothic structure."—Ruskin in 'Stones of Venice'.

36.

Shall I be alive that morning the scaffold
　　Is broken away, and the long-pent fire,
Like the golden hope of the world, unbaffled
　　Springs from its sleep, and up goes the spire,
While, "God and the People" plain for its motto,
　　Thence the new tricolor flaps at the sky?
At least to foresee that glory of Giotto
　　And Florence together, the first am I!

———

St. 36. and up goes the spire: Giotto's plan included a spire of 100 feet, but the project was abandoned by Taddeo Gaddi, who carried on the work after the death of Giotto in 1336.

"The mountains from without
In silence listen for the word said next.
What word will men say,—here where Giotto planted
His Campanile like an unperplexed
Fine question heaven-ward, touching the things granted
A noble people, who, being greatly vexed
In act, in aspiration keep undaunted?"

—Mrs. Browning's 'Casa Guidi Windows',
Pt. I., vv. 66-72.

Pictor Ignotus.

[Florence, 15—.]

I could have painted pictures like that youth's
    Ye praise so. How my soul springs up! No bar
Stayed me—ah, thought which saddens while it soothes!
    —Never did fate forbid me, star by star,
To outburst on your night, with all my gift
    Of fires from God: nor would my flesh have shrunk
From seconding my soul, with eyes uplift
    And wide to heaven, or, straight like thunder, sunk
To the centre, of an instant; or around
    Turned calmly and inquisitive, to scan   [10]
The license and the limit, space and bound,
    Allowed to truth made visible in man.
And, like that youth ye praise so, all I saw,
    Over the canvas could my hand have flung,
Each face obedient to its passion's law,
    Each passion clear proclaimed without a tongue:
Whether Hope rose at once in all the blood,
    A-tiptoe for the blessing of embrace,

Or Rapture drooped the eyes, as when her brood
    Pull down the nesting dove's heart to its place;   [20]
Or Confidence lit swift the forehead up,
    And locked the mouth fast, like a castle braved,—
O human faces! hath it spilt, my cup?
    What did ye give me that I have not saved?
Nor will I say I have not dreamed (how well!)
    Of going—I, in each new picture,—forth,
As, making new hearts beat and bosoms swell,
    To Pope or Kaiser, East, West, South, or North,
Bound for the calmly satisfied great State,
    Or glad aspiring little burgh, it went,   [30]
Flowers cast upon the car which bore the freight,
    Through old streets named afresh from the event,
Till it reached home, where learned age should greet
    My face, and youth, the star not yet distinct
Above his hair, lie learning at my feet!—
    Oh, thus to live, I and my picture, linked
With love about, and praise, till life should end,
    And then not go to heaven, but linger here,
Here on my earth, earth's every man my friend,
    The thought grew frightful, 'twas so wildly dear!   [40]
But a voice changed it. Glimpses of such sights
    Have scared me, like the revels through a door
Of some strange house of idols at its rites!
    This world seemed not the world it was, before:
Mixed with my loving trusting ones, there trooped
    . . . Who summoned those cold faces that begun
To press on me and judge me? Though I stooped
    Shrinking, as from the soldiery a nun,
They drew me forth, and spite of me . . . enough!
    These buy and sell our pictures, take and give,   [50]
Count them for garniture and household-stuff,
    And where they live needs must our pictures live
And see their faces, listen to their prate,
    Partakers of their daily pettiness,
Discussed of,—"This I love, or this I hate,
    This likes me more, and this affects me less!"
Wherefore I chose my portion. If at whiles

My heart sinks, as monotonous I paint
These endless cloisters and eternal aisles
    With the same series, Virgin, Babe, and Saint,   [60]
With the same cold calm beautiful regard,—
    At least no merchant traffics in my heart;
The sanctuary's gloom at least shall ward
    Vain tongues from where my pictures stand apart:
Only prayer breaks the silence of the shrine
    While, blackening in the daily candle-smoke,
They moulder on the damp wall's travertine,
    'Mid echoes the light footstep never woke.
So, die my pictures! surely, gently die!
    O youth, men praise so,—holds their praise its worth?   [70]
Blown harshly, keeps the trump its golden cry?
    Tastes sweet the water with such specks of earth?

———

3. ah, thought which saddens while it soothes: the thought saddens him that he has not realized his capabilities, and soothes him that he has resisted the temptations to earthly fame, and been true to his soul.

14-22. he could have expressed Hope, Rapture, Confidence, and all other passions, in the human face, each clear proclaimed without a tongue.

23. hath it spilt, my cup?: the cup of his memory.

24. What did ye give me that I have not saved?: he has retained all the impressions he has received from human faces.

25 et seq.: Nor will I say I have not dreamed (how well I have dreamed!) of going forth in each new picture, as it went to Pope or Kaiser, etc., making new hearts beat and bosoms swell.

34. the star not yet distinct above his hair: his fame not having yet shone brightly out; "his" refers to "youth".

35. lie learning: and should lie.

41. But a voice changed it: the voice of his secret soul.

67. travertine: coating of lime; properly a limestone.
Lat., 'lapis Tiburtinus', found near Tibur, now Tivoli.

Andrea del Sarto.

[Called "The Faultless Painter".]

But do not let us quarrel any more,
No, my Lucrezia! bear with me for once:
Sit down and all shall happen as you wish.
You turn your face, but does it bring your heart?
I'll work then for your friend's friend, never fear,
Treat his own subject after his own way,
Fix his own time, accept too his own price,
And shut the money into this small hand
When next it takes mine. Will it? tenderly?
Oh, I'll content him,—but to-morrow, Love!   [10]
I often am much wearier than you think,
This evening more than usual: and it seems
As if—forgive now—should you let me sit
Here by the window, with your hand in mine,
And look a half hour forth on Fiesole,
Both of one mind, as married people use,
Quietly, quietly the evening through,
I might get up to-morrow to my work
Cheerful and fresh as ever. Let us try.
To-morrow, how you shall be glad for this!   [20]
Your soft hand is a woman of itself,
And mine, the man's bared breast she curls inside.
Don't count the time lost, neither; you must serve
For each of the five pictures we require:
It saves a model. So! keep looking so—
My serpentining beauty, rounds on rounds!
—How could you ever prick those perfect ears,
Even to put the pearl there! oh, so sweet—
My face, my moon, my everybody's moon,
Which everybody looks on and calls his,   [30]
And, I suppose, is looked on by in turn,
While she looks—no one's: very dear, no less.
You smile? why, there's my picture ready made,
That's what we painters call our harmony!

A common grayness silvers every thing,—
All in a twilight, you and I alike
—You, at the point of your first pride in me
(That's gone, you know)—but I, at every point;
My youth, my hope, my art, being all toned down
To yonder sober pleasant Fiesole.   [40]
There's the bell clinking from the chapel-top;
That length of convent-wall across the way
Holds the trees safer, huddled more inside;
The last monk leaves the garden; days decrease,
And autumn grows, autumn in every thing.
Eh? the whole seems to fall into a shape,
As if I saw alike my work and self
And all that I was born to be and do,
A twilight-piece. Love, we are in God's hand.
How strange now, looks the life he makes us lead;   [50]
So free we seem, so fettered fast we are!
I feel he laid the fetter: let it lie!
This chamber, for example—turn your head—
All that's behind us! You don't understand
Nor care to understand about my art,
But you can hear at least when people speak:
And that cartoon, the second from the door
—It is the thing, Love! so such things should be:
Behold Madonna!—I am bold to say.
I can do with my pencil what I know,   [60]
What I see, what at bottom of my heart
I wish for, if I ever wish so deep—
Do easily, too—when I say, perfectly,
I do not boast, perhaps: yourself are judge,
Who listened to the Legate's talk last week;
And just as much they used to say in France.
At any rate 'tis easy, all of it!
No sketches first, no studies, that's long past:
I do what many dream of, all their lives,
—Dream? strive to do, and agonize to do,   [70]
And fail in doing. I could count twenty such
On twice your fingers, and not leave this town,
Who strive—you don't know how the others strive

To paint a little thing like that you smeared
Carelessly passing with your robes afloat,—
Yet do much less, so much less, Someone says,
(I know his name, no matter)—so much less!
Well, less is more, Lucrezia: I am judged.
There burns a truer light of God in them,
In their vexed beating stuffed and stopped-up brain, [80]
Heart, or whate'er else, than goes on to prompt
This low-pulsed forthright craftsman's hand of mine.
Their works drop groundward, but themselves, I know,
Reach many a time a heaven that's shut to me,
Enter and take their place there sure enough,
Though they come back and cannot tell the world.
My works are nearer heaven, but I sit here.
The sudden blood of these men! at a word—
Praise them, it boils, or blame them, it boils too.
I, painting from myself and to myself,   [90]
Know what I do, am unmoved by men's blame
Or their praise either. Somebody remarks
Morello's outline there is wrongly traced,
His hue mistaken; what of that? or else,
Rightly traced and well ordered; what of that?
Speak as they please, what does the mountain care?
Ah, but a man's reach should exceed his grasp,
Or what's a heaven for? All is silver-gray,
Placid and perfect with my art: the worse!
I know both what I want and what might gain;   [100]
And yet how profitless to know, to sigh
"Had I been two, another and myself,
Our head would have o'erlooked the world!" No doubt.
Yonder's a work now, of that famous youth
The Urbinate who died five years ago.
('Tis copied, George Vasari sent it me.)
Well, I can fancy how he did it all,
Pouring his soul, with kings and popes to see,
Reaching, that heaven might so replenish him,
Above and through his art—for it gives way;   [110]
That arm is wrongly put—and there again—
A fault to pardon in the drawing's lines,

259

Its body, so to speak: its soul is right,
He means right—that, a child may understand.
Still, what an arm! and I could alter it:
But all the play, the insight and the stretch—
Out of me, out of me! And wherefore out?
Had you enjoined them on me, given me soul,
We might have risen to Rafael, I and you.
Nay, Love, you did give all I asked, I think—   [120]
More than I merit, yes, by many times.
But had you—oh, with the same perfect brow,
And perfect eyes, and more than perfect mouth,
And the low voice my soul hears, as a bird
The fowler's pipe, and follows to the snare—
Had you, with these the same, but brought a mind!
Some women do so. Had the mouth there urged
"God and the glory! never care for gain.
The present by the future, what is that?
Live for fame, side by side with Agnolo!   [130]
Rafael is waiting: up to God, all three!"
I might have done it for you. So it seems:
Perhaps not. All is as God over-rules.
Beside, incentives come from the soul's self;
The rest avail not. Why do I need you?
What wife had Rafael, or has Agnolo?
In this world, who can do a thing, will not;
And who would do it, cannot, I perceive:
Yet the will's somewhat—somewhat, too, the power—
And thus we half-men struggle. At the end,   [140]
God, I conclude, compensates, punishes.
'Tis safer for me, if the award be strict,
That I am something underrated here,
Poor this long while, despised, to speak the truth.
I dared not, do you know, leave home all day,
For fear of chancing on the Paris lords.
The best is when they pass and look aside;
But they speak sometimes; I must bear it all.
Well may they speak! That Francis, that first time,
And that long festal year at Fontainebleau!   [150]
I surely then could sometimes leave the ground,

260

Put on the glory, Rafael's daily wear,
In that humane great monarch's golden look,—
One finger in his beard or twisted curl
Over his mouth's good mark that made the smile,
One arm about my shoulder, round my neck,
The jingle of his gold chain in my ear,
I painting proudly with his breath on me,
All his court round him, seeing with his eyes,
Such frank French eyes, and such a fire of souls   [160]
Profuse, my hand kept plying by those hearts,—
And, best of all, this, this, this face beyond,
This in the background, waiting on my work,
To crown the issue with a last reward!
A good time, was it not, my kingly days?
And had you not grown restless . . . but I know—
'Tis done and past; 'twas right, my instinct said;
Too live the life grew, golden and not gray:
And I'm the weak-eyed bat no sun should tempt
Out of the grange whose four walls make his world. [170]
How could it end in any other way?
You called me, and I came home to your heart.
The triumph was, to have ended there; then, if
I reached it ere the triumph, what is lost?
Let my hands frame your face in your hair's gold,
You beautiful Lucrezia that are mine!
"Rafael did this, Andrea painted that;
The Roman's is the better when you pray,
But still the other's Virgin was his wife"—
Men will excuse me. I am glad to judge   [180]
Both pictures in your presence; clearer grows
My better fortune, I resolve to think.
For, do you know, Lucrezia, as God lives,
Said one day Agnolo, his very self,
To Rafael . . . I have known it all these years . . .
(When the young man was flaming out his thoughts
Upon a palace-wall for Rome to see,
Too lifted up in heart because of it)
"Friend, there's a certain sorry little scrub
Goes up and down our Florence, none cares how,   [190]

Who, were he set to plan and execute
As you are, pricked on by your popes and kings,
Would bring the sweat into that brow of yours!"
To Rafael's!—And indeed the arm is wrong.
I hardly dare . . . yet, only you to see,
Give the chalk here—quick, thus the line should go!
Ay, but the soul! he's Rafael! rub it out!
Still, all I care for, if he spoke the truth,
(What he? why, who but Michel Agnolo?
Do you forget already words like those?)   [200]
If really there was such a chance so lost,—
Is, whether you're—not grateful—but more pleased.
Well, let me think so. And you smile indeed!
This hour has been an hour! Another smile?
If you would sit thus by me every night
I should work better, do you comprehend?
I mean that I should earn more, give you more.
See, it is settled dusk now; there's a star;
Morello's gone, the watch-lights show the wall,
The cue-owls speak the name we call them by.   [210]
Come from the window, love,—come in, at last,
Inside the melancholy little house
We built to be so gay with. God is just.
King Francis may forgive me: oft at nights
When I look up from painting, eyes tired out,
The walls become illumined, brick from brick
Distinct, instead of mortar, fierce bright gold,
That gold of his I did cement them with!
Let us but love each other. Must you go?
That cousin here again? he waits outside?   [220]
Must see you—you, and not with me? Those loans?
More gaming debts to pay? you smiled for that?
Well, let smiles buy me! have you more to spend?
While hand and eye and something of a heart
Are left me, work's my ware, and what's it worth?
I'll pay my fancy. Only let me sit
The gray remainder of the evening out,
Idle, you call it, and muse perfectly
How I could paint, were I but back in France,

One picture, just one more—the Virgin's face, [230]
Not your's this time! I want you at my side
To hear them—that is, Michel Agnolo—
Judge all I do and tell you of its worth.
Will you? To-morrow, satisfy your friend.
I take the subjects for his corridor,
Finish the potrait out of hand—there, there,
And throw him in another thing or two
If he demurs; the whole should prove enough
To pay for this same cousin's freak. Beside,
What's better and what's all I care about, [240]
Get you the thirteen scudi for the ruff!
Love, does that please you? Ah, but what does he,
The cousin! what does he to please you more?

I am grown peaceful as old age to-night.
I regret little, I would change still less.
Since there my past life lies, why alter it?
The very wrong to Francis!—it is true
I took his coin, was tempted and complied,
And built this house and sinned, and all is said.
My father and my mother died of want. [250]
Well, had I riches of my own? you see
How one gets rich! Let each one bear his lot.
They were born poor, lived poor, and poor they died:
And I have labored somewhat in my time
And not been paid profusely. Some good son
Paint my two hundred pictures—let him try!
No doubt, there's something strikes a balance. Yes,
You loved me quite enough, it seems to-night.
This must suffice me here. What would one have?
In heaven, perhaps, new chances, one more chance— [260]
Four great walls in the New Jerusalem,
Meted on each side by the angel's reed,
For Leonard, Rafael, Agnolo, and me
To cover—the three first without a wife,
While I have mine! So—still they overcome
Because there's still Lucrezia,—as I choose.

Again the cousin's whistle! Go, my love.

———

29. My face, my moon:

"Once, like the moon, I made
The ever-shifting currents of the blood
According to my humour ebb and flow."
>   —Cleopatra, in Tennyson's 'A Dream of Fair
>   Women'.

"You are the powerful moon of my blood's sea,
To make it ebb or flow into my face
As your looks change."
>   —Ford and Decker's 'Witch of Edmonton'.

35. A common grayness: Andrea del Sarto was distinguished for his skill in chiaro-oscuro.

82. low-pulsed forthright craftsman's hand: "Andrea del Sarto's was, after all, but the 'low-pulsed forthright craftsman's hand', and therefore his perfect art does not touch our hearts like that of Fra Bartolommeo, who occupies about the same position with regard to the great masters of the century as Andrea del Sarto. Fra Bartolommeo spoke from his heart. He was moved by the spirit, so to speak, to express his pure and holy thoughts in beautiful language, and the ideal that presented itself to his mind, and from which he, equally with Raphael, worked, approached almost as closely as Raphael's to that abstract beauty after which they both longed. Andrea del Sarto had no such longing: he was content with the loveliness of earth. This he could understand and imitate in its fullest perfection, and therefore he troubled himself but little about the 'wondrous paterne' laid up in heaven. Many of his Madonnas have greater beauty, strictly speaking, than those of Bartolommeo, or even of Raphael; but we miss in them that mysterious spiritual loveliness that gives the latter their chief charm." —Heaton's History of Painting.

93. Morello: the highest of the spurs of the Apennines to the north of Florence.

96. Speak as they please, what does the mountain care?: it's beyond their criticism.

105. The Urbinate: Raphael Santi, born 1483, in Urbino. Andrea sees in Raphael, whose technique was inferior to his own, his superior, as he reached above and through his art—for it gives way.

106. George Vasari: see note under St. 9 of 'Old Pictures in Florence'.

120. Nay, Love, you did give all I asked: it must be understood that his wife has replied with pique, to what he said in the two preceding lines.

129. by the future: when placed by, in comparison with, the future.

130. Agnolo: Michael Angelo (more correctly, Agnolo) Buonarotti. See note under St. 30 of 'Old Pictures in Florence'.

146. For fear of chancing on the Paris lords: by reason of his breaking the faith he had pledged to Francis I. of France, and using for his own purposes, or his wife's, the money with which the king had entrusted him to purchase works of art in Italy.

149-165. That Francis, that first time: he thinks with regret of the king and of his honored and inspiring stay at his court.

161. by those hearts: along with, by the aid of.

173. The triumph was . . . there: i.e., in your heart.

174. ere the triumph: in France.

177. Rafael did this, . . . was his wife: a remark ascribed to some critic.

198. If he spoke the truth: i.e., about himself.

199. What he: do you ask?

202. all I care for . . . is whether you're.

209. Morello's gone: its outlines are lost in the dusk. See v. 93.

218. That gold of his: see note to v. 146.

220. That cousin here again?: one of Lucrezia's gallants is referred to, to pay whose gaming debts, it appears, she has obtained money of her husband. It must be understood that this gallant whistles here. See last verse of the monologue.

263. Leonard: Leonardo da Vinci.

Fra Lippo Lippi.

I am poor brother Lippo, by your leave!
You need not clap your torches to my face.
Zooks, what's to blame? you think you see a monk!
What, 'tis past midnight, and you go the rounds,
And here you catch me at an alley's end
Where sportive ladies leave their doors ajar?
The Carmine's my cloister: hunt it up,
Do,—harry out, if you must show your zeal,
Whatever rat, there, haps on his wrong hole,
And nip each softling of a wee white mouse,   [10]
'Weke, weke', that's crept to keep him company!
Aha! you know your betters? Then, you'll take
Your hand away that's fiddling on my throat,
And please to know me likewise. Who am I?
Why, one, sir, who is lodging with a friend
Three streets off—he's a certain . . . how d'ye call?
Master—a . . . Cosimo of the Medici,
I' the house that caps the corner. Boh! you were best!
Remember and tell me, the day you're hanged,
How you affected such a gullet's-gripe!   [20]
But you, sir, it concerns you that your knaves
Pick up a manner, nor discredit you:
Zooks, are we pilchards, that they sweep the streets
And count fair prize what comes into their net?
He's Judas to a tittle, that man is!
Just such a face! Why, sir, you make amends.
Lord, I'm not angry! Bid your hangdogs go
Drink out this quarter-florin to the health
Of the munificent House that harbors me
(And many more beside, lads! more beside!)   [30]
And all's come square again. I'd like his face—
His, elbowing on his comrade in the door
With the pike and lantern,—for the slave that holds
John Baptist's head a-dangle by the hair
With one hand ("Look you, now", as who should say)
And his weapon in the other, yet unwiped!
It's not your chance to have a bit of chalk,

A wood-coal or the like? or you should see!
Yes, I'm the painter, since you style me so.
What, brother Lippo's doings, up and down,   [40]
You know them, and they take you? like enough!
I saw the proper twinkle in your eye—
'Tell you, I liked your looks at very first.
Let's sit and set things straight now, hip to haunch.
Here's spring come, and the nights one makes up bands
To roam the town and sing out carnival,
And I've been three weeks shut within my mew,
A-painting for the great man, saints and saints
And saints again. I could not paint all night—
Ouf! I leaned out of window for fresh air.   [50]
There came a hurry of feet and little feet,
A sweep of lute-strings, laughs, and whifts of song—
'Flower o' the broom,
Take away love, and our earth is a tomb!
Flower o' the quince,
I let Lisa go, and what good in life since?
Flower o' the thyme'—and so on. Round they went.
Scarce had they turned the corner when a titter
Like the skipping of rabbits by moonlight,—three slim shapes,
And a face that looked up . . . zooks, sir, flesh and blood,   [60]
That's all I'm made of! Into shreds it went,
Curtain and counterpane and coverlet,
All the bed-furniture—a dozen knots,
There was a ladder! Down I let myself,
Hands and feet, scrambling somehow, and so dropped,
And after them. I came up with the fun
Hard by Saint Lawrence, hail fellow, well met,—
'Flower o' the rose,
If I've been merry, what matter who knows?'
And so, as I was stealing back again,   [70]
To get to bed and have a bit of sleep
Ere I rise up to-morrow and go work
On Jerome knocking at his poor old breast
With his great round stone to subdue the flesh,
You snap me of the sudden. Ah, I see!
Though your eye twinkles still, you shake your head—

Mine's shaved—a monk, you say—the sting's in that!
If Master Cosimo announced himself,
Mum's the word naturally; but a monk!
Come, what am I a beast for? tell us, now!   [80]
I was a baby when my mother died
And father died and left me in the street.
I starved there, God knows how, a year or two
On fig-skins, melon-parings, rinds and shucks,
Refuse and rubbish. One fine frosty day,
My stomach being empty as your hat,
The wind doubled me up and down I went.
Old aunt Lapaccia trussed me with one hand
(Its fellow was a stinger, as I knew),
And so along the wall, over the bridge,   [90]
By the straight cut to the convent. Six words there,
While I stood munching my first bread that month:
"So, boy, you're minded," quoth the good fat father
Wiping his own mouth, 'twas refection-time,—
"To quit this very miserable world?
Will you renounce" . . ."the mouthful of bread?" thought I;
By no means! Brief, they made a monk of me;
I did renounce the world, its pride and greed,
Palace, farm, villa, shop, and banking-house,
Trash, such as these poor devils of Medici   [100]
Have given their hearts to—all at eight years old.
Well, sir, I found in time, you may be sure,
'Twas not for nothing—the good bellyful,
The warm serge and the rope that goes all round,
And day-long blessed idleness beside!
"Let's see what the urchin's fit for"—that came next.
Not overmuch their way, I must confess.
Such a to-do! They tried me with their books:
Lord, they'd have taught me Latin in pure waste!
'Flower o' the clove,   [110]
All the Latin I construe is, "Amo" I love!'
But, mind you, when a boy starves in the streets
Eight years together as my fortune was,
Watching folk's faces to know who will fling
The bit of half-stripped grape-bunch he desires,

And who will curse or kick him for his pains,—
Which gentleman processional and fine,
Holding a candle to the Sacrament,
Will wink and let him lift a plate and catch
The droppings of the wax to sell again,   [120]
Or holla for the Eight and have him whipped,—
How say I?—nay, which dog bites, which lets drop
His bone from the heap of offal in the street,—
Why, soul and sense of him grow sharp alike,
He learns the look of things, and none the less
For admonition from the hunger-pinch.
I had a store of such remarks, be sure,
Which, after I found leisure, turned to use:
I drew men's faces on my copy-books,
Scrawled them within the antiphonary's marge,   [130]
Joined legs and arms to the long music-notes,
Found eyes and nose and chin for A's and B's,
And made a string of pictures of the world
Betwixt the ins and outs of verb and noun,
On the wall, the bench, the door. The monks looked black.
"Nay," quoth the Prior, "turn him out, d'ye say?
In no wise. Lose a crow and catch a lark.
What if at last we get our man of parts,
We Carmelites, like those Camaldolese
And Preaching Friars, to do our church up fine   [140]
And put the front on it that ought to be!"
And hereupon he bade me daub away.
Thank you! my head being crammed, the walls a blank,
Never was such prompt disemburdening.
First every sort of monk, the black and white,
I drew them, fat and lean: then, folks at church,
From good old gossips waiting to confess
Their cribs of barrel-droppings, candle-ends,—
To the breathless fellow at the altar-foot,
Fresh from his murder, safe and sitting there   [150]
With the little children round him in a row
Of admiration, half for his beard, and half
For that white anger of his victim's son
Shaking a fist at him with one fierce arm,

Signing himself with the other because of Christ
(Whose sad face on the cross sees only this
After the passion of a thousand years),
Till some poor girl, her apron o'er her head
(Which the intense eyes looked through), came at eve
On tiptoe, said a word, dropped in a loaf,   [160]
Her pair of ear-rings and a bunch of flowers
(The brute took growling), prayed, and so was gone.
I painted all, then cried, "'Tis ask and have;
Choose, for more's ready!"—laid the ladder flat,
And showed my covered bit of cloister-wall.
The monks closed in a circle and praised loud
Till checked, taught what to see and not to see,
Being simple bodies,—"That's the very man!
Look at the boy who stoops to pat the dog!
That woman's like the Prior's niece who comes   [170]
To care about his asthma: it's the life!"
But there my triumph's straw-fire flared and funked;
Their betters took their turn to see and say:
The prior and the learned pulled a face
And stopped all that in no time. "How? what's here?
Quite from the mark of painting, bless us all!
Faces, arms, legs, and bodies like the true
As much as pea and pea! it's devil's game!
Your business is not to catch men with show,
With homage to the perishable clay,   [180]
But lift them over it, ignore it all,
Make them forget there's such a thing as flesh.
Your business is to paint the souls of men—
Man's soul, and it's a fire, smoke . . . no, it's not . . .
It's vapor done up like a new-born babe—
(In that shape when you die it leaves your mouth),
It's . . . well, what matters talking, it's the soul!
Give us no more of body than shows soul!
Here's Giotto, with his Saint a-praising God,
That sets us praising,—why not stop with him?   [190]
Why put all thoughts of praise out of our head
With wonder at lines, colors, and what not?
Paint the soul, never mind the legs and arms!

Rub all out, try at it a second time!
Oh, that white smallish female with the breasts,
She's just my niece . . . Herodias, I would say,—
Who went and danced, and got men's heads cut off!
Have it all out!" Now, is this sense, I ask?
A fine way to paint soul, by painting body
So ill, the eye can't stop there, must go further   [200]
And can't fare worse! Thus, yellow does for white
When what you put for yellow's simply black,
And any sort of meaning looks intense
When all beside itself means and looks naught.
Why can't a painter lift each foot in turn,
Left foot and right foot, go a double step,
Make his flesh liker and his soul more like,
Both in their order? Take the prettiest face,
The Prior's niece . . . patron-saint—is it so pretty
You can't discover if it means hope, fear,   [210]
Sorrow or joy? won't beauty go with these?
Suppose I've made her eyes all right and blue,
Can't I take breath and try to add life's flash,
And then add soul and heighten them threefold?
Or say there's beauty with no soul at all—
(I never saw it—put the case the same—)
If you get simple beauty and naught else,
You get about the best thing God invents:
That's somewhat: and you'll find the soul you have missed,
Within yourself, when you return him thanks.   [220]
"Rub all out!" Well, well, there's my life, in short,
And so the thing has gone on ever since.
I'm grown a man no doubt, I've broken bounds:
You should not take a fellow eight years old
And make him swear to never kiss the girls.
I'm my own master, paint now as I please—
Having a friend, you see, in the Corner-house!
Lord, it's fast holding by the rings in front—
Those great rings serve more purposes than just
To plant a flag in, or tie up a horse!   [230]
And yet the old schooling sticks, the old grave eyes
Are peeping o'er my shoulder as I work,

The heads shake still—"It's art's decline, my son!
You're not of the true painters, great and old;
Brother Angelico's the man, you'll find;
Brother Lorenzo stands his single peer:
Fag on at flesh, you'll never make the third!"
'Flower o' the pine,
You keep your mistr . . . manners, and I'll stick to mine!'
I'm not the third, then: bless us, they must know!   [240]
Don't you think they're the likeliest to know,
They with their Latin? So, I swallow my rage,
Clinch my teeth, suck my lips in tight, and paint
To please them—sometimes do, and sometimes don't;
For, doing most, there's pretty sure to come
A turn, some warm eve finds me at my saints—
A laugh, a cry, the business of the world—
('Flower o' the peach,
Death for us all, and his own life for each!')
And my whole soul revolves, the cup runs over,   [250]
The world and life's too big to pass for a dream,
And I do these wild things in sheer despite,
And play the fooleries you catch me at,
In pure rage! The old mill-horse, out at grass
After hard years, throws up his stiff heels so,
Although the miller does not preach to him
The only good of grass is to make chaff.
What would men have? Do they like grass or no—
May they or mayn't they? all I want's the thing
Settled forever one way. As it is,   [260]
You tell too many lies and hurt yourself:
You don't like what you only like too much,
You do like what, if given you at your word,
You find abundantly detestable.
For me, I think I speak as I was taught;
I always see the garden, and God there
A-making man's wife: and, my lesson learned,
The value and significance of flesh,
I can't unlearn ten minutes afterwards.

You understand me: I'm a beast, I know.   [270]
But see, now—why, I see as certainly
As that the morning-star's about to shine,
What will hap some day. We've a youngster here
Comes to our convent, studies what I do,
Slouches and stares and lets no atom drop:
His name is Guidi—he'll not mind the monks—
They call him Hulking Tom, he lets them talk—
He picks my practice up—he'll paint apace,
I hope so—though I never live so long,
I know what's sure to follow. You be judge!   [280]
You speak no Latin more than I, belike;
However, you're my man, you've seen the world
—The beauty and the wonder and the power,
The shapes of things, their colors, lights, and shades,
Changes, surprises,—and God made it all!
—For what? Do you feel thankful, ay or no,
For this fair town's face, yonder river's line,
The mountain round it and the sky above,
Much more the figures of man, woman, child,
These are the frame to? What's it all about?   [290]
To be passed over, despised? or dwelt upon,
Wondered at? oh, this last of course!—you say.
But why not do as well as say,—paint these
Just as they are, careless what comes of it?
God's works—paint any one, and count it crime
To let a truth slip. Don't object, "His works
Are here already; nature is complete:
Suppose you reproduce her—(which you can't)
There's no advantage! you must beat her, then."
For, don't you mark? we're made so that we love   [300]
First when we see them painted, things we have passed
Perhaps a hundred times nor cared to see;
And so they are better, painted—better to us,
Which is the same thing. Art was given for that;
God uses us to help each other so,
Lending our minds out. Have you noticed, now
Your cullion's hanging face? A bit of chalk,
And trust me but you should, though! How much more

273

If I drew higher things with the same truth!
That were to take the Prior's pulpit-place,   [310]
Interpret God to all of you! Oh, oh,
It makes me mad to see what men shall do
And we in our graves! This world's no blot for us,
Nor blank; it means intensely, and means good:
To find its meaning is my meat and drink.
"Ay, but you don't so instigate to prayer!"
Strikes in the Prior: "when your meaning's plain
It does not say to folks—remember matins,
Or, mind your fast next Friday!" Why, for this
What need of art at all? A skull and bones,   [320]
Two bits of stick nailed cross-wise, or, what's best,
A bell to chime the hour with, does as well.
I painted a Saint Laurence six months since
At Prato, splashed the fresco in fine style:
"How looks my painting, now the scaffold's down?"
I ask a brother: "Hugely," he returns—
"Already not one phiz of your three slaves
Who turn the Deacon off his toasted side,
But's scratched and prodded to our heart's content,
The pious people have so eased their own   [330]
With coming to say prayers there in a rage:
We get on fast to see the bricks beneath.
Expect another job this time next year,
For pity and religion grow i' the crowd—
Your painting serves its purpose!" Hang the fools!

—That is—you'll not mistake an idle word
Spoke in a huff by a poor monk, Got wot,
Tasting the air this spicy night which turns
The unaccustomed head like Chianti wine!
Oh, the church knows! don't misreport me, now!   [340]
It's natural a poor monk out of bounds
Should have his apt word to excuse himself:
And hearken how I plot to make amends.
I have bethought me: I shall paint a piece
. . . There's for you! Give me six months, then go, see
Something in Sant' Ambrogio's! Bless the nuns!

They want a cast o' my office. I shall paint
God in the midst, Madonna and her babe,
Ringed by a bowery, flowery angel-brood,
Lilies and vestments and white faces, sweet   [350]
As puff on puff of grated orris-root
When ladies crowd to church at midsummer.
And then i' the front, of course a saint or two—
Saint John, because he saves the Florentines,
Saint Ambrose, who puts down in black and white
The convent's friends and gives them a long day,
And Job, I must have him there past mistake,
The man of Uz (and Us without the z,
Painters who need his patience). Well, all these
Secured at their devotion, up shall come   [360]
Out of a corner when you least expect,
As one by a dark stair into a great light,
Music and talking, who but Lippo! I!—
Mazed, motionless, and moon-struck—I'm the man!
Back I shrink—what is this I see and hear?
I, caught up with my monk's things by mistake,
My old serge gown and rope that goes all round,
I, in this presence, this pure company!
Where's a hole, where's a corner for escape?
Then steps a sweet angelic slip of a thing   [370]
Forward, puts out a soft palm—"Not so fast!"
—Addresses the celestial presence, "nay—
He made you and devised you, after all,
Though he's none of you! could Saint John there, draw—
His camel-hair make up a painting-brush?
We come to brother Lippo for all that,
Iste perfecit opus!" So, all smile—
I shuffle sideways with my blushing face
Under the cover of a hundred wings
Thrown like a spread of kirtles when you're gay   [380]
And play hot cockles, all the doors being shut,
Till, wholly unexpected, in there pops
The hot-head husband! Thus I scuttle off
To some safe bench behind, not letting go
The palm of her, the little lily thing

That spoke the good word for me in the nick,
Like the Prior's niece . . . Saint Lucy, I would say.
And so all's saved for me, and for the church
A pretty picture gained. Go, six months hence!
Your hand, sir, and good-bye: no lights, no lights!   [390]
The street's hushed, and I know my own way back,
Don't fear me! There's the gray beginning. Zooks!

———

17. Cosimo of the Medici: Cosimo, or Cosmo, de' Medici, surnamed the Elder, a celebrated Florentine statesman, and a patron of learning and the arts; b. 1389, d. 1464.

23. pilchards: a kind of fish.

34. John Baptist's head: an imaginary picture.

67. Saint Lawrence: church of San Lorenzo, in Florence, famous for the tombs of the Medici, adorned with Michel Angelo's Day and Night, Morning and Evening, etc. See 'Hawthorne's Italian Note-Books'.

88. Old aunt Lapaccia: Mona Lapaccia, his father's sister.

121. the Eight: 'gli Otto di guerra', surnamed 'i Santi', the Saints; a magistracy composed of Eight citizens, instituted by the Florentines, during their war with the Church, in 1376, for the administration of the city government. Two were chosen from the 'Signori', three, from the 'Mediocri' (Middle Classes), and three, from the 'Bassi' (Lower Classes). For their subsequent history, see 'Le Istorie Fiorentine di Niccolo Machiavelli'.

122. How say I?:—nay, worse than that, which dog bites, etc.

127. remarks: observations.

139. Camaldolese: monks of the celebrated convent of Camaldoli.

143. Thank you!: there's a remark interposed here by one of the men, perhaps "YOU'RE no dauber", to which he replies, "Thank you".

145 et seq. The realistic painter, who disdains nothing, is shown here.

189. Giotto di Bondone (1266-1337): a pupil of Cimabue, and regarded as the principal reviver of art in Italy. He was a personal friend of Dante. See note under 'Old Pictures in Florence', St. 2.

223. I'm grown a man no doubt, I've broken bounds: all the editions are so punctuated; but it seems the comma should be after "man", connecting "no doubt" with "I've broken bounds".

235. "Giovanni da Fiesole, better known as Fra Angelico (1387-1455). Angelico was incomparably the greatest of the distinctively mediaeval school, whose 'dicta' the Prior in the poem has all at his tongue's end. To 'paint the souls of men', to 'make them forget there's such a thing as flesh', was the end of his art. And, side by side with Angelico, Masaccio painted. His short life taught him a different lesson—'the value and significance of flesh'. He would paint by preference the BODIES of men, and would give us NO MORE OF SOUL than the body can reveal. So he 'laboured', saith the chronicler, 'in nakeds', and his frescoes mark an epoch in art."—Ernest Bradford (B. S. Illustrations).

"One artist in the seclusion of his cloister, remained true to the traditions and mode of expression of the middle ages, into which, nevertheless, the incomparable beauty and feeling of his nature breathed fresh life. Fra Giovanni Angelico, called da Fiesole from the place of his birth, occupies an entirely exceptional position. He is the late-blooming flower of an almost by-gone time amid the pulsations of a new life. Never, in the whole range of pictorial art, have the inspired fervor of Christian feeling, the angelic beauty and purity of which the soul is capable, been so gloriously interpreted as in his works. The exquisite atmosphere of an almost supernaturally ideal life surrounds his pictures, irradiates the rosy features of his youthful faces, or greets us, like the peace of God, in the dignified figures of his devout old men. His prevailing themes are the humility of soul of those who have joyfully accepted the will of God, and the tranquil Sabbath calm of those who are lovingly consecrated to the service of the Highest. The movement and the changing course of life, the energy of passion and action concern him not."—'Outlines of the History of Art'. By Dr. Wilh. Luebke.

236. Lorenzo Monaco: a monk of the order of Camaldoli; a conservative artist of the time, who adhered to the manner of Taddeo Gaddi and his disciples, but Fra Angelico appears likewise to have influenced him.

238. Flower o' the pine, etc.: this snatch of song applies to what he has just been talking about: you have your own notions of art, and I have mine.

276. Tommaso Guidi (1401-1428), better known as Masaccio, i.e., Tommasaccio, Slovenly or Hulking Tom. "From his time, and forward," says Mr. Ernest Radford (B. S. Illustrations), "religious painting in the old sense was at an end. Painters no longer attempted to transcend nature, but to copy her, and to copy her in her loveliest aspects. The breach between the old order and the new was complete." The poet makes him learn of Lippi, not, as Vasari states, Lippi of him.

"When Browning wrote this poem, he knew that the mastership or pupilship of Fra Lippo to Masaccio (called 'Guidi' in the poem), and vice versa, was a moot point; but in making Fra Lippi the master, he followed the best authority he had access to, the last edition of Vasari, as he stated in a Letter to the 'Pall Mall' at the time, in answer to M. Etienne [a writer in the 'Revue des deux Mondes'.] Since then, he finds that the latest enquirer into the subject, Morelli, believes the fact is the other way, and that Fra Lippo was the pupil."—B. Soc. Papers, Pt. II, p. 160.

The letter to the 'Pall Mall Gazette' I have not seen. M. Etienne's Article is in Tome 85, pp. 704-735, of the 'Revue des Deux Mondes', 1870, and the letter probably appeared soon after its publication. What edition of Vasari is referred to, in the above note, as the last, is uncertain; but in Vasari's own editions of 1550 and 1568, and in Mrs. Foster's translation, 1855, Lippi is made the pupil, and not the master, of Masaccio.

323. Saint Laurence: suffered martyrdom in the reign of the Emperor Valerian, A.D. 258. He was broiled to death on a gridiron.

327. Already not one phiz of your three slaves . . . but's scratched: the people are so indignant at what they are doing, in the life-like picture.

336. That is—: he fears he has spoken too plainly, and will be reported.

339. Chianti: a wine named from the part of Italy so called.

345. There's for you: he tips them.

346. Sant' Ambrogio's: a convent in Florence.

354. Saint John: John the Baptist is meant; see v. 375.

355. Saint Ambrose: born about 340; made archbishop of Milan in 374; died 397; instituted the 'Ambrosian Chant'.

377. Iste perfecit opus!: this is on a scroll, in the picture, held by the "sweet angelic slip of a thing".

389. The picture referred to is 'The Coronation of the Virgin', in the 'Accademia delle Belle Arti', in Florence. There is a photograph of it in 'Illustrations to Browning's Poems', Part I., published by the Browning Society, with an interesting description of the picture, by Mr. Ernest Radford. There's no "babe" in the picture.

392. Zooks!: it's high time I was back and in bed, that my night-larking be not known.

A Face.

If one could have that little head of hers
Painted upon a background of pale gold,
Such as the Tuscan's early art prefers!
No shade encroaching on the matchless mould
Of those two lips, which should be opening soft
In the pure profile; not as when she laughs,
For that spoils all: but rather as if aloft
Yon hyacinth, she loves so, leaned its staff's
Burthen of honey-colored buds, to kiss
And capture 'twixt the lips apart for this.   [10]
Then her lithe neck, three fingers might surround,
How it should waver, on the pale gold ground,
Up to the fruit-shaped, perfect chin it lifts!
I know, Correggio loves to mass, in rifts
Of heaven, his angel faces, orb on orb
Breaking its outline, burning shades absorb:
But these are only massed there, I should think,
Waiting to see some wonder momently
Grow out, stand full, fade slow against the sky
(That's the pale ground you'd see this sweet face by),   [20]
All heaven, meanwhile, condensed into one eye
Which fears to lose the wonder, should it wink.

1. If one could have: Oh, if one could only have, etc.

9, 10. to kiss and capture: gerundives: to be kissed and captured.

14. Correggio: Antonio Allegri da Correggio, born 1494, died 1534. "He was the first master—the Venetians notwithstanding—to take a scheme of color and chiaro-scuro as the 'raison d'etre' of a complete composition, and his brush, responding to the idea, blends light and shade in delicious harmony."—Woltmann and Woermann's 'History of Painting'.

The Bishop orders his Tomb.

[Rome, 15—.]

—

* The tomb is imaginary; though it is said to be pointed out to visitors to Saint Praxed's who desire particularly to see it.

—

Vanity, saith the preacher, vanity!
Draw round my bed: is Anselm keeping back?
Nephews—sons mine . . . ah God, I know not! Well—
She, men would have to be your mother once,
Old Gandolf envied me, so fair she was!
What's done is done, and she is dead beside,
Dead long ago, and I am Bishop since,
And as she died so must we die ourselves,
And thence ye may perceive the world's a dream.
Life, how and what is it? As here I lie   [10]
In this state-chamber, dying by degrees,
Hours and long hours in the dead night, I ask
"Do I live, am I dead?" Peace, peace seems all.
Saint Praxed's ever was the church for peace;
And so, about this tomb of mine. I fought
With tooth and nail to save my niche, ye know:
—Old Gandolf cozened me, despite my care;
Shrewd was that snatch from out the corner South
He graced his carrion with, God curse the same!

Yet still my niche is not so cramped but thence   [20]
One sees the pulpit on the epistle-side,
And somewhat of the choir, those silent seats,
And up into the aery dome where live
The angels, and a sunbeam's sure to lurk;
And I shall fill my slab of basalt there,
And 'neath my tabernacle take my rest,
With those nine columns round me, two and two,
The odd one at my feet where Anselm stands:
Peach-blossom marble all, the rare, the ripe
As fresh-poured red wine of a mighty pulse.   [30]
—Old Gandolf with his paltry onion-stone,
Put me where I may look at him! True peach,
Rosy and flawless: how I earned the prize!
Draw close: that conflagration of my church
—What then? So much was saved if aught were missed!
My sons, ye would not be my death? Go dig
The white-grape vineyard where the oil-press stood,
Drop water gently till the surface sink,
And if ye find . . . Ah God, I know not, I! . . .
Bedded in store of rotten fig-leaves soft,   [40]
And corded up in a tight olive-frail,
Some lump, ah God, of lapis lazuli,
Big as a Jew's head cut off at the nape,
Blue as a vein o'er the Madonna's breast . . .
Sons, all have I bequeathed you, villas, all,
That brave Frascati villa with its bath,
So, let the blue lump poise between my knees,
Like God the Father's globe on both his hands
Ye worship in the Jesu Church so gay,
For Gandolf shall not choose but see and burst!   [50]
Swift as a weaver's shuttle fleet our years:
Man goeth to the grave, and where is he?
Did I say, basalt for my slab, sons? Black—
'Twas ever antique-black I meant! How else
Shall ye contrast my frieze to come beneath?
The bas-relief in bronze ye promised me,
Those Pans and Nymphs ye wot of, and perchance
Some tripod, thyrsus, with a vase or so,

The Saviour at his sermon on the mount,
Saint Praxed in a glory, and one Pan   [60]
Ready to twitch the Nymph's last garment off,
And Moses with the tables . . . but I know
Ye mark me not! What do they whisper thee,
Child of my bowels, Anselm? Ah, ye hope
To revel down my villas while I gasp
Bricked o'er with beggar's mouldy travertine
Which Gandolf from his tomb-top chuckles at!
Nay, boys, ye love me—all of jasper, then!
'Tis jasper ye stand pledged to, lest I grieve
My bath must needs be left behind, alas!   [70]
One block, pure green as a pistachio-nut,
There's plenty jasper somewhere in the world—
And have I not Saint Praxed's ear to pray
Horses for ye, and brown Greek manuscripts,
And mistresses with great smooth marbly limbs?
—That's if ye carve my epitaph aright,
Choice Latin, picked phrase, Tully's every word,
No gaudy ware like Gandolf's second line—
Tully, my masters? Ulpian serves his need!
And then how I shall lie through centuries,   [80]
And hear the blessed mutter of the mass,
And see God made and eaten all day long,
And feel the steady candle-flame, and taste
Good strong thick stupefying incense-smoke!
For as I lie here, hours of the dead night,
Dying in state and by such slow degrees,
I fold my arms as if they clasped a crook,
And stretch my feet forth straight as stone can point,
And let the bedclothes, for a mortcloth, drop
Into great laps and folds of sculptor's work: [90]
And as yon tapers dwindle, and strange thoughts
Grow, with a certain humming in my ears,
About the life before I lived this life,
And this life too, popes, cardinals, and priests,
Saint Praxed at his sermon on the mount,
Your tall pale mother with her talking eyes,
And new-found agate urns as fresh as day,

And marble's language, Latin pure, discreet,
—Aha, ELUCESCEBAT quoth our friend?
No Tully, said I, Ulpian at the best!   [100]
Evil and brief hath been my pilgrimage.
All lapis, all, sons! Else I give the Pope
My villas! Will ye ever eat my heart?
Ever your eyes were as a lizard's quick,
They glitter like your mother's for my soul,
Or ye would heighten my impoverished frieze,
Piece out its starved design, and fill my vase
With grapes, and add a visor and a Term,
And to the tripod ye would tie a lynx
That in his struggle throws the thyrsus down,   [110]
To comfort me on my entablature
Whereon I am to lie till I must ask
"Do I live, am I dead?" There, leave me, there!
For ye have stabbed me with ingratitude
To death: ye wish it—God, ye wish it! Stone—
Gritstone, a-crumble! Clammy squares which sweat
As if the corpse they keep were oozing through—
And no more lapis to delight the world!
Well go! I bless ye. Fewer tapers there,
But in a row: and, going, turn your backs   [120]
—Ay, like departing altar-ministrants,
And leave me in my church, the church for peace,
That I may watch at leisure if he leers—
Old Gandolf, at me, from his onion-stone,
As still he envied me, so fair she was!

—

1. Vanity, saith the preacher, vanity!: "The Bishop on his death-bed has reached Solomon's conclusion that 'all is vanity'. So he proceeds to specify his particular vanity in the choice of a tombstone." —N. Brit. Rev. 34, p. 367. "In 'The Palace of Art', Mr. Tennyson has shown the despair and isolation of a soul surrounded by all luxuries of beauty, and living in and for them; but in the end the soul is redeemed and converted to the simple humanities of earth. Mr. Browning has shown that such a sense of isolation and such despair are by no means inevitable; there is a death in life which

consists in tranquil satisfaction, a calm pride in the soul's dwelling among the world's gathered treasures of stateliness and beauty. . . . So the unbelieving and worldly spirit of the dying Bishop, who orders his tomb at Saint Praxed's, his sense of the vanity of the world simply because the world is passing out of his reach, the regretful memory of the pleasures of his youth, the envious spite towards Gandolf, who robbed him of the best position for a tomb, and the dread lest his reputed sons should play him false and fail to carry out his designs, are united with a perfect appreciation of Renaissance art, and a luxurious satisfaction, which even a death-bed cannot destroy, in the splendor of voluptuous form and color."
—Edward Dowden.

46. Frascati: a town of central Italy, near the site of the ancient Tusculum, ten or twelve miles S. E. of Rome; it has many fine old villas.

53. Did I say, basalt for my slab, sons?: Note how all things else, even such reflections as are expressed in the two preceding verses, are incidental with the Bishop; his poor, art-besotted mind turns abruptly to the black basalt which he craves for the slab of his tomb; and see vv. 101, 102.

66. travertine: see note to v. 67 of 'Pictor Ignotus'.

71. pistachio-nut: or, green almond.

79. Ulpian: Domitius Ulpianus, one of the greatest of Roman jurists, and chief adviser of the emperor, Alexander Severus; born about 170, died 228; belongs to the Brazen age of Roman literature.

95. Saint Praxed at his sermon on the mount: the poor dying Bishop, in the disorder of his mind, makes a 'lapsus linguae' here; see v. 59.

99. elucescebat: "he was beginning to shine forth"; a late Latin word not found in the Ciceronian vocabulary, and therefore condemned by the Bishop; this word is, perhaps, what is meant by the "gaudy ware" in the second line of Gandolf's epitaph, referred to in v. 78.

A Toccata of Galuppi's.

1.

Oh Galuppi, Baldassaro, this is very sad to find!
I can hardly misconceive you; it would prove me deaf and blind;
But, although I take your meaning, 'tis with such a heavy mind!

—

St. 1. Galuppi, Baldassaro (rather Baldassare): b. 1703, in
Burano, an island near Venice, and thence called Buranello; d. 1785;
a distinguished composer, whose operas, about fifty in number, and
mostly comic, were at one time the most popular in Italy; Galuppi
is regarded as the father of the Italian comic opera.

2.

Here you come with your old music, and here's all the good it
    brings.
What, they lived once thus at Venice where the merchants were the
    kings,
Where Saint Mark's is, where the Doges used to wed the sea with
    rings?

—

St. 2. Saint Mark's: see Ruskin's description of this glorious
basilica, in 'The Stones of Venice'.

3.

Ay, because the sea's the street there; and 'tis arched by . . .
    what you call
. . . Shylock's bridge with houses on it, where they kept the
    carnival:
I was never out of England—it's as if I saw it all.

4.

Did young people take their pleasure when the sea was warm in
    May?
Balls and masks begun at midnight, burning ever to mid-day,
When they made up fresh adventures for the morrow, do you say?

5.

Was a lady such a lady, cheeks so round and lips so red,—
On her neck the small face buoyant, like a bell-flower on its bed,
O'er the breast's superb abundance where a man might base his
    head?

6.

Well, and it was graceful of them: they'd break talk off and afford
—She, to bite her mask's black velvet, he, to finger on his sword,
While you sat and played Toccatas, stately at the clavichord?

—

    St. 6. Toccatas: the Toccata was a form of musical composition
for the organ or harpsichord, somewhat in the free and brilliant
style of the modern fantasia or capriccio; clavichord: "a keyed
stringed instrument, now superseded by the pianoforte {now called
a piano}."—Webster.

7.

What? Those lesser thirds so plaintive, sixths diminished, sigh on
    sigh,
Told them something? Those suspensions, those solutions—"Must
    we die?"
Those commiserating sevenths—"Life might last! we can but try!"

St. 7. The musical technicalities used in this stanza, any musician can explain and illustrate.

8.

"Were you happy?"—"Yes."—"And are you still as happy?"—"Yes.
    And you?"
—"Then, more kisses!"—"Did I stop them, when a million seemed
    so few?"
Hark, the dominant's persistence till it must be answered to!

—

St. 8. The questions in this stanza must be supposed to be caused by the effect upon the revellers of the "plaintive lesser thirds", the "diminished sixths", the "commiserating sevenths", etc., of the preceding stanza.

9.

So, an octave struck the answer. Oh, they praised you, I dare say!
"Brave Galuppi! that was music! good alike at grave and gay!
I can always leave off talking when I hear a master play!"

10.

Then they left you for their pleasure: till in due time, one by one,
Some with lives that came to nothing, some with deeds as well
    undone,
Death stepped tacitly, and took them where they never see the
    sun.

11.

But when I sit down to reason, think to take my stand nor swerve,
While I triumph o'er a secret wrung from nature's close reserve,
In you come with your cold music till I creep through every nerve.

———

St. 11. While I triumph o'er a secret wrung from nature's close
reserve: the secret of the soul's immortality.

12.

Yes, you, like a ghostly cricket, creaking where a house was
burned:
"Dust and ashes, dead and done with, Venice spent what Venice
earned.
The soul, doubtless, is immortal—where a soul can be discerned.

13.

"Yours for instance: you know physics, something of geology,
Mathematics are your pastime; souls shall rise in their degree;
Butterflies may dread extinction,—you'll not die, it cannot be!

———

St. 13. The idea is involved in this stanza that the soul's
continued existence is dependent on its development in this life; the
ironic character of the stanza is indicated by the merely intellectual
subjects named, physics, geology, mathematics, which do not of
themselves, necessarily, contribute to SOUL-development. All
from the 2d verse of the 12th stanza down to "Dust and ashes"
in the 15th, is what the music, "like a ghostly cricket, creaking
where a house was burned", says to the speaker, in the monologue,
of the men and women for whom life meant simply a butterfly
enjoyment.

14.

"As for Venice and her people, merely born to bloom and drop,
Here on earth they bore their fruitage, mirth and folly were the
     crop:
What of soul was left, I wonder, when the kissing had to stop?

15.

"Dust and ashes!" So you creak it, and I want the heart to scold.
Dear dead women, with such hair, too—what's become of all the
     gold
Used to hang and brush their bosoms? I feel chilly and grown old.

Abt Vogler.

(After he has been extemporizing upon the Musical Instrument
of his Invention.)

1.

Would that the structure brave, the manifold music I build,
     Bidding my organ obey, calling its keys to their work,
Claiming each slave of the sound, at a touch, as when Solomon
     willed
     Armies of angels that soar, legions of demons that lurk,
Man, brute, reptile, fly,—alien of end and of aim,
     Adverse, each from the other heaven-high, hell-deep
     removed,—
Should rush into sight at once as he named the ineffable Name,
     And pile him a palace straight, to pleasure the princess he
     loved!

—

     St. 1. The leading sentence, "Would that the structure brave",
etc., is interrupted by the comparison, "as when Solomon willed",
etc., and continued in the 2d stanza, "Would it might tarry like his",
etc.; the construction of the comparison is, "as when Solomon

willed that armies of angels, legions of devils, etc., should rush into
sight and pile him a palace straight"; the reference is to the legends
of the Koran in regard to Solomon's magical powers.

2.

Would it might tarry like his, the beautiful building of mine,
    This which my keys in a crowd pressed and importuned to
    raise!
Ah, one and all, how they helped, would dispart now and now
    combine,
    Zealous to hasten the work, heighten their master his praise!
And one would bury his brow with a blind plunge down to hell,
    Burrow a while and build, broad on the roots of things,
Then up again swim into sight, having based me my palace well,
    Founded it, fearless of flame, flat on the nether springs.

———

St. 2. the beautiful building of mine: "Of all our senses,
hearing seems to be the most poetical; and because it requires most
imagination. We do not simply listen to sounds, but whether they
be articulate or inarticulate, we are constantly translating them into
the language of sight, with which we are better acquainted; and
this is a work of the imaginative faculty."—'Poetics: an Essay on
Poetry'. By E. S. Dallas.
    The idea expressed in the above extract is beautifully embodied
in the following lines from Coleridge's 'Kubla Khan':—

    "It was a miracle of rare device,
    A sunny pleasure-dome, with caves of ice!
    A damsel with a dulcimer
    In a vision once I saw:
    It was an Abyssinian maid,
    And on her dulcimer she played,
    Singing of Mount Abora.
    Could I revive within me
    Her symphony and song,
    To such a deep delight 'twould win me,
    That with music loud and long,

I would build that dome in air,
That sunny dome! those caves of ice!
And all who HEARD should SEE them there", etc.

3.

And another would mount and march, like the excellent minion
    he was,
    Ay, another and yet another, one crowd but with many a crest,
Raising my rampired walls of gold as transparent as glass,
    Eager to do and die, yield each his place to the rest:
For higher still and higher (as a runner tips with fire,
    When a great illumination surprises a festal night—
Outlining round and round Rome's dome from space to spire)
    Up, the pinnacled glory reached, and the pride of my soul was
    in sight.

4.

In sight? Not half! for it seemed, it was certain, to match man's
    birth,
    Nature in turn conceived, obeying an impulse as I;
And the emulous heaven yearned down, made effort to reach the
    earth,
    As the earth had done her best, in my passion, to scale the
    sky:
Novel splendors burst forth, grew familiar and dwelt with mine,
    Not a point nor peak but found, but fixed its wandering star;
Meteor-moons, balls of blaze: and they did not pale nor pine,
    For earth had attained to heaven, there was no more near nor
    far.

5.

Nay more; for there wanted not who walked in the glare and glow,
    Presences plain in the place; or, fresh from the Protoplast,
Furnished for ages to come, when a kindlier wind should blow,

Lured now to begin and live, in a house to their liking at last;
Or else the wonderful Dead who have passed through the body and gone,
But were back once more to breathe in an old world worth their new:
What never had been, was now; what was, as it shall be anon;
And what is,—shall I say, matched both? for I was made perfect too.

6.

All through my keys that gave their sounds to a wish of my soul,
All through my soul that praised as its wish flowed visibly forth,
All through music and me! For think, had I painted the whole,
Why, there it had stood, to see, nor the process so wonder-worth.
Had I written the same, made verse—still, effect proceeds from cause,
Ye know why the forms are fair, ye hear how the tale is told;
It is all triumphant art, but art in obedience to laws,
Painter and poet are proud, in the artist-list enrolled:—

7.

But here is the finger of God, a flash of the will that can,
Existent behind all laws: that made them, and, lo, they are!
And I know not if, save in this, such gift be allowed to man,
That out of three sounds he frame, not a fourth sound, but a star.
Consider it well: each tone of our scale in itself is naught;
It is everywhere in the world—loud, soft, and all is said:
Give it to me to use! I mix it with two in my thought,
And, there! Ye have heard and seen: consider and bow the head!

8.

Well, it is gone at last, the palace of music I reared;
    Gone! and the good tears start, the praises that come too
    slow;
For one is assured at first, one scarce can say that he feared,
    That he even gave it a thought, the gone thing was to go.
Never to be again! But many more of the kind
    As good, nay, better perchance: is this your comfort to me?
To me, who must be saved because I cling with my mind
    To the same, same self, same love, same God: ay, what was,
    shall be.

9.

Therefore to whom turn I but to thee, the ineffable Name?
    Builder and maker, thou, of houses not made with hands!
What, have fear of change from thee who art ever the same?
    Doubt that thy power can fill the heart that thy power
    expands?
There shall never be one lost good! What was, shall live as before;
    The evil is null, is naught, is silence implying sound;
What was good, shall be good, with, for evil, so much good more;
    On the earth the broken arcs; in the heaven, a perfect round.

10.

All we have willed or hoped or dreamed of good, shall exist;
    Not its semblance, but itself; no beauty, nor good, nor power
Whose voice has gone forth, but each survives for the melodist,
    When eternity affirms the conception of an hour.
The high that proved too high, the heroic for earth too hard,
    The passion that left the ground to lose itself in the sky,
Are music sent up to God by the lover and the bard;
    Enough that he heard it once: we shall hear it by-and-by.

11.

And what is our failure here but a triumph's evidence
    For the fulness of the days? Have we withered or agonized?
Why else was the pause prolonged but that singing might issue
    thence?
    Why rushed the discords in, but that harmony should be
    prized?
Sorrow is hard to bear, and doubt is slow to clear,
    Each sufferer says his say, his scheme of the weal and woe:
But God has a few of us whom he whispers in the ear;
    The rest may reason and welcome; 'tis we musicians know.

——

St. 11. And what is our failure here: "As long as effort is directed to the highest, that aim, though it is out of reach, is the standard of hope. The existence of a capacity, cherished and quickened, is a pledge that it will find scope. The punishment of the man who has fixed all his thoughts upon earth, a punishment felt on reflection to be overwhelming in view of possibilities of humanity, is the completest gratification of desires unworthily limited:—

    "'Thou art shut
Out of the heaven of spirit; glut
Thy sense upon the world: 'tis thine
For ever—take it!' ('Easter Day', xx.).

On the other hand, the soul which has found in success not rest but a starting-point, which refuses to see in the first-fruits of a partial victory the fulness of its rightful triumph, has ever before it a sustaining and elevating vision:—

    "'What stops my despair?
This:—'tis not what man Does which exalts him, but what man
    Would do!' ('Saul', 18).

"'What I aspired to be,
And was not, comforts me;

A brute I might have been, but would not sink i' the scale.'"
  ('Rabbi Ben Ezra', 7).—Rev. Prof. Westcott on Browning's
  View of Life ('Browning Soc. Papers', iv., 405, 406).

12.

Well, it is earth with me; silence resumes her reign:
  I will be patient and proud, and soberly acquiesce.
Give me the keys. I feel for the common chord again,
  Sliding by semitones, till I sink to the minor,—yes,
And I blunt it into a ninth, and I stand on alien ground,
  Surveying a while the heights I rolled from into the deep;
Which, hark, I have dared and done, for my resting-place is found,
  The C Major of this life: so, now I will try to sleep.

"Touch him ne'er so lightly."

[Epilogue to Dramatic Idyls. Second Series.]

—

* See 'Pages from an Album', in 'The Century Illustrated Monthly Magazine' (Scribner's), for November 1882, pp. 159, 160, where is given a fac-simile of the poet's Ms. of these verses and of the ten verses he afterwards added, in response, it seems, to a carping critic.

—

"Touch him ne'er so lightly, into song he broke:
Soil so quick-receptive,—not one feather-seed,
Not one flower dust fell but straight its fall awoke
Vitalizing virtue: song would song succeed
Sudden as spontaneous—prove a poet-soul!"
  Indeed?
Rock's the song-soil rather, surface hard and bare:
Sun and dew their mildness, storm and frost their rage
Vainly both expend,—few flowers awaken there:

Quiet in its cleft broods—what the after age
Knows and names a pine, a nation's heritage.

Memorabilia.

1.

Ah, did you once see Shelley plain,
  And did he stop and speak to you,
And did you speak to him again?
  How strange it seems, and new!

2.

But you were living before that,
  And also you are living after;
And the memory I started at—
  My starting moves your laughter!

3.

I crossed a moor, with a name of its own
  And a certain use in the world, no doubt,
Yet a hand's-breadth of it shines alone
  'Mid the blank miles round about:

4.

For there I picked up on the heather
  And there I put inside my breast
A moulted feather, an eagle-feather!
  Well, I forget the rest.

How it strikes a Contemporary.

I only knew one poet in my life:
And this, or something like it, was his way.

You saw go up and down Valladolid,
A man of mark, to know next time you saw.
His very serviceable suit of black
Was courtly once and conscientious still,
And many might have worn it, though none did:
The cloak, that somewhat shone and showed the threads,
Had purpose, and the ruff, significance.
He walked, and tapped the pavement with his cane,   [10]
Scenting the world, looking it full in face:
An old dog, bald and blindish, at his heels.
They turned up, now, the alley by the church,
That leads no whither; now, they breathed themselves
On the main promenade just at the wrong time.
You'd come upon his scrutinizing hat,
Making a peaked shade blacker than itself
Against the single window spared some house
Intact yet with its mouldered Moorish work,—
Or else surprise the ferrel of his stick   [20]
Trying the mortar's temper 'tween the chinks
Of some new shop a-building, French and fine.
He stood and watched the cobbler at his trade,
The man who slices lemons into drink,
The coffee-roaster's brazier, and the boys
That volunteer to help him turn its winch.
He glanced o'er books on stalls with half an eye,
And fly-leaf ballads on the vendor's string,
And broad-edge bold-print posters by the wall.
He took such cognizance of men and things,   [30]
If any beat a horse, you felt he saw;
If any cursed a woman, he took note;
Yet stared at nobody,—you stared at him,
And found, less to your pleasure than surprise,
He seemed to know you and expect as much.
So, next time that a neighbor's tongue was loosed,
It marked the shameful and notorious fact,
We had among us, not so much a spy,
As a recording chief-inquisitor,
The town's true master if the town but knew!   [40]
We merely kept a governor for form,

While this man walked about and took account
Of all thought, said and acted, then went home,
And wrote it fully to our Lord the King
Who has an itch to know things, he knows why,
And reads them in his bedroom of a night.
Oh, you might smile! there wanted not a touch,
A tang of . . . well, it was not wholly ease,
As back into your mind the man's look came.
Stricken in years a little, such a brow   [50]
His eyes had to live under!—clear as flint
On either side o' the formidable nose
Curved, cut and colored like an eagle's claw.
Had he to do with A.'s surprising fate?
When altogether old B. disappeared,
And young C. got his mistress,—was't our friend,
His letter to the King, that did it all?
What paid the bloodless man for so much pains?
Our Lord the King has favorites manifold,
And shifts his ministry some once a month;   [60]
Our city gets new governors at whiles,—
But never word or sign, that I could hear,
Notified, to this man about the streets,
The King's approval of those letters conned
The last thing duly at the dead of night.
Did the man love his office? Frowned our Lord,
Exhorting when none heard—"Beseech me not!
Too far above my people,—beneath me!
I set the watch,—how should the people know?
Forget them, keep me all the more in mind!"   [70]
Was some such understanding 'twixt the two?

I found no truth in one report at least—
That if you tracked him to his home, down lanes
Beyond the Jewry, and as clean to pace,
You found he ate his supper in a room
Blazing with lights, four Titians on the wall,
And twenty naked girls to change his plate!
Poor man, he lived another kind of life
In that new stuccoed third house by the bridge,

Fresh-painted, rather smart than otherwise!   [80]
The whole street might o'erlook him as he sat,
Leg crossing leg, one foot on the dog's back,
Playing a decent cribbage with his maid
(Jacynth, you're sure her name was) o'er the cheese
And fruit, three red halves of starved winter-pears,
Or treat of radishes in April. Nine,
Ten, struck the church clock, straight to bed went he.

My father, like the man of sense he was,
Would point him out to me a dozen times;
"St—St," he'd whisper, "the Corregidor!"   [90]
I had been used to think that personage
Was one with lacquered breeches, lustrous belt,
And feathers like a forest in his hat,
Who blew a trumpet and proclaimed the news,
Announced the bull-fights, gave each church its turn,
And memorized the miracle in vogue!
He had a great observance from us boys;
We were in error; that was not the man.

I'd like now, yet had haply been afraid,
To have just looked, when this man came to die,   [100]
And seen who lined the clean gay garret sides,
And stood about the neat low truckle-bed,
With the heavenly manner of relieving guard.
Here had been, mark, the general-in-chief,
Thro' a whole campaign of the world's life and death,
Doing the King's work all the dim day long,
In his old coat and up to knees in mud,
Smoked like a herring, dining on a crust,—
And, now the day was won, relieved at once!
No further show or need of that old coat,   [110]
You are sure, for one thing! Bless us, all the while
How sprucely we are dressed out, you and I!
A second, and the angels alter that.
Well, I could never write a verse,—could you?
Let's to the Prado and make the most of time.

"Transcendentalism":

A Poem in Twelve Books.

—

* Transcendentalism: a poem in twelve books. It must be understood that the poet addressed has written a long poem under this title, and a brother-poet, while admitting that it contains "true thoughts, good thoughts, thoughts fit to treasure up", raises the objection that they are naked, instead of being draped, as they should be, in sights and sounds.

—

Stop playing, poet! May a brother speak?
'Tis you speak, that's your error. Song's our art:
Whereas you please to speak these naked thoughts
Instead of draping them in sights and sounds.
—True thoughts, good thoughts, thoughts fit to treasure up!
But why such long prolusion and display,
Such turning and adjustment of the harp,
And taking it upon your breast, at length,
Only to speak dry words across its strings?
Stark-naked thought is in request enough: [10]
Speak prose and hollo it till Europe hears!
The six-foot Swiss tube, braced about with bark,
Which helps the hunter's voice from Alp to Alp—
Exchange our harp for that,—who hinders you?
But here's your fault; grown men want thought, you think;
Thought's what they mean by verse, and seek in verse;
Boys seek for images and melody,
Men must have reason—so, you aim at men.
Quite otherwise! Objects throng our youth, 'tis true;
We see and hear and do not wonder much: [20]
If you could tell us what they mean, indeed!
As German Boehme never cared for plants
Until it happed, a-walking in the fields,
He noticed all at once that plants could speak,
Nay, turned with loosened tongue to talk with him.
That day the daisy had an eye indeed—

Colloquized with the cowslip on such themes!
We find them extant yet in Jacob's prose.
But by the time youth slips a stage or two
While reading prose in that tough book he wrote,   [30]
(Collating and emendating the same
And settling on the sense most to our mind)
We shut the clasps and find life's summer past.
Then, who helps more, pray, to repair our loss—
Another Boehme with a tougher book
And subtler meanings of what roses say,—
Or some stout Mage like him of Halberstadt,
John, who made things Boehme wrote thoughts about?
He with a "look you!" vents a brace of rhymes,
And in there breaks the sudden rose herself,   [40]
Over us, under, round us every side,
Nay, in and out the tables and the chairs
And musty volumes, Boehme's book and all,—
Buries us with a glory, young once more,
Pouring heaven into this shut house of life.
So come, the harp back to your heart again!
You are a poem, though your poem's naught.
The best of all you showed before, believe,
Was your own boy-face o'er the finer chords
Bent, following the cherub at the top   [50]
That points to God with his paired half-moon wings.

—

22. German Boehme: Jacob Boehme (or Behmen), a shoemaker
and a famous theosophist, b. 1575, at Old Seidenberg, a village near
Goerlitz; d. 1624. The 24th verse of the poem, "He noticed all at
once that plants could speak", may refer to a remarkable experience
of Boehme, related in Dr. Hans Lassen Martensen's 'Jacob Boehme:
his life and teaching, or studies in theosophy: translated from the
Danish by T. Rhys Evans', London, 1885: "Sitting one day in his
room, his eye fell upon a burnished pewter dish, which reflected
the sunshine with such marvellous splendor that he fell into an
inward ecstasy, and it seemed to him as if he could now look into
the principles and deepest foundations of things. He believed that
it was only a fancy, and in order to banish it from his mind he went

out upon the green. But here he remarked that he gazed into the very heart of things, the very herbs and grass, and that actual nature harmonized with what he had inwardly seen." Martensen, in his biography, follows that by Frankenberg, in which the experience may be given more in detail.

37-40. him of Halberstadt, John: "It is not a thinker like Boehme, who will compensate us for the lost summer of our life; but a magician like John of Halberstadt, who can, at any moment, conjure roses up."

"The 'magic' symbolized, is that of genuine poetry; but the magician, or 'Mage', is an historical person; and the special feat imputed to him was recorded of other magicians in the Middle Ages, if not of himself. 'Johannes Teutonicus, a canon of Halberstadht in Germany, after he had performed a number of prestigious feats almost incredible, was transported by the Devil in the likeness of a black horse, and was both seen and heard upon one and the same Christmas day, to say mass in Halberstadht, in Mayntz, and in Cologne' ('Heywood's Hierarchy', Bk. IV., p. 253). The 'prestigious feat' of causing flowers to appear in winter, was a common one." —Mrs. Sutherland Orr's 'Handbook to the works of Robert Browning', p. 209.

It may be said that the advice given in this poem, Browning has not sufficiently followed in his own poetry. On this point, a writer in the 'British Quarterly Review' (Vol. 23, p. 162) justly remarks: "Browning's thought is always that of a poet. Subtle, nimble, and powerful as is the intellect, and various as is the learning, all is manifested through the imagination, and comes forth shaped and tinted by it. Thus, even in the foregoing passages [cited from 'Transcendentalism' and 'Bishop Blougram's Apology'], where the matter is almost as purely as it can be the produce of the mere understanding, it is still evident that the method of the thought is poetic. The notions take the form of images. For example, the poet means to say that Prose is a good and mighty vehicle in its way, but that it is not Poetry; and how does the conception shape itself in his mind? Why, in an image. All at once it is not Prose that is thought about, but a huge six-foot speaking-trumpet braced round with bark, through which the Swiss hunters help their voices from Alp to Alp— Poetry, on the other hand, being no such big and blaring instrument, but a harp taken to the breast of youth and swept by ecstatic fingers. And so with the images of Boehme and his book, and John of Halberstadt with his magic rose—still a concrete body to enshrine an abstract meaning."

Apparent Failure.

"We shall soon lose a celebrated building."
               —Paris Newspaper.

1.

No, for I'll save it! Seven years since,
    I passed through Paris, stopped a day
To see the baptism of your Prince;
    Saw, made my bow, and went my way:
Walking the heat and headache off,
    I took the Seine-side, you surmise,
Thought of the Congress, Gortschakoff,
    Cavour's appeal and Buol's replies,
So sauntered till—what met my eyes?

—

St. 1. To see the baptism of your Prince: the Prince Imperial, son of Napoleon III. and the Empress Eugenie, born March 16, 1856. the Congress: the Congress of Paris.

Gortschakoff: Prince Alexander Michaelowitsch Gortschakoff; while representing Russia at the Court of Vienna, he kept Austria neutral during the Crimean War.

Cavour: Count Camillo Benso di Cavour, Italian statesman, b. 1810; at the Congress of Paris, brought forward the question of the political consolidation of Italy, which led to the invasion of Italy by the Austrians, who were defeated; d. 6th June, 1861.

Buol: Karl Ferdinand von Buol-Schauenstein, Austrian diplomatist, and minister of foreign affairs from 1852 to 1859.

2.

Only the Doric little Morgue!
    The dead-house where you show your drowned:

Petrarch's Vaucluse makes proud the Sorgue,
　　Your Morgue has made the Seine renowned.
One pays one's debt in such a case;
　　I plucked up heart and entered,—stalked,
Keeping a tolerable face
　　Compared with some whose cheeks were chalked:
Let them! No Briton's to be balked!

—

St. 2. Petrarch's Vaucluse makes proud the Sorgue: Fontaine
de Vaucluse, a celebrated fountain, in the department of Vaucluse,
in Southern France, the source of the Sorgues. The village named
after it was for some time the residence of Petrarch.

3.

First came the silent gazers; next,
　　A screen of glass, we're thankful for;
Last, the sight's self, the sermon's text,
　　The three men who did most abhor
Their life in Paris yesterday,
　　So killed themselves: and now, enthroned
Each on his copper couch, they lay
　　Fronting me, waiting to be owned.
I thought, and think, their sin's atoned.

4.

Poor men, God made, and all for that!
　　The reverence struck me; o'er each head
Religiously was hung its hat,
　　Each coat dripped by the owner's bed,
Sacred from touch: each had his berth,
　　His bounds, his proper place of rest,
Who last night tenanted on earth
　　Some arch, where twelve such slept abreast,—
Unless the plain asphalte seemed best.

5.

How did it happen, my poor boy?
    You wanted to be Buonaparte
And have the Tuileries for toy,
    And could not, so it broke your heart?
You, old one by his side, I judge,
    Were, red as blood, a socialist,
A leveller! Does the Empire grudge
    You've gained what no Republic missed?
Be quiet, and unclinch your fist!

6.

And this—why, he was red in vain,
    Or black,—poor fellow that is blue!
What fancy was it, turned your brain?
    Oh, women were the prize for you!
Money gets women, cards and dice
    Get money, and ill-luck gets just
The copper couch and one clear nice
    Cool squirt of water o'er your bust,
The right thing to extinguish lust!

7.

It's wiser being good than bad;
    It's safer being meek than fierce:
It's fitter being sane than mad.
    My own hope is, a sun will pierce
The thickest cloud earth ever stretched;
    That, after Last, returns the First,
Though a wide compass round be fetched;
    That what began best, can't end worst,
Nor what God blessed once, prove accurst.

Rabbi Ben Ezra.

1.

Grow old along with me!
The best is yet to be,
The last of life, for which the first was made:
Our times are in His hand
Who saith, "A whole I planned,
Youth shows but half; trust God: see all, nor be afraid!"

———

St. 1. Grow old along with me!: I understand that the aged Rabbi is addressing some young friend. The best is yet to be, the last of life:

> "By the spirit, when age shall o'ercome thee, thou still shalt
>   enjoy
> More indeed, than at first when, unconscious, the life of
>   a boy."
>
> —'Saul', 162, 163.

2.

Not that, amassing flowers,
Youth sighed, "Which rose make ours,
Which lily leave and then as best recall?"
Not that, admiring stars,
It yearned, "Nor Jove, nor Mars;
Mine be some figured flame which blends, transcends them
    all!"

3.

Not for such hopes and fears
Annulling youth's brief years,
Do I remonstrate: folly wide the mark!
Rather I prize the doubt

Low kinds exist without,
Finished and finite clods, untroubled by a spark.

—

St. 2, 3. The construction is, I do not remonstrate that youth, amassing flowers, sighed, Which rose make ours, which lily leave, etc., nor that, admiring stars, it (youth) yearned, etc.

4.

Poor vaunt of life indeed,
Were man but formed to feed
On joy, to solely seek and find and feast;
Such feasting ended, then
As sure an end to men;
Irks care the crop-full bird? Frets doubt the maw-crammed beast?

—

St. 4. Irks care: does care irk . . . does doubt fret . . .

5.

Rejoice we are allied
To That which doth provide
And not partake, effect and not receive!
A spark disturbs our clod;
Nearer we hold of God
Who gives, than of His tribes that take, I must believe.

—

St. 5. Nearer we hold of God: have title to a nearer relationship. See Webster, s.v. Hold, v.i. def. 3. {No edition is given.}

6.

Then, welcome each rebuff
That turns earth's smoothness rough,
Each sting that bids nor sit nor stand but go!

Be our joys three-parts pain!
Strive, and hold cheap the strain;
Learn, nor account the pang; dare, never grudge the throe!

7.

For thence,—a paradox
Which comforts while it mocks,—
Shall life succeed in that it seems to fail:
What I aspired to be,
And was not, comforts me:
A brute I might have been, but would not sink i' the scale.

—

St. 7. What I aspired to be: "'tis not what man Does which exalts him, but what man Would do."—'Saul', v. 296.

8.

What is he but a brute
Whose flesh hath soul to suit,
Whose spirit works lest arms and legs want play?
To man, propose this test—
Thy body at its best,
How far can that project thy soul on its lone way?

—

St. 8. Thy body at its best, How far, etc.: "In our flesh grows the branch of this life, in our soul it bears fruit."—'Saul', v. 151.

9.

Yet gifts should prove their use:
I own the Past profuse
Of power each side, perfection every turn:
Eyes, ears took in their dole,
Brain treasured up the whole;
Should not the heart beat once "How good to live and
    learn"?

—

St. 9. the Past: he means the past of his own life.

10.

Not once beat "Praise be Thine!
I see the whole design,
I, who saw Power, see now Love perfect too:
Perfect I call Thy plan:
Thanks that I was a man!
Maker, remake, complete,—I trust what Thou shalt do!"

—

St. 10. The original reading of the 3d verse was, "I, who saw Power, SHALL see Love perfect too." The change has cleared up a difficulty. The All-Great is now to me, in my age, the All-Loving too. Maker, remake, complete: there seems to be an anticipation here of the metaphor of the Potter's wheel, in stanzas 25-32, and see Jer. 18:4.

11.

For pleasant is this flesh;
Our soul, in its rose-mesh
Pulled ever to the earth, still yearns for rest:
Would we some prize might hold
To match those manifold
Possessions of the brute,—gain most, as we did best!

12.

Let us not always say
"Spite of this flesh to-day
I strove, made head, gained ground upon the whole!"
As the bird wings and sings,
Let us cry "All good things
Are ours, nor soul helps flesh more, now, than flesh helps soul!"

13.

Therefore I summon age
To grant youth's heritage,
Life's struggle having so far reached its term:
Thence shall I pass, approved
A man, for aye removed
From the developed brute, a God though in the germ.

St. 13. Thence shall I pass, etc.: It will be observed that here
and in some of the following stanzas, the Rabbi speaks in the
person of youth; so youth should say to itself.

14.

And I shall thereupon
Take rest, ere I be gone
Once more on my adventure brave and new:
Fearless and unperplexed,
When I wage battle next,
What weapons to select, what armor to indue.

15.

Youth ended, I shall try
My gain or loss thereby;
Leave the fire ashes, what survives is gold:
And I shall weigh the same,
Give life its praise or blame:
Young, all lay in dispute; I shall know, being old.

16.

For, note when evening shuts,
A certain moment cuts
The deed off, calls the glory from the gray:
A whisper from the west

Shoots—"Add this to the rest,
Take it and try its worth: here dies another day."

17.

So, still within this life,
Though lifted o'er its strife,
Let me discern, compare, pronounce at last,
"This rage was right i' the main,
That acquiescence vain:
The Future I may face now I have proved the Past."

18.

For more is not reserved
To man, with soul just nerved
To act to-morrow what he learns to-day:
Here, work enough to watch
The Master work, and catch
Hints of the proper craft, tricks of the tool's true play.

19.

As it was better, youth
Should strive, through acts uncouth,
Toward making, than repose on aught found made:
So, better, age, exempt
From strife, should know, than tempt
Further. Thou waitedst age: wait death, nor be afraid!

20.

Enough now, if the Right
And Good and Infinite
Be named here, as thou callest thy hand thine own,
With knowledge absolute,
Subject to no dispute
From fools that crowded youth, nor let thee feel alone.

St. 20. knowledge absolute: soul knowledge, which is reached through direct assimilation by the soul of the hidden principles of things, as distinguished from intellectual knowledge, which is based on the phenominal, and must be more or less subject to dispute.

21.

Be there, for once and all,
Severed great minds from small,
Announced to each his station in the Past!
Was I, the world arraigned,
Were they, my soul disdained,
Right? Let age speak the truth and give us peace at last!

—

St. 21, vv. 4, 5. The relatives are suppressed;—Was I whom the world arraigned, or were they whom my soul disdained, right?

22.

Now, who shall arbitrate?
Ten men love what I hate,
Shun what I follow, slight what I receive;
Ten, who in ears and eyes
Match me: we all surmise,
They, this thing, and I, that: whom shall my soul believe?

23.

Not on the vulgar mass
Called "work", must sentence pass,
Things done, that took the eye and had the price;
O'er which, from level stand,
The low world laid its hand,
Found straightway to its mind, could value in a trice:

24.

But all, the world's coarse thumb
And finger failed to plumb,
So passed in making up the main account:
All instincts immature,
All purposes unsure,
That weighed not as his work, yet swelled the man's amount:

25.

Thoughts hardly to be packed
Into a narrow act,
Fancies that broke through language and escaped:
All I could never be,
All, men ignored in me,
This, I was worth to God, whose wheel the pitcher shaped.

26.

Ay, note that Potter's wheel,
That metaphor! and feel
Why time spins fast, why passive lies our clay,—
Thou, to whom fools propound,
When the wine makes its round,
"Since life fleets, all is change; the Past gone, seize to-day!"

—

St. 26. Potter's wheel: "But now, O Lord, thou art our Father:
we are the clay, and thou our Potter; and we are all the work of thy
hand."—Is. 64:8; and see Jer. 18:2-6.

27.

Fool! All that is, at all,
Lasts ever, past recall;
Earth changes, but thy soul and God stand sure:
What entered into thee,

THAT was, is, and shall be:
Time's wheel runs back or stops: Potter and clay endure.

28.

He fixed thee mid this dance
Of plastic circumstance,
This Present, thou, forsooth, wouldst fain arrest:
Machinery just meant
To give thy soul its bent,
Try thee, and turn thee forth sufficiently impressed.

29.

What though the earlier grooves
Which ran the laughing loves
Around thy base, no longer pause and press?
What though, about thy rim,
Skull-things in order grim
Grow out, in graver mood, obey the sterner stress?

30.

Look not thou down but up!
To uses of a cup,
The festal board, lamp's flash, and trumpet's peal,
The new wine's foaming flow,
The Master's lips aglow!
Thou, heaven's consummate cup, what needst thou with
    earth's wheel?

31.

But I need, now as then,
Thee, God, who mouldest men!
And since, not even while the whirl was worst,
Did I,—to the wheel of life
With shapes and colors rife,
Bound dizzily,—mistake my end, to slake Thy thirst:

32.

So, take and use Thy work,
Amend what flaws may lurk,
What strain o' the stuff, what warpings past the aim!
My times be in Thy hand!
Perfect the cup as planned!
Let age approve of youth, and death complete the same!

A Grammarian's Funeral.

Shortly after the Revival of Learning in Europe.

Let us begin and carry up this corpse,
    Singing together.
Leave we the common crofts, the vulgar thorpes,
    Each in its tether
Sleeping safe in the bosom of the plain,
    Cared-for till cock-crow:
Look out if yonder be not day again
    Rimming the rock-row!
That's the appropriate country; there, man's thought,
    Rarer, intenser,   [10]
Self-gathered for an outbreak, as it ought,
    Chafes in the censer.
Leave we the unlettered plain its herd and crop;
    Seek we sepulture
On a tall mountain, citied to the top,
    Crowded with culture!
All the peaks soar, but one the rest excels;
    Clouds overcome it;
No, yonder sparkle is the citadel's
    Circling its summit.   [20]
Thither our path lies; wind we up the heights!
    Wait ye the warning?
Our low life was the level's and the night's:
    He's for the morning.
Step to a tune, square chests, erect each head,

'Ware the beholders!
This is our master, famous, calm, and dead,
  Borne on our shoulders.

Sleep, crop and herd! sleep, darkling thorpe and croft
  Safe from the weather!   [30]
He, whom we convoy to his grave aloft,
  Singing together,
He was a man born with thy face and throat,
  Lyric Apollo!
Long he lived nameless: how should spring take note
  Winter would follow?
Till lo, the little touch, and youth was gone!
  Cramped and diminished,
Moaned he, "New measures, other feet anon!
  "My dance is finished?"   [40]
No, that's the world's way; (keep the mountain-side,
  Make for the city!)
He knew the signal, and stepped on with pride
  Over men's pity;
Left play for work, and grappled with the world
  Bent on escaping:
"What's in the scroll," quoth he, "thou keepest furled?
  Show me their shaping,
Theirs who most studied man, the bard and sage,—
  Give!"—So, he gowned him,   [50]
Straight got by heart that book to its last page:
  Learned, we found him.
Yea, but we found him bald too, eyes like lead,
  Accents uncertain:
"Time to taste life," another would have said,
  "Up with the curtain!"
This man said rather, "Actual life comes next?
  Patience a moment!
Grant I have mastered learning's crabbed text,
  Still there's the comment.   [60]
Let me know all! Prate not of most or least,
  Painful or easy!
Even to the crumbs I'd fain eat up the feast,

Ay, nor feel queasy."
Oh, such a life as he resolved to live,
    When he had learned it,
When he had gathered all books had to give!
    Sooner, he spurned it.
Image the whole, then execute the parts—
    Fancy the fabric   [70]
Quite, ere you build, ere steel strike fire from quartz,
    Ere mortar dab brick!

(Here's the town-gate reached; there's the market-place
    Gaping before us.)
Yea, this in him was the peculiar grace
    (Hearten our chorus!)
That before living he'd learn how to live—
    No end to learning:
Earn the means first—God surely will contrive
    Use for our earning.   [80]
Others mistrust and say, "But time escapes!
    Live now or never!"
He said, "What's time? Leave Now for dogs and apes!
    Man has Forever."
Back to his book then: deeper drooped his head:
    CALCULUS racked him:
Leaden before, his eyes grew dross of lead:
    TUSSIS attacked him.
"Now, master, take a little rest!"—not he!
    (Caution redoubled!   [90]
Step two abreast, the way winds narrowly!)
    Not a whit troubled,
Back to his studies, fresher than at first,
    Fierce as a dragon
He (soul-hydroptic with a sacred thirst)
    Sucked at the flagon.
Oh, if we draw a circle premature,
    Heedless of far gain,
Greedy for quick returns of profit, sure
    Bad is our bargain!   [100]
Was it not great? did not he throw on God

(He loves the burthen)—
God's task to make the heavenly period
    Perfect the earthen?
Did not he magnify the mind, show clear
    Just what it all meant?
He would not discount life, as fools do here,
    Paid by instalment.
He ventured neck or nothing—heaven's success
    Found, or earth's failure: [110]
"Wilt thou trust death or not?" He answered, "Yes!
    Hence with life's pale lure!"
That low man seeks a little thing to do,
    Sees it and does it:
This high man, with a great thing to pursue,
    Dies ere he knows it.
That low man goes on adding one to one,
    His hundred's soon hit:
This high man, aiming at a million,
    Misses an unit.   [120]
That, has the world here—should he need the next,
    Let the world mind him!
This, throws himself on God, and unperplexed
    Seeking shall find him.
So, with the throttling hands of death at strife,
    Ground he at grammar;
Still, through the rattle, parts of speech were rife:
    While he could stammer
He settled HOTI's business—let it be!—
    Properly based OUN—   [130]
Gave us the doctrine of the enclitic 'De',
    Dead from the waist down.
Well, here's the platform, here's the proper place:
    Hail to your purlieus,
All ye highfliers of the feathered race,
    Swallows and curlews!
Here's the top-peak; the multitude below
    Live, for they can, there:
This man decided not to Live but Know—
    Bury this man there?   [140]

Here—here's his place, where meteors shoot, clouds form,
  Lightnings are loosened,
Stars come and go! Let joy break with the storm,
  Peace let the dew send!
Lofty designs must close in like effects:
  Loftily lying,
Leave him—still loftier than the world suspects,
  Living and dying.

  —

18. overcome: pass over, overhang, overshadow; used as in Macbeth III. IV. 3, "overcome us like a summer's cloud".

39, 40. New measures, . . . finished?: do you say? not at all.

42. All in parentheses, throughout the poem, is addressed by the speaker directly to his companions.

57. Actual life comes next: do you say? No. I have more to do first.

86. Calculus: the stone.

88. Tussis: a cough.

95. hydroptic: hydropic, dropsical.

129. Hoti: the Greek particle '/Oti, conj. that, etc.

130. Oun: Greek particle Ou^'n, then, now then, etc.

131. the enclitic De: Greek De {Delta epsilon}; in regard to this, the following letter by Browning appeared in the London 'Daily News' of Nov. 21, 1874: "To the Editor of 'The Daily News'. Sir,— In a clever article this morning you speak of 'the doctrine of the enclitic De'—'which, with all deference to Mr. Browning, in point of fact does not exist.' No, not to Mr. Browning: but pray defer to Herr Buttmann, whose fifth list of 'enclitics' ends 'with the inseparable De'—or to Curtius, whose fifth list ends also with 'De (meaning 'towards' and as a demonstrative appendage)'. That this is not to be confounded with the accentuated 'De, meaning BUT", was the 'doctrine' which the Grammarian bequeathed to those capable of receiving it.— I am, sir, yours obediently, R. B."—'Browning Soc. Papers', Part I., p. 56.

An Epistle containing the Strange Medical Experience of Karshish, the Arab Physician.

Karshish, the picker-up of learning's crumbs,
The not-incurious in God's handiwork
(This man's-flesh he hath admirably made,
Blown like a bubble, kneaded like a paste,
To coop up and keep down on earth a space
That puff of vapor from his mouth, man's soul)
—To Abib, all-sagacious in our art,
Breeder in me of what poor skill I boast,
Like me inquisitive how pricks and cracks
Befall the flesh through too much stress and strain,   [10]
Whereby the wily vapor fain would slip
Back and rejoin its source before the term,—
And aptest in contrivance (under God)
To baffle it by deftly stopping such:—
The vagrant Scholar to his Sage at home
Sends greeting (health and knowledge, fame with peace)
Three samples of true snake-stone—rarer still,
One of the other sort, the melon-shaped
(But fitter, pounded fine, for charms than drugs),
And writeth now the twenty-second time.   [20]

My journeyings were brought to Jericho:
Thus I resume. Who, studious in our art,
Shall count a little labor unrepaid?
I have shed sweat enough, left flesh and bone
On many a flinty furlong of this land.
Also, the country-side is all on fire
With rumors of a marching hitherward:
Some say Vespasian cometh, some, his son.
A black lynx snarled and pricked a tufted ear;
Lust of my blood inflamed his yellow balls: [30]
I cried and threw my staff, and he was gone.
Twice have the robbers stripped and beaten me,
And once a town declared me for a spy;
But at the end, I reach Jerusalem,
Since this poor covert where I pass the night,

This Bethany, lies scarce the distance thence
A man with plague-sores at the third degree
Runs till he drops down dead. Thou laughest here!
'Sooth, it elates me, thus reposed and safe,
To void the stuffing of my travel-scrip,   [40]
And share with thee whatever Jewry yields.
A viscid choler is observable
In tertians, I was nearly bold to say;
And falling-sickness hath a happier cure
Than our school wots of: there's a spider here
Weaves no web, watches on the ledge of tombs,
Sprinkled with mottles on an ash-gray back;
Take five and drop them . . . but who knows his mind,
The Syrian runagate I trust this to?
His service payeth me a sublimate   [50]
Blown up his nose to help the ailing eye.
Best wait: I reach Jerusalem at morn,
There set in order my experiences,
Gather what most deserves, and give thee all—
Or I might add, Judaea's gum-tragacanth
Scales off in purer flakes, shines clearer-grained,
Cracks 'twixt the pestle and the porphyry,
In fine exceeds our produce. Scalp-disease
Confounds me, crossing so with leprosy:
Thou hadst admired one sort I gained at Zoar—   [60]
But zeal outruns discretion. Here I end.

Yet stay! my Syrian blinketh gratefully,
Protesteth his devotion is my price—
Suppose I write what harms not, though he steal?
I half resolve to tell thee, yet I blush,
What set me off a-writing first of all.
An itch I had, a sting to write, a tang!
For, be it this town's barrenness,—or else
The Man had something in the look of him,—
His case has struck me far more than 'tis worth.   [70]
So, pardon if—(lest presently I lose,
In the great press of novelty at hand,
The care and pains this somehow stole from me)

I bid thee take the thing while fresh in mind,
Almost in sight—for, wilt thou have the truth?
The very man is gone from me but now,
Whose ailment is the subject of discourse.
Thus then, and let thy better wit help all!

'Tis but a case of mania: subinduced
By epilepsy, at the turning-point   [80]
Of trance prolonged unduly some three days;
When, by the exhibition of some drug
Or spell, exorcization, stroke of art
Unknown to me and which 'twere well to know,
The evil thing, out-breaking, all at once,
Left the man whole and sound of body indeed,—
But, flinging (so to speak) life's gates too wide,
Making a clear house of it too suddenly,
The first conceit that entered might inscribe
Whatever it was minded on the wall   [90]
So plainly at that vantage, as it were
(First come, first served), that nothing subsequent
Attaineth to erase those fancy-scrawls
The just-returned and new-established soul
Hath gotten now so thoroughly by heart
That henceforth she will read or these or none.
And first—the man's own firm conviction rests
That he was dead (in fact they buried him)
—That he was dead and then restored to life
By a Nazarene physician of his tribe: [100]
—'Sayeth, the same bade "Rise", and he did rise.
"Such cases are diurnal", thou wilt cry.
Not so this figment!—not, that such a fume,
Instead of giving way to time and health,
Should eat itself into the life of life,
As saffron tingeth flesh, blood, bones, and all!
For see, how he takes up the after-life.
The man—it is one Lazarus a Jew,
Sanguine, proportioned, fifty years of age,
The body's habit wholly laudable,   [110]
As much, indeed, beyond the common health

322

As he were made and put aside to show.
Think, could we penetrate by any drug
And bathe the wearied soul and worried flesh,
And bring it clear and fair, by three days' sleep!
Whence has the man the balm that brightens all?
This grown man eyes the world now like a child.
Some elders of his tribe, I should premise,
Led in their friend, obedient as a sheep,
To bear my inquisition. While they spoke,   [120]
Now sharply, now with sorrow,—told the case,—
He listened not except I spoke to him,
But folded his two hands and let them talk,
Watching the flies that buzzed: and yet no fool.
And that's a sample how his years must go.
Look if a beggar, in fixed middle-life,
Should find a treasure,—can he use the same
With straitened habits and with tastes starved small,
And take at once to his impoverished brain
The sudden element that changes things,   [130]
That sets the undreamed-of rapture at his hand,
And puts the cheap old joy in the scorned dust?
Is he not such an one as moves to mirth—
Warily parsimonious, when no need,
Wasteful as drunkenness at undue times?
All prudent counsel as to what befits
The golden mean, is lost on such an one:
The man's fantastic will is the man's law.
So here—we call the treasure knowledge, say,
Increased beyond the fleshly faculty—   [140]
Heaven opened to a soul while yet on earth,
Earth forced on a soul's use while seeing heaven:
The man is witless of the size, the sum,
The value in proportion of all things,
Or whether it be little or be much.
Discourse to him of prodigious armaments
Assembled to besiege his city now,
And of the passing of a mule with gourds—
'Tis one! Then take it on the other side,
Speak of some trifling fact,—he will gaze rapt   [150]

With stupor at its very littleness
(Far as I see), as if in that indeed
He caught prodigious import, whole results;
And so will turn to us the by-standers
In ever the same stupor (note this point),
That we, too, see not with his opened eyes.
Wonder and doubt come wrongly into play,
Preposterously, at cross purposes.
Should his child sicken unto death,—why, look
For scarce abatement of his cheerfulness,   [160]
Or pretermission of the daily craft!
While a word, gesture, glance from that same child
At play or in the school or laid asleep,
Will startle him to an agony of fear,
Exasperation, just as like. Demand
The reason why—"'tis but a word," object—
"A gesture"—he regards thee as our lord
Who lived there in the pyramid alone,
Looked at us (does thou mind?) when, being young,
We both would unadvisedly recite   [170]
Some charm's beginning, from that book of his,
Able to bid the sun throb wide and burst
All into stars, as suns grown old are wont.
Thou and the child have each a veil alike
Thrown o'er your heads, from under which ye both
Stretch your blind hands and trifle with a match
Over a mine of Greek fire, did ye know!
He holds on firmly to some thread of life—
(It is the life to lead perforcedly)
Which runs across some vast, distracting orb   [180]
Of glory on either side that meagre thread,
Which, conscious of, he must not enter yet—
The spiritual life around the earthly life:
The law of that is known to him as this,
His heart and brain move there, his feet stay here.
So is the man perplext with impulses
Sudden to start off crosswise, not straight on,
Proclaiming what is right and wrong across,
And not along, this black thread through the blaze—

"It should be" balked by "here it cannot be".   [190]
And oft the man's soul springs into his face
As if he saw again and heard again
His sage that bade him "Rise", and he did rise.
Something, a word, a tick o' the blood within
Admonishes: then back he sinks at once
To ashes, who was very fire before,
In sedulous recurrence to his trade
Whereby he earneth him the daily bread;
And studiously the humbler for that pride,
Professedly the faultier that he knows   [200]
God's secret, while he holds the thread of life.
Indeed the especial marking of the man
Is prone submission to the heavenly will—
Seeing it, what it is, and why it is.
'Sayeth, he will wait patient to the last
For that same death which must restore his being
To equilibrium, body loosening soul
Divorced even now by premature full growth:
He will live, nay, it pleaseth him to live
So long as God please, and just how God please.   [210]
He even seeketh not to please God more
(Which meaneth, otherwise) than as God please.
Hence, I perceive not he affects to preach
The doctrine of his sect whate'er it be,
Make proselytes as madmen thirst to do:
How can he give his neighbor the real ground,
His own conviction? Ardent as he is—
Call his great truth a lie, why, still the old
"Be it as God please" re-assureth him.
I probed the sore as thy disciple should: [220]
"How, beast," said I, "this stolid carelessness
Sufficeth thee, when Rome is on her march
To stamp out like a little spark thy town,
Thy tribe, thy crazy tale and thee at once?"
He merely looked with his large eyes on me.
The man is apathetic, you deduce?
Contrariwise, he loves both old and young,
Able and weak, affects the very brutes

And birds—how say I? flowers of the field—
As a wise workman recognizes tools   [230]
In a master's workshop, loving what they make.
Thus is the man as harmless as a lamb:
Only impatient, let him do his best,
At ignorance and carelessness and sin—
An indignation which is promptly curbed:
As when in certain travel I have feigned
To be an ignoramus in our art
According to some preconceived design,
And happed to hear the land's practitioners
Steeped in conceit sublimed by ignorance,   [240]
Prattle fantastically on disease,
Its cause and cure—and I must hold my peace!

Thou wilt object—Why have I not ere this
Sought out the sage himself, the Nazarene
Who wrought this cure, inquiring at the source,
Conferring with the frankness that befits?
Alas! it grieveth me, the learned leech
Perished in a tumult many years ago,
Accused,—our learning's fate,—of wizardry,
Rebellion, to the setting up a rule   [250]
And creed prodigious as described to me.
His death, which happened when the earthquake fell
(Prefiguring, as soon appeared, the loss
To occult learning in our lord the sage
Who lived there in the pyramid alone),
Was wrought by the mad people—that's their wont!
On vain recourse, as I conjecture it,
To his tried virtue, for miraculous help—
How could he stop the earthquake? That's their way!
The other imputations must be lies: [260]
But take one, though I loath to give it thee,
In mere respect for any good man's fame.
(And after all, our patient Lazarus
Is stark mad; should we count on what he says?
Perhaps not: though in writing to a leech
'Tis well to keep back nothing of a case.)

This man so cured regards the curer, then,
As—God forgive me! who but God himself,
Creator and sustainer of the world,
That came and dwelt in flesh on it a while!   [270]
—'Sayeth that such an one was born and lived,
Taught, healed the sick, broke bread at his own house,
Then died, with Lazarus by, for aught I know,
And yet was . . . what I said nor choose repeat,
And must have so avouched himself, in fact,
In hearing of this very Lazarus
Who saith—but why all this of what he saith?
Why write of trivial matters, things of price
Calling at every moment for remark?
I noticed on the margin of a pool   [280]
Blue-flowering borage, the Aleppo sort,
Aboundeth, very nitrous. It is strange!

Thy pardon for this long and tedious case,
Which, now that I review it, needs must seem
Unduly dwelt on, prolixly set forth!
Nor I myself discern in what is writ
Good cause for the peculiar interest
And awe indeed this man has touched me with.
Perhaps the journey's end, the weariness
Had wrought upon me first. I met him thus: [290]
I crossed a ridge of short sharp broken hills
Like an old lion's cheek teeth. Out there came
A moon made like a face with certain spots
Multiform, manifold, and menacing:
Then a wind rose behind me. So we met
In this old sleepy town at unaware,
The man and I. I send thee what is writ.
Regard it as a chance, a matter risked
To this ambiguous Syrian: he may lose,
Or steal, or give it thee with equal good.   [300]
Jerusalem's repose shall make amends
For time this letter wastes, thy time and mine;
Till when, once more thy pardon and farewell!

The very God! think, Abib; dost thou think?
So, the All-Great, were the All-Loving too—
So, through the thunder comes a human voice
Saying, "O heart I made, a heart beats here!
Face, my hands fashioned, see it in myself!
Thou hast no power nor may'st conceive of mine:
But love I gave thee, with myself to love,   [310]
And thou must love me who have died for thee!"
The madman saith He said so: it is strange.

—

1. Karshish . . . To Abib. {that is, phrase finishes on line 7.}

17. snake-stone: a certain kind of stone supposed to be efficacious when placed upon the bite of a snake, in absorbing or charming away the poison.

21. My journeyings were brought to Jericho: i.e., in his last letter.

28. Vespasian: T. Flavius Sabinus Vespasianus, Roman emperor, A.D. 70-79; sent by Nero in 66 to conduct the war against the Jews; when proclaimed emperor, left his son Titus to continue the war.

24-33. his ardent scientific interest has caused him to brave all dangers.

49. The Syrian runagate: perhaps I'm writing for nothing in trusting my letter to him.

60. Thou hadst: wouldst have. Zoar: one of the "cities of the plain", S. E. of the Dead Sea (Gen. 19:22).

65-78. Though he's deeply impressed with the subject, he approaches it with extreme diffidence, writing to the "all-sagacious" Abib.

82. exhibition: used in its medical sense of administering a remedy.

103. fume: vaporish fancy.

106. As saffron tingeth: Chaucer uses "saffron" metaphorically as a verb:—

"And in Latyn I speke a wordes fewe,
To saffron with my predicacioun,

And for to stire men to devocioun."—'The Pardoner's
   Prologue'.

113. Think, could WE penetrate by any drug.

141, 142. "Browning has drawn the portraiture of one to
whom the eternal is sensibly present, whose spirit has gained
prematurely absolute predominance: . . . and the result is . . . a
being 'Professedly the faultier that he knows God's secret, while he
holds the thread of life' (vv. 200, 201). Lazarus therefore, while he
moves in the world, has lost all sense of proportion in things about
him, all measure of and faculty of dealing with that which sways
his fellows. He has no power or will to win them to his faith, but he
simply stands among men as a patient witness of the overwhelming
reality of the divine: a witness whose authority is confessed, even
against his inclination, by the student of nature, who turns again
and again to the phenomenon which he affects to disparage.

"In this crucial example Browning shows how the exclusive
dominance of the spirit destroys the fulness of human life, its uses
and powers, while it leaves a passive life, crowned with an unearthly
beauty. On the other hand, he shows in his study of Cleon that
the richest results of earth in art and speculation, and pleasure and
power, are unable to remove from life the desolation of final gloom
. . . The contrast is of the deepest significance. The Jewish peasant
endures earth, being in possession of heaven: the Greek poet, in
possession of earth, feels that heaven, some future state,

   'Unlimited in capability
   For joy, as this is in desire for joy',

is a necessity for man; but no,

   'Zeus has not yet revealed it; and alas,
   He must have done so, were it possible!'

But we must not pause to follow out the contrast into details. It is enough to see broadly that flesh and spirit each claim recognition in connection with their proper spheres, in order that the present life may bear its true result."—Rev. Prof. Westcott on 'Browning's View of Life' ('B. Soc. Papers', IV., pp. 401, 402).

166. object: offer in opposition; see v. 243.

167. our lord: some sage under whom they had learned; see v. 254.

174. Thou and the child have: i.e., for him, Lazarus.

177. Greek fire: see Gibbon, chap. 52. {a flammable liquid, kept so secret that its exact constitution is still unknown.}

281. Aleppo: a city of Syria; the blue-flowering borage was supposed to possess valuable medicinal virtues and exhilarating qualities.

301. Jerusalem's repose shall make amends: he will avail himself of it to write a better letter than this one.

A Martyr's Epitaph.

(From 'Easter Day'.)

I was born sickly, poor, and mean,
A slave: no misery could screen
The holders of the pearl of price
From Caesar's envy; therefore twice
I fought with beasts, and three times saw
My children suffer by his law;
At last my own release was earned:
I was some time in being burned,
But at the close a Hand came through
The fire above my head, and drew   [10]
My soul to Christ, whom now I see.
Sergius, a brother, writes for me
This testimony on the wall—
For me, I have forgot it all.

Soliloquy of the Spanish Cloister.

1.

Gr-r-r—there go, my heart's abhorrence!
　　Water your damned flower-pots, do!
If hate killed men, Brother Lawrence,
　　God's blood, would not mine kill you!
What? your myrtle-bush wants trimming?
　　Oh, that rose has prior claims—
Needs its leaden vase filled brimming?
　　Hell dry you up with its flames!

2.

At the meal we sit together:
　　'Salve tibi!' I must hear
Wise talk of the kind of weather,
　　Sort of season, time of year:
'Not a plenteous cork-crop: scarcely
　　Dare we hope oak-galls, I doubt:
What's the Latin name for "parsley"?'
　　What's the Greek name for Swine's Snout?

3.

Whew! We'll have our platter burnished,
　　Laid with care on our own shelf!
With a fire-new spoon we're furnished,
　　And a goblet for ourself,
Rinsed like something sacrificial
　　Ere 'tis fit to touch our chaps—
Marked with L. for our initial!
　　(He-he! There his lily snaps!)

4.

SAINT, forsooth! While brown Dolores
    Squats outside the Convent bank
With Sanchicha, telling stories,
    Steeping tresses in the tank,
Blue-black, lustrous, thick like horse-hairs,
    —Can't I see his dead eye glow,
Bright as 'twere a Barbary corsair's?
    (That is, if he'd let it show!)

5.

When he finishes refection,
    Knife and fork he never lays
Cross-wise, to my recollection,
    As do I, in Jesu's praise.
I the Trinity illustrate,
    Drinking watered orange-pulp—
In three sips the Arian frustrate;
    While he drains his at one gulp.

—

St. 5. the Arian: a follower of Arius (died 336 A.D.), who denied
that the Son was co-essential and co-eternal with the Father.

6.

Oh, those melons? If he's able
    We're to have a feast! so nice!
One goes to the Abbot's table,
    All of us get each a slice.
How go on your flowers? None double?
    Not one fruit-sort can you spy?
Strange!—And I, too, at such trouble,
    Keep them close-nipped on the sly!

7.

There's a great text in Galatians,
    Once you trip on it, entails
Twenty-nine distinct damnations,
    One sure, if another fails:
If I trip him just a-dying,
    Sure of heaven as sure can be,
Spin him round and send him flying
    Off to hell, a Manichee?

———

St. 7. text in Galatians: chap. 5, vv. 19-21, where are enumerated "the works of the flesh". There are seventeen named; he uses twenty-nine indefinitely; it's common in French to use trente-six (36) for any pretty big number. If I trip him: What if I; and so in next stanza. a Manichee: a follower of Mani, who aimed to unite Parseeism, or Parsism, with Christianity.

8.

Or, my scrofulous French novel
    On gray paper with blunt type!
Simply glance at it, you grovel
    Hand and foot in Belial's gripe:
If I double down its pages
    At the woful sixteenth print,
When he gathers his greengages,
    Ope a sieve and slip it in't?

9.

Or, there's Satan!—one might venture
    Pledge one's soul to him, yet leave
Such a flaw in the indenture
    As he'd miss till, past retrieve,
Blasted lay that rose-acacia
    We're so proud of! Hy, Zy, Hine . . .

'St, there's Vespers! Plena gratia
  Ave, Virgo! Gr-r-r—you swine!

—

St. 9. Hy, Zy, Hine: represent the sound of the vesper bell.

Holy-Cross Day.

On which the Jews were forced to attend an Annual Christian
Sermon in Rome.

—

* "By a bull of Gregory XIII. in the year 1584, all Jews above
the age of twelve years were compelled to listen every week to
a sermon from a Christian priest; usually an exposition of some
passages of the Old Testament, and especially those relating to the
Messiah, from the Christian point of view. This burden is not yet
wholly removed from them; and to this day, several times in the
course of a year, a Jewish congregation is gathered together in the
church of S. Angelo in Pescheria, and constrained to listen to a
homily from a Dominican friar, to whom, unless his zeal have eaten
up his good feelings and his good taste, the ceremony must be as
painful as to his hearers. In the same spirit of vulgar persecution,
there is upon the gable of a church, opposite one of the gates of
the Ghetto, a fresco painting of the Crucifixion, and, underneath,
an inscription in Hebrew and Latin, from the 2d and 3d verses
of the 65th chapter of Isaiah— 'I have spread out my hands all
the day unto a rebellious people, which walketh in a way that was
not good, after their own thoughts; a people that provoketh me to
anger continually to my face.'" —George S. Hillard's Six Months in
Italy. (1853.)

—

["Now was come about Holy-Cross Day, and now must my
lord preach his first sermon to the Jews: as it was of old cared for
in the merciful bowels of the Church, that, so to speak, a crumb,
at least, from her conspicuous table here in Rome, should be,
though but once yearly, cast to the famishing dogs, under-trampled
and bespitten-upon beneath the feet of the guests. And a moving

sight in truth, this, of so many of the besotted blind restif and ready-to-perish Hebrews! now maternally brought —nay (for He saith, 'Compel them to come in'), haled, as it were, by the head and hair, and against their obstinate hearts, to partake of the heavenly grace. What awakening, what striving with tears, what working of a yeasty conscience! Nor was my lord wanting to himself on so apt an occasion; witness the abundance of conversions which did incontinently reward him: though not to my lord be altogether the glory."—Diary by the Bishop's Secretary, 1600.]

What the Jews really said, on thus being driven to church, was rather to this effect:—

1.

Fee, faw, fum! bubble and squeak!
Blessedest Thursday's the fat of the week.
Rumble and tumble, sleek and rough,
Stinking and savory, smug and gruff,
Take the church-road, for the bell's due chime
Gives us the summons—'tis sermon-time!

2.

Boh, here's Barnabas! Job, that's you?
Up stumps Solomon—bustling too?
Shame, man! greedy beyond your years
To handsel the bishop's shaving-shears?
Fair play's a jewel! Leave friends in the lurch?
Stand on a line ere you start for the church!

3.

Higgledy piggledy, packed we lie,
Rats in a hamper, swine in a sty,
Wasps in a bottle, frogs in a sieve,
Worms in a carcass, fleas in a sleeve.
Hist! square shoulders, settle your thumbs
And buzz for the bishop—here he comes.

4.

Bow, wow, wow—a bone for the dog!
I liken his Grace to an acorned hog.
What, a boy at his side, with the bloom of a lass,
To help and handle my lord's hour-glass!
Didst ever behold so lithe a chine?
His cheek hath laps like a fresh-singed swine.

5.

Aaron's asleep—shove hip to haunch,
Or somebody deal him a dig in the paunch!
Look at the purse with the tassel and knob,
And the gown with the angel and thingumbob!
What's he at, quotha? reading his text!
Now you've his curtsey—and what comes next?

6.

See to our converts—you doomed black dozen—
No stealing away—nor cog nor cozen!
You five, that were thieves, deserve it fairly;
You seven, that were beggars, will live less sparely;
You took your turn and dipped in the hat,
Got fortune—and fortune gets you; mind that!

7.

Give your first groan—compunction's at work;
And soft! from a Jew you mount to a Turk.
Lo, Micah,—the selfsame beard on chin
He was four times already converted in!
Here's a knife, clip quick—it's a sign of grace—
Or he ruins us all with his hanging-face.

8.

Whom now is the bishop a-leering at?
I know a point where his text falls pat.
I'll tell him to-morrow, a word just now
Went to my heart and made me vow
To meddle no more with the worst of trades:
Let somebody else play his serenades!

9.

Groan all together now, whee—hee—hee!
It's a-work, it's a-work, ah, woe is me!
It began, when a herd of us, picked and placed,
Were spurred through the Corso, stripped to the waist;
Jew brutes, with sweat and blood well spent
To usher in worthily Christian Lent.

10.

It grew, when the hangman entered our bounds,
Yelled, pricked us out to his church like hounds:
It got to a pitch, when the hand indeed
Which gutted my purse, would throttle my creed:
And it overflows, when, to even the odd,
Men I helped to their sins, help me to their God.

11.

But now, while the scapegoats leave our flock,
And the rest sit silent and count the clock,
Since forced to muse the appointed time
On these precious facts and truths sublime,—
Let us fitly employ it, under our breath,
In saying Ben Ezra's Song of Death.

12.

For Rabbi Ben Ezra, the night he died,
Called sons and sons' sons to his side,
And spoke, "This world has been harsh and strange;
Something is wrong: there needeth a change.
But what, or where? at the last or first?
In one point only we sinned, at worst.

—

St. 12. Rabbi Ben Ezra: see biographical sketch subjoined to
the Argument of the Monologue entitled 'Rabbi Ben Ezra'.

13.

"The Lord will have mercy on Jacob yet,
And again in his border see Israel set.
When Judah beholds Jerusalem,
The stranger-seed shall be joined to them:
To Jacob's house shall the Gentiles cleave,
So the Prophet saith and his sons believe.

14.

"Ay, the children of the chosen race
Shall carry and bring them to their place:
In the land of the Lord shall lead the same,
Bondsmen and handmaids. Who shall blame,
When the slaves enslave, the oppressed ones o'er
The oppressor triumph for evermore!

15.

"God spoke, and gave us the word to keep:
Bade never fold the hands nor sleep
'Mid a faithless world,—at watch and ward,
Till Christ at the end relieve our guard.
By his servant Moses the watch was set:
Though near upon cock-crow, we keep it yet.

16.

"Thou! if thou wast he, who at mid-watch came,
By the starlight, naming a dubious name!
And if, too heavy with sleep—too rash
With fear—O thou, if that martyr-gash
Fell on thee coming to take thine own,
And we gave the Cross, when we owed the Throne—

17.

"Thou art the Judge. We are bruised thus.
But, the Judgment over, join sides with us!
Thine too is the cause! and not more thine
Than ours, is the work of these dogs and swine,
Whose life laughs through and spits at their creed,
Who maintain thee in word, and defy thee in deed!

18.

"We withstood Christ then? Be mindful how
At least we withstand Barabbas now!
Was our outrage sore? But the worst we spared,
To have called these—Christians, had we dared!
Let defiance to them pay mistrust of thee,
And Rome make amends for Calvary!

19.

"By the torture, prolonged from age to age,
By the infamy, Israel's heritage,
By the Ghetto's plague, by the garb's disgrace,
By the badge of shame, by the felon's place,
By the branding-tool, the bloody whip,
And the summons to Christian fellowship,—

—

St. 19. Ghetto: the Jews' quarter in Rome, Venice, and other cities. The name is supposed to be derived from the Hebrew 'ghet', meaning division, separation, divorce.

20.

"We boast our proof that at least the Jew
Would wrest Christ's name from the Devil's crew.
Thy face took never so deep a shade
But we fought them in it, God our aid!
A trophy to bear, as we march, thy band
South, East, and on to the Pleasant Land!"

[The late Pope abolished this bad business of the sermon.—R. B.]
—

The late Pope: Gregory XVI.

Saul.

1.

Said Abner, "At last thou art come! Ere I tell, ere thou speak,
Kiss my cheek, wish me well!" Then I wished it, and did kiss his
    cheek.
And he, "Since the King, O my friend, for thy countenance sent,
Neither drunken nor eaten have we; nor until from his tent
Thou return with the joyful assurance the King liveth yet,
Shall our lip with the honey be bright, with the water be wet.
For out of the black mid-tent's silence, a space of three days,
Not a sound hath escaped to thy servants, of prayer nor of praise,
To betoken that Saul and the spirit have ended their strife,
And that, faint in his triumph, the monarch sinks back upon life.
                               [10]

2.

"Yet now my heart leaps, O beloved! God's child with his dew
On thy gracious gold hair, and those lilies still living and blue
Just broken to twine round thy harp-strings, as if no wild heat
Were now raging to torture the desert!"

3.

    Then I, as was meet,
Knelt down to the God of my fathers, and rose on my feet,
And ran o'er the sand burnt to powder. The tent was unlooped;
I pulled up the spear that obstructed, and under I stooped;
Hands and knees on the slippery grass-patch, all withered and
    gone,
That extends to the second enclosure, I groped my way on   [20]
Till I felt where the foldskirts fly open. Then once more I prayed,
And opened the foldskirts and entered, and was not afraid
But spoke, "Here is David, thy servant!" And no voice replied.
At the first I saw naught but the blackness; but soon I descried
A something more black than the blackness—the vast, the upright
Main prop which sustains the pavilion: and slow into sight
Grew a figure against it, gigantic and blackest of all.
Then a sunbeam, that burst through the tent-roof, showed Saul.

4.

He stood as erect as that tent-prop, both arms stretched out wide
On the great cross-support in the centre, that goes to each side;
    [30]
He relaxed not a muscle, but hung there as, caught in his pangs
And waiting his change, the king serpent all heavily hangs,
Far away from his kind, in the pine, till deliverance come
With the spring-time,—so agonized Saul, drear and stark, blind and
    dumb.

5.

Then I tuned my harp,—took off the lilies we twine round its
    chords
Lest they snap 'neath the stress of the noontide—those sunbeams
    like swords!
And I first played the tune all our sheep know, as, one after one,
So docile they come to the pen-door till folding be done.
They are white, and untorn by the bushes, for lo, they have fed
Where the long grasses stifle the water within the stream's bed;

                                                              [40]

And now one after one seeks its lodging, as star follows star
Into eve and the blue far above us,—so blue and so far!

6.

—Then the tune, for which quails on the cornland will each leave
    his mate
To fly after the player; then, what makes the crickets elate
Till for boldness they fight one another: and then, what has
    weight
To set the quick jerboa a-musing outside his sand house—
There are none such as he for a wonder, half bird and half
    mouse!
God made all the creatures and gave them our love and our fear,
To give sign, we and they are his children, one family here.

7.

Then I played the help-tune of our reapers, their wine-song, when
    hand   [50]
Grasps at hand, eye lights eye in good friendship, and great hearts
    expand
And grow one in the sense of this world's life.—And then, the last
    song
When the dead man is praised on his journey—"Bear, bear him
    along
With his few faults shut up like dead flowerets! Are balm seeds not
    here

To console us? The land has none left such as he on the bier.
Oh, would we might keep thee, my brother!"—And then, the glad
    chant
Of the marriage,—first go the young maidens, next, she whom we
    vaunt
As the beauty, the pride of our dwelling.—And then, the great
    march
Wherein man runs to man to assist him and buttress an arch
Naught can break; who shall harm them, our friends?—Then,
    the chorus intoned [60]
As the Levites go up to the altar in glory enthroned.
But I stopped here: for here in the darkness Saul groaned.

    8.

And I paused, held my breath in such silence, and listened apart;
And the tent shook, for mighty Saul shuddered: and sparkles 'gan
    dart
From the jewels that woke in his turban at once with a start
All its lordly male-sapphires, and rubies courageous at heart.
So the head: but the body still moved not, still hung there erect.
And I bent once again to my playing, pursued it unchecked,
As I sang,—

    9.

    "Oh, our manhood's prime vigor! No spirit feels waste,
Not a muscle is stopped in its playing nor sinew unbraced.   [70]
Oh, the wild joys of living! the leaping from rock up to rock,
The strong rending of boughs from the fir-tree, the cool silver
    shock
Of the plunge in a pool's living water, the hunt of the bear,
And the sultriness showing the lion is couched in his lair.
And the meal, the rich dates yellowed over with gold dust divine,
And the locust-flesh steeped in the pitcher, the full draught of
    wine,
And the sleep in the dried river-channel where bulrushes tell
That the water was wont to go warbling so softly and well.
How good is man's life, the mere living! how fit to employ

All the heart and the soul and the senses forever in joy!   [80]
Hast thou loved the white locks of thy father, whose sword thou
        didst guard
When he trusted thee forth with the armies, for glorious reward?
Didst thou see the thin hands of thy mother, held up as men sung
The low song of the nearly departed, and hear her faint tongue
Joining in while it could to the witness, 'Let one more attest,
I have lived, seen God's hand through a lifetime, and all was for
        best!'
Then they sung through their tears in strong triumph, not much,
        but the rest.
And thy brothers, the help and the contest, the working whence
        grew
Such result as, from seething grape-bundles, the spirit strained
        true:
And the friends of thy boyhood—that boyhood of wonder and
        hope,   [90]
Present promise and wealth of the future beyond the eye's
        scope,—
Till lo, thou art grown to a monarch; a people is thine;
And all gifts, which the world offers singly, on one head combine!
On one head, all the beauty and strength, love and rage (like the
        throe
That, a-work in the rock, helps its labor and lets the gold go)
High ambition and deeds which surpass it, fame crowning them,—
        all
Brought to blaze on the head of one creature—King Saul!"

        10.

And lo, with that leap of my spirit,—heart, hand, harp, and voice,
Each lifting Saul's name out of sorrow, each bidding rejoice
Saul's fame in the light it was made for—as when, dare I say, [100]
The Lord's army, in rapture of service, strains through its array,
And upsoareth the cherubim-chariot—"Saul!" cried I, and
        stopped,
And waited the thing that should follow. Then Saul, who hung
        propped
By the tent's cross-support in the centre, was struck by his name.

Have ye seen when Spring's arrowy summons goes right to the
    aim,
And some mountain, the last to withstand her, that held (he alone,
While the vale laughed in freedom and flowers) on a broad bust
    of stone
A year's snow bound about for a breastplate,—leaves grasp of the
    sheet?
Fold on fold all at once it crowds thunderously down to his feet,
And there fronts you, stark, black, but alive yet, your mountain of
    old,   [110]
With his rents, the successive bequeathings of ages untold—
Yea, each harm got in fighting your battles, each furrow and scar
Of his head thrust 'twixt you and the tempest—all hail, there they
    are!
—Now again to be softened with verdure, again hold the nest
Of the dove, tempt the goat and its young to the green on his
    crest
For their food in the ardors of summer. One long shudder thrilled
All the tent till the very air tingled, then sank and was stilled
At the King's self left standing before me, released and aware.
What was gone, what remained? All to traverse 'twixt hope and
    despair.
Death was past, life not come: so he waited. Awhile his right hand
                              [120]
Held the brow, helped the eyes, left too vacant, forthwith to
    remand
To their place what new objects should enter: 'twas Saul as before.
I looked up and dared gaze at those eyes, nor was hurt any more
Than by slow pallid sunsets in autumn, ye watch from the shore,
At their sad level gaze o'er the ocean—a sun's slow decline
Over hills which, resolved in stern silence, o'erlap and intwine
Base with base to knit strength more intensely: so, arm folded arm
O'er the chest whose slow heavings subsided.

    11.

    What spell or what charm
(For, a while there was trouble within me), what next should I
    urge

To sustain him where song had restored him?—Song filled to the
    verge [130]
His cup with the wine of this life, pressing all that it yields
Of mere fruitage, the strength and the beauty: beyond, on what
    fields,
Glean a vintage more potent and perfect to brighten the eye
And bring blood to the lip, and commend them the cup they put
    by?
He saith, "It is good"; still he drinks not: he lets me praise life,
Gives assent, yet would die for his own part.

    12.

    Then fancies grew rife
Which had come long ago on the pasture, when round me the
    sheep
Fed in silence—above, the one eagle wheeled slow as in sleep;
And I lay in my hollow and mused on the world that might lie
'Neath his ken, though I saw but the strip 'twixt the hill and the
    sky.   [140]
And I laughed—"Since my days are ordained to be passed with my
    flocks,
Let me people at least, with my fancies, the plains and the rocks,
Dream the life I am never to mix with, and image the show
Of mankind as they live in those fashions I hardly shall know!
Schemes of life, its best rules and right uses, the courage that
    gains,
And the prudence that keeps what men strive for." And now these
    old trains
Of vague thought came again; I grew surer; so, once more the
    string
Of my harp made response to my spirit, as thus—

    13.

    "Yea, my King,"
I began—"thou dost well in rejecting mere comforts that spring
From the mere mortal life held in common by man and by brute:
                [150]

In our flesh grows the branch of this life, in our soul it bears fruit.
Thou hast marked the slow rise of the tree,—how its stem trembled
    first
Till it passed the kid's lip, the stag's antler; then safely outburst
The fan-branches all round; and thou mindest when these too, in
    turn
Broke a-bloom and the palm-tree seemed perfect: yet more was to
    learn,
E'en the good that comes in with the palm-fruit. Our dates shall
    we slight,
When their juice brings a cure for all sorrow? or care for the plight
Of the palm's self whose slow growth produced them? Not so!
    stem and branch
Shall decay, nor be known in their place, while the palm-wine shall
    stanch
Every wound of man's spirit in winter. I pour thee such wine.
[160]
Leave the flesh to the fate it was fit for! the spirit be thine!
By the spirit, when age shall o'ercome thee, thou still shalt enjoy
More indeed, than at first when, inconscious, the life of a boy.
Crush that life, and behold its wine running! Each deed thou hast
    done
Dies, revives, goes to work in the world; until e'en as the sun
Looking down on the earth, though clouds spoil him, though
    tempests efface,
Can find nothing his own deed produced not, must everywhere
    trace
The results of his past summer-prime,—so, each ray of thy will,
Every flash of thy passion and prowess, long over, shall thrill
Thy whole people, the countless, with ardor, till they too give
    forth   [170]
A like cheer to their sons: who in turn, fill the South and the
    North
With the radiance thy deed was the germ of. Carouse in the past!
But the license of age has its limit; thou diest at last.
As the lion when age dims his eyeball, the rose at her height,
So with man—so his power and his beauty forever take flight.
No! Again a long draught of my soul-wine! Look forth o'er the
    years!

Thou hast done now with eyes for the actual; begin with the
    seer's!
Is Saul dead? In the depth of the vale make his tomb—bid arise
A gray mountain of marble heaped four-square, till, built to the
    skies,
Let it mark where the great First King slumbers: whose fame would
    ye know?
Up above see the rock's naked face, where the record shall go
                              [181]
In great characters cut by the scribe,—Such was Saul, so he did;
With the sages directing the work, by the populace chid,—
For not half, they'll affirm, is comprised there! Which fault to
    amend,
In the grove with his kind grows the cedar, whereon they shall
    spend
(See, in tablets 'tis level before them) their praise, and record
With the gold of the graver, Saul's story,—the statesman's great
    word
Side by side with the poet's sweet comment. The river's a-wave
With smooth paper-reeds grazing each other when prophet-winds
    rave:
So the pen gives unborn generations their due and their part
                              [190]
In thy being! Then, first of the mighty, thank God that thou art!"

    14.

And behold while I sang . . . but O Thou who didst grant me, that
    day,
And, before it, not seldom hast granted thy help to essay,
Carry on and complete an adventure,—my shield and my sword
In that act where my soul was thy servant, thy word was my
    word,—
Still be with me, who then at the summit of human endeavor
And scaling the highest, man's thought could, gazed hopeless as
    ever
On the new stretch of heaven above me—till, mighty to save,
Just one lift of thy hand cleared that distance—God's throne from
    man's grave!

Let me tell out my tale to its ending—my voice to my heart [200]
Which can scarce dare believe in what marvels last night I took
    part,
As this morning I gather the fragments, alone with my sheep!
And still fear lest the terrible glory evanish like sleep,
For I wake in the gray dewy covert, while Hebron upheaves
The dawn struggling with night on his shoulder, and Kidron
    retrieves
Slow the damage of yesterday's sunshine.

    15.

    I say then,—my song
While I sang thus, assuring the monarch, and, ever more strong,
Made a proffer of good to console him—he slowly resumed
His old motions and habitudes kingly. The right hand replumed
His black locks to their wonted composure, adjusted the swathes
                            [210]
Of his turban, and see—the huge sweat that his countenance
    bathes,
He wipes off with the robe; and he girds now his loins as of yore,
And feels slow for the armlets of price, with the clasp set before.
He is Saul, ye remember in glory,—ere error had bent
The broad brow from the daily communion; and still, though much
    spent
Be the life and the bearing that front you, the same, God did
    choose,
To receive what a man may waste, desecrate, never quite lose.
So sank he along by the tent-prop, till, stayed by the pile
Of his armor and war-cloak and garments, he leaned there awhile,
And sat out my singing,—one arm round the tent-prop, to raise
                            [220]
His bent head, and the other hung slack—till I touched on the
    praise
I foresaw from all men in all time, to the man patient there;
And thus ended, the harp falling forward. Then first I was 'ware
That he sat, as I say, with my head just above his vast knees
Which were thrust out on each side around me, like oak-roots
    which please

To encircle a lamb when it slumbers. I looked up to know
If the best I could do had brought solace: he spoke not, but slow
Lifted up the hand slack at his side, till he laid it with care
Soft and grave, but in mild settled will, on my brow: through my
    hair
The large fingers were pushed, and he bent back my head, with
    kind power—
All my face back, intent to peruse it, as men do a flower.
[231]
Thus held he me there with his great eyes that scrutinized mine—
And oh, all my heart how it loved him! but where was the sign?
I yearned—"Could I help thee, my father, inventing a bliss,
I would add, to that life of the past, both the future and this;
I would give thee new life altogether, as good, ages hence,
As this moment,—had love but the warrant, love's heart to
    dispense!"

    16.

Then the truth came upon me. No harp more—no song more!
    outbroke—

    17.

"I have gone the whole round of creation: I saw and I spoke;
I, a work of God's hand for that purpose, received in my brain
[240]
And pronounced on the rest of his handwork—returned him
    again
His creation's approval or censure: I spoke as I saw.
I report, as a man may of God's work—all's love, yet all's law.
Now I lay down the judgeship he lent me. Each faculty tasked
To perceive him, has gained an abyss, where a dewdrop was asked.
Have I knowledge? confounded it shrivels at Wisdom laid bare.
Have I forethought? how purblind, how blank, to the Infinite
    Care!
Do I task any faculty highest, to image success?
I but open my eyes,—and perfection, no more and no less,

In the kind I imagined, full-fronts me, and God is seen God

[250]

In the star, in the stone, in the flesh, in the soul and the clod.
And thus looking within and around me, I ever renew
(With that stoop of the soul which in bending upraises it too)
The submission of man's nothing-perfect to God's all-complete,
As by each new obeisance in spirit, I climb to his feet.
Yet with all this abounding experience, this deity known,
I shall dare to discover some province, some gift of my own.
There's a faculty pleasant to exercise, hard to hoodwink,
I am fain to keep still in abeyance (I laugh as I think),
Lest, insisting to claim and parade in it, wot ye, I worst

[260]

E'en the Giver in one gift.—Behold, I could love if I durst!
But I sink the pretension as fearing a man may o'ertake
God's own speed in the one way of love: I abstain for love's sake.
—What, my soul? see thus far and no farther? when doors great
   and small,
Nine-and-ninety flew ope at our touch, should the hundredth
   appal?
In the least things have faith, yet distrust in the greatest of all?
Do I find love so full in my nature, God's ultimate gift,
That I doubt his own love can compete with it? Here the parts
   shift?
Here, the creature surpass the creator,—the end, what began?
Would I fain in my impotent yearning do all for this man,

[270]

And dare doubt he alone shall not help him, who yet alone can?
Would it ever have entered my mind, the bare will, much less
   power,
To bestow on this Saul what I sang of, the marvellous dower
Of the life he was gifted and filled with? to make such a soul,
Such a body, and then such an earth for insphering the whole?
And doth it not enter my mind (as my warm tears attest)
These good things being given, to go on, and give one more, the
   best?
Ay, to save and redeem and restore him, maintain at the height
This perfection,—succeed, with life's dayspring, death's minute of
   night?

Interpose at the difficult minute, snatch Saul, the mistake,
[280]
Saul, the failure, the ruin he seems now,—and bid him awake
From the dream, the probation, the prelude, to find himself set
Clear and safe in new light and new life,—a new harmony yet
To be run and continued, and ended—who knows?—or endure!
The man taught enough by life's dream, of the rest to make sure;
By the pain-throb, triumphantly winning intensified bliss,
And the next world's reward and repose, by the struggles in this.

    18.

"I believe it! 'Tis thou, God, that givest, 'tis I who receive:
In the first is the last, in thy will is my power to believe.
All's one gift: thou canst grant it moreover, as prompt to my
     prayer,   [290]
As I breathe out this breath, as I open these arms to the air.
From thy will, stream the worlds, life and nature, thy dread
     Sabaoth:
I will?—the mere atoms despise me! Why am I not loth
To look that, even that in the face too? Why is it I dare
Think but lightly of such impuissance? What stops my despair?
This;—'tis not what man Does which exalts him, but what man
     Would do!
See the King—I would help him, but cannot, the wishes fall
     through.
Could I wrestle to raise him from sorrow, grow poor to enrich,
To fill up his life, starve my own out, I would—knowing which,
I know that my service is perfect. Oh, speak through me now!
[300]
Would I suffer for him that I love? So wouldst thou—so wilt thou!
So shall crown thee the topmost, ineffablest, uttermost crown—
And thy love fill infinitude wholly, nor leave up nor down
One spot for the creature to stand in! It is by no breath,
Turn of eye, wave of hand, that salvation joins issue with death!
As thy love is discovered almighty, almighty be proved
Thy power, that exists with and for it, of being beloved!
He who did most, shall bear most; the strongest shall stand the
     most weak.

'Tis the weakness in strength, that I cry for! my flesh, that I seek
In the Godhead! I seek and I find it. O Saul, it shall be

[310]

A Face like my face that receives thee; a Man like to me,
Thou shalt love and be loved by, forever: a Hand like this hand
Shall throw open the gates of new life to thee! See the Christ
    stand!"

    19.

I know not too well how I found my way home in the night.
There were witnesses, cohorts about me, to left and to right,
Angels, powers, the unuttered, unseen, the alive, the aware:
I repressed, I got through them as hardly, as strugglingly there,
As a runner beset by the populace famished for news—
Life or death. The whole earth was awakened, hell loosed with her
    crews;
And the stars of night beat with emotion, and tingled and shot

[320]

Out in fire the strong pain of pent knowledge: but I fainted not,
For the Hand still impelled me at once and supported, suppressed
All the tumult, and quenched it with quiet, and holy behest,
Till the rapture was shut in itself, and the earth sank to rest.
Anon at the dawn, all that trouble had withered from earth—
Not so much, but I saw it die out in the day's tender birth;
In the gathered intensity brought to the gray of the hills;
In the shuddering forests' held breath; in the sudden wind-thrills;
In the startled wild beasts that bore oft, each with eye sidling still
Though averted with wonder and dread; in the birds stiff and chill

[330]

That rose heavily as I approached them, made stupid with awe:
E'en the serpent that slid away silent—he felt the new law.
The same stared in the white humid faces upturned by the
    flowers;
The same worked in the heart of the cedar and moved the vine-
    bowers:
And the little brooks witnessing murmured, persistent and low,
With their obstinate, all but hushed voices—"E'en so, it is so!"

320 et seq.: see note to St. 37, 38, of 'By the Fireside'.

A Death in the Desert.

[Supposed of Pamphylax the Antiochene:
It is a parchment, of my rolls the fifth,
Hath three skins glued together, is all Greek
And goeth from Epsilon down to Mu:
Lies second in the surnamed Chosen Chest,   [5]
Stained and conserved with juice of terebinth,
Covered with cloth of hair, and lettered Xi,
From Xanthus, my wife's uncle, now at peace:
Mu and Epsilon stand for my own name.
I may not write it, but I make a cross   [10]
To show I wait His coming, with the rest,
And leave off here: beginneth Pamphylax.]

——

1-12. The bracketed prefatory lines, explanatory of the parchment on which are recorded the last hours and last talk of St. John with his devoted attendants, purport to have been written by one who was at the time the owner of the parchment. It appears to have come into his possession through his wife, a niece of the Xanthus who, with Pamphylax of Antioch, the supposed author of the narrative (he having told it on the eve of his martyrdom to a certain Phoebas, v. 653), and two others, is represented therein as waiting on the dying apostle, and who afterwards "escaped to Rome, was burned, and could not write the chronicle." (vv. 56, 57.)

4. And goeth from Epsilon down to Mu: the reference is to some numbering on the parchment.

6. terebinth: the turpentine tree.

——

I said, "If one should wet his lips with wine,
And slip the broadest plantain-leaf we find,
Or else the lappet of a linen robe,   [15]
Into the water-vessel, lay it right,

354

And cool his forehead just above the eyes,
The while a brother, kneeling either side,
Should chafe each hand and try to make it warm,—
He is not so far gone but he might speak." [20]
This did not happen in the outer cave,
Nor in the secret chamber of the rock,
Where, sixty days since the decree was out,
We had him, bedded on a camel-skin,
And waited for his dying all the while; [25]
But in the midmost grotto: since noon's light
Reached there a little, and we would not lose
The last of what might happen on his face.

—

23. the decree: of persecution of the Christians, perhaps that
under Domitian. The poet probably did not think of any particular
persecution.

—

I at the head, and Xanthus at the feet,
With Valens and the Boy, had lifted him, [30]
And brought him from the chamber in the depths,
And laid him in the light where we might see:
For certain smiles began about his mouth,
And his lids moved, presageful of the end.

Beyond, and half way up the mouth o' the cave, [35]
The Bactrian convert, having his desire,
Kept watch, and made pretence to graze a goat
That gave us milk, on rags of various herb,
Plantain and quitch, the rocks' shade keeps alive:
So that if any thief or soldier passed [40]
(Because the persecution was aware),
Yielding the goat up promptly with his life,
Such man might pass on, joyful at a prize,
Nor care to pry into the cool o' the cave.
Outside was all noon and the burning blue. [45]

36. the Bactrian convert: in vv. 649, 650, he is spoken of as "but a wild childish man, and could not write nor speak, but only loved." Bactria was a kingdom in Central Asia; the modern name is Balkh {a district in northern Afghanistan as of 1995}. having his desire: as a new convert, the simple man was eager to serve, even unto death.

41. aware: on the lookout; exercising a strict espionage.

—

"Here is wine", answered Xanthus,—dropped a drop;
I stooped and placed the lap of cloth aright,
Then chafed his right hand, and the Boy his left:
But Valens had bethought him, and produced
And broke a ball of nard, and made perfume.   [50]
Only, he did—not so much wake, as—turn
And smile a little, as a sleeper does
If any dear one call him, touch his face—
And smiles and loves, but will not be disturbed.

Then Xanthus said a prayer, but still he slept: [55]
It is the Xanthus that escaped to Rome,
Was burned, and could not write the chronicle.

Then the Boy sprang up from his knees, and ran,
Stung by the splendor of a sudden thought,
And fetched the seventh plate of graven lead   [60]
Out of the secret chamber, found a place,
Pressing with finger on the deeper dints,
And spoke, as 'twere his mouth proclaiming first,
"I am the Resurrection and the Life."

—

60. the seventh plate of graven lead: one of the plates on which John's Gospel was graven. It contained, it appears, the 11th chapter, in which Jesus says to Martha, 25th verse, "I am the Resurrection and the Life." The Boy uttered the words with such expression as 'twere HIS mouth first proclaiming them.

—

Whereat he opened his eyes wide at once,   [65]
And sat up of himself, and looked at us;
And thenceforth nobody pronounced a word:
Only, outside, the Bactrian cried his cry
Like the lone desert-bird that wears the ruff,
As signal we were safe, from time to time.   [70]

———

69. the lone desert-bird: the ruff may possibly be referred to.
See Webster, s.v.

———

First he said, "If a man declared to me,
This my son Valens, this my other son,
Were James and Peter,—nay, declared as well
This lad was very John,—I could believe!
—Could, for a moment, doubtlessly believe: [75]
So is myself withdrawn into my depths,
The soul retreated from the perished brain
Whence it was wont to feel and use the world
Through these dull members, done with long ago.
Yet I myself remain; I feel myself: [80]
And there is nothing lost. Let be, awhile!"

———

76. withdrawn into my depths: into the depths of his absolute
being, of the "what Is"; see the doctrine of the trinal unity of man
which follows.

———

[This is the doctrine he was wont to teach,
How divers persons witness in each man,
Three souls which make up one soul: first, to wit,
A soul of each and all the bodily parts,   [85]
Seated therein, which works, and is what Does,
And has the use of earth, and ends the man
Downward; but, tending upward for advice,
Grows into, and again is grown into

By the next soul, which, seated in the brain,   [90]
Useth the first with its collected use,
And feeleth, thinketh, willeth,—is what Knows:
Which, duly tending upward in its turn,
Grows into, and again is grown into
By the last soul, that uses both the first,   [95]
Subsisting whether they assist or no,
And, constituting man's self, is what Is
And leans upon the former, makes it play,
As that played off the first: and, tending up,
Holds, is upheld by, God, and ends the man   [100]
Upward in that dread point of intercourse,
Nor needs a place, for it returns to Him.
What Does, what Knows, what Is; three souls, one man.
I give the glossa of Theotypas.]

———

82-104. The supposed narrator, Pamphylax, gives in these
bracketed verses, on the authority of an imagined Theotypas, a
doctrine John was wont to teach, of the trinal unity of man— the
third "person" of which unity, "what Is", being man's essential,
absolute nature. The dying John is represented as having won his
way to the Kingdom of the "what Is", the Kingdom of eternal
truth within himself. In Luke 17:20-21, we read: "And when he
was demanded of the Pharisees, when the Kingdom of God
should come, he answered them and said, The Kingdom of God
cometh not with observation: neither shall they say, Lo here! or,
Lo there! for, behold, the Kingdom of God is within you." In
harmony with which, Paracelsus is made to say, in Browning's
poem, "Truth is within ourselves; . . . there is an inmost centre
in us all, where truth abides in fulness"; etc. See pp. 24 and 25 of
this volume. {In this etext, see Chapter I, 'The Spiritual Ebb and
Flow, etc.', of the Introduction. Excerpt is shortly before the poem
'Popularity'.} "Life, you've granted me, develops from within. But
INNERMOST OF THE INMOST, MOST INTERIOR OF THE
INTERNE, GOD CLAIMS HIS OWN, DIVINE HUMANITY
RENEWING NATURE" (Mrs. Browning's 'Aurora Leigh'). Mrs.
M. G. Glazebrook, in her paper on 'A Death in the Desert', read
at the 48th meeting of the Browning Society, Feb. 25th, 1887,

paraphrases these lines: "The first and lowest [soul] is that which has to do with earth and corporeal things, the animal soul, which receives primary sensations and is the immediate cause of action —'what Does'. The second is the intellect, and has its seat in the brain: it is superior to the first, but dependent on it, since it receives as material the actual experience which the animal soul supplies; it is the feeling, thinking, willing soul —'what Knows'. The third, and highest, is the spirit of man, the very principle of life, the divine element in man linking him to God, which is self-subsistent and therefore independent of sensation and knowledge, but nevertheless makes use of them, and gives them existence and energy—'what Is'."

—

And then, "A stick, once fire from end to end;   [105]
Now, ashes save the tip that holds a spark!
Yet, blow the spark, it runs back, spreads itself
A little where the fire was: thus I urge
The soul that served me, till it task once more
What ashes of my brain have kept their shape,   [110]
And these make effort on the last o' the flesh,
Trying to taste again the truth of things"—
(He smiled)—"their very superficial truth;
As that ye are my sons, that it is long
Since James and Peter had release by death,   [115]
And I am only he, your brother John,
Who saw and heard, and could remember all.
Remember all! It is not much to say.
What if the truth broke on me from above
As once and oft-times? Such might hap again: [120]
Doubtlessly He might stand in presence here,
With head wool-white, eyes, flame, and feet like brass,
The sword and the seven stars, as I have seen—
I who now shudder only and surmise
'How did your brother bear that sight and live?'   [125]

—

113. superficial truth: phenomenal, relative truth; that which is arrived at through the senses, and belongs to the domain of the

"what Knows". Essential, absolute truth can be known only through a response thereto of the essential, the absolute, the "what Is", in man's nature. John has attained to a measure of absolute truth, and smiles on reverting to the very superficial truth of things.

121-123. See The Revelation of St. John, chap. 1.

125. your brother: he means himself, of course.

——

"If I live yet, it is for good, more love
Through me to men: be naught but ashes here
That keep awhile my semblance, who was John,—
Still, when they scatter, there is left on earth
No one alive who knew (consider this!)   [130]
—Saw with his eyes and handled with his hands
That which was from the first, the Word of Life.
How will it be when none more saith 'I saw'?

"Such ever was love's way: to rise, it stoops.
Since I, whom Christ's mouth taught, was bidden teach, [135]
I went, for many years, about the world,
Saying, 'It was so; so I heard and saw',
Speaking as the case asked: and men believed.
Afterward came the message to myself
In Patmos isle; I was not bidden teach.   [140]
But simply listen, take a book and write,
Nor set down other than the given word.
With nothing left to my arbitrament
To choose or change: I wrote, and men believed.
Then, for my time grew brief, no message more,   [145]
No call to write again, I found a way,
And, reasoning from my knowledge, merely taught
Men should, for love's sake, in love's strength, believe;
Or I would pen a letter to a friend,
And urge the same as friend, nor less nor more: [150]
Friends said I reasoned rightly, and believed.
But at the last, why, I seemed left alive
Like a sea-jelly weak on Patmos strand,
To tell dry sea-beach gazers how I fared
When there was mid-sea, and the mighty things;   [155]

Left to repeat, 'I saw, I heard, I knew',
And go all over the old ground again,
With Antichrist already in the world,
And many Antichrists, who answered prompt
'Am I not Jasper as thyself art John?   [160]
Nay, young, whereas through age thou mayest forget:
Wherefore, explain, or how shall we believe?'
I never thought to call down fire on such,
Or, as in wonderful and early days,
Pick up the scorpion, tread the serpent dumb;   [165]
But patient stated much of the Lord's life
Forgotten or misdelivered, and let it work:
Since much that at the first, in deed and word,
Lay simply and sufficiently exposed,
Had grown (or else my soul was grown to match,   [170]
Fed through such years, familiar with such light,
Guarded and guided still to see and speak)
Of new significance and fresh result;
What first were guessed as points, I now knew stars,
And named them in the Gospel I have writ.   [175]
For men said, 'It is getting long ago:
Where is the promise of His coming?'—asked
These young ones in their strength, as loth to wait,
Of me who, when their sires were born, was old.
I, for I loved them, answered, joyfully,   [180]
Since I was there, and helpful in my age;
And, in the main, I think such men believed.
Finally, thus endeavoring, I fell sick.
Ye brought me here, and I supposed the end,
And went to sleep with one thought that, at least,   [185]
Though the whole earth should lie in wickedness,
We had the truth, might leave the rest to God.
        Yet now I wake in such decrepitude
As I had slidden down and fallen afar,
Past even the presence of my former self,   [190]
Grasping the while for stay at facts which snap,
Till I am found away from my own world,
Feeling for foot-hold through a blank profound,
Along with unborn people in strange lands,

Who say—I hear said or conceive they say—   [195]
'Was John at all, and did he say he saw?
Assure us, ere we ask what he might see!'

———

156. I saw, I heard, I knew: expressions which occur throughout
John's Revelation.

188-197. The poet provides, in these lines, for the prophetic
character of John's discourse, its solution of the difficulties destined
to beset Christianity in the future, and especially of those which have
been raised in our own times. The historical bulwarks which the
Strausses and the Renans have endeavored to destroy, Christianity,
in its essential, absolute character, its adaptiveness to spiritual
vitality, and the wants of the soul, can do without. Indeed, there
will be much gained when the historical character of Christianity
is generally disregarded. Its impregnable fortress, namely, the
Personality, Jesus Christ, will remain, and mankind will forever seek
and find refuge in it. Arthur Symons, in his 'Introduction to the
Study of Browning', remarks: . . ."it is as a piece of ratiocination—
suffused, indeed, with imagination— that the poem seems to have
its raison d'etre. The bearing of this argument on contemporary
theories, may to some appear a merit, to others a blemish. To make
the dying John refute Strauss or Renan, handling their propositions
with admirable dialectical skill, is certainly, on the face of it,
somewhat hazardous. But I can see no real incongruity in imputing
to the seer of Patmos a prophetic insight into the future—no real
inconsequence in imagining the opponent of Cerinthus spending
his last breath in the defence of Christian truth against a foreseen
scepticism."

———

"And how shall I assure them? Can they share
—They, who have flesh, a veil of youth and strength
About each spirit, that needs must bide its time,   [200]
Living and learning still as years assist
Which wear the thickness thin, and let man see—
With me who hardly am withheld at all,
But shudderingly, scarce a shred between,
Lie bare to the universal prick of light?   [205]

Is it for nothing we grow old and weak,
We whom God loves? When pain ends, gain ends too.
To me, that story—ay, that Life and Death
Of which I wrote 'it was'—to me, it is;
—Is, here and now: I apprehend naught else.   [210]
Is not God now i' the world His power first made?
Is not His love at issue still with sin,
Visibly when a wrong is done on earth?
Love, wrong, and pain, what see I else around?
Yea, and the Resurrection and Uprise   [215]
To the right hand of the throne—what is it beside,
When such truth, breaking bounds, o'erfloods my soul,
And, as I saw the sin and death, even so
See I the need yet transiency of both,
The good and glory consummated thence?   [220]
I saw the Power; I see the Love, once weak,
Resume the Power: and in this word 'I see',
Lo, there is recognized the Spirit of both
That moving o'er the spirit of man, unblinds
His eye and bids him look. These are, I see;   [225]
But ye, the children, His beloved ones too,
Ye need,—as I should use an optic glass
I wondered at erewhile, somewhere i' the world,
It had been given a crafty smith to make;
A tube, he turned on objects brought too close,   [230]
Lying confusedly insubordinate
For the unassisted eye to master once:
Look through his tube, at distance now they lay,
Become succinct, distinct, so small, so clear!
Just thus, ye needs must apprehend what truth   [235]
I see, reduced to plain historic fact,
Diminished into clearness, proved a point
And far away: ye would withdraw your sense
From out eternity, strain it upon time,
Then stand before that fact, that Life and Death,   [240]
Stay there at gaze, till it dispart, dispread,
As though a star should open out, all sides,
Grow the world on you, as it is my world.

202. "Oh, not alone when life flows still do truth and power emerge, but also when strange chance ruffles its current; in unused conjuncture, when sickness breaks the body—hunger, watching, excess, or languor— oftenest death's approach—peril, deep joy, or woe." —Browning's 'Paracelsus'.

"The soul's dark cottage, battered and decayed,
Lets in new light through chinks that Time has made.
Stronger by weakness, wiser men become,
As they draw near to their eternal home.
Leaving the old, both worlds at once they view,
That stand upon the threshold of the new."
                                        —Edmund Waller.

"Drawing near her death, she sent most pious thoughts as harbingers to heaven; and her soul saw a glimpse of happiness through the chinks of her sickness-broken body." Fuller's 'Holy and Profane State', Book I., chap. 2.

203. With me: connect with 'share', v. 198.

208-209. See p. 62 of this volume. {In this etext, Part II, Section 3 in the Introduction. It is shortly before an excerpt from 'Christmas Eve'.}

221-225. See stanzas 9 and 10 of 'Rabbi Ben Ezra'.

227. an optic glass: perhaps anachronistic.

—

"For life, with all it yields of joy and woe,
And hope and fear,—believe the aged friend,—   [245]
Is just our chance o' the prize of learning love,
How love might be, hath been indeed, and is;
And that we hold thenceforth to the uttermost
Such prize despite the envy of the world,
And, having gained truth, keep truth: that is all.   [250]
But see the double way wherein we are led,
How the soul learns diversely from the flesh!
With flesh, that hath so little time to stay,
And yields mere basement for the soul's emprise,

Expect prompt teaching. Helpful was the light,   [255]
And warmth was cherishing and food was choice
To every man's flesh, thousand years ago,
As now to yours and mine; the body sprang
At once to the height, and staid: but the soul,—no!
Since sages who, this noontide, meditate   [260]
In Rome or Athens, may descry some point
Of the eternal power, hid yestereve;
And, as thereby the power's whole mass extends,
So much extends the ether floating o'er
The love that tops the might, the Christ in God.   [265]
Then, as new lessons shall be learned in these
Till earth's work stop and useless time run out,
So duly, daily, needs provision be
For keeping the soul's prowess possible,
Building new barriers as the old decay,   [270]
Saving us from evasion of life's proof,
Putting the question ever, 'Does God love,
And will ye hold that truth against the world?'
Ye know there needs no second proof with good
Gained for our flesh from any earthly source: [275]
We might go freezing, ages,—give us fire,
Thereafter we judge fire at its full worth,
And guard it safe through every chance, ye know!
That fable of Prometheus and his theft,
How mortals gained Jove's fiery flower, grows old   [280]
(I have been used to hear the pagans own)
And out of mind; but fire, howe'er its birth,
Here is it, precious to the sophist now
Who laughs the myth of Aeschylus to scorn,
As precious to those satyrs of his play,   [285]
Who touched it in gay wonder at the thing.
While were it so with the soul,—this gift of truth
Once grasped, were this our soul's gain safe, and sure
To prosper as the body's gain is wont,—
Why, man's probation would conclude, his earth   [290]
Crumble; for he both reasons and decides,
Weighs first, then chooses: will he give up fire
For gold or purple once he knows its worth?

Could he give Christ up were His worth as plain?
Therefore, I say, to test man, the proofs shift, [295]
Nor may he grasp that fact like other fact,
And straightway in his life acknowledge it,
As, say, the indubitable bliss of fire.
Sigh ye, 'It had been easier once than now?'
To give you answer I am left alive; [300]
Look at me who was present from the first!
Ye know what things I saw; then came a test,
My first, befitting me who so had seen:
'Forsake the Christ thou sawest transfigured, Him
Who trod the sea and brought the dead to life? [305]
What should wring this from thee?'—ye laugh and ask.
What wrung it? Even a torchlight and a noise,
The sudden Roman faces, violent hands,
And fear of what the Jews might do! Just that,
And it is written, 'I forsook and fled': [310]
There was my trial, and it ended thus.
Ay, but my soul had gained its truth, could grow:
Another year or two,—what little child,
What tender woman that had seen no least
Of all my sights, but barely heard them told, [315]
Who did not clasp the cross with a light laugh,
Or wrap the burning robe round, thanking God?
Well, was truth safe forever, then? Not so.
Already had begun the silent work
Whereby truth, deadened of its absolute blaze, [320]
Might need love's eye to pierce the o'erstretched doubt.
Teachers were busy, whispering 'All is true
As the aged ones report; but youth can reach
Where age gropes dimly, weak with stir and strain,
And the full doctrine slumbers till to-day.' [325]
Thus, what the Roman's lowered spear was found,
A bar to me who touched and handled truth,
Now proved the glozing of some new shrewd tongue,
This Ebion, this Cerinthus or their mates,
Till imminent was the outcry 'Save our Christ!' [330]
Whereon I stated much of the Lord's life
Forgotten or misdelivered, and let it work.

Such work done, as it will be, what comes next?
What do I hear say, or conceive men say,
'Was John at all, and did he say he saw?   [335]
Assure us, ere we ask what he might see!'

—

284. the myth of Aeschylus: embodied in his 'Prometheus Bound'.

295. the proofs shift: see pp. 37 and 38. {In etext, shortly before two excerpts from 'A Death in the Desert', Chapter II, Section 1 of Introduction.} Objective proofs, in spiritual matters, need reconstruction, again and again; and whatever may be their character, they are inadequate, and must finally, in the Christian life, be superseded by subjective proofs— by man's winning his way to the kingdom of eternal truth within himself —the kingdom of the "what Is".

307-310. See Matt. 26:56; Mark 14:50; John 18:3.

326-328. what the Roman's lowered spear was found [to be, namely], a bar, [etc.,] now proved [to be, etc.].

329. This Ebion, this Cerinthus: see 'Gibbon's History of the Decline and Fall of the Roman Empire', Chaps. 15, 21, 47. And see, especially, the able articles, "Cerinthus" and "Ebionism and Ebionites", in the 'Dictionary of Christian Biography', etc., edited by Dr. William Smith and Professor Wace. "'Ebion' as a name first personified by Tertullian, was said to have been a pupil of Cerinthus, and the Gospel of St. John to have been as much directed against the former as the latter. St. Paul and St. Luke were asserted to have spoken and written against Ebionites. The 'Apostolical Constitutions' (vi. c. 6) traced them back to Apostolic times; Theodoret (Haer. fab. II. c. 2) assigned them to the reign of Domitian (A.D. 81-96). The existence of an 'Ebion' is, however, now surrendered." From Art. Ebionism in 'Dict. of Christian Biography'.

And see Prof. George P. Fisher's 'Beginnings of Christianity', 1877.

"Cerinthus, a man who was educated in the wisdom of the Egyptians, taught that the world was not made by the primary God, but by a certain power far separated from him, and at a distance from that Principality who is supreme over the universe, and ignorant of him who is above all. He represented Jesus as having not been born of a virgin, but as being the son of Joseph and Mary according to the ordinary course of human generation, while he nevertheless was more righteous, prudent, and wise than other men. Moreover, after his baptism, Christ descended upon him in the form of a dove from the Supreme Ruler, and that then he proclaimed the unknown Father, and performed miracles. But at last Christ departed from Jesus, and that then Jesus suffered and rose again, while Christ remained impassible, inasmuch as he was a spiritual being." 'The Writings of Irenaeus, transl. by Rev. Alexander Roberts, D.D., and Rev. W. H. Rambaut, A.B.', Edinburgh, 1868. Vol. I., Book I., Chap xxvi.

—

"Is this indeed a burthen for late days,
And may I help to bear it with you all,
Using my weakness which becomes your strength?
For if a babe were born inside this grot,   [340]
Grew to a boy here, heard us praise the sun,
Yet had but yon sole glimmer in light's place,—
One loving him and wishful he should learn,
Would much rejoice himself was blinded first
Month by month here, so made to understand   [345]
How eyes, born darkling, apprehend amiss:
I think I could explain to such a child
There was more glow outside than gleams he caught,
Ay, nor need urge 'I saw it, so believe!'
It is a heavy burthen you shall bear   [350]
In latter days, new lands, or old grown strange,
Left without me, which must be very soon.
What is the doubt, my brothers? Quick with it!
I see you stand conversing, each new face,
Either in fields, of yellow summer eves,   [355]
On islets yet unnamed amid the sea;
Or pace for shelter 'neath a portico
Out of the crowd in some enormous town
Where now the larks sing in a solitude;
Or muse upon blank heaps of stone and sand   [360]
Idly conjectured to be Ephesus:

And no one asks his fellow any more
'Where is the promise of His coming?' but
'Was He revealed in any of His lives,
As Power, as Love, as Influencing Soul?'　　　　　[365]

———

346. darkling: an old adverbial form; in the dark. See 'Paradise
Lost', III. 39. "O, wilt thou darkling leave me?" Sh's 'M. N. D.', II.
2. 86; "So, out went the candle, and we were left darkling." 'Lear', I.
4. 237; also 'A. and C.', IV. 15. 10.

353. What is the doubt, my brothers?: He addresses his
brothers of the far future. The eight following verses are very
beautiful.

362-365. The question, "Where is the promise of His coming?"
asked in John's own day, gives place in the far future to which the
ken of the dying Apostle extends, to the question whether God
was indeed revealed in Christ, 'As Power, as Love, as Influencing
Soul', or whether, man having already love in himself, Christ were
not a mere projection from man's inmost mind (v. 383)? If so there
is nothing to fall back on but force, or natural law. This anticipated
questioning and reasoning extends from v. 370 to v. 421.

———

"Quick, for time presses, tell the whole mind out,
And let us ask and answer and be saved!
My book speaks on, because it cannot pass;
One listens quietly, nor scoffs but pleads
'Here is a tale of things done ages since:　　　　　[370]
What truth was ever told the second day?
Wonders, that would prove doctrine, go for naught.
Remains the doctrine, love; well, we must love,
And what we love most, power and love in one,
Let us acknowledge on the record here,　　　　　[375]
Accepting these in Christ: must Christ then be?
Has He been? Did not we ourselves make Him?
Our mind receives but what it holds, no more.
First of the love, then; we acknowledge Christ—
A proof we comprehend His love, a proof　　　　　[380]
We had such love already in ourselves,

369

Knew first what else we should not recognize.
'Tis mere projection from man's inmost mind,
And, what he loves, thus falls reflected back,
Becomes accounted somewhat out of him;   [385]
He throws it up in air, it drops down earth's,
With shape, name, story added, man's old way.
How prove you Christ came otherwise at least?
Next try the power: He made and rules the world:
Certes there is a world once made, now ruled,   [390]
Unless things have been ever as we see.
Our sires declared a charioteer's yoked steeds
Brought the sun up the east and down the west,
Which only of itself now rises, sets,
As if a hand impelled it and a will,—   [395]
Thus they long thought, they who had will and hands:
But the new question's whisper is distinct,
Wherefore must all force needs be like ourselves?
We have the hands, the will; what made and drives
The sun is force, is law, is named, not known,   [400]
While will and love we do know; marks of these.
Eye-witnesses attest, so books declare—
As that, to punish or reward our race,
The sun at undue times arose or set
Or else stood still: what do not men affirm?   [405]
But earth requires as urgently reward
Or punishment to-day as years ago,
And none expects the sun will interpose:
Therefore it was mere passion and mistake,
Or erring zeal for right, which changed the truth.   [410]
Go back, far, farther, to the birth of things;
Ever the will, the intelligence, the love,
Man's!—which he gives, supposing he but finds,
As late he gave head, body, hands, and feet,
To help these in what forms he called his gods.   [415]
First, Jove's brow, Juno's eyes were swept away,
But Jove's wrath, Juno's pride continued long;
At last, will, power, and love discarded these,
So law in turn discards power, love, and will.
What proveth God is otherwise at least?   [420]
All else, projection from the mind of man!'

—

367. And let us ask and answer: John's talk, it must be understood, is with future people, not with the attendants.

368. My book speaks on: that is, to people of all futures, because it cannot pass away.

371. What truth, etc.: that is, truth is soon perverted, obscured, and often turned into positive untruth.

372. Wonders, that would prove doctrine: that is, whose purpose was to prove.

385. Comes to be considered as something outside of, and distinct from, himself.

—

"Nay, do not give me wine, for I am strong,
But place my gospel where I put my hands.

"I say that man was made to grow, not stop;
That help, he needed once, and needs no more,   [425]
Having grown but an inch by, is withdrawn:
For he hath new needs, and new helps to these.
This imports solely, man should mount on each
New height in view; the help whereby he mounts,
The ladder-rung his foot has left, may fall,   [430]
Since all things suffer change save God the Truth.
Man apprehends Him newly at each stage
Whereat earth's ladder drops, its service done;
And nothing shall prove twice what once was proved.
You stick a garden-plot with ordered twigs   [435]
To show inside lie germs of herbs unborn,
And check the careless step would spoil their birth;
But when herbs wave, the guardian twigs may go,
Since should ye doubt of virtues, question kinds,
It is no longer for old twigs ye look,   [440]
Which proved once underneath lay store of seed,
But to the herb's self, by what light ye boast,
For what fruit's signs are. This book's fruit is plain,
Nor miracles need prove it any more.
Doth the fruit show? Then miracles bade 'ware   [445]

At first of root and stem, saved both till now
From trampling ox, rough boar, and wanton goat.
What? Was man made a wheelwork to wind up,
And be discharged, and straight wound up anew?
No!—grown, his growth lasts; taught, he ne'er forgets: [450]
May learn a thousand things, not twice the same.
This might be pagan teaching: now hear mine.

———

424. Here John's answer begins to the questioning and reasoning contained in vv. 370-421.

In vv. 424-434, is contained a favorite teaching of Browning. It appears in various forms throughout his poetry. See the quotation from 'Luria', p. 38.

428. This imports solely: this is the one all important thing.

428-430. A similar comparison is used in 'Julius Caesar', A. II., S. I., 22-27:

> . . . "lowliness is young ambition's ladder,
> Whereto the climber-upward turns his face;
> But when he once attains the upmost round,
> He then unto the ladder turns his back,
> Looks in the clouds, scorning the base degrees
> By which he did ascend."

452. This might be pagan teaching: that is, even pagan teaching might go so far as this.

———

"I say, that as the babe, you feed awhile,
Becomes a boy and fit to feed himself,
So, minds at first must be spoon-fed with truth: [455]
When they can eat, babe's nurture is withdrawn.
I fed the babe whether it would or no:
I bid the boy or feed himself or starve.
I cried once, 'That ye may believe in Christ,
Behold this blind man shall receive his sight!' [460]
I cry now, 'Urgest thou, FOR I AM SHREWD,

AND SMILE AT STORIES HOW JOHN'S WORD COULD
   CURE—
REPEAT THAT MIRACLE AND TAKE MY FAITH?'
I say, that miracle was duly wrought
When, save for it, no faith was possible.   [465]
Whether a change were wrought i' the shows o' the world,
Whether the change came from our minds which see
Of shows o' the world so much as and no more
Than God wills for His purpose,—(what do I
See now, suppose you, there where you see rock   [470]
Round us?)—I know not; such was the effect,
So faith grew, making void more miracles
Because too much: they would compel, not help.
I say, the acknowledgment of God in Christ
Accepted by thy reason, solves for thee   [475]
All questions in the earth and out of it,
And has so far advanced thee to be wise.
Wouldst thou unprove this to re-prove the proved?
In life's mere minute, with power to use that proof,
Leave knowledge and revert to how it sprung?   [480]
Thou hast it; use it and forthwith, or die!

———

472. So faith grew, making void more miracles: the outward manifestations of spiritual powers (du/namis, 'power', 'act of power', and shmei^on, 'sign', 'token', are the original words in the N. T., which are translated 'miracle') gave place to subjective proof. Christianity was endorsed by man's own soul. To this may be added, that even the historical bulwarks of Christianity may, ere long, be dispensed with.

474-481. These verses may be taken as presenting Browning's own conclusion as to the whole duty of man, in a spiritual direction. And see the quotation from 'Christmas Eve' and the remarks which follow, on pp. 63 and 64. {In etext, Chapter II, Section 3 of Introduction.}

———

"For I say, this is death and the sole death,
When a man's loss comes to him from his gain,

Darkness from light, from knowledge ignorance,
And lack of love from love made manifest;   [485]
A lamp's death when, replete with oil, it chokes;
A stomach's when, surcharged with food, it starves.
With ignorance was surety of a cure.
When man, appalled at nature, questioned first
'What if there lurk a might behind this might?'   [490]
He needed satisfaction God could give,
And did give, as ye have the written word:
But when he finds might still redouble might,
Yet asks, 'Since all is might, what use of will?'
—Will, the one source of might,—he being man   [495]
With a man's will and a man's might, to teach
In little how the two combine in large,—
That man has turned round on himself and stands,
Which in the course of nature is, to die.

"And when man questioned, 'What if there be love   [500]
Behind the will and might, as real as they?'—
He needed satisfaction God could give,
And did give, as ye have the written word:
But when, beholding that love everywhere,
He reasons, 'Since such love is everywhere,   [505]
And since ourselves can love and would be loved,
We ourselves make the love, and Christ was not',—
How shall ye help this man who knows himself,
That he must love and would be loved again,
Yet, owning his own love that proveth Christ,   [510]
Rejecteth Christ through very need of Him?
The lamp o'erswims with oil, the stomach flags
Loaded with nurture, and that man's soul dies.

"If he rejoin, 'But this was all the while
A trick; the fault was, first of all, in thee,   [515]
Thy story of the places, names and dates,
Where, when, and how the ultimate truth had rise,
—Thy prior truth, at last discovered none,
Whence now the second suffers detriment.
What good of giving knowledge if, because   [520]

O' the manner of the gift, its profit fail?
And why refuse what modicum of help
Had stopped the after-doubt, impossible
I' the face of truth—truth absolute, uniform?
Why must I hit of this and miss of that,   [525]
Distinguish just as I be weak or strong,
And not ask of thee and have answer prompt,
Was this once, was it not once?—then and now
And evermore, plain truth from man to man.
Is John's procedure just the heathen bard's?   [530]
Put question of his famous play again
How for the ephemerals' sake, Jove's fire was filched,
And carried in a cane and brought to earth:
THE FACT IS IN THE FABLE, cry the wise,
MORTALS OBTAINED THE BOON, SO MUCH IS FACT,
                                                           [535]
THOUGH FIRE BE SPIRIT AND PRODUCED ON EARTH.
As with the Titan's, so now with thy tale:
Why breed in us perplexity, mistake,
Nor tell the whole truth in the proper words?'

———

514-539. John anticipates another objection that will be made
to his Gospel, namely, that so many things therein are not cleared
up, that the whole truth is not told in the proper words, the sceptic
claiming that everything should have been so proved

"That the probation bear no hinge nor loop
To hang a doubt on";

that all after-doubt, impossible in the face of truth—truth
absolute, uniform, might have been stopped.

523. Had stopped: would have stopped.
530. the heathen bard's: Aeschylus'.
531. famous play: 'Prometheus Bound'.
532. ephemerals': mortals'.
537. Titan's: Prometheus'.

———

"I answer, Have ye not to argue out   [540]
The very primal thesis, plainest law,
—Man is not God but hath God's end to serve,
A master to obey, a course to take,
Somewhat to cast off, somewhat to become?
Grant this, then man must pass from old to new,   [545]
From vain to real, from mistake to fact,
From what once seemed good, to what now proves best.
How could man have progression otherwise?
Before the point was mooted 'What is God?'
No savage man inquired 'What is myself?'   [550]
Much less replied, 'First, last, and best of things.'
Man takes that title now if he believes
Might can exist with neither will nor love,
In God's case—what he names now Nature's Law—
While in himself he recognizes love   [555]
No less than might and will: and rightly takes.
Since if man prove the sole existent thing
Where these combine, whatever their degree,
However weak the might or will or love,
So they be found there, put in evidence,—   [560]
He is as surely higher in the scale
Than any might with neither love nor will,
As life, apparent in the poorest midge
(When the faint dust-speck flits, ye guess its wing),
Is marvellous beyond dead Atlas' self—   [565]
Given to the nobler midge for resting-place!
Thus, man proves best and highest—God, in fine,
And thus the victory leads but to defeat,
The gain to loss, best rise to the worst fall,
His life becomes impossible, which is death.   [570]

———

540-633. All that John says in these verses, in reply to the anticipated objections urged in vv. 514-539, are found, substantially, in several passages in Browning's poetry. See remarks on pp. 36-38 beginning, "The human soul is regarded in Browning's poetry", etc. {Chapter II, Section 1 in this etext.} An infallible guide, which would render unnecessary any struggles on man's part, after light and truth, would torpify his powers. And see vv. 582-633 of the present poem.

552. Man takes that title now: that is, of 'First, last, and best of things", if, etc. See sections 17 and 18 of 'Saul', and stanza 10 of 'Rabbi Ben Ezra'. And see the grand dying speech of Paracelsus, which concludes Browning's poem.

554. "A law of nature means nothing to Mr. Browning if it does not mean the immanence of power, and will, and love. He can pass with ready sympathy into the mystical feeling of the East, where in the unclouded sky, in the torrent of noonday light, God is so near

> 'He glows above
> With scarce an intervention, presses close
> And palpitatingly, His soul o'er ours.'

But the wisdom of a Western 'savant' who in his superior intellectuality replaces the will of God by the blind force of nature, seems to Mr. Browning to be science falsely so called, a new ignorance founded upon knowledge,

> 'A lamp's death when, replete with oil, it chokes.'

To this effect argues the prophet John in 'A Death in the Desert', anticipating with the deep prevision of a dying man the doubts and questionings of modern days. And in the third of those remarkable poems which form the epilogue of the 'Dramatis Personae', the whole world rises in the speaker's imagination into one vast spiritual temple, in which voices of singers, and swell of trumpets, and cries of priests are heard going up to God no less truly than in the old Jewish worship, while the face of Christ, instinct with divine will and love, becomes apparent, as that of which all nature is a type or an adumbration." —Prof. Edward Dowden in his Comparative Study of Browning and Tennyson (Studies in Literature, 1789-1877).

—

"But if, appealing thence, he cower, avouch
He is mere man, and in humility

Neither may know God nor mistake himself;
I point to the immediate consequence
And say, by such confession straight he falls   [575]
Into man's place, a thing nor God nor beast,
Made to know that he can know and not more:
Lower than God who knows all and can all,
Higher than beasts which know and can so far
As each beast's limit, perfect to an end,   [580]
Nor conscious that they know, nor craving more;
While man knows partly but conceives beside,
Creeps ever on from fancies to the fact,
And in this striving, this converting air
Into a solid he may grasp and use,   [585]
Finds progress, man's distinctive mark alone,
Not God's, and not the beasts': God is, they are,
Man partly is and wholly hopes to be.
Such progress could no more attend his soul
Were all it struggles after found at first   [590]
And guesses changed to knowledge absolute,
Than motion wait his body, were all else
Than it the solid earth on every side,
Where now through space he moves from rest to rest.
Man, therefore, thus conditioned, must expect   [595]
He could not, what he knows now, know at first;
What he considers that he knows to-day,
Come but to-morrow, he will find misknown;
Getting increase of knowledge, since he learns
Because he lives, which is to be a man,   [600]
Set to instruct himself by his past self:
First, like the brute, obliged by facts to learn,
Next, as man may, obliged by his own mind,
Bent, habit, nature, knowledge turned to law.
God's gift was that man should conceive of truth,   [605]
And yearn to gain it, catching at mistake,
As midway help till he reach fact indeed.
The statuary ere he mould a shape
Boasts a like gift, the shape's idea, and next
The aspiration to produce the same;   [610]
So, taking clay, he calls his shape thereout,

Cries ever 'Now I have the thing I see':
Yet all the while goes changing what was wrought,
From falsehood like the truth, to truth itself.
How were it had he cried 'I see no face,   [615]
No breast, no feet i' the ineffectual clay?'
Rather commend him that he clapped his hands,
And laughed, 'It is my shape and lives again!'
Enjoyed the falsehood, touched it on to truth,
Until yourselves applaud the flesh indeed ·   [620]
In what is still flesh-imitating clay.
Right in you, right in him, such way be man's!
God only makes the live shape at a jet.
Will ye renounce this pact of creatureship?
The pattern on the Mount subsists no more,   [625]
Seemed awhile, then returned to nothingness;
But copies, Moses strove to make thereby,
Serve still and are replaced as time requires:
By these, make newest vessels, reach the type!
If ye demur, this judgment on your head,   [630]
Never to reach the ultimate, angels' law,
Indulging every instinct of the soul
There where law, life, joy, impulse are one thing!
"Such is the burthen of the latest time.
I have survived to hear it with my ears,   [635]
Answer it with my lips: does this suffice?
For if there be a further woe than such,
Wherein my brothers struggling need a hand,
So long as any pulse is left in mine,
May I be absent even longer yet,   [640]
Plucking the blind ones back from the abyss,
Though I should tarry a new hundred years!"

But he was dead: 'twas about noon, the day
Somewhat declining: we five buried him
That eve, and then, dividing, went five ways,   [645]
And I, disguised, returned to Ephesus.

By this, the cave's mouth must be filled with sand.
Valens is lost, I know not of his trace;

The Bactrian was but a wild childish man,
And could not write nor speak, but only loved: [650]
So, lest the memory of this go quite,
Seeing that I to-morrow fight the beasts,
I tell the same to Phoebas, whom believe!
For many look again to find that face,
Beloved John's to whom I ministered,   [655]
Somewhere in life about the world; they err:
Either mistaking what was darkly spoke
At ending of his book, as he relates,
Or misconceiving somewhat of this speech
Scattered from mouth to mouth, as I suppose.   [660]
Believe ye will not see him any more
About the world with his divine regard!
For all was as I say, and now the man
Lies as he lay once, breast to breast with God.

---

652. Pamphylax tells the story to Phoebas, on the eve of his
    martyrdom.
654-660. See Gospel of St. John 21:20-24.
662. regard: look.

"To whom thus Michael, with regard benign:" P. L., XI.,
    34.
"From that placid aspect and meek regard."—P. R., III.,
    217.

De Quincey remarks (Milton vs. Southey and Landor) in reply
to Landor's demurring that "meek regard conveys no new idea to
placid aspect": "But ASPECT is the countenance of Christ when
passive to the gaze of others; REGARD is the same countenance
in active contemplation of those others whom he loves or pities.
The PLACID ASPECT expresses, therefore, the divine rest; the
MEEK REGARD expresses the divine benignity; the one is
the self-absorption of the total Godhead, the other the external
emanation of the Filial Godhead."

[Cerinthus read and mused; one added this:— [665]

"If Christ, as thou affirmest, be of men
Mere man, the first and best but nothing more,—
Account Him, for reward of what He was,
Now and forever, wretchedest of all.
For see; Himself conceived of life as love,   [670]
Conceived of love as what must enter in,
Fill up, make one with His each soul He loved:
Thus much for man's joy, all men's joy for Him.
Well, He is gone, thou sayest, to fit reward.
But by this time are many souls set free,   [675]
And very many still retained alive:
Nay, should His coming be delayed awhile,
Say, ten years longer (twelve years, some compute)
See if, for every finger of thy hands,
There be not found, that day the world shall end,   [680]
Hundreds of souls, each holding by Christ's word
That He will grow incorporate with all,
With me as Pamphylax, with him as John,
Groom for each bride! Can a mere man do this?
Yet Christ saith, this He lived and died to do.   [685]
Call Christ, then, the illimitable God,
Or lost!"

But 'twas Cerinthus that is lost.]

—

665. Cerinthus read and mused: It must be supposed that an opportunity had been afforded Cerinthus of reading the MS. by the one who added the postscript, which is addressed to him, and who sought his conversion.

683. That is, 'With me as [with] Pamphylax, with him as [with] John': See Gospel of John, 17:11,21-23.

—

- - - - - - -

"In the critical examination of the evangelical records, the fourth Gospel suffered most. Strauss—in this instance following his early master and later antagonist, Baur—denied that St. John had anything to do with its composition. The author, he held, was neither St. John nor any one else who had personally known Christ: nor, in accordance with a widely accepted theory, did he believe it to be the work of a pupil of St. John, who, after the death of his master, related, from memory or from fragmentary notes, traditions and sayings which had been taught him, and made out of them a continuous history. Strauss pronounced it to be a controversial work, written late in the second century after Christ, by a profound theologian of the Greek Gnostic and anti-Jewish school, whose design was not to add another to the existing biographies of Christ, not to represent him as a real man, nor to give an account of any human life, but to produce an elaborate theological work in which, under the veil of allegory, the Neo-platonic conception of Christ as the Logos, the realized Word of God, the divine principle of light and life, should be developed. With this purpose, the writer made a free selection from the sayings and doings of Christ as recorded in the three Gospels already written, and as freely invented others. All the events, all the words, of the Gospel thus composed, are subordinate to the main design, which was worked out by the author with an artistic completeness most ingeniously traced by his German interpreters. Each miracle symbolizes some important dogma, and its narration must be understood to mean that it embodies some deep spiritual truth, not, necessarily, that it ever actually took place. The author manifests, throughout, his ignorance of Jewish customs, and his antagonism to Jewish sentiments."

* * * * *

"The general purport of the poem can scarcely be doubted, as we look back upon it as a whole and consider its main conclusions. The tendency of the argument is to diminish the importance of the original events—historical or traditional—on which the Christian religion is based. 'It is not worth while,' the writer seems to say to Strauss and his followers, 'to occupy ourselves with discussions about miracles and events which are said to have taken place a long time ago, and can now neither be denied or proved. What we are concerned with, is, Christianity as it is now: as a religion which the human mind has through many generations developed, purified, spiritualized; and which has reacted upon human nature and made it wiser and nobler. Shall we give up this faith which has been so great a power for good in the world, and which, its whole past history justifies us in concluding, will continue its work of improvement, because our belief in certain events is shaken or destroyed? It would be vain, indeed, thus to build our religion on a foundation so unstable as material evidence. For human sensations are not infallible; they very often deceive us; we think we see objects, which are really the illusions of our own brain; others we see in part only, or distorted; others we fail to perceive at all. Our faith, essential as it is to the well-being of the deepest parts of our nature, must not be dependent on such controlling powers as these.'"

* * * * *

"He [Browning] was, we may suppose, offended by Strauss's ruthless attack on much that mankind has held sacred for ages. His religious sense was revolted by the assumption that there was nothing in Christianity which could survive the destruction of the miraculous and supernatural elements in its history. He desired to represent Christianity as an entirely spiritual religion, independent of external, material agencies. In order to make his argument as powerful as possible, he chose for his mouth-piece one of the personal followers of Christ, on whom, it might be supposed, the actual human life of his master had made a permanent and lively impression. With the details of Biblical criticism he had nothing to do; his principles were unaffected by discussions about the authenticity of the various parts of Gospels; so, in defiance of Strauss, the disciple he chose was that very John, whose personality, as recognized by long tradition, had been so much discredited. He showed how even in one of the disciples the recollection of wonders and signs could be transcended, and at last obliterated, by a spiritual faith which was sustained by the needs and faculties of the soul. The poem is, in effect, an eloquent protest in defence of 'the breath and finer spirit of all knowledge'."

From Mrs. M. G. Glazebrook's paper on 'A Death in the Desert', read before the London Browning Society.

A LIST OF CRITICISMS OF
BROWNING'S WORKS.

(Selected from Dr. Frederick J. Furnivall's 'Bibliography of Robert Browning', contained in 'The Browning Society's Papers', Part I., with additions in Part II.)

1833.   The Monthly Mag., N. S., V. 7, pp. 254-262: Review of 'Pauline', by W. J. Fox.

1835.   The Examiner, Sept. 6, pp. 563-565: on 'Paracelsus', by John Forster.

1835.   Monthly Repository, Nov., pp. 716-727: Review of 'Paracelsus', by W. J. Fox.

1836.   New Monthly Mag., March, Vol. 46, pp. 289-308: 'Evidences of a New Genius for Dramatic Poetry.—No. 1.' On 'Paracelsus', by John Forster.

1837.   Edinburgh Rev., July, Vol. 66, pp. 132-151: 'Strafford'.

1848.   N. A. Rev., April, Vol. 66, pp. 357-400: B.'s 'Plays and Poems', by James Russell Lowell.

1849.   Eclectic Rev., London, 4th S. V. 26, pp. 203-214: on 1. the 'Poems', 2 vols. 1849, and 2. 'Sordello', 1840. A sympathetic and excellent review.

1850.   Massachusetts Quarterly Rev., No. XI. June, Art. IV. 'Browning's Poems'. 1. 'Poems', 2 vols., Boston, 1850. 2. 'Christmas Eve' and 'Easter Day', London, 1850.

1850.   Littell's Living Age, Vol. 25, pp. 403-409: on 'Christmas Eve' and 'Easter Day'.

1857.   The Christian Remembrancer, N. S., Vol. 39, pp. 361-390.

1861.   North British Rev., May, pp. 350-374: on 'The Poems and Plays of R. B.', by F. H. Evans.

1863.   Fraser's Mag., Feb., pp. 240-256.

1863.   The Eclectic Rev., No. 23, N. S., May, pp. 436-454.

1863.   National Rev., Oct., Vol. 47, pp. 417-446. Poetical Works of R. B., 3 vols., 3d ed., by R. H. Hutton; republ. in Hutton's 'Literary Essays, 1871'.

1864.   The Eclectic and Congregational Rev., July, pp. 61-72: on 'Dramatis Personae', by E. Paxton Hood.

1864.   Edinburgh Rev., Oct., pp. 537-565: on 'Poems', 1863, and 'Dramatis Personae', 1864.

1864.   National Rev., N. S., Nov., 1864; Wordsworth, Tennyson, and Browning; or Pure, Ornate, and Grotesque Art in English Poetry; republ. in 'Literary Studies', by Walter Bagshot.

1865.   Quarterly Rev., July, Vol. 118, pp. 77-105: on 'Dramatis Personae', 1864, and 'Poems', 3 vols., 1863.

1867.   Contemporary Rev., Jan. and Feb., 1867, Vol. 4, pp. 1-15, 133-148. Thoughtful and able articles.

1867.   Fraser's Mag., Oct., pp. 518-530: 'Sordello', by Edward Dowden.

1868.   Athenaeum, Dec. 26, pp. 875, 876: 'The Ring and the Book', Vol. 1. by Robert Buchanan; revised and publ. in his 'Master Spirits', 1873.

1868.   Eclectic and Congregational Rev., Dec., Art. II. 'Poetical Works', 6 vols., 1868, by E. Paxton Hood. See under 1864.

1868.   Essays on B.'s poetry, by J. T. Nettleship.

1869.   Athenaeum, March 20, pp. 399, 400: on 'The Ring and the Book', Vols. 2, 3, and 4.

1869.   Fortnightly Rev., March, Vol. 5, N. S., pp. 331-343: on 'The Ring and the Book', by John Morley. An able and generous article.

1869.   Quarterly Rev., April, pp. 328-359: on Mod. Eng. Poets; a few pages are on B.'s poems and 'The Ring and the Book'.

1869.   Edinburgh Rev., July, Vol. 130, pp. 164-186: on 'The Ring and the Book'.

1869.   London Quarterly Rev., July, on B.'s Poetry— all then published.

1869.   N. Brit. Rev., Oct., pp. 97-128: B.'s Latest Poetry ('The Ring and the Book').

1871.   Saint Paul's Mag., Dec., 1870, and Jan., 1871, Vol. 7, pp. 257-276, 377-397: 'Poems' and 'The Ring and the Book', by E. J. Hasell.

1871.   Athenaeum, Aug. 12, pp. 199, 200: on 'Balaustion's Adventure'.

1871.   Contemporary Rev., Sept., pp. 284-296, on 'Balaustion's Adventure', by Matthew Browne (pseudonym).

1871.   The Times, Oct. 6: a long review of 'Balaustion's Adventure'.

1871.   'Our Living Poets: an Essay in Criticism'. By H. Buxton Forman. 4th chap. on B., pp. 103-152.

1871.   Fortnightly Rev., Oct., Vol. 10, N. S., pp. 478-490: on 'Balaustion's Adventure', by Sidney Colvin.

1871.   The Dark Blue Mag., Oct. and Nov., Vol. 2, pp. 171-184, 305-319: 'Browning as a Preacher', by Miss E. Dickinson West. An admirable essay.

1872.   Edinburgh Rev., Jan., Vol. 135, pp. 221-249: on 'Balaustion's Adventure'.

1872.   Academy, Jan. 15: on 'Hohenstiel-Schwangau'.

1872.   Academy, July 1: on 'Fifine at the Fair', by F. Wedmore.

1873.   Athenaeum, May 10: on 'Red Cotton Night-Cap Country'.

1873.   Academy, June 2: on 'Red Cotton Night-Cap Country', by G. A. Simcox.

1873.   'Master Spirits', by Robert Buchanan; contains, pp. 89-109, a revised reprint of the Athenaeum reviews of 'The Ring and the Book', Dec., 1869, and March, 1870.

1875.   Academy, April 17: on 'Aristophanes' Apology', by J. A. Symonds.

1875.   Athenaeum, April 17, pp. 513, 514: on 'Aristophanes' Apology'.

1875.   Athenaeum, Nov. 27, pp. 701, 702: on 'The Inn Album'.

1876.   Academy, July 29: on 'Pacchiarotto', by Edward Dowden.

1876.   Macmillan's Mag., Feb., Vol. 33, pp. 347-354: on 'Inn Album', by A. C. Bradley.

1876.   'Victorian Poets. By Edmund Clarence Stedman'. Boston: 1876. Chap. IX., pp. 292-341, devoted to Browning.

1877.   Academy, Nov. 3: on 'The Agamemnon of Aeschylus', by J. A. Symonds.

1878. Church Quarterly Rev., Oct., pp. 65-92: on B.'s Poems, by the Hon. and Rev. Arthur Lyttleton. An article to be read by all students of Browning.

1878. Academy, June 1: on 'La Saisiaz', and 'The Two Poets of Croisic', by G. A. Simcox.

1878. Athenaeum, May 25, pp. 661-664: on 'La Saisiaz', by W. Theodore Watts.

1879. 'Studies in Literature, 1789-1877. By Edward Dowden, LL.D.' London: C. Kegan Paul & Co., pp. 191-239: 'Mr. Tennyson and Mr. Browning. A comparative study'. Ranks with the very best of Browning criticisms.

1879. Athenaeum, May 10: on 'Dramatic Idyls', I., by Walter Theodore Watts.

1879. Academy, May 10: on 'Dramatic Idyls', I., by F. Wedmore.

1880. Athenaeum, July 10, pp. 39-41: on 'Dramatic Idyls', 2d S., by W. Th. Watts.

1881. Gentleman's Mag., Dec., pp. 682-695: on 'The Ring and the Book', by James Thomson.

1881. Scribner's Century Mag., Dec. 1, pp. 189-200: on 'The Early Writings of R. B.', by E. W. Gosse.

1881. The Cambridge Review, Dec. 7, Vol. 3, pp. 146, 147: a review of 'Rabbi ben Ezra' and 'Abt Vogler', by A. W.

Some of the most valuable criticism of Browning's Poetry has been produced and published by The Browning Society of London, founded in 1881 by Dr. F. J. Furnivall, and still in active operation. Dr. Furnivall's 'Bibliography of Robert Browning', occupying Part I. of 'The Browning Society's Papers', and continued in Part II., is a storehouse of valuable information, of all kinds, pertaining to Browning's Poetry, and to Browning the man. Every Browning student should possess a copy of it. The following papers, among others, have been published by the Society:—

Introductory Address to the Browning Society. By the Rev. J. Kirkman, M.A., Queen's Coll., Cambridge, Oct. 28, 1881.

On 'Pietro of Abano' and the leading ideas of 'Dramatic Idyls', second series, 1880. By the Rev. J. Sharpe, M.A. Read Nov. 25, 1881.

On Browning's 'Fifine at the Fair'. By J. T. Nettleship, Esq. Read Feb. 24, 1882.

Notes on the Genius of Robert Browning. By James Thomson. Read Jan. 27, 1882.

Browning's Philosophy. By John Bury, Trin. Coll., Dublin. Read April 28, 1882.

On 'Bishop Blougram's Apology'. By the Rev. Prof. E. Johnson, M.A. Read May 26, 1882.

The Idea of Personality, as embodied in Robert Browning's Poetry. By Prof. Hiram Corson, LL.D., Cornell University. Read June 23, 1882. (Contained in this volume.)

The Religious Teaching of Browning. By Dorothea Beale. Read Oct. 27, 1882.

An Account of Abbe Vogler. (From Fetis & Nisard.) By Miss Eleanor Marx.

Conscience and Art in Browning. By the Rev. Prof. E. Johnson, M.A.

Browning's Intuition, specially in regard of Music and the Plastic Arts. By J. T. Nettleship. Read Feb. 23, 1883.

On some Points in Browning's View of Life. By the Rev. Prof. B. F. Westcott, D.D. Read before the Cambridge Browning Soc., Nov., 1882.

One aspect of Browning's Villains. By Miss E. D. West. Read April 27, 1883.

Browning's Poems on God and Immortality as bearing on life here. By William F. Revell. Read March 30, 1883.

James Lee's Wife. By Rev. J. H. Bulkeley. Read May 25, 1883.

Abt Vogler. By Mrs. Turnbull. Read June 22, 1883.

On some prominent points of Browning's teaching. By W. A. Raleigh, Esq., of King's College, Cambridge. Read Feb. 22, 1884.

'Caliban upon Setebos', with some notes on Browning's subtlety and humor. By J. Cotter Morison, Esq. Read April 25, 1884.

In a Balcony. By Mrs. Turnbull. Read July 4, 1884.

On 'Mr. Sludge the Medium'. By Edwin Johnson, M.A. Read March 27, 1885.

Browning as a Scientific Poet. By Edward Berdoe, M.R.C.S. (Eng.), L.R.C.P. (Ed.). Read April 24, 1885.

On the development of Browning's genius in his capacity as Poet or Maker. By J. T. Nettleship, Esq. Read Oct. 30, 1885.
On 'Aristophanes' Apology'. By John B. Bury, B.A., Trin. Coll., Dublin. Read Jan. 29, 1886.
Andrea Del Sarto. By Albert Fleming. Read Feb. 26, 1886.
The reasonable rhythm of some of Browning's Poems. By the Rev. H. J. Bulkeley, M.A. Read May 28, 1886.

The following works should be mentioned:—

Stories from Robert Browning. By Frederic May Holland. With an Introduction by Mrs. Sutherland Orr. London: 1882.
Strafford: a Tragedy. By Robert Browning. With notes and preface by Emily H. Hickey [First Hon. Sec. of the Browning Society]. And an Introduction by Samuel R. Gardiner, LL.D., Professor of Modern History, King's College, London. London: 1884.
A Handbook to the works of Robert Browning. By Mrs. Sutherland Orr. London: 1885. A good reference book.
Poets and Problems. By George Willis Cooke. Boston: 1886. pp. 269-388 devoted to Browning.
Essays on Poetry and Poets. By the Hon. Roden Noel. London: 1886. pp. 256-282 devoted to Browning.
Select Poems of Robert Browning. By W. J. Rolfe. Boston.

Important works published since the first edition of this book:—

Sordello's Story retold in prose. By Annie Wall. Boston and New York: 1886.
Browning's Women. By Mary E. Burt. With an introduction by Rev. Edward Everett Hale, D.D., LL.D. Chicago: 1887.
Studies in the Poetry of Robert Browning. By James Fotheringham. London: 1887.
An Introduction to the Poetry of Robert Browning. By William John Alexander, Ph.D. Boston: 1889.
Sordello: an outline analysis of Mr. Browning's poem. By Jeanie Morison. Edinburgh and London: 1889.
Robert Browning Personalia. By Edmund Gosse. Boston and New York: 1890.

Robert Browning: Essays and Thoughts. By John T. Nettleship. New York: 1890.

Browning's Message to his Time: his Religion, Philosophy, and Science. By Edward Berdoe. London: 1890.

A Guide-Book to the poetic and dramatic works of Robert Browning. By George Willis Cooke. Boston: 1891.

Life and Letters of Robert Browning. By Mrs. Sutherland Orr. Boston: 1891.

Browning as a philosophical and religious teacher. By Henry Jones, M.A. New York: 1891.

Some additional papers of the Browning Society, published since the first edition of this book:—

"A Death in the Desert". By Mrs. M. G. Glazebrook. Read February 25, 1887.

Some Notes on Browning's poems referring to music. By Helen J. Ormerod. Read May 27, 1887.

"Saul". By Anna M. Stoddart. Read May 25, 1888.

Andrea del Sarto and Abt Vogler. By Helen J. Ormerod. Read November 30, 1888.

La Saisiaz. By Rev. W. Robertson. Read January 25, 1889.

On the difficulties and obscurities encountered in a study of Browning's poems. By James Bertram Oldham, B.A. Read February 22, 1889.

Taurello Salinguerra: historical details illustrative of Browning's Sordello. Muratori and Browning compared. By W. M. Rossetti. Read November 29, 1889.

The value of Browning's work. By William F. Revell. Read May 30, 1890.

The student will find much other valuable material in the Browning Society papers.

For Articles in Periodical Literature, the student should consult Poole's Indexes.

BIBLIOBAZAAR

The essential book market!

Did you know that you can get any of our titles in large print?

Did you know that we have an ever-growing collection of books in many languages?

Order online:
www.bibliobazaar.com

Find all of your favorite classic books!

Stay up to date with the latest government reports!

At BiblioBazaar, we aim to make knowledge more accessible by making thousands of titles available to you- *quickly and affordably*.

Contact us:
BiblioBazaar
PO Box 21206
Charleston, SC 29413

773282

Printed in Great Britain by
Amazon.co.uk, Ltd.,
Marston Gate.